"Looking for a romance that will have you laughing out loud while recognizing the impact of ever-changing seasons in our lives? *Every Girl Gets Confused* is romantic comedy at its best. A sweet romance. A wonderful band of supporting family and friends. And enough humor to keep me smiling on each page. This book is a great next chapter in Katie and Brady's story and a welcome addition to my library. I highly recommend it!"

—**Cara Putman**, award-winning author of
Shadowed by Grace and *Where Treetops Glisten*

"*Every Girl Gets Confused* is a delightful mix of romance, inspiration, and humor, woven together with Thompson's trademark Texas storytelling and a happily-ever-after ending that will make you want to swoon."

—**Judy Christie**, author of *Wreath,*
A Girl in the Wreath Willis series

"Janice Thompson tosses her readers into a humorous whirl of romantic possibilities with characters I swear I've met in small-town Texas. Fun!"

—**Julianna Deering**, author of the
Drew Farthering Mystery series

Books by Janice Thompson

WEDDINGS BY BELLA

Fools Rush In

Swinging on a Star

It Had to Be You

That's Amore

BACKSTAGE PASS

Stars Collide

Hello, Hollywood!

The Director's Cut

WEDDINGS BY DESIGN

Picture Perfect

The Icing on the Cake

The Dream Dress

A Bouquet of Love

BRIDES WITH STYLE

Every Bride Needs a Groom

Every Girl Gets Confused

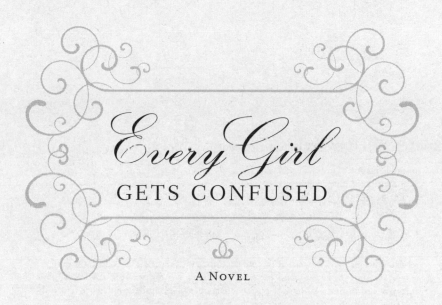

Every Girl
GETS CONFUSED

A NOVEL

JANICE
THOMPSON

Revell

a division of Baker Publishing Group
Grand Rapids, Michigan

© 2015 by Janice Thompson

Published by Revell
a division of Baker Publishing Group
P.O. Box 6287, Grand Rapids, MI 49516-6287
www.revellbooks.com

Printed in the United States of America

Library of Congress Cataloging-in-Publication Data
Thompson, Janice A.
    Every girl gets confused : a novel / Janice Thompson.
       pages ; cm.— (Brides with style ; #2)
  · ISBN 978-0-8007-2400-9 (pbk.)
      1. Dating (Social customs)—Fiction. 2. Man-woman relationships—Fiction.
I. Title.
PS3620.H6824E95 2015
813′.6—dc23   2015020726

The author is represented by MacGregor Literary, Inc.

15   16   17   18   19   20   21   7   6   5   4   3   2   1

*To one of my favorite singers
of all time, past, present, or future: the
incomparable Doris Day. What joy to base
this book on someone I've admired since
childhood, and how fun to use her songs
and movies as my chapter titles.*

*In loving memory of our precious Evie Joy.
You were not long for this earth, little one,
but remain forever in our hearts.
Can't wait to see you in heaven,
where all will be well.*

1

ℋoop-Dee-Doo

I always feel a rise in my scalp or in the backs of my wrists
when something is special, whether it be a song or a man.

Doris Day

If anyone had told this small-town, freckle-faced girl that
she'd end up gracing the cover of a big-city bridal magazine wearing the world's most beautiful wedding gown,
she would've said they were crazy. But that was just what
happened.

Through a series of unfortunate—er, fortunate—events, I
found myself plucked up from my predictable life in Fairfield,
Texas, a quaint little town where Pop ran the local hardware

store and Mama led the choir at the Baptist church. In less time than it took to say, "Hey, let's all go to Dairy Queen for a Blizzard," I was transported to a whole new world in the Dallas–Fort Worth metroplex, that of Cosmopolitan Bridal.

From there, I somehow landed on the cover of *Texas Bride* magazine wearing an exquisite gown that had been specifically designed for me by none other than Nadia James, Texas's most renowned dress designer. All of this because of a contest for brides-to-be, a contest I had no right entering in the first place since I wasn't exactly engaged. Oh, I'd come close to having a ring on my finger, but my now ex-boyfriend, Casey Lawson, had left me high and dry in the eleventh hour. My ringless finger still ached, and I shuddered whenever I thought about the pain and embarrassment our very public breakup had caused back in Fairfield.

Not that anyone at Cosmopolitan Bridal seemed to care about my lack of a groom. They were far too busy celebrating the upswing in sales after the October issue of *Texas Bride* hit the stands. I was now firmly planted in the happiest place on earth. Or at least the happiest place in the state of Texas. Groom or no groom, I was destined to be surrounded by gowns, veils, and bridesmaid dresses every day. Goodbye, Dairy Queen. Hello, big-city life.

Settling into my new job turned out to be easier than I'd imagined once Brady James, the shop's interim manager, welcomed me with open arms. After a brief getting-to-know-you season, he also welcomed me with a few sweet kisses. But my budding relationship with the pro basketball player turned bridal shop manager didn't necessarily mean I'd be wearing that gorgeous wedding gown for real, at least not anytime soon. Still, a girl could daydream, right?

That was exactly what I found myself doing near the close

of the day on the first Monday in November. A firm voice brought me back to reality.

"Katie, did you place that ad in the *Tribune*?"

I startled to attention as our head salesclerk's voice sounded from outside my office door. Before I could respond, Madge entered the room, her arms loaded with bolts of fabric—tulle, lace, and the prettiest eggshell-hued satin I'd ever laid eyes on. The bolt on top started to slide, and I bounded from my seat to grab the slippery satin before the whole pile went tumbling to the ground. I caught it just in time and secured its spot atop the others.

"Thanks." Madge shifted her position, nearly losing her grip on the bolts once more. "So, did you place the ad or not?"

"I did." I gave her a confident smile. No one could accuse Katie Fisher of falling down on the job. No sir. I aimed to please.

"Ah. I see." Madge's nose wrinkled. "Nadia wants to talk to you about that. She's on the phone."

"O-oh?" I still flinched whenever my boss's name was spoken. Working for one of the country's top designers still made me a tad nervous. Okay, a *lot* nervous. "It's almost midnight in Paris. Why is she calling so late?"

"It's important."

I gave Madge a nod and reached for the phone. Seconds later, I was engaged in a lively conversation with Nadia. I assured her that the ad had been placed in the *Tribune*, as per her earlier instructions.

Instead of celebrating that fact, she groaned. "Oh no. I was hoping you hadn't placed it yet."

"Why?"

"Because we're backlogged. Madge says we've taken over sixty orders for the Loretta Lynn gown just since I left the

Dallas area. They've come in like a flood and I'm not there to build a dam."

"I see." Although her dam analogy left images of beavers running through my mind.

"I didn't think about what this would do to our business, to be honest." Nadia's voice was laced with anxiety. Weird. She rarely let her worries shine through. "I mean, I expected sales, of course, but we'll have to mass-produce to keep up with the demand. We've been busy in the past, but never like this."

"What can I do, Nadia?" I reached for my pen and paper.

She hesitated and then released a little sigh. "That's the problem. I don't know."

My pen hovered above the paper, awaiting its cue.

"I've talked to Dahlia. Even with the extra seamstresses she's hired, she just can't keep up." The exhaustion in Nadia's voice rang through. "It's a happy problem, I guess. Growing pains. But I truly don't know what I'm going to do. There's no way we can continue taking orders for dresses if we can't fill those orders."

I set my pen down, ready to offer all the assurance I could. "Don't worry, Nadia. We'll figure it out, I promise. I'm sure Brady has a plan in mind."

"I hope so. That boy of mine is a whiz—on and off the court."

"Yes, he is." Only, he wouldn't be on the court anytime soon. With his knee injury requiring a second surgery, Brady had already missed out on most of the season. Heartbreaking.

"When you see him, please give him my love." Nadia released a yawn. "I'd better hit the hay. Long day tomorrow."

"Of course."

I'd just started to say goodbye when she jumped back in. "And Katie, in case I haven't said it often enough, we're tickled

10

to have you on board at Cosmopolitan Bridal. I credit our recent successes to you."

"To me?" I was just the one who'd pretended to be engaged so I could enter a contest.

"Yes. I truly believe God brought you to us. And you're doing a fantastic job with the marketing end of things."

"Maybe a little *too* good?" I countered.

She chuckled. "Never thought I'd say so, but yes. Do you think you can pull the ad from the *Tribune* before it goes live?"

I glanced at the clock. Five minutes till five. I'd have to get right on it. "I'll give it my best shot, Nadia. I'll shoot you an email after I find out."

"Thanks, hon. Talk to you later."

"Bye."

I put in a call to the advertising rep at the paper and asked him to pull the ad. No telling what he would put in its place, but that wasn't my concern. I needed to keep my focus where it belonged—on the shop.

And on the handsome fella now standing in the door of my office. I felt the edges of my lips turn up when I saw Brady standing there. Mr. Tall, Dark, and Handsome took a couple of steps in my direction and I rose to meet him. He extended his arms as if to offer me an embrace, but I shook my head and whispered, "We're on the clock."

"It's six minutes after five." He gave me a knowing look and then pulled me into a warm hug. "And you . . ." He kissed me on the cheek. "Need . . ." He gave me two more kisses on the other cheek. "A break." These words were followed by the sweetest kiss on the lips and I was transported to a happy place.

Until Madge cleared her throat from out in the hall.

Brady brushed the tip of his finger across my cheek and

then took a step back just as she entered the room, clucking her tongue in motherly fashion.

"Are you two at it again?" Madge rolled her eyes. "I thought we agreed to no PDA."

"PDA?" Crinkles formed between Brady's dark brows.

"Public displays of affection," Madge and I said in unison.

"Makes the customers nervous," she added.

Brady crossed his arms. "Let me understand this. You're telling me that the sight of a man kissing a woman makes happy-go-lucky brides-to-be nervous?"

"Well, in the workplace, I mean." Madge shook her head. "Anyway, I suppose it's really none of my business."

"Yep." Brady pulled me back into his arms. "And we're off the clock. So you just tell any nervous bride to worry about her own love life, not mine."

Love life?

Did he really just say *love* life?

I gazed up, up, up into Brady's gorgeous blue eyes, my heart soaring to the skies above—okay, the ceiling above—as he gave me a kiss that erased any doubts.

Madge left the room, muttering all the way. I couldn't seem to rid myself of the giddy sensation that threatened to weaken my knees. Just about the time I'd leveraged the distance between heaven and earth, my cell phone rang. I hated to interrupt such a tender moment, but it might be Nadia calling again.

Strange, though, that she would call me on my cell and not the office phone.

Brady stopped kissing me and gave me a little shrug as I reached for my purse. Seconds later, as the phone rang for the third time, I finally held it in my grip. When I read the name *Casey Lawson* on the screen, it took everything inside of me not to toss the foul thing into the trash can on the far side of the room—a perfect three-point shot.

Instead, with my heart in my throat, I pushed the button on the phone and tried to offer the most normal-sounding hello that a once-jilted girlfriend who'd just been caught kissing a new fella could give.

2

My Dreams Are Getting Better All the Time

We all knew you were going to have a meteoric rise and be a very big star. Nobody had any doubt of it.

Janis Paige to Doris Day

My hands trembled as I clutched my phone. Out of the corner of my eye I could see Brady watching me with that "you okay?" look in his eyes. From the other end of the line I heard my ex-boyfriend's voice ring out. "Katie? You there?"

I hated the way Casey's voice made me feel. He'd broken my heart months ago and I'd moved on. So why did my stomach still jolt when I heard that smoother-than-velvet voice now? Ugh. I'd never had much of a poker face and couldn't seem to control the nervous edge to my voice either.

"Y-yes." I shifted the phone to my other ear. "Yeah, I'm here." *Here in Dallas, with the guy I adore. Not there with you. Not anymore.*

"Hey." Casey had never been the talkative sort, but "hey" seemed a little bland, even for him.

Brady gave me a curious look and I mouthed, "Casey."

I must've actually said that out loud, because my ex responded with a nervous chuckle. "At least you haven't forgotten my name."

"Of course not, Casey. We grew up together. I'll never forget you."

This garnered an eyebrow raise from Brady, who decided this would be a good time to slip out of the room. I'd have to explain later. I certainly hadn't asked for this call, nor did I mean anything by the "I'll never forget you" line.

"I heard about Queenie." Casey cleared his throat. "That's some news. Who would've guessed your grandmother would get married this late in life? Crazy, right?"

Okay, conversation about my family. I could deal with that. Nothing too personal. "I wouldn't say it's crazy. It's pretty awesome, if you want my opinion. Not every woman has the chance to get married in her golden years. I'm thrilled for her. The whole family is."

"I didn't mean crazy. Not really." An uncomfortable pause followed his words. "So, Mama said the wedding's next month. Two weeks before Christmas?"

"Right. December 12th. Invitations just went out."

"And she's getting married at the Baptist church?"

"From what I understand, yes. But Casey, Queenie has only

been engaged a little while. How in the world do you know all of that?"

He chuckled. "Well, Bessie May told Ophelia Edwards and Ophelia told Prissy Moyer up at the Methodist church. Prissy told Jimmy Lee, the Methodist pastor's son, who, by the way, got a new job stocking the shelves at Brookshire Brothers. Jimmy Lee told the manager—did you know that old man Peterson retired and his son has taken his place?—and then Mr. Peterson told my mom when she was in the checkout line buying some apples for a homemade apple pie. Oh, and Mama called me. Naturally."

"Naturally." I glanced toward the door to see if Brady had reappeared. Nope. "Glad to see the party line is alive and well in Fairfield."

Casey laughed. "You know how it is, Katie. Nothing ever changes."

"Except my eighty-two-year-old grandmother marrying a minister who's secretly had the hots for her for years. And she's done the unthinkable—switched denominations. Other than that, everything's just as it always was."

"Yeah, that's a little different." Casey hesitated and I could almost envision the wrinkles in his brow as he thought through this conversation. I knew every detail of that handsome face, after all. Caring for a fella for over ten years meant memorizing his expressions, his vocal inflections, even his quirks.

"Tell me about it." I glanced toward the doorway, wondering where Brady had gone. "And other things are changing too. My father doesn't run the hardware store anymore. He—"

"Passed it to your brother. Heard that too. I saw Jasper last time I was in town."

"Ah. Well, maybe you heard that Jasper is engaged to—"

"That Crystal girl. The one he met at the bridal shop. She's from Georgia. They're talking about getting married in the spring after he renovates the store."

"Wow." I gave a little whistle. "I guess news really does spread. And I had no idea my brother was talking about renovating the hardware store."

"He is," Casey said. "There's only one thing I'm not sure about. You said Queenie's converted? She's a Presbyterian now, right?"

"Yep."

"Does her move to the Presbyterian church have the Baptists in an uproar?"

I paused to think through my response, though this small talk was really wearing on me. "Not really." I shifted the phone to my other ear and noticed my hands were a little sweaty. "I think everyone is happy for her, to be honest. So no uproar." *Except the obvious one you caused in my heart when you skipped out on me five months ago.*

Where did *that* come from?

"Are you coming home for the wedding?" he asked.

"Home? You mean Fairfield?" Was this some sort of joke? Did he really think I'd miss my grandmother's big day?

"Of course Fairfield."

The surprise in his voice threw me a little. I poked my finger in my free ear to drown out the sound of Madge hollering something to Brady just outside the office door. "I'm just surprised to hear you call Fairfield home, Casey. You live in Oklahoma now, don't you?"

"Y-yes." He hesitated. "Anyway, just wondered if I'd see you at the wedding."

Okay, now this had reached a ridiculous point. "She's my grandmother. I wouldn't miss her wedding for the world, Casey. You know that. I'm headed back to Fairfield this coming

Saturday to help plan her shower. I'm even helping her pick out a gown."

"Right. You do the wedding gown thing now."

"The wedding gown thing?"

"Well, you know. You work at that shop," he said. "And you're living with your aunt Alva, Queenie's sister. Heard about that too. I just wondered if you were coming home for the big day, is all. But you've answered that question . . . and I'm glad. Really glad. It'll be great to see you again. I mean that. I really do."

This whole conversation was beyond strange. Why would Casey Lawson care if I worked at a bridal shop, or if I came home for my grandmother's wedding? Why did it matter if I was living with my aunt in Dallas? The guy couldn't care less about me. He'd made that obvious months ago . . . hadn't he?

"So, are you bringing that guy with you?" Casey's words startled me back to attention.

"Brady?" Now I hesitated. "Not sure if he can come to the wedding. He'll be having another surgery on his knee soon, so I guess it depends on how he's healing. If he's well enough I'm sure he'd love to come. He adores Queenie, and vice versa."

"Right. I read all about it online." He laughed. "I mean, I heard that he's having surgery, not that he adores Queenie. I guess we can count the Mavericks out for the playoffs this year if Brady's not coming back to the game." Off Casey went on a tangent, talking about basketball. As if this call had anything to do with that.

I waited until I just couldn't take it anymore before interrupting him. "Why did you call again, Casey?"

"I . . . I just miss your voice, Katie. We used to do everything together. We were the dynamic duo. Now I'm stuck here in Oklahoma in the middle of an oil field and I'm—"

"Lonely." We spoke the word together.

"Yeah." He sighed. "I guess it was inevitable. Or maybe I had it coming to me."

He had it coming to him, all right. But that was none of my business. Not anymore. Still, maybe I should encourage the guy. "I happen to know there are a ton of available girls in Tulsa. We get a lot of bridesmaids from that area. Just look around you, Casey. God will bring the right person."

"He did." Casey cleared his throat. "I mean, he will."

That first part totally threw me. If my ex was trying to send me some sort of signals, they were mixed at best.

At that moment the hallway outside my office door came alive with activity. Dahlia and her team of sewing aficionados came out of the studio at the back of the hallway, voices raised in some sort of argument. Nothing unusual about that these days. From the doorway, I heard Brady talking to them. Scolding, really. No doubt he was ready to leave. And though the sound of my ex-boyfriend's voice held some appeal, I found far more reason to end the call when I turned and saw the "come hither" look in Brady's eyes.

So I ditched Casey. Quickly. And after a couple of deep breaths I wondered why I'd even bothered to take the call in the first place. Everything about it just felt wrong.

"Do I even want to know?" Brady stepped into the room and I could read the concern in his eyes.

I tossed my phone into my purse and tidied up my desk, preparing to leave. "Casey."

"Yeah, gathered that much. What's his deal?" Brady's gorgeous blue eyes narrowed a bit.

"I think he's lonely."

"Lonely?" Brady pulled me into his arms and planted kisses in my hair. "He's going to have to call someone else to ease his pain. Want me to tell him that? I'll be happy to." He ran his fingertips along my hairline and I rested my head against his shoulder.

I shook my head and didn't respond. Doggone it. I didn't want to be affected by Casey's call, but something about the sound of his voice still got to me.

"We've been best friends since we were little," I said. "It's hard to shake off a best friend."

"I don't mind a little friendship, but if he thinks . . ." Brady's voice tightened. "If he thinks . . ."

"Surely not."

Then again, Casey *had* sounded odd. And what was up with that stuff about being lonely? Some sort of subliminal message?

"When you're used to talking to someone every day and then you don't talk anymore, it gets weird." I gave a little shrug. "I think he's just at that inevitable stage where he's adjusting to his new normal."

Brady still didn't look convinced. "I'm perfectly adjusted to my new normal, and he'd better not mess it up. He had his chance and he blew it. His loss is my gain."

"Mine too." I smiled up at him, my heart feeling more at home than ever before. Ah, that handsome face! It won me over, not just because of the perfect job God had done in creating it, but because of the emotion behind it. The edges of my sweetie's lips curled up in a delicious grin, and a little shiver ran through me as he leaned down, his breath warm against my cheek.

"Good. Because I'm laying claim to you, Katie Sue."

I couldn't help but laugh. "Sounds like a country song. Someone reach for a guitar."

"Yep." He faked a heavy drawl as he warbled, "I'm layin' claim to you, Katie Sue. Yer purty face makes me want to . . .

to . . ." He raked his fingers through his hair. "I've never been very good at rhyming, sorry."

"Ha-ha. It's okay."

"What do you think? Will they play my song on the radio?"

"Well, you *are* Brady James, basketball star. Maybe they'll play it on the Dallas stations because you're already famous in these here parts." I winked.

In an instant his expression shifted from lighthearted to sad. Ack.

"I guess it's time to stop calling me a basketball player, don't you think?" He gestured to his left knee. "Once I have the second surgery on this knee, I'll be out of commission for a long time. Maybe for good. You know what's going to happen. They'll release me from my contract for this season, at the very least. No going back."

"More time to work on the lyrics of my song?" I forced a smile but he only shrugged. "I'm sorry, Brady. I'm just trying to make things less painful."

"Here's one thing that can help make things less painful: if I know that Casey isn't trying to force his way back into your life. You don't think he will, do you?"

"He's never been one to commit to anything. Learned that the hard way. Maybe he's at the wishy-washy stage with his new job. Surely it's just a phase."

"Yeah, well, I'd like to show him a phase." Brady's eyes narrowed and he raised his fists as if ready for a fight. For whatever reason, the image of the two guys in the ring got me tickled.

"What?" Brady feigned surprise. "You don't think I can take him?"

"Oh, you could take him, all right. But right now, I'd rather you take me . . . to dinner."

"Mmm. Dinner." He reached to grab my coat off the rack

and slipped it over my shoulders. "You had me at chicken-fried steak."

"Um, I never said 'chicken-fried steak.'"

"Yes you did. Just this minute." He grinned and kissed me. "And I'm all in, trust me."

Okay then. I'd eat two platefuls of chicken-fried steak for this guy. I might even throw in some mashed potatoes, gravy, and a biscuit. As long as he kept kissing me like that, we'd burn off the calories in no time.

3

Everybody Loves a Lover

Wrinkles are hereditary. Parents get them from their children.

Doris Day

No one loved my hometown of Fairfield as much as my grandmother, Queenie Fisher. She never left unless one of two things happened: the Lord spoke in an audible voice or she had to visit her orthopedist in Dallas to tend to her titanium knee. On the first Thursday in November she had an appointment with the knee doctor. Ironic, since her knee doc was Brady's knee doc too. Small world, orthopedics.

She'd deliberately scheduled her appointment on the same day as Brady's so we could all meet up. Her plan? Visit the doc, grab lunch, and then pick out her wedding gown. With

my help, of course. I couldn't get over the fact that my grandmother was getting married. Crazy! I couldn't wait to spend
time with her and with her groom-to-be.

It would take some getting used to, seeing Reverend Bradford with her, but there he was, his eyes shimmering with
adoration for my grandmother as he helped her out of the
car and into the building. Minutes later, the four of us sat in
the rather sterile waiting room of Metroplex Orthopedics,
Queenie and I catching up on the goings-on back in Fairfield
while the fellas talked about basketball.

Out of the corner of my eye I could see the pained expression on Brady's face as the good reverend talked about the
Mavericks. Missing out on this was killing him, especially
since the team seemed to be struggling. I sensed Brady's pain,
though he rarely spoke of it. The fans were missing him too,
if one could judge from the outpouring of love and concern
every time Brady went out in public.

"Dr. Jennings will get him fixed up in a hurry." Queenie's
words startled me back to the present. I turned to her, my
spirits lifting as I picked up on her zeal. The edges of her lips
had curled up in a soft smile, emphasizing the wrinkles on her
cheeks. At eighty-two years of age she still had the prettiest
skin of anyone I knew, though it was tissue-paper thin. And
she was a whiz with the makeup brush, adding just the right
amount of blush and lipstick. As always, practically perfect
in every way.

"Oh, I know, Queenie. This next surgery should take care
of everything."

Reverend Bradford glanced our way. "Hoping she doesn't
have to have a second surgery, Katie."

"We weren't talking about me, Paul." Queenie patted her
titanium knee. "I'm just here for a checkup. Gotta figure out

why these metal parts are giving me such fits. Do you think it's possible to be allergic to titanium?"

"I suppose anything's possible, but let's hope it's not that." I glanced up as a new patient entered the waiting room. He approached the sliding glass window and carried on a conversation with the receptionist, then took a seat.

"Just got to make sure before the big day." Queenie's voice reminded me that we were mid-conversation. "I don't want my right knee to lock up while I'm cruising down the aisle toward Prince Charming here." She gave Reverend Bradford a little wink, which he returned. I couldn't help the chuckle that escaped. I'd witnessed the stern side of my grandmother for years. And the bossy side. But the romantic side? This was a new one. And the image of her cruising down the aisle on her titanium knee got me tickled. I'd seen her hobbling, but never cruising.

Brady chimed in, talking about a friend of his, a guy from church, who had a titanium knee. Reverend Bradford countered with a story about a guy who had a prosthetic hip. Before long we were all cracking jokes about mechanical body parts. Then the nurse called my grandmother's name.

She rose, albeit slowly—no cruising whatsoever. "Let's see what he's got to say about this old gal, whether she's fit to travel down the aisle or not."

"Or—or not?" Reverend Bradford looked alarmed as he stood and took her arm, pointing her toward the inner office door. "Do you really think he'll advise you not to marry?"

"Kidding, kidding!" Queenie gave him a gentle kiss on the cheek. "Just wanted to see the look on your face. You're getting me, Paul Bradford, for better or for worse, in sickness and in health. And I'm fit as a fiddle." She took a couple of steps toward the nurse, but her knee didn't cooperate, so she stopped. "Maybe not fit as a fiddle, but alive and well."

Seconds later they disappeared back into the doctor's inner sanctum, and we awaited Brady's turn. He centered his conversation on Queenie, but I had a feeling there was more going on in that anxious brain of his.

After a few moments I couldn't take it anymore. I reached for his hand. "Brady? Can I ask a question?"

He gave me a thoughtful look. "Of course, Katie. I don't have any secrets from you."

I hesitated to think through my next words. "Dr. Jennings is going to do a second surgery on your knee, right?"

Brady fidgeted in his seat. "Well, he suggested it at my last visit if the tear wasn't healing up. The knee keeps giving out on me. So . . . " A look of sadness came over him. "Yeah. I guess so."

"You said we could talk about anything, and we do. But not that. We hardly ever talk about your knee. Or basketball. I mean, you talk about the other players and about Stan."

"Stan? That old coot? You know how he is, Katie. It's an agent's job to worry about his players."

"Who said anything about worrying? And just for the record, he's not the only one who's anxious." I leaned in close to whisper those words so as not to draw the attention of others around us. "I want you to be okay, Brady, and I don't just mean your knee. I want to know for sure that you're okay not playing this season. Emotionally, I mean. If you ever opened up and talked about it, I wouldn't fret, but you're so . . . so . . . closed off."

He shrugged and I saw his expression harden. "I've reconciled myself to the fact that I can't play, so I'll stay at Cosmopolitan and work. It's a pretty sedentary job. I'm handling it all right." He lowered his voice as the fellow in the seat across from us looked our way.

"There's a difference between handling something and enjoying it," I said in a strained whisper. "I hope you'll reach the point where you're okay at the bridal shop. I don't want it to be something you just tolerate. You know?"

"Yeah."

I felt the sting of tears as I added, "I just worry about you. I want you to be happy."

When Brady looked me in the eyes, I saw the most reflective expression there. He reached over and gripped my hand. "I'm learning to be happy no matter my circumstances. We don't always get what we want, but God promises to make all things work together for our good. And look at what he's done. If I hadn't come to work at Cosmopolitan, I would never have gotten to know you. And knowing you has changed my life forever. I'm crazy about basketball. Always have been. But I've found something I'm a lot crazier about, Katie, so put your mind at ease. I can tolerate just about anything if you're with me."

If that didn't make a girl feel good about herself, nothing would! And the kiss that followed—right there in the waiting room of Metroplex Orthopedics—certainly did. Must've been a doozy even for the onlookers, because applause broke out when he stopped kissing me. The guy across from us hollered, "Three-point shot!" and then let out a whoop.

An older woman to our left called out, "Looks like the lips aren't broken, even if the knee is."

Brady laughed, then went on to describe his knee injury. "It's a torn meniscus. Doc Jennings operated months ago, but it's still not stable."

"Looks like you've found something a little more stable, eh?" The woman's eyes shimmered with mischief and we all laughed. This opened up the floor to conversation, and soon

Brady was himself again, chatting with the other patients as if they were old friends. I drew in a cleansing breath, happy to have my fella back to normal.

Minutes later the nurse called Brady back. "Do . . . do you want me to go with you?" I asked.

"Of course." He raised his voice, making quite the production out of his next statement. "He's not a proctologist. He's just examining my knee."

This got another laugh out of the other patients, who were all looking and feeling more like family now.

Turned out the doctor might as well have been a proctologist. Brady had to change into a gown before being examined, something he clearly hadn't counted on. I stepped outside of the room while he made the transition from pants to hospital gown, then came back in when he called out, "You may enter."

I'd seen my very tall, very handsome fella in just about every kind of clothing, but not this. The gown, obviously meant for someone much shorter, came up to mid-thigh. With his legs exposed, the scar on his left knee from the previous surgery jumped out at me. I'd never paid much attention to it before—really, I rarely saw it unless Brady happened to be wearing shorts—but today it seemed to grab my attention.

Brady took a seat on the table and groaned. "Promise you won't take any pictures of me in this getup. Stan would have a field day if anyone released this image to the press."

"I promise, I promise." I winked. "But you are awfully cute, if my opinion means anything."

"Cute?" He looked surprised.

"Er, handsome. Very, very handsome. And great legs." I gave a little whistle.

"If you don't count the knee." He ran his fingers along his knee as he tried to flex it. My gaze shifted to his face as he grimaced.

28

"Sorry, Brady. And I promise, no photos."

He turned his attention to a poster on the wall—a detailed look at the human knee—then looked back at me. "I just don't think I'm ready for photos of me in this getup to hit the airwaves."

Through the wall I could hear Queenie laughing in the next room. She must've gotten good news from the surgeon. Either that or they were sharing some sort of private joke. I thought about how much my grandmother had changed over the past several months since admitting her affection for Reverend Bradford. She'd morphed from a cranky old lady to a feisty bride-to-be filled with life and laughter. Even her physical appearance had changed. Once terse and stern, she now appeared softer around the edges. Love had a way of doing that to a person.

Ah, love.

I glanced up at Brady, who seemed a little preoccupied with his gown, which he attempted to tuck under his thighs. I would've laughed and made a comment about miniskirts, but it didn't seem appropriate. Instead, I focused on matters of the heart.

We hadn't done the "I love you" thing yet. I mean, we hadn't spoken the words. He showed me with every move, every encouraging word, that he adored me. In fact, I'd never been treated better or felt more affirmed. But he hadn't come out and said it yet. Maybe he was just taking his time.

I didn't have time to think about it very long because Doc Jennings entered the room and dove into a jovial conversation with Brady about the Mavericks. The older fellow did the examination while talking, and I could tell he wasn't pleased with the outcome of the last surgery. Over and over again he asked Brady to move his knee, then to put pressure on it while bending and flexing. I could read the pain in Brady's eyes, especially when he stood and placed most of his weight on that leg. He took a seat once more, relief flooding his face as the pressure was lifted.

After the lighthearted conversation, the surgeon's expression shifted to one of concern, and he wrote something down on Brady's chart. "I think we've let this go long enough, Brady," he said. "I've looked at your most recent MRI and I don't like what I see. Things are getting worse, not better. Sometimes it takes more than one surgery to get these tears under control." He pointed to the poster on the wall and began a lengthy, elaborate explanation of what he planned to do to the inside of Brady's knee. I pinched my eyes shut, unable to fathom it.

"We need to get you on the calendar as soon as possible. I'll send my nurse in to schedule you." The doctor reached out his hand, and Brady shook it but didn't say anything.

Turned out he didn't have to. From outside the closed door Queenie's voice rang out. "Yoo-hoo! Katie Sue? You in there?"

I peeked my head out of the door and nodded. "Yes, almost done."

"Praise the Lord, I can get married!" Queenie giggled. "Doc even said I'd be good to walk all the way down the aisle without another surgery."

Ironic.

"We're headed out to lunch." Reverend Bradford looped his arm through my grandmother's. "Still want to join us?"

I glanced back at Brady, who was now engaged in quiet conversation with the doctor about his surgery.

"Maybe not this time."

Queenie's joyous expression saddened. "Ah. Gotcha. When we're done with lunch I'll meet you at Cosmopolitan to pick out my wedding dress. What time do you think you'll be back up there?"

"Maybe an hour? I wouldn't miss it for the world. Aunt Alva's coming too, right?"

"Yep. We're swinging by the house to pick her up. I wouldn't want to pick out my wedding gown without my sister's help, that's for sure. She'll be honest about how I look." Queenie gazed with adoration at Reverend Bradford. "Just have to ditch this handsome fella before I come. Don't want him to see me in my gown before the big day."

"You're going to be a radiant bride, Queenie." He gave her a kiss on the tip of her nose. "A vision of loveliness. I'm counting every moment until our wedding day. You'll be a princess floating down the aisle."

"More like a marshmallow waddling down the aisle, but let's not go there just yet. Doc Jennings says with a little therapy he'll have me walking better in time for the big day. Isn't that right, Doc?"

The orthopedist turned to give her a smile and a nod.

Queenie's gaze traveled through the opening in the door to Brady still seated on the examining table. She looked back at me and leaned in close to whisper, "I'll be praying for Brady, honey. He'll do just fine. Trust me when I say that things don't always work out like you think." She glanced up at Reverend Bradford. "Sometimes they work out better."

The good reverend gave a nod, and seconds later the happy couple sauntered—okay, hobbled—out of the office, Queenie's cane tap-tap-tapping on the wooden floor. I turned my attention back to the guy in the hospital gown, determined to keep a smile on my face, even if his faded under the pressure. With the Lord's help, I could surely keep my fella's spirits up.

4

$\mathscr{A}$ren't You Glad You're You

I think it was films. I loved all those Doris Day visuals of her being a tomboy and then changing into this gorgeous girl in a ballgown.

> Stella McCartney, on being asked why
> she became a fashion designer

B rady didn't have much to say on the drive back to the bridal shop. I knew he was silently focused on the November 19th surgery. I did my best to listen quietly to the radio and contemplate my schedule for the rest of the day. Nevertheless, I kept glancing at the calendar app on my phone, distracted by the surgery date.

Two weeks. Just two short weeks until the man was operated

on . . . again. Two weeks to get past the chaos at the shop, the goings-on in Fairfield, and the feeling of anxiety that gripped my heart whenever I thought about the operation that would put Brady through more pain. I needed to come up with a way to encourage him, both before the surgery and after. My guy was going to need me more than ever.

Not that he wanted my input. No, right now he just wanted silence, obviously. I reached over and patted his arm. He glanced my way and shrugged. "It's okay, Katie. God's got this."

"Yep." Not much of an answer, but the right answer just the same. "You sure you're all right driving?"

"Of course. I'm fine as long as I'm sitting. Mostly." He fixed his gaze on the road.

"Just checking." I shoved my phone back in my purse, determined to shift my focus to Queenie.

He glanced at me again and I could read the concern in his eyes. "I'll be okay, Katie, I promise. Just give Queenie the attention she deserves. It's her special day. Let's make sure she has the dress of her dreams."

"I will. She's probably already waiting for me at the shop. I hope Twiggy doesn't mind helping me with the fitting." A feeling of comfort wrapped around me as I spoke the young salesclerk's name. Though I'd only known Twiggy a few months, she'd already won my heart. She'd won my brother Beau's heart too. Their budding relationship made me so happy.

"Twiggy won't mind." Brady eased on the brake and turned right onto Jackson Street. "You know how easygoing she is."

"I'm glad someone is. The design and alterations crew back in the studio . . ."

"Yeah, they're a different story altogether. Whatever you do, don't ask Dahlia for help. She's overwhelmed. Her whole team is."

His words were confirmed the moment we arrived back at the shop. Brady headed to his office to make some calls. I didn't find Queenie, but I did see Twiggy and Madge at the register waiting on a customer. I waved and motioned to the studio as I called out, "Going to grab some lunch."

Twiggy put her hand up as if to stop me. "Do. Not. Go. Back. There."

"What?"

"Do. Not. Go. Back. There." Her words were so forceful that even the customer looked alarmed.

I took a few steps in Twiggy's direction to explain. "I *have* to go back there. I have some leftovers in the fridge that need to be eaten today or they'll go bad. We were supposed to go to lunch with Queenie but it didn't work out, so I'm starving."

Twiggy's eyes widened and she shook her head. "Go ahead and starve. Let the leftovers go bad. Do yourself a favor and skip lunch or go out. You can thank me later for giving you that advice. But whatever you do . . . Don't. Go. Into. The. Studio."

"Twiggy, that's just plain silly. I know they're busy, but . . . seriously?"

She finished waiting on the customer, then turned back to me. "Seriously. Enter at your own risk. You have been warned."

I let out a nervous laugh, but I couldn't get my feet to cooperate. Maybe I'd better not attempt it after all.

"I've been avoiding the studio for days," Madge interjected. "The tension is so thick you could cut it with a knife. And you don't even want to know what happened between Eduardo and Hibiscus earlier. It's really bad back there right now."

"Eduardo and Hibiscus?" I stopped to reflect on two of our newest designers. "But they've always gotten along so well."

"Until now."

With a wave of my hand I tried to dismiss her concerns.

"Well, I know they're in rough shape trying to get caught up with orders. That's why I encouraged Queenie to pick something off the rack. Not that there's time to design a new gown anyway. Her wedding is in five weeks. Crazy."

"Hey, no point in waiting when you're eighty-two." Twiggy flashed a smile and I felt my anxieties ease.

"I know, right?" Before I could decide what to do about my food, the door to the shop opened and Queenie stepped inside with Aunt Alva on her heels. Oh well. So much for eating lunch.

"We drove all the way to Alva's house, but she wasn't there," Queenie explained. "Even called her phone, but she didn't answer."

"But she's here now." I gestured to my great-aunt, who fished around in her purse.

"I don't even know why I bought that ridiculous cell phone. I can never remember where I put it." Alva shrugged and closed her purse. "And I guess I forgot that Queenie was coming by to get me."

"So how did you get here?" I asked, still feeling perplexed by this conversation.

"Lori-Lou came by and got me." Alva shifted her oversized purse to her other shoulder. "She dropped me off on her way to her OB visit. I met up with Queenie in the parking lot. She really gave me the what-for since I ignored her call, but I think maybe I left my phone at home."

Nothing new there.

"Can you take me home later?" Alva asked.

"Of course. If you don't mind hanging around until I'm done working." I had to admit, I cringed a little when she mentioned my cousin. Not that I had anything against Lori-Lou. Not at all. She'd welcomed me to the Dallas–Fort Worth area a few months back, after all. But her rambunctious children could be very difficult at times. They'd been known to create chaos at Cosmopolitan in days past. Probably for the best that she hadn't stayed today, what with tempers flaring all around us already.

Still, I was thrilled to see Queenie and Alva getting along so well. The two sisters were inseparable these days, quite a contrast from the past several years when they'd barely spoken.

Today they gabbed with Twiggy as if they'd never had a care in the world. Brady popped his head out of his office to say hello and then disappeared back inside the inner sanctum once again. Not that I blamed him. Staying away from all of the estrogen was probably a good thing, especially with so much on his mind. And the next few hours were all about my grandmother anyway.

"Where did Reverend Bradford go after he dropped you off, Queenie?" I asked.

My grandmother waggled her finger. "You know, Katie Sue, you're going to have to stop calling him Reverend Bradford at some point. He's going to be your grandfather in a few short weeks."

"True." I pursed my lips as I thought about that. "But *Grandpa* just doesn't seem right."

"No, of course not. What about something like Pap-Paul?"

"Pap-Paul?" Seemed a little . . . informal for a reverend. "I'll think about it, Queenie, I promise. Maybe I'll come up with my own name for him."

"You could call him Paul," Alva suggested. "That's a very twenty-first-century approach to the problem. Just call folks by their name. That's what I always do."

"Or you could call him Grampy," Twiggy said. "That's what I call my step-grandfather."

"None of that step-stuff here," Queenie scolded. "But we

don't need to settle on a name today. As long as it's not 'hey you,' I think we'll be fine. But let's cut the reverend stuff, okay? Paul is family now." Her eyes glistened as she looked around the shop. "At least he will be once I find a dress and sashay down the aisle to take his hand."

"So, where did Reverend—er, Pap-Paul—go?" I asked.

Queenie walked over to a rack of dresses and started looking through them, nearly dropping her large purse. "He dropped me off and headed over to Starbucks to work on his sermon for this Sunday. We're doing a whole series on the prodigal son."

"We? You're *preaching* at the Presbyterian church now?"

"No, no." With a wave of her hand she corrected me. "That sweet man just asks for my help with his messages. I think he values my input."

"Sure he does, Queenie. You're a wealth of knowledge."

"When you're eighty-two years old, you should be. I like to think of my brain as a big file box with millions of dusty files inside just waiting to be brushed off and used."

"Paul is lucky to have you," I said. "Truly."

"No, honey . . ." She reached over and took my hand, her eyes brimming with tears. "I'm the lucky one. I never thought I'd have the opportunity to find love again, and I've done it. We've done it. We've defied the odds."

They had defied the odds, all right. To marry at eighty-two? Who had that sort of blissful second chance?

Second chance. That was what I'd been given with Brady. Maybe my grandmother wasn't the only one with a fresh opportunity.

"That's a blessing," I said.

Queenie gave me a knowing look. "Yep. That's our December sermon series, honey: God's abundant blessings. But we can talk more about that later. Now let's look for my dress, shall we? It won't do me any good to plan a wedding if I'm walking naked down the aisle."

Ew.

She guffawed and slapped her thigh. "Now, wouldn't that be a sight?"

It'd be a sight, all right, and not one the Baptists or the Presbyterians would stop talking about anytime soon.

"Let's get this show on the road." Queenie gestured to the rows and rows of gowns. "Shopping for a wedding dress isn't something I do every day. In fact, it's been fifty-plus years since I looked at gowns like this."

"Fashions have surely changed a bit since then." Twiggy took Queenie by the arm. "And I have a vested interest in your gown, Queenie, so I want to help you in any way I can."

"Oh?" My grandmother gave the young woman a suspicious look. "And why is that?"

"Because I might need you to return the favor someday."

A collective gasp went up from all in attendance. "Are you saying that grandson of mine has proposed?" Queenie clasped her hands together in apparent glee. "God bless Beau for seeing the light."

"Not exactly. But I feel sure it'll come any day now. I think Beau's settling into his new job with Stan before he pops the question."

"What exactly does he do with that Stan man, anyway?" my grandmother asked.

"Stan is Brady's agent," I explained. "And he's training Beau to become a sports agent too."

"But right now Beau mostly manages things for Stan," Twiggy said.

"Someone needs to manage Stan," Madge chimed in. "That old fart has been unmanageable for as long as I've known him."

"Oh, I don't know." Alva shrugged. "He seems pretty great to me."

"The point is, Beau and Stan are doing well with the agency, so I don't think it'll be long before he pops the question." Twiggy giggled. "Beau, not Stan."

Madge slapped herself on the forehead.

I tried not to sigh, but Beau and Twiggy had known each other less time than Brady and I. They'd passed the "I love you" stage a couple months back, and Brady and I were just now at the "I love being with you" one.

"I'm just saying that one day I'll be a happy bride too, so Queenie and I can lean on each other." Twiggy fussed with some of the gowns on a nearby rack. "And Katie too."

I put my hands up. "Oh, I don't really have any experience with wedding planning. Not really. I mean, I've never been a bride."

"She just played one on TV." Queenie laughed and slapped her thigh. "That's pretty funny, if I do say so myself."

I didn't particularly find it that funny but offered a strained laugh just to feel like part of the crowd. "I've never been on TV, Queenie," I said. "Well, unless you count that one time when Pop filmed a homemade commercial for the hardware store. But I was only seven."

"True, but you looked mighty cute in that painter's apron and tool belt. Folks in Fairfield are still talking about that."

"Painter's apron?" Twiggy asked. "Tool belt?"

"Don't ask." I groaned. "And please, whatever you do, never bring it up around my mama. She and Pop almost got divorced over that one. He made her wear a placard that promoted a new toilet line. She was humiliated."

"Your parents never came close to divorce, Katie Sue." Queenie clucked her tongue. "What an exaggeration."

"You didn't hear all of the goings-on behind the scenes. But we're not here to talk about that. Today is all about you, Queenie—nothing else."

"Oh, right."

"You might not've played a bride on television, Katie, but you looked pretty convincing on the cover of *Texas Bride* in that magnificent Loretta Lynn gown last month," Twiggy said. "So I'd say you fit the role nicely."

"Yes, indeed. And perhaps it won't be long before some fella snaps to attention and pops the question." Alva gave me a pointed look and then hobbled over to the rack to finger a taffeta gown.

Twiggy rolled her eyes. "Some men are so clueless. But thankfully Beau isn't. He's the sweetest thing since processed sugar. And you should hear the lovely things he said to me just this morning."

Seemed like the perfect time to change the subject. I clapped my hands together and smiled with all the confidence I could muster. "We'd better get back to business, folks. Queenie's only got a couple of hours before she has to get back to Fairfield."

"Oh my, yes." My grandmother glanced at her watch. "The WOP-pers are meeting tonight to pray for an urgent need."

"WOP-pers?" Madge looked perplexed. "Like the candy?"

"Women of Prayer. It's the name of our prayer group in Fairfield," Queenie explained. "Anyway, there's an urgent need at the Baptist church, so we're gathering together in one accord to pray in the hopes that the Lord will intervene."

"What sort of urgent need, Queenie?" I asked.

"Well now, it's extremely confidential. I can't really say." She leaned in close and whispered, "But it might have a little something to do with my wedding planner, Joni Milford." She gave me a knowing look. "Something along those lines."

40

"Joni Milford? As in, the Joni who graduated the year before me? The one who played softball?"

"The one and only. She's a fabulous wedding planner, I might add."

"Wow." I hardly knew what to say in response to this revelation. My memories of Joni Milford were slanted, and not in the best direction. She'd always been a little . . . manly. Hardly the wedding planner type.

"Is she married?" I asked. "Does she have any experience with weddings?"

"Not married yet, but that is the reason for the confidential prayer request. I can't say anything else, except perhaps to add that she's got her eye on a certain young man who might just have his eye on her as well."

My goodness. I'd have to get caught up on this information when I returned to Fairfield on Saturday to help plan Queenie's shower. Right now? Well, with the clock ticking, we needed to stay focused on my grandmother's dress!

5

Falling in Love Again

She [Doris Day] had a pretty serious attitude toward her work, and life in general, but that did not keep her from having a very pleasant disposition and always making others around her feel good.

Leo Fuchs

Picking out the right gown for my grandmother turned out to be tougher than I'd imagined, what with so many women chiming in at once. After a bit of browsing I decided to go straight to the bride-to-be for her opinion.

"What sort of gown are you looking for, Queenie?" I asked.

She turned away from several Paris-inspired dresses to give me a little shrug. "Obviously something off the rack, because

I don't think Dahlia would have time to make a dress on such a tight deadline."

"Dahlia." Twiggy released a slow breath and glanced toward the back of the store where the designers worked in their studio. "Do. Not. Go. Back. There."

"Oh, I won't." Queenie put her hands up in the air. "Just getting something off the rack, as I said. Though I haven't a clue what would look good on me."

"And she's got to look picture-perfect on her wedding day," Alva chimed in. "We want Paul's heart to go pitter-patter when he sees her."

"At our age, we just hope the pitter-patter doesn't come grinding to a halt." Queenie chuckled. "So, nothing over the top. Just a pretty dress that flatters my physique." She pointed to her rounded hips and thighs. "Perhaps a bit of camouflage."

"We've got some lovely options right here." I pointed at a long row of gowns, and my grandmother's eyes appeared to glaze over as she looked at one of the price tags attached.

"My goodness." She dropped the tag as if it had burned her.

"Remember, Queenie, you'll get my discount—40 percent. So don't fret. And it won't be 40 percent off that price either. It's 40 percent off the wholesale price."

"Yes, well . . ." She held her hand away from the dresses as though afraid to touch them.

"Let's start with color. Will you be radiant in white, confident in cream, or flirty in fuchsia?" Twiggy giggled. "Sorry. Trying to picture you in a hot pink dress. It's just not coming to me."

"Um, no." Queenie's face flushed. "Now, I've given this a lot of thought. I was married for nearly fifty years to your grandpa, Katie. I wouldn't feel right starting over in a white dress. People would think I was nuts, playing the role of the virginal bride."

I cleared my throat and pushed that image right out of my head. "So, cream?" I asked.

"I just don't know if that's appropriate either. Back in my day, the only women who wore cream or ivory dresses were women who were, well . . ." Her nose wrinkled. "Compromised."

"Compromised?" the rest of us said in unison.

"Oh my." Twiggy's eyes widened. "You're certainly not compromised."

"Certainly not." Queenie fanned herself with a church bulletin she'd pulled out of her purse. "Unless you count the part where I was married and had children. But I've never considered children a compromise."

"What color are you thinking then?" I asked her.

The prettiest smile turned up the edges of her lips. "I've always been partial to pale blue. A really soft blue like the color of the powder puff in my lavender-scented dusting powder." She pressed the bulletin back in her purse.

I knew the dusting powder well. It was as much a part of her physique as her short silver hair and soft pink lipstick.

"Oh, I see." Twiggy appeared to be thinking. "I've got just the ticket. There's a line of bridesmaid dresses just in from New York. One of them is a pale blue number that's gorgeous. I'd never given thought to using it as a wedding gown, but it's floor-length and has the prettiest neckline. Let me show you."

Minutes later she pulled out one of our newest additions to the shop, an adorable soft blue dress in satin crepe with a sheer overlay on the skirt.

"Oh, it's beautiful." Queenie ran her fingers across the thin overlay and smiled. "And such a soft shade of blue . . . just what I had in mind." Then her brows wrinkled. "But do you think people will realize I'm the bride?"

"Oh, trust me, Queenie, everyone in Fairfield is looking forward to seeing you marry Reverend Bradford," I said. "They'll all know you're the bride. You'll be the one marching down the center aisle, straight into his arms."

"Speaking of which, I have a question." Alva put her hands on her hips. "When one marries a reverend, who performs the ceremony? I mean, he can't exactly be groom and pastor at the same time, can he? The poor fella will get whiplash playing two roles at once."

"Actually, our pastor at the Baptist church is performing the ceremony." Queenie continued to run her fingers along the fabric of the blue gown. "And we're getting married at the Baptist church. That's where I've spent most of my life, after all." She took the gown from Twiggy and held it up in front of herself as if trying to see the fit.

"You're marrying the Presbyterian pastor at the Baptist church?" Twiggy laughed. "In my neck of the woods that would be grounds for excommunication."

"Well, not in Fairfield." Queenie put the dress back on the rack. "In Fairfield we don't discriminate."

"Unless you happen to root for the Texans instead of the Cowboys," I added. "Then it's time for all-out war."

"Oh my, yes. Or you're a Spurs fan instead of Mavericks," Queenie added. "You don't want to get me started. I still remember the time Dave Peterson, the owner up at Brookshire Brothers, told everyone he was rooting for the Spurs. I thought Bessie May was going to have a conniption. You wouldn't believe how much business the store lost over that one. Next thing you know, they have a Mavericks poster hanging in the front window. Shrewd businessman, that Peterson boy." She glanced at the gown. "Now, about this dress." She looked a bit nervous as she held it up again. "What size is this one?"

Twiggy checked the tag and I could see the concern etched between her brows. "Oh, it's an 8."

"I'm guessing we'll need to double that." Queenie gave a nervous chuckle. "Maybe triple."

"No way. Let's start by trying a . . ." Twiggy stepped back and squinted, obviously attempting to eyeball Queenie's measurements. "Yes, we'll start by trying a 12. And we'll go from there."

"I haven't seen a 12 since I was twelve years old," my grandmother muttered. "But if she thinks it's worth a shot, who am I to argue?"

Half an hour later Queenie stood in front of the mirror wearing a size 16. It was a wee bit loose in the shoulders, but I knew Dahlia and her team could remedy that. Someday. Not today. Still, I could hardly believe my eyes as I took in the beautiful cut of the gown and the way it was perfectly fitted to my grandmother's waistline. And I loved the crystals on the bodice. They provided just enough glitz and glam to make the dress a wedding gown.

"Queenie, you look radiant." I clasped my hands together, thoroughly delighted at Twiggy's find.

She couldn't seem to formulate any words—rare for my grandmother. She stared at her reflection with tears in her eyes. "Do you think Paul will like it?"

"He'll love it!" Twiggy said. "Who wouldn't? You look like Cinderella, Queenie! Same color of dress and everything."

She squinted to give herself a closer look. "More like the fairy godmother, but I guess that's okay. Every woman deserves to look radiant on her wedding day, even if she is a little fluffy."

Her words struck me right in the heart. I'd wanted to look radiant on my wedding day too. That was why I'd entered the contest at Cosmopolitan Bridal in the first place, so I would look lovely for Casey. Only, I hadn't married Casey. And these days I hardly paused long enough to think about my own one-day wedding. I was too focused on living my life and growing my relationship with Brady to fret over all that.

"Don't you think, Katie?"

"Hmm?"

My grandmother swished her skirt. "Oh, I was asking if you thought this skirt was full enough. Twiggy suggested adding a petticoat underneath to give it some fullness."

"Awesome idea," I said. "We have a great line of petticoats. You don't even have to buy one. You can borrow it. We have a line of loaners."

"Goodness. Makes 'em sound like automobiles," Alva said. She started telling a story about a Buick she'd rented back in the seventies but lost Queenie after a moment or two.

"I don't want to end up looking like Scarlett O'Hara," my grandmother said. "Maybe I should rethink the petticoat? I need to fit down the aisle. That's already going to be a challenge, being a size 16 and all."

"Don't be silly. It's all going to be perfect. Well, after a few alterations on the shoulders." Twiggy fussed with the loose shoulders on the gown. "We'll have to take you back to visit with Dahlia and her team."

We all feel into a silent trance at that proclamation.

"Sure." Queenie nodded. "I'll be happy to see Dahlia again. It's been ages since she and Dewey came to Fairfield for a visit."

"She's been rather busy," I said.

"Yes. Indeed." Twiggy paled. "The moment has arrived at last. I've been avoiding the studio all day, as I'm sure you've noticed. Dahlia's in a snit. And don't even get me started on Eduardo."

"Eduardo? Who's Eduardo?" Queenie looked perplexed. "I don't remember anyone with that name."

"He's new," Twiggy said. "Relatively new, anyway."

"He works for Dahlia in the studio," I explained. "Quite the character, but one of the most amazing designers I've ever met. And we've got a couple of new girls back there too—Hibiscus and Jane."

"Hibiscus? Someone named Hibiscus works here now?" Queenie looked more confused now.

"Yes," Twiggy said. "In fact, let's do this—I'll send you back to Hibiscus for your alterations. Of all the designers, she's the least emotional. I think she'll be perfect." She clasped her hands together. "What do you think?"

"Less emotional is good." Queenie laughed. "Trust me, there's enough emotion going on in my heart already." Her eyes flooded with tears. She pressed the chiffon down with her wrinkled hands, then looked at Alva. "What do you think, sister? And be honest."

Alva's own eyes filled with tears. She stood next to Queenie, the two of them gazing into their reflections in the mirror, and tried to force out a few words. "I . . . I . . ." She swiped at her eyes with the back of her hand. "I think you're lovely."

"Lovely?" Queenie snorted. "Now there's a word rarely used to describe me. Hardheaded, sure. Tough as nails, clearly. But, lovely?"

Alva put her hand on her sister's arm. "Oh, but you are, Queenie, and that dress is perfect for the wedding."

"Remind me again why I'm not running away to elope?" My grandmother looked at her reflection in the mirror, and I could read the concern in her eyes. "I was married for fifty years. I don't need a big, fancy wedding. People will think I'm being selfish."

"S-selfish?" Alva sputtered. "Girl, this relationship with Paul is a new beginning, and this is just the dress to take you there. Every woman deserves that." She slapped Queenie on the backside. "Now stop carrying on like that."

"Good gravy." My grandmother swished her skirt as she stared at her reflection in the mirror. "If you say so."

"I say so." The two sisters gazed in the mirror together. In that moment, I saw just how alike they were. Same basic height. Same body shape. Similar skin tone. These sisters were two peas in a pod.

Twiggy interrupted the moment. "Queenie, if you've got your heart set on this blue one, we'll get Hibiscus started on the alterations. If you change your mind about the color, we have this same dress in a beautiful shade of eggshell."

"It's not really eggshell," Madge reminded her. "More like buff."

Queenie cleared her throat as she turned her back on the mirror. "Speaking of buff, that reminds me that I'm absolutely dreading the wedding night."

A collective gasp went up from all in attendance. Well, all but Twiggy, who released a nervous laugh.

"For pity's sake, why?" Alva put her hands on her hips and stared at her sister. "Like you said, you were married for fifty years. It's not like playing the piano. You don't forget."

"Yes, but my sweet husband watched this old body of mine disintegrate slowly, over time. Paul is going to see it—all of it, in its glory—for the first time. Ever." Queenie shuddered. "Horrifying thought."

Yes, it was a horrifying thought just to imagine my grandmother in a negligee. No doubt with her titanium knee and arthritic hips, the honeymoon night could prove to be problematic, but I'd never ask about it. Never. Ever.

As she talked about her hubby-to-be with such an affectionate expression on her face, I couldn't help but think that their golden years would be filled with amazing opportunities to find comfort, love, and joy.

Off in the distance Brady passed by. I hoped he would look our way, chime in about how lovely Queenie looked.

But he didn't.

He kept moving slowly toward the front of the store, a somber expression on his face. I could almost read his troubling thoughts: *Surgery. Again. Basketball career over.*

It's just a season, I reminded myself. One that would end soon.

I hoped.

In the meantime, I'd better stay focused on the bride-to-be. With a forced smile I turned back to my grandmother, ready to brave the alterations department.

6

*N*o Two People

Doris Day was such a big movie and TV star, people overlooked
her singing. The proof is in the package. She's one of the best
singers there ever was.

Margaret Whiting

Things at Cosmopolitan Bridal continued to intensify
over the next twenty-four hours, especially in the studio, where Dahlia and her team worked against the
clock to turn out gowns for customers. I managed to get Hibiscus started on Queenie's alterations, then turned my attention to the upcoming Christmas promotions in the *Tribune*.

Up front Madge and Twiggy kept the customers happy.
In the studio out back, Dahlia and her team continued their

work. Nestled in a tiny office between the store and the studio, I did my best to promote the shop and to run interference with customers who weren't thrilled that their dresses were taking longer than expected. Of course, I spent a good deal of time glancing through the open doorway into the office across the hall, occupied by my handsome chicken-fried-steak-eatin' man.

Not that we had a chance to talk about anything other than work. With such a crazy flurry of customers, who had time to think about food? Or take a break? We certainly didn't talk about the obvious thing—Brady's upcoming surgery. No matter how I tried to open that Pandora's box, he kept it tightly sealed. But with his pre-surgery appointment approaching, he'd have to talk about it soon.

I thought about that as I took a call from a newshound Friday morning. The reporter—if one could call him that—tried to wheedle information out of me about the condition of Brady's knee, but I refused to play along. No one could accuse Katie Fisher of having loose lips.

On Friday morning, midway into composing an email to the local paper, I received a phone call from my brother Jasper in Fairfield. His first words threw me a little. "Houston, we have a problem."

"Um, my name is Katie, and I live in Fairfield. Er, Dallas."

"Whatever." Jasper grunted. "We still have a problem."

"What's up?" I leaned back in my chair and closed my laptop.

"Mom and Pop are out of the country. Again. This is their second trip in less than a month."

"Right. Galápagos. Turtles."

"Yeah. Trying to picture Mom with the turtles, but it's just not coming to me."

"Me either. But that's not why you called," I reminded him.

"True. Okay, it's almost the holiday season, as I'm sure you're aware." Suddenly he sounded very businesslike.

"I am." A quick glance at the calendar to my right proved it: Friday, November 6th. "And . . . ?"

"And I've never done the display window at the hardware store before. That was always your job."

"Oh, it's really not that big of a deal. You just—"

"You're coming back to Fairfield tomorrow to help the other ladies plan Queenie's shower, right?"

"Yes. And . . . ?"

"Aw, c'mon, Katie. I was kind of hoping you'd stop by the hardware store and help me. You're the creative one."

"I don't know, Jasper. I've got a full day. After we plan Queenie's shower, I've got to go to her place to deal with my dress."

"Your dress?"

"You know, the one I won in the contest."

"What do you mean, deal with it?"

"I'm putting it in Queenie's cedar closet."

"Ah." The long pause that followed was probably his way of saying, "So, you're not wearing it anytime soon?"

"Anyway, I can swing by the hardware store after that if you like, but you probably won't really need my help. I'm pretty sure you guys can handle a window display without me."

"Not sure about that. I need some tips. Ideas."

"It's easy," I said. "Just go up into the attic and look for the lights and tree and tinsel and stuff."

"Well, yeah . . ." He left to ring up a customer and then returned about twenty seconds later. "Sorry about that. How do I make hammers and saws and toilet brushes look festive? That's the real question."

"Put Crystal to work on it."

"You want me to ask my bride-to-be to make a toilet brush look festive?" My brother snorted. "Seriously?"

"Not a toilet brush, Jasper. There are a ton of things you can use in the window. Put her on the phone and I'll give her some ideas."

Seconds later my future sister-in-law was on the line, sounding more than a little concerned. "I hate to see him frettin' like this, Katie," she said. "I've *neh*-vuh seen this side of Jasper before. He's *so* worked up about that silly window display."

"Yeah. I hate to say it, but my brothers have been very dependent on me. Everyone has. But it's okay. I'll tell you what to do. If you'd like me to stop by tomorrow afternoon when I'm done planning for Queenie's shower, just call, okay? If you still need my help, I'll be happy to give it."

"Oh, thank you, honey!" Crystal released a sigh. "I feel *so* much *bet*-uh knowin' you're nearby!"

I shared some thoughts and suggestions. Before long Crystal sounded excited about the project ahead.

"Oh, I can see it now, Katie!" She chuckled. "What if we stacked up the boxes of *nay*-uhls and screws to form the shape of a Christmas tree and then *cuh*-vuhed them in lights and tinsel? And on the *uh*-thuh side of the window I could put Santa Claus comin' out of that fake fireplace thing that's *neh*-vuh sold. What do you think of *them* apples?"

"I think it sounds lovely."

"Oh, you've got my mind *ree*-lun, Katie Sue! I just cain't wait to dive in! And maybe I won't even need you to stop by after all!"

As I listened to her excitement grow, I felt a strange mixture of emotions—jealousy, because she seemed to be a natural at something I'd worked hard to be mediocre at, and relief, because my services were no longer needed.

Probably a little more jealousy than relief.

We ended the call and I went back to work on my emails as I pondered the window display here at Cosmopolitan Bridal. Hopefully I'd be able to get busy on it. Maybe one day later this month, if things slowed down.

Slowed down. That was funny. I dove back into my work, not coming up for air until Madge popped her head in the door at noon. "You should eat something."

"I'm so busy, Madge."

"You need sustenance. We all do." She put her hands on her broad hips. "In theory, anyway."

"Okay, thanks. I'll figure it out. In a minute."

"All work and no play makes for a dull boy. Er, girl." Madge leaned against the doorjamb and I could read the exhaustion in her eyes. I knew just how she felt.

I glanced down at the pile of papers on my desk, brushed my hair out of my face, and sighed. "Do you think I'm dispensable, Madge?"

She stared at me for a moment before responding. "Is that some kind of a joke?"

"No, I'm being serious. Nadia said I'm doing too good of a job. My cover shoot brought in too many customers. So remind me again why she's paying me to do press releases and PR for the shop when we're already drowning in work?"

"Because . . ." Madge plopped down in the chair across from my desk. "It won't always be this way. Trust me when I say that we go through seasons of plenty and seasons of want."

"Like in the Bible? Feast or famine?"

"Yes. We're in a feasting season right now, but there's usually a famine around the corner. So having a plan to promote the business long-term is wise, don't you think?"

"When you put it like that, yes. And I guess I see what you

mean. It was the same at the hardware store. In the summertime everyone wanted to fix up their yards, their kiddie pools, their swing sets, etc., so our shop had a steady stream of customers. And in the fall people bought rakes and wheelbarrows. The crowd slowed down in winter, which was why we tried to think outside the box and give our customers a Christmas experience. We drew them in with creativity. Everyone wanted to see what sort of window display we'd come up with next."

"Which reminds me, you need to get with Dahlia to discuss our window display. Nadia loved your idea about doing something old-fashioned."

"Like the old windows Macy's used to do."

"Yes, love it. So you and Dahlia will have to decide which gowns to use. White, obviously. And you'll have to create some sort of backdrop. Winter wonderland, maybe?"

"Sure. No problem. But before I can think about all of that, I do need some food. Did I hear you tell Twiggy that you ordered some sort of sandwich platter?"

"Yes. Had it delivered to the studio. But . . . Do. Not. Go. Back. There."

"Oh, the food's just for the sewing crew?"

"It's not that. Tempers are just . . . well . . . flaring back in the studio today. Do yourself a favor and order a pizza."

"Madge, really?"

Her eyes widened and she nodded. "I made the mistake of carrying the platter back there. I thought I'd seen Dahlia in every state of mind, but I've never seen her like this."

"Might have to go back there now, just to see for myself." I gave a nervous laugh.

"Eat at your own risk. You were warned."

I thought about what Madge had said about the seasons as I made my way back to the studio. We really did go through seasons of plenty and seasons of want. I'd done the same in my personal life. Not so very long ago I was in a season of want, wondering if I'd ever find happiness. Today I was in a season of plenty, wrapped in the arms of a great guy and overloaded with so much work I barely had time to sleep.

Now, to talk to Dahlia about that window display. Entering the studio midday might prove to be dangerous, what with everyone working against the clock, but I had no choice. My lunch was in the refrigerator back there.

As I entered the room, Dahlia looked up at me and grunted. Quite the greeting.

I found the usually gorgeous blonde in a messy state, her hair wound up in a knot and with very little makeup on. Quite a contrast to the practically-perfect-in-every-way version we usually got. In place of her usual beautiful clothes and high heels, she wore a blouse that looked slept in, sweatpants, and tennis shoes. Worse still, she snapped at everyone as she worked, her words laced with angst.

I tried to remedy this with kind words. "You guys should eat something. All work and no play . . . well, you know."

"Like we have time to eat." She rolled her eyes and spread out a bolt of crepe satin to be cut. "I have a bride coming at three for a fitting and I've barely started her dress. And don't even get me started on the gown I just finished. The bride came in for her final fitting and wants the sweetheart neckline changed to fit her new physique."

"New physique?" I asked.

Dahlia gestured to her chest. "Breast reduction. Why oh why don't these brides tell me before I start my alterations that they're about to have surgery?"

I couldn't answer that question. Didn't even want to try. Instead, I gestured to the platter of cold cuts and cheese slices that Madge had delivered moments earlier. "Please eat. I'll feel so much better if you do." And I'd feel better eating too if someone would join me. I reached for a slice of ham and popped it into my mouth. Yum.

No one seemed to notice. Dahlia and her team kept up an angst-filled conversation as they continued their work. I found myself mesmerized by all of them, but particularly Eduardo, an elderly fellow with a thick Spanish accent. The guy had to be in his seventies, but he had been Nadia's top choice to help Dahlia with dress design and production. I'd met a few guys over the years who sewed, but not many of them had the masculine swagger thing down. Eduardo was as swaggerly as a fella could get in his golden years.

And talk about golden! I hadn't seen that color hair since Queenie's favorite televangelist was forced off the air for accosting a woman in an airport. Eduardo's silver hair had a gold sheen to it. No doubt he paid a pretty penny for that 'do.

While Eduardo proved his masculinity with every move, one of our other new seamstresses offered a counterbalance in femininity. Hibiscus was as light and flowery as her name. The twenty-something was straight out of fashion school, a petite little thing who flitted around the sewing room as light as a feather. She rarely bothered with makeup. Her clothing and hairstyle reminded me of the hippies I'd seen in a documentary about the sixties. Her free spirit provided great fodder for Eduardo, who took delight in everything she did.

Unfortunately, Dahlia didn't. Poor Dahlia. OCD drove her every move, especially now, with so much work on her plate. She had no room for flightiness.

And then there was Jane. Quirky, over-the-top Jane. She'd only been working for Cosmopolitan for six weeks, but she'd already changed her hair and makeup a couple of times. One day a platinum blonde, the next a redhead. One day thick eyeliner and dark cherry lipstick, the next soft peach.

No, nothing ever stayed the same with Jane. Except for her choice in lunch foods. Every day with a peanut butter sandwich and chips, which she consumed even now with reckless abandon. She seemed to get emotional as Dahlia scolded her about the crumbs from the potato chips, but she quickly cleaned up after herself and got back to work, clearly delighted by the very process of sewing.

I sometimes watched the designers at work and wondered what it would be like to be so in the zone that you didn't care what went on around you. You simply dove into your art and created, created, created, lost in a world that no one could penetrate.

Me? I could tell they didn't even realize I was still in the room, so after a few more bites of food, I headed out to the shop to check on Madge and Twiggy, who were working the front desk. Madge, who often was terse, appeared to be in a more aggravated state than usual.

"Houston, we have a problem," she said.

"What sort of problem?"

"You're not going to believe it. Remember that bride with the pierced eyebrow and purple hair?"

"How could I forget her? Nothing we did was right." I groaned as the memories flooded over me. "What about her?"

"She's taken her story to the media."

"W-what?" Ack. "Madge, what is she saying?"

"She said that our shop is poorly run and that we owe her."

"But she got her dress, and we even knocked five hundred dollars off the price," Twiggy said. "Didn't we?"

Madge nodded. "We went above and beyond. She's nuts."

"And she got the dress on time, in spite of the ten thousand changes she asked for along the way," I added.

Madge crossed her arms. "I know. I remember it well."

"So what's her beef?" Twiggy asked. "What does she really want?"

"A new dress. She's saying that the dress doesn't look like the original design."

"But that's the point," I argued. "She didn't want the original design. She started with the Loretta Lynn but wanted to add a zillion things to it. And she wanted the bodice altered completely. Dahlia did exactly what she asked."

"Dahlia went above and beyond, just like she's doing now with all of the other orders." Twiggy looked a bit like a mother hen. No doubt she'd take down any customer who messed with her friends in the studio. "I'm already worried about her. She's so overworked."

"I know. I'm worried about her too." In fact, I secretly wondered if Dahlia would make it through this crazy season. With so many orders to fill, she was already frazzled.

"Is that crazy bride really involving the media?" Twiggy asked. "If so, do we get to tell our side of the story?"

"Wait, media?" Brady's voice sounded from behind me. "Who's called the media?"

"A discontented customer." Madge quickly filled him in, and my sweet guy started pacing the front of the shop. Well, as much as he could pace with a bum knee.

"We'll have to do some work to eradicate this."

I put my hand up. "Here's my opinion—not that anyone asked for it. Whenever you have an unhappy customer, it does no good to tell your side. It just keeps the hype going. You respond, she kicks back. I say we do something wonderful for the community. Some sort of big event for brides-to-be. The media will come and watch and our reputation will be golden again."

"When would we find time?" Brady looked concerned. "We're already flooded with work."

"It doesn't have to be something big. Maybe we do an event where the first ten brides to show up on Black Friday get a free gown. Off the rack, I mean. Ready-made. Could we afford to give up ten gowns?"

He shrugged. "Might be okay, but we'd have to pull some of our more expensive gowns ahead of time and put them in the back room. In other words, limit the availability. It might work, though."

"Sure it'll work. Except we'll have a mob scene outside and women will be fighting each other to get in." Madge smacked herself on the forehead. "You see my point? It can't be the first ten in line. They'll be camping outside the night before. Maybe we do a drawing as they come in. Everyone wins . . . something. Some will win a gown, others a veil, that sort of thing. And like you said, Brady, we can limit our stock by only putting out what we can afford to give away."

"Last season's dresses, for instance," I suggested.

"Right." Madge nodded and looked around the room as if doing inventory. "They're gorgeous but they're not selling, so why not give them up? And the same with some of the shoes we've had in stock for a while. And tiaras. If we open this up to the public and a lot of brides come away winners, people will be happy. And I have a feeling they'll buy a lot of other stuff if we do deep discounts. The goal here would be to get rid of all of the inventory from last season."

I paused to think as she spoke the word "season." Out with the old, in with the new. Kind of like so many areas of my life lately.

An idea developed. "Ooh, we can have a wedding reception. We can get cake decorators and other vendors to come."

"Cake and punch? In the store?" Brady said. "No way."

"We'll do it out front. Set up a tent. If we involve vendors, then it'll turn the whole thing into an extravaganza." I snapped my fingers. "That's it! A Black Friday bridal extravaganza. What do you think?"

"What if it's cold?" Madge asked. "Should we still do it in a tent out front?"

"Sure! People won't care. They're crazy on Black Friday. They'll do anything to save a few bucks. And if we bring in vendors, then we're all patting one another on the back and helping the whole wedding community out. Right?"

Twiggy didn't look convinced. "Sounds like a lot of work."

"It won't be so bad," I said. "Just a matter of getting organized ahead of time and having the right things out on display."

"And bringing in a tent, and contacting vendors, and . . ." Madge groaned.

I put my hand up. "That's why you have me. I'll arrange for all of that. I'll get an ad in the paper and update our website with the details." Suddenly I could hardly wait. We'd host a real wedding extravaganza, right here at Cosmopolitan Bridal!

Wait—what was I thinking? I was already in wedding planning mode, helping Queenie. And then there was Brady's surgery on the 19th. He wouldn't be in any shape to help with the extravaganza just one week after the fact, would he?

With God's help, I'd get 'er done, as Queenie often said. And I'd do it for our customers, to prove once and for all that Cosmopolitan Bridal was the place to be, even when discontented customers aired their grievances.

On the other hand, planning a big event the day after Thanksgiving when I'd be in Fairfield with my family on Thanksgiving Day? I must be nuts.

Maybe we could set up the shop on Wednesday. Yes, that

would work. Set up the shop on Wednesday night, drive to Fairfield on Thursday, spend the day with family, sleep a few hours at my parents' place, drive back in the wee hours Friday morning in time to greet the vendors, help them get set up in the tent . . .

Whew! I was tired just thinking about it!

Oh well. I could do it. And when I did, I would prove myself to Nadia and the others. Not that I really needed to prove anything, but I'd make Cosmopolitan Bridal look good to the media and hopefully erase any negative image that crazy bride had caused.

As I detailed my plans for the extravaganza, Brady gave me an admiring look. "I told my mom you're the best thing that's ever happened to Cosmopolitan Bridal, Katie, and it's true."

"Th-thank you, Brady." I gazed up, up, up into his gorgeous blue eyes and smiled. Now, if only he would add, "You're the best thing that's ever happened to me."

"*And* you're the best thing that's ever happened to me." His smile broadened with each word.

Whoa! Had the boy read my mind or what? I gave him a little wink and he leaned down to kiss me on the cheek.

Madge cleared her throat and muttered, "No PDA," but I barely heard her.

In that moment, wrapped in Brady's arms, I truly felt invincible. Empowered by his kisses, I could slay dragons, battle frustrated designers, sell a thousand bridal gowns.

Okay, maybe not a thousand. But we would bring in a crowd for Black Friday like Cosmopolitan Bridal had never seen before. And we would do it all with yours truly at the helm. If I could just get my knees to stop shaking long enough to put a plan in motion, anyway.

7

Please Don't Eat the Daisies

I had the best costars you could ever have, and I miss them so much. We had such a great time working together.

Doris Day

Pretty much everyone in my hometown of Fairfield revered Queenie, so it came as no surprise that they were pulling out all the stops for her big day. Her best friend, Bessie May, was planning a surprise lingerie shower. Like anything in Fairfield would stay a secret for long. Thankfully, I wasn't invited. And Ophelia, a lifelong friend of my grandmother's, had offered her services as cake baker and decorator. Every time I pictured the elderly Ophelia carrying a four-tiered cake,

I got the shivers, though I couldn't fault her for wanting to contribute. Prissy Moyer, one of Queenie's friends from the Methodist church, offered to make the punch—she claimed it was an old family recipe. Even Brother Krank, fellow Baptist church elder and director at the local retirement home, was in a charitable mood, offering his services as a deejay. Yes, my grandmother certainly had a lot of friends, and they were all in a celebratory frame of mind.

Most everyone, at least. The members of the Baptist church seemed a bit perplexed that Queenie had transferred her membership to First Presbyterian. Other than that, the whole town of Fairfield celebrated her good news. And with the ceremony coming up so quickly—two weeks before Christmas—we had a lot of planning to do, starting with the obvious: a bridal shower.

I'd thrown a few of those in my day, but never for a woman in her eighties. What did one buy an octogenarian bride? My mind reeled with possibilities as I made the drive from Dallas to Fairfield the first Saturday in November. To my right, Alva dozed in the passenger seat—not unusual on a long drive like this. Well, she dozed until the car's Bluetooth rang. I did my best not to wake her as I pushed the button on the steering wheel to answer, but it couldn't be helped.

"Hello?"

"Hello, Katie," Alva said, half-asleep, then rolled her head toward the window.

"Is this Katie Fisher?" An unfamiliar female voice sounded from the other end of the line.

"It is. How may I help you?"

Alva stirred in her seat and her eyes popped open. "It would be a big help if you'd stop at the next gas station. My bladder's about to burst." She let out an exaggerated groan.

Ack.

"My name is Carrie Sanders," the woman on the phone said. "I live in San Antonio."

"Ooh, San Antonio, home of the Spurs!" Alva seemed to come fully awake at this point. She lit into a lengthy dissertation about the team, then glanced my way and put her hand over her mouth. "Now, don't you go telling Brady I said all of that, all right? As far as he's concerned, my loyalty is to the Mavericks. And it is, naturally. But the Spurs are a great team too, and they tend to make the playoffs. A lot. So it's hard not to be a fan, if you know what I mean."

I gave her a strained look in the hopes that she would remember the woman on the other end of the phone, then returned my gaze to the highway.

"Oh, I agree," the woman said. "Though I have no particular loyalties either way. My family is really into basketball, though, so I can totally relate to the passion over a particular team." She chuckled. "Have I caught you at a bad time?"

"Oh, I'm just driving home to Fairfield, but I'm free to talk. I've got you on speaker, so we're good. Did you need to make an appointment?"

"Well, I just needed to change the time. I'm coming this Thursday to choose a gown. I talked to a lady named Madge just now and she referred me to you. She said you're in charge of the schedule?"

"Yes, that's right." Except I didn't have access to my schedule while driving. "I'm sure we'll work it out." *I hope.*

"Honestly, I wouldn't mind getting something from a store here in San Antonio, but my dad wants me to have the dress of my dreams. He does well for himself, so he says money is no object."

Wow. I couldn't imagine my father, a hardworking hardware store owner, ever using the words, "Money is no object." My gaze shifted to the rearview mirror. I caught a glimpse of my wedding gown—the dress I'd won in the contest—hanging in the backseat. Hauling it to Queenie's cedar closet still seemed a bit sad.

"Anyway, the reason I'm calling is because I wanted to give you a heads-up about my family before I get there. I tried to explain to Madge, but she seemed a little distracted."

"Oh? Your family will be with you?" I asked.

"Yes, several of them."

Alarm bells went off in my head. "How many are we talking?"

"Oh, six or seven. Maybe eight, if Nonna comes. But I wouldn't count on her. She doesn't like road trips anymore because she has an overactive bladder."

"That reminds me . . ." Alva tapped me on the arm. "If you please. Next exit."

I did my best not to sigh. "So, you're coming with the family. We'll be happy to meet everyone."

"There's a little more to it than that. See, they're really, well . . ."

Alva tapped me again and whispered, "Pull off here, Katie," as she gestured to the upcoming exit.

"I'm marrying the best guy in the world," Carrie said. "His name is Jimmy. But it's safe to say his family and mine don't always get along. And I don't just mean about the big stuff. They can't seem to agree on anything."

"Oh, I'm sorry to hear that." I took the exit and pulled into a service station parking lot. I'd no sooner brought the car to a stop than Alva bounded out and headed to the ladies' room. I had to give it to her—she sure moved fast when motivated.

"Sorrier than you know." Carrie's voice brought me back to the conversation. "Because they're all coming with me to pick out a dress and it's bound to be a fiasco. I wish I could've gotten out of this—trust me, I do—but both families want to be involved. One big happy family. That's us. Only, we're not. Happy, I mean. We are big." She sighed. "And what I said isn't 100 percent accurate. My parents are perfectly happy as long as his parents aren't around, and vice versa. To be honest, they can't stand one another. At all. And it can get a little explosive when we're all together, especially during the playoffs."

"Playoffs?"

"Yeah. Trust me."

Oh boy. We'd had this scenario before. Things rarely ended well with both families involved. But what could I do? I promised Carrie that we would do our best to make the experience fun, and she ended the call with a cheerful, "See you soon!"

A few minutes later Alva approached the car holding two sodas and two candy bars. She opened her door and grinned as she passed some of the goodies my way. "Figure I owed 'em my business since they loaned me their toilet."

If that didn't make a girl feel like eating chocolate while drinking Diet Root Beer, nothing would. We sat in the parking lot a moment as we nibbled on the goodies.

Alva wiped a glob of chocolate off her lip and tossed the candy bar wrapper into the trash bag. "Not trying to be nosy, but who was that gal on the radio?"

"Radio?" I gave my aunt a curious look.

"Well, sure. Her voice was coming straight through the radio. Strangest thing . . . it was almost like she was talking to you. Never heard of a radio that worked like that before. But I suppose there's a lot of stuff I don't understand about technology these days."

I bit back laughter as I said, "It's a Bluetooth."

"Bluetooth?" She pulled down her visor and gazed into the little vanity mirror, her mouth wide open. She seemed to be examining the inside of her mouth, then she glanced my way and shrugged. "Don't see anything on my teeth at all, Katie Sue. It was only on my lip. And it wasn't blue. It was chocolate."

"No, I meant . . . oh, never mind." I put the car in gear and headed back to the highway, determined to get this show back on the road.

"So, that gal on the radio talk show . . . she's part of a wedding story or something?"

"She's a bride-to-be and is getting her dress from our shop."

"That's what it sounded like to me, but I couldn't be sure. Pretty good PR for Cosmopolitan, having a big radio star like that on board. And she's coming all the way from San Antonio?"

"Yes." No point in explaining the rest.

"And bringing the family?"

"Yes, the whole family, and from what she said right before you left the car, they don't get along. At all." I shook my head. "Might make good fodder for a TV show, but it's rarely fun in person, trust me. I've seen more brides lose it over family members, and vice versa. It's hard all the way around."

"Then let's you and me make a pact." Alva reached over and patted my hand. "We'll agree to demonstrate the opposite spirit."

"What do you mean?"

"We won't be one of those families. When it comes to planning my sister's wedding, we're all in, 100 percent. And there won't be any squabbling."

"That's sweet, Alva."

My aunt's eyes flooded and her voice quivered. "I plan to keep my trap shut, no matter what she chooses. Even if she picks a hot pink minidress for the ceremony. She's the bride. It's all about her."

Um, you were there when she went with the light blue . . .
"She'll look lovely on her big day. No doubt about it."

"Right. Beautiful golden-years bride." Alva leaned back against the seat, her eyes fluttering closed. "I'm an old spinster. No wedding in sight for me. So don't worry, sweet girl. You'll never have to keep your trap shut on my account. If there's really such a thing as Prince Charming, he somehow missed his exit and met up with some other prettier, younger chick."

The strangest feelings swept over me at her words. I wanted to respond with a lecture about how life was filled with possibilities no matter your age. I would use Queenie as an example. But before I could open my mouth, Alva was snoring loudly.

I thought about her words as I drove. She considered herself an old maid. Likely people around her did too. She was eighty-plus years old and had never married. But not everyone was meant to, right?

I pushed that thought out of my head and gave the wedding dress another glance in my rearview mirror. It seemed to mock me. I released a slow breath and tried to deal with the strange emotions stirring in me. I'd already worn that beautiful gown on the cover of a famous magazine. I would wear it for real one day as I walked down the aisle toward Brady. I would. In the meantime, I'd keep my spirits up by focusing on Queenie's big day.

The rest of the drive, Alva talked in her sleep about some of the strangest things I'd ever heard. My thoughts shifted back to the bride-to-be, Carrie Sanders. What would it be like to have two families dueling instead of cooperating? Awkward.

Then again, I understood awkward, didn't I? Hadn't my ex-boyfriend just called a few days back to tell me how much he missed me?

I refused to let my thoughts linger on Casey. Instead, I focused my attention on the road. And on my schedule. With Brady's surgery coming up, I needed to put everything down on my calendar.

Suddenly the idea of Brady heading into surgery made my heart skip a beat. I couldn't see past the image of the man I loved undergoing something so painful.

The man I loved.

I did love him. I did. And in spite of the fact that he'd never come out and said the words, I prayed he loved me too.

8

On Moonlight Bay

I would crawl over the mountains of Beverly Hills on my hands
and knees if I could do a movie with Doris Day!

John Wayne

I headed south on I-45, breathing a sigh of relief as I came
to the Fairfield exit. I couldn't help myself. I had to stop at
Cooper Farms to buy some peach preserves and talk to the
owner, who was providing vegetables for Queenie's wedding
reception. Gratis, naturally. Was the whole town of Fairfield
offering their services at no cost?

After this I pointed the car in the direction of Dairy Queen,
where my cousin and the other ladies would be waiting. The
strangest emotions took hold of me as I pulled into the park-

ing spot. I felt glued to my seat. How many times had I come here with Casey over the years? Dozens? No, hundreds was more like it.

"Ooh, a Blizzard. I can't wait. It's been ages since I had a Blizzard." Alva giggled. "I don't care how cold it is outside, I love ice cream."

"Me too." First, though, I had to shake the chill that gripped me as I got out of the car.

As soon as we walked inside, my gaze traveled to the booth where Casey and I had sat so many times, enjoying Blizzards. There in that spot sat my cousin Lori-Lou with her three children, the oldest two girls seated on the bench next to her and baby Joshie in a high chair at the end of the table.

"You made it!" She gestured for me to join them.

"Of course I made it, girl. We've got a lot of planning to do."

I took a seat across from them, and the oldest two children immediately slithered under the table and popped up on my side. They jumped in my lap at the same time.

"I miss you, Aunt Katie!" Mariela's pigtails slapped me in the face as she snuggled up close.

"Me miss you too," Gilly added as she flung her arms around my neck, nearly suffocating her older sister underneath.

"Get off me, Gilly," Mariela scolded.

"No, you move!" Gilly shouted.

"No, you!"

The squabble escalated until Lori-Lou threatened to take away their electronics. That settled it. They calmed down, Gilly on my right, Mariela on my left.

Alva took a seat next to Lori-Lou and clucked her tongue at the children. "Are my babies being naughty?"

"Them? Naughty?" Lori-Lou snorted.

"I'm so happy this week is behind me." I eased my way out

of my jacket, nearly hitting Gilly in the head with my elbow. "It's been crazy."

"Girl, you haven't experienced crazy until you've tried to potty train one kid while pulling another one off the bottle. It's a nightmare, I tell you."

"It'd be a toss-up. Things are nuts at the shop right now. Glad to be here instead of there."

"Oh? Planning an ooh-la-la bridal shower for your grandmother is more appealing than dealing with angry customers?" Alva asked.

"Actually, the ooh-la-la shower is the one Bessie May's planning." My cousin's eyes grew large. "You don't even want to know the particulars on that one, trust me. Just thank your lucky stars it's only for Queenie's bridesmaids."

Alva raised her hand and smiled. "I'm the maid of honor, and I can't wait!"

"What's ooh-la-la, Mommy?" Mariela asked.

"It's something grown-ups say." Aunt Alva gave her a knowing look. "Now, I'm going to get myself some chicken strips and French fries. You hungry, Katie?"

I nodded and she trotted off to the register to order.

"I hope you don't mind that the kids are here," Lori-Lou said. "I tried to get Josh to watch them, but he couldn't take any more days off. We've got a house payment to cover now."

"I understand. I've got a new car payment myself."

"So happy for you." She glanced through the window at my new SUV. "It's beautiful, Katie. And no one deserves it more than you. That old clunker of yours was something else."

"It wasn't worth much as a trade-in, but I'm glad to be rid of it."

"We're still driving the minivan. Guess we'll run it into the ground. No fancy bells and whistles, but it'll do until we can afford something newer."

"I understand. I drove my old car until it nearly gave up the ghost. Brady helped me pick out the SUV."

"How is Brady?" Her smile morphed into a look of concern. "Scheduled for surgery?"

"Yeah. November 19th."

"Ack. That's close."

"Yes, and you'll never believe what I did. I scheduled a big event at the bridal shop on Black Friday. He won't be back up and running by then. I don't know what I was thinking, but I can't go back on my word now." I filled her in on the details while we waited for the other ladies to show up.

"You'll manage, Katie," she said when I finished. "You can do anything you put your mind to."

"Obviously you can too." I motioned to the children, who were coloring their paper menus. I gave Lori-Lou an admiring look. "How are you feeling, anyway?"

She rubbed her pregnant belly and groaned. "I think maybe I'm too old for this."

"Don't be silly. You're only thirty-two."

"Just feels a lot harder this time. Maybe because I have my hands so full with the others. No idea how I'm going to hold this one once she gets here."

"*She?* It's a girl?"

"Oops!" She put her hand over her mouth. "I was supposed to be keeping that a secret until we do the big reveal on Facebook. We just had the ultrasound yesterday. Want to see the picture?"

Before I could say, "Of course!" she opened her purse.

"It's in here somewhere." She pulled out a pacifier and a sippy cup, then a wrinkled piece of paper, which she unfolded.

"Mariela painted this for you, by the way." She passed the artwork my way and continued to pull items out of her purse: tissues, diaper wipes, a random pink sock, and a headband. Finally, she gave up. "Sorry. I thought I had it." She pulled out an electronic tablet and passed it to Mariela. Seconds later the girls were squabbling over who got to use it first.

"It's okay. You can show me next time." I opened the painting from Mariela and a photo fell out. The ultrasound photo.

"Ooh, there it is!" Lori-Lou picked it up and groaned. "Wait, let me wipe it off. It's sticky. I think it has grape jelly on it. Joshie had jelly this morning."

When she finally got the picture clean, she passed it my way and pointed. "See there? Those are her girl parts, plain as day."

Hmm. What I was looking at certainly didn't look like a baby, and I'd be hard-pressed to label anything girl parts. I just nodded and smiled, which I often did.

On either side of me, Mariela and Gilly still fought over the tablet. This put me squarely in the middle of their argument. The tone of Lori-Lou's voice changed as the turned to the girls. "Gilly, stop fighting with your sister or you won't get your turn." She turned back to me and sighed. "I just can't wait to have a sweet little baby girl. I'm sure she'll be adorable."

Mariela reached across me to smack Gilly on the arm and the youngster started wailing. "She hit me!"

Lori-Lou was so distracted by the ultrasound photo that she didn't seem to notice any of this. She carried on and on about the baby, about how precious little girls were.

Mariela yanked the tablet from Gilly's hands, causing a screaming fit to ensue. At this point an elderly man in the booth behind us got up and left, glaring all the while. Not that Lori-Lou noticed. She just kept staring at that picture in my hands.

"So, did you want me to keep this?" I asked.

"Yep. We have one just like it on the fridge."

Perfect place to put something that looked like a work of abstract art. I pressed it into my purse and glanced up at the register where Alva stood gabbing with the manager.

"Who else is coming to this meeting?" I asked.

"Bessie May and Ophelia. Prissy Moyer was going to come, but she's got grandchildren in town." Lori-Lou reached out and grabbed the tablet from Mariela and threatened to put it away for good if they didn't stop fighting. That slowed things down—for a moment.

"That should be fun." I did my best not to roll my eyes. "Are we the only young ones?"

"No. Joni Milford is the wedding coordinator at the Baptist church now. Did you know?"

"That's right. Queenie did tell me that. Am I the only one who's surprised that she's . . . well . . . planning weddings?"

"I was a little shocked, if you want my opinion, but stranger things have happened. And hey, it'll be good to have a friend who knows a little something about wedding planning. Won't be long before we're doing this for you and Brady."

I cleared my throat.

Lori-Lou shoved her items back in her purse. "Oh, you know what I mean, Katie. You're dating someone, so you're well on your way to the altar."

"Katie Sue's headed to the altar?" Aunt Alva appeared at the table. "Well, praise the Lord! I've prayed every day that Brady would pop the question. How did he do it, Katie? And why wasn't I the first to know? I'm your roommate, after all."

I put my hand up. "No, no, no. Brady hasn't proposed."

"Eh? What's that you say? Brady proposed?"

I turned to discover that Bessie May and Ophelia had entered.

"Who's Brady, anyway?" Bessie May added. "That football fella?"

"Basketball, Bessie May." Lori-Lou closed her purse and shoved it onto the bench. "He plays basketball."

"Brady is Katie's fiancé." Alva scooted back into her spot across from me. "But I had no idea they were engaged. That calls for double Blizzards all the way around."

"No. He has not proposed."

I must've said it too loudly because Mariela piped up with, "Don't worry, Aunt Katie. You'll get married someday. I'll be your flower girl." Her little nose wrinkled as she added, "If I'm not too old by then."

I groaned.

"I thought you were marrying that Lawson boy." Ophelia looked more than a little perplexed. "Did you break it off?"

"They broke it off ages ago, Ophelia." Bessie May rolled her eyes. "Honestly. No one pays attention to anything around here."

"Today is supposed to be about Queenie, not me," I said.

"Speaking of Queenie, where is she?" Lori-Lou glanced toward the door.

"She's up at the church, talking to Joni about the ceremony," Bessie May said. "But she'll be here shortly. I just talked to Joni a few minutes ago. She'll be driving Queenie over just as soon as they've gone over the to-do list."

"Where's a person supposed to sit for this meeting anyway?" Ophelia looked down at our messy table.

"You kids scoot to the next table," Lori-Lou said. "Take the tablet with you." She reached into her purse and came out with a coloring book and crayons. "Here, take these too."

The girls scooted into the booth the elderly man had vacated, and Mariela started eating the French fries he'd left

behind. Lovely. Bessie May and Ophelia squeezed in next
to me.

"Now we're ready to roll," Alva said.

"Hardly." Bessie May grumbled about the sticky table, so
Lori-Lou pulled out a wipe and went to town cleaning it.

I couldn't stop thinking about Joni, former star softball
player on the Fairfield girls' team. We'd never been terribly
close, but that had more to do with the fact that she'd been
busy playing ball and I'd been a cheerleader. And Fairfield
Peach Queen. And Casey's date to the prom. And I hated to
state the obvious, but she hadn't really been the sort of girl to
gravitate toward my group of friends. We were more the giddy
sleepover types. She was the athletic type. Seemed strange
that she would be coordinating my grandmother's wedding.
The rumors that had followed her in school were, well, not
terribly flattering.

Rumors.

"What about rumors, Katie?" Ophelia asked.

"Oh, sorry." I startled to attention. "Didn't realize I'd said
that out loud."

"If you're asking for the latest on Joni, you've come to the
right place." Bessie May squeezed some hand sanitizer into
her palms, then passed the bottle to Ophelia. "But I'll have to
lower my voice. Norah Harrison is sitting just three booths
behind us and the woman couldn't keep her lips shut if her
life depended on it. Now, what was I going to tell you again?"

"Bessie May, you are the worship leader at the Baptist church
now." I clucked my tongue at her. "You can't go around spreading rumors. It's not godly."

She leaned in close as she rubbed the sanitizer into her
hands. "I'm not *spreading* anything. What I'm about to tell
you is common knowledge."

"Then why are we whispering?" Lori-Lou responded in hushed tones.

"Because it's a surprise." Bessie May gave us a wink. "Top secret."

"Just like Queenie's lingerie shower?" Alva quirked a brow.

Bessie May glared at her. "Anyway, most folks still don't know. Did you hear that Levi Nash and Joni are dating?"

This certainly got my attention. "Oh, wow. Levi and Joni?" Well, if that wasn't a strange match.

"Yep." Bessie May nodded. "Well, I guess it's not verifiable. No one's caught 'em smooching or anything like that, so it wouldn't hold up in a court of law."

"Yet," Ophelia added.

"Yet." Bessie May's face turned pink. "But they spend a lot of time together. Thick as thieves, those two. Just thought you'd want to know. But whatever you do, don't mention it. I don't think anyone is supposed to know."

"You said it was common knowledge."

"Common knowledge to me. And the other WOP-pers. You know how we are, Katie Sue."

Yes, I knew all right.

"We're tight with the Lord and we have a spiritual sense about these things. So you can take what I've said to the bank. But don't try to cash the check just yet. Not until they make it public."

"I won't say a word, I promise." The idea of Joni and Levi as a couple seemed strange at best. They didn't seem to have much in common. Interesting.

"All this talk about folks falling in love is making me hungry." Alva glanced at the register. "I'm going to eat my weight in chicken strips, fries, and ice cream. If they ever get my order filled, I mean. I'd better go find out what's keeping them."

"Might as well order, myself." Bessie May scooted to the edge of the bench and attempted to stand. Alva tried to give her a hand but nearly took a tumble in the process. Then Ophelia joined them and they all headed over to the register.

"I'm sorry about all of that, Katie," Lori-Lou said.

"All of what?"

"That misunderstanding about Brady proposing."

"Oh, no biggie." With a wave of my hand I did my best to dismiss any concerns.

She gave me a sympathetic look. "You and Brady are a match made in heaven. He'll pop the question soon."

"You think?" I considered her words. "You used to say that about Casey too, remember? In fact, it was less than six months ago. I was sitting in my car, right out there . . ." I pointed out the plate-glass window to the parking lot beyond.

At that very moment the door of Dairy Queen opened and a man stepped inside.

A familiar man.

Casey Lawson.

9

Anyone Can Fall in Love

If it's true that men are such beasts, this must account for the fact that most women are animal lovers.

Doris Day

Katie?" Casey approached our booth and stared at me, a smile curling up the edges of his lips—those same lips I'd kissed a thousand times. "You're back in town?"

I could've asked him the very same question. Instead, I nodded. "Yeah. We're planning Queenie's bridal shower." *Didn't I just tell you all of this when we talked on the phone?*

"Ah." He glanced down at our table. The table where we'd talked about our hopes, our dreams, our aspirations. The table where we'd held hands, dipped French fries in ketchup, and talked about what we wanted to be when we grew up.

Only, now we *were* grown up. And he was no longer at the table. That idea should've suited me just fine, especially since I had the best guy in the world waiting for me back in Dallas, but for some reason I couldn't seem to see past the familiar boyfriend—er, ex-boyfriend—standing right in front of me.

Alva walked up with my basket of food in her hand, which she plopped on the table in front of me. It looked and smelled amazing, the crispy fries tantalizing me at once and the chicken strips the perfect shade of golden brown. Behind her, Bessie May and Ophelia arrived with food in hand as well. They all took their seats and dove right in.

Casey glanced down and smiled. "You're eating the chicken strips. Might've guessed."

"I ordered you an M&M Blizzard too, Katie." Alva gave me a knowing look. "It'll be ready as soon as you're done with the chicken."

"M&M?" Casey looked shocked. "You always had the Oreo."

"Things change, Casey." I gave him a piercing look and hoped he would take the hint. "*Preferences* change."

"Ah. Got it. Well, you ladies have a nice day. I need to go order my Blizzard and burger. I'm in town for the whole weekend." He paused as if waiting for me to respond in some way. I didn't. I just offered him a polite smile and got busy eating my chicken strips.

I couldn't help but watch as he sauntered to the register and ordered the Oreo Blizzard. I knew he would, of course. He'd always had the Oreo. His tastes obviously hadn't changed. I tried not to read too much into that notion.

Even after Queenie arrived, my thoughts kept traveling back

to Casey. I did my best to push them aside as I greeted my grandmother.

Now, I'd obviously known Queenie all my life, but I had never seen her this happy. Truly, the past few months had transformed her, not just internally but externally as well. For a woman of eighty-two, she looked blissfully young.

For that matter, so did the young woman who'd come with her. Joni. The once-tough softball player had apparently softened around the edges. She looked downright feminine. And peaceful. I'd rarely seen her looking this at ease.

Alva pulled baby Joshie out of the high chair and nudged it away from the table. Queenie and Joni pulled a couple of chairs into the spot and settled into place. Alva bounced the baby up and down on her knee and spoke in baby talk to him. Until he slobbered all over her blouse. Then she passed him to his mother.

Yep. We were definitely ready for our meeting. And with so many women seated at the end of our table, I could barely see past them to Casey. Not that I wanted to see Casey, exactly.

"Okay, let's get this show on the road. I've got a long day ahead of me." Queenie put her hands on the table. "Lots of work to get done."

Joni pulled an iPad out of her bag and fired it up. "Everything's under control. No worries." She'd condensed everything into a spreadsheet, which she handled with grace and ease. All the while she kept us laughing and smiling, not an easy task with Ophelia hollering, "Eh? What'd you say? I left my hearing aid at home, girl!"

"Queenie and I have worked out the logistics of the event, and invitations have gone out," Joni explained. "The ceremony will be at ten in the morning. Bridesmaids will be Alva, Bessie May, Ophelia, and Prissy Moyer—who, by the way, is sorry she couldn't be with us today."

"All WOP-pers but Alva," Bessie May said, the pride in her voice evident. "And we're making her an honorary WOP-per."

"Gee, thanks." Alva continued to wipe the spit-up off her blouse. "I feel so special."

I flinched a little when my name wasn't listed as a brides-maid, until I realized all of the bridesmaids were over the age of seventy. Perhaps it was a blessing not to be added to that group just yet, though I did feel myself aging as Bessie May went off on a tangent about how she hoped her irritable bowel syndrome wouldn't prove to be problematic on the big day. Lovely. At the next table Gilly and Mariela took to fighting over the colors. They both wanted red.

"I'll be seeing red if those two keep it up," Ophelia mut-tered. "Could someone please do something about them?"

Naturally, this offended Lori-Lou, who snapped at the kids and then focused on her phone instead of the meeting.

Joni finally managed to pull the conversation back on track. I gave her an admiring look, pausing to gaze at her lovely makeup job. The Joni I'd known hadn't worn makeup. Or smelled like perfume. Sure, she was still taller than most of the other girls I knew. And yes, her shoulders were broader too, possibly from all of that softball playing. But I was looking at a woman transformed. Fascinating.

Joni's face lit into a smile as she noticed Casey across the room. "Hey, look who's back in town."

I glanced over and sighed as I realized his eyes were still on me. Ack. "Yeah. I've already talked to him." I kept my atten-tion on the to-do list, unwilling to let myself get caught in Casey's gaze once more.

"I haven't yet. If you ladies don't mind, I'm going to order some food and say hello."

"Don't mind a bit," I said. I watched as she walked over to Casey's table and stood next to him.

"Isn't she the sweetest thing?" Queenie gave her an admiring look. "I daresay she's one of the most talented girls in town. And kindhearted too. Sweeter than peaches."

"I say we nominate her for Peach Queen this spring," Ophelia said. "What do you think of them apples?"

"I'd say you're a few years too late, Ophelia," Bessie May said. "You have obviously forgotten that Ms. Peach has to be no older than nineteen years of age. Joni is older than that."

"She graduated the year before me," I said. "So she's probably a little too old. But other than that she sure seems like a shoo-in." I watched her easygoing conversation with Casey. "Looks like she's won Casey over, and that's not easy these days."

"She's got a way about her." Queenie smiled. "It just goes to show you a little love goes a long, long way. It wasn't that long ago—a few months, really—when Joni was on the fringes. No friends. No social life. I believe she was in a depression, if you want the truth of it. But thanks to Levi Nash—God bless that sweet boy—she found her place. And there's no turning back."

"Right."

Laughter rang out from Joni and Casey, who appeared to be sharing some sort of joke. I watched them with interest. I realized I'd judged her unfairly in the past, mostly because of physical appearance and mannerisms. She might be a little, er, manly. A little rough around the edges. But something had softened her. As I saw her with Casey, watching the crinkles around her eyes when she laughed, she looked beautiful.

"So, tell me what we're lacking, Queenie." I turned my attention back to my grandmother. "How can I help with the wedding?"

"I can't think of a thing, sweet girl. The whole town has swept in around me to fill every need, right down to the chicken finger appetizers at the reception." She gave a nod to the Dairy Queen manager, who tipped his hat at her.

"Is he providing Blizzards too?" I asked.

My grandmother chuckled. "Well, no, but that's a lovely idea. Do you think I should ask him?"

"Nah, that wasn't my point." I laughed. "But you are truly the most loved woman I've ever known. Everyone wants your day to be special, and that does my heart good."

"You don't know the half of it, Katie. Ginger Harris has offered to loan me all of the tablecloths she bought for her daughter's wedding. And Ophelia here is making my cake— each of the four tiers a different flavor."

Ophelia looked up from her chicken finger basket. "White with strawberry filling. Chocolate with caramel filling. Italian cream cake and . . . what's the fourth one again, Queenie?"

"Lemon raspberry."

"Yes. Lemon raspberry." Ophelia took another bite of chicken and a look of satisfaction came over her. "Though I personally don't think as many people will eat the lemon."

"I heard you were making the cake, Ophelia," I said. "I've been wondering how you planned to transport it to the church."

"Oh, I'm bringing it in layers. Bessie May is swinging by to pick me up in her SUV. I believe we'll have enough space for all four tiers. I just hope it's enough cake for all of the guests we're expecting. This is going to be the shindig of the year."

"The year?" Queenie laughed. "The decade is more like it."

"True. Anyone who's anyone'll be there," Bessie May interjected. "The invitations just went out a few days ago and we've already had more than 80 percent of the potential guests RSVP."

"You're well loved for sure, Queenie." Lori-Lou fished around in her purse for lipstick.

"But don't you worry about how I'll put the cake together, Katie," Ophelia said. "I'll assemble it at the church and then add the trim work. And if it looks like the crowd is growing, I'll add a fifth tier. I'll make it a marbled cake. Folks love that."

"She's really a wonder, Katie," my grandmother said. "You'd be surprised at how gifted some of us golden-years ladies are."

"Oh, not surprised by that at all," I said. "I hope to be half the woman you are when I'm your age."

"Not much chance of that if you keep swallowing down those chicken strips." Bessie May pursed her lips. "But what were we talking about?"

"Talking about how well loved I am," Queenie said. "Katie's brothers are going to help set up the tables in the reception hall, and her father is giving me away."

"I'm sure he feels so honored to be able to do that," I said.

"Maybe. From what your mother told me a while back, he's put on so much weight from their cruises that he barely fits into his suit anymore."

"Oh, I can get him fitted with a tuxedo." I scribbled that down on my paper so I wouldn't forget. "No problem."

"Your father in a tuxedo? That'll be the day. Anyway, everything's coming together and I couldn't be happier." She released a contented sigh. "I really mean that. I don't recall being happier in my entire life."

"I'm so glad, Queenie."

She leaned forward and gave me a compassionate look. "I want the same for you, honey-bun. I want you to marry Brady and let us lavish you with blessings too."

"Oh, I . . . well . . ."

"I know, I know. But he's going to propose soon."

"That's what we all said about Casey too, remember?" I caught a glimpse of my ex out of the corner of my eye, still laughing and talking with Joni, who had apparently forgotten the reason she'd come to Dairy Queen in the first place.

"Yes, well . . ." With a wave of her hand Queenie dismissed that idea. "I never thought the two of you were much of a match."

I lowered my voice to keep from being overheard. "You could have mentioned that at any time during the many years we were dating."

"Would it have done any good? You were blinded by love." Queenie's nose wrinkled. "Or you were blinded by the idea of being *in* love. It doesn't hurt your feelings if I say it like that, does it, Katie?"

I shrugged. "I think I really loved Casey. He's a great guy. Just not *the* guy."

"And now you've found *the* guy?" Bessie May gave me a curious look. "That football fella? The one with the broken arm?"

"Basketball," Alva said. "Knee."

"Yeah, I've been having trouble with my knee all week," Ophelia said. "But it has nothing to do with basketball."

I sighed. "Just keep praying for Brady, Queenie. He's in so much pain with his knee. I know you know what that's like. But I think there's a lot going on in his head that he's not sharing with me."

"He's disappointed that he's unable to go back to playing basketball, you mean."

"I guess. A couple of months back he seemed reconciled to the idea, so I'm kind of confused that it's suddenly bugging him so much again. But it is."

"He can always go back to football," Bessie May said.

"Though I never understood why those fellas felt the need to run around the field in those tight pants. Just seems so . . . girlie. Patting one another on the fannies and such." She fanned herself with her napkin. "Strange behaviors."

Joni picked that exact moment to return to our table, food in hand. "What did I miss?"

"You don't want to know." Lori-Lou looked up from her phone. "But it was interesting, to say the least."

Moments later Casey rose from his table and walked our direction. "Great to see you ladies again." He offered my grandmother a warm smile. "And congratulations, Queenie. I'm so happy for you. We all are."

"Why, thank you, Casey. That means a lot."

"You still working in Tulsa, Casey?" Ophelia licked the chicken finger crumbs from her fingers.

"Yes. For now, anyway. Not sure how long that'll last, though. I might end up back in Fairfield. My father needs help on the property and I really miss everyone." He gave me a piercing look. "Kind of feels like I left pieces of my heart back here. You know?"

The whole table grew eerily silent as all eyes shifted to me. I cleared my throat and turned my gaze out the window.

"Just praying about it," Casey said. "I feel sure the Lord will let me know."

I couldn't help but look his way at this point. Was he really thinking about moving back home? And what was that stuff about helping his father? This couldn't be the same guy who'd called Fairfield a two-bit town just six months ago, could it?

We somehow got the meeting back on track. Less than an hour later, Queenie's shower was planned and I'd gained an entirely new perspective about Joni. In fact, I had a new perspective about a lot of things—the women who'd gathered around my grandmother, for instance. And the business owners who'd gone out of their way to lavish her with love and support.

There was much to be said about small-town living. I'd almost forgotten.

Not that I'd trade my life in the big city for any of it. No, I'd made up my mind. Cosmopolitan Bridal was my new home away from home, and that was where I was meant to be, at least for now.

10

Everywhere You Go

Any girl can look glamorous . . . just stand there and look stupid.

Doris Day

When the meeting ended, Alva and I gave Queenie a lift back to her house. I carried my bagged gown inside to put into the cedar closet.

My grandmother gave me a curious look as I walked down the hallway with it. "What's in the bag, Katie Sue?"

I bit back the temptation to say, "My wedding dress," and settled for, "The dress I wore for the magazine cover shoot. I was wondering if I could put it into your cedar closet so it stays safe."

"Surely it won't need to be stored away for long." She gave me a wink. "Won't be long before Brady James pops the question, after all."

"Maybe, but I'd like the dress to be safe. Things just hold up better in the cedar closet, right?"

"Right." Queenie still looked a bit confused.

"I told her she could keep it at my place, but I don't have a cedar closet." Alva went into a discussion about the benefits of cedar closets and completely lost me. Still, I couldn't help but notice the sympathetic expression on her face as I carried the dress out of the room, and it raised several questions in my mind. Was I one of those people who was never meant to get married?

We spent the rest of the evening visiting and having dinner at Sam's. Seemed strange to eat at Sam's without my mom and dad, but they were out to sea. Afterward Alva and I headed back to my parents' place to spend the night. It felt kind of weird calling it "my parents' place," but it wasn't my home anymore. Though it sure felt like it as I drifted off to sleep in the comfort of my own bed. Wow. Pure bliss!

On Sunday morning we attended the early service at the Baptist church, but nothing felt right about it. Queenie was a Presbyterian now, so her spot in the pew was empty. Beau was in Dallas, and so was Dewey. That left Jasper and Crystal, but they'd both defected to the second service, which was more contemporary. Mama wasn't leading the choir anymore now that she and Pop were out of town so much. Bessie May, God bless her, gave it the old college try, but even Alva squirmed in her seat when the choir attempted an off-key rendition of the "Hallelujah Chorus." Yikes.

Speaking of college, I couldn't help but notice the college- and career-aged folks coming into the sanctuary for the second service, the contemporary one. Turned out Levi and Joni led worship for that one. In fact, the whole stage was transformed in a matter of minutes as a keyboard and several guitars filled the space where the choir had stood just moments before.

I stuck around a few minutes to listen in and smiled when I heard one of my favorite songs coming through the PA system. Even from out in the foyer, I could tell they sounded great. To me, anyway. I'd always known Levi could sing—I mean, the guy won our tenth grade talent show at Fairfield High, after all—but Joni? Who knew she had such a rich alto voice? Their harmonies sounded remarkable. Almost like they were meant to be. Just more confirmation that the WOP-pers were right about this happy duo.

Alva didn't appear to enjoy the contemporary music. She stuck her fingers in her ears. "I don't know why they have to put on a rock-and-roll show in church. It's irreverent."

"It's not rock and roll, Alva," I explained. "It's contemporary praise and worship and it sounds great."

"Well, I don't like it." She walked out into the parking lot, mumbling about the noise. As we got into the car, she continued carrying on about the instruments. "Back in my day we didn't allow loud instruments in the church."

"Um, Alva . . . didn't they have an organ?"

"Of course."

"And didn't the organ play loudly?"

"I don't remember it being loud, but it wouldn't have mattered. The organ is God's favorite instrument, so it's a moot point."

This certainly got my attention. "Oh?"

"Yes, and I can prove it in the Scriptures. Look it up."

"I'll do that as soon as I get back home."

"Yes, look it up. It's in the Old Testament four times. God

loves the rich sound of a pipe organ as it pushes out the melody of 'In the Garden.' It's in Deuteronomy. Second chapter."

"But Aunt Alva, the pipe organ wasn't invented until . . . Oh, never mind." No point in getting her riled up.

Thinking about pipe organs reminded me that I'd promised Queenie we'd stop by the Presbyterian church to say goodbye before leaving town. We were just in time for their second service, so in we went for round two of Sunday in Fairfield. Well, round three if you counted the five minutes of listening to Levi and Joni sing.

The Presbyterian service was quite a bit different than the Baptist. For one thing, the pastor— my grandfather to-be— wore a long black robe with a collar. The service kicked off with an organ prelude. A *loud* organ prelude. I put my fingers in my ears and did my best not to groan at the pain it caused.

"See there, Katie Sue?" Alva nudged me with her elbow when it ended. "God's smiling down on this service. I have it on good authority he's a fan of the organ. Deuteronomy chapter four."

"Ah." Either the chapters were changing or the Bible had a lot to say about pipe organs.

I was so busy examining the inside of the sanctuary that I almost got lost in the experience. I'd been in here a couple of times before, but never on a Sunday morning. The grand arches and white wainscoting were breathtaking, especially with the sun shining through the brilliant colors in the stained-glass windows.

An elderly fellow led us in a responsive reading and we sang a hymn. Alva nodded and smiled, then leaned over and said, "A beautiful hymn. Just what we should be singing in church, Katie Sue."

I had to admit it was lovely. But again I was distracted, this time staring at Casey Lawson, who'd entered late and took a seat with his parents.

We all recited the Apostles' Creed, sang another hymn, and watched as the children went forward for a kid-friendly sermonette from the pastor. Then it was time for the announcements. Lo and behold if they didn't announce Queenie and Reverend Bradford's wedding just like it was an ordinary church event.

"Join us next Sunday for a potluck, followed by homemade apple pie from Sister Susie. And don't miss out on the upcoming nuptials of our own dear Reverend Bradford as he ties the knot with Queenie Fisher on December 12th. You're all invited."

You're all invited? No doubt Ophelia would have to add a fifth tier to that cake after all.

Queenie turned all shades of red as they asked her to stand. She did—albeit slowly, thanks to the titanium knee—then took a seat, mumbling about how embarrassed she was.

She wasn't, of course. The old girl loved the attention. No doubt she would make an amazing first lady for First Presbyterian. If they didn't mind the fact that she didn't know all the words to the Apostles' Creed by heart.

Reverend Bradford took his place at the podium and began an enlightening sermon on the prodigal son, but I was a little distracted by a humming sound coming from my purse. I reached for my phone to make sure I'd turned off the ringer and happened to notice several texts coming through from Casey. I turned around to make sure he was still sitting a few pews behind me, and he was. Weird.

I glanced at the phone, but Queenie put her hand over it as if in warning: *Don't you dare get on that telephone during service, Katie Sue!* She didn't even have to speak the words. I heard them loud and clear when her hand clamped over mine. I shoved the phone back in my purse and spent the next few minutes trying to figure out what was so important that Casey would have to text me in church.

When the service ended, folks gathered in the foyer to visit. Many made their plans to have lunch at Sam's or Lone Star Grill. Me? I just wanted to get out of there and get back home to Dallas.

Home. Dallas.

Weird but true. I somehow made it out of the church without alerting Casey, who appeared to be distracted by Reverend Bradford. Alva could barely keep up with me as I trucked across the parking lot.

"Wait up, Katie Sue! I'm no spring chicken." I could hear her huffing and puffing behind me as she tried to keep up. "Ooh, chicken! Let's stop and have some lunch before we drive back. They've got great fried chicken at Sam's."

"But we just ate there last night. Besides, the lunch crowd at Sam's will be terrible, Alva." I turned back to look at her. "If you really want chicken, then what about KFC?"

"Yeah." She sighed. "I guess some people get their chicken there."

I had barely made it inside my car when Casey caught up with me. I reluctantly rolled the window down so as not to look rude.

"Leaving so soon?" he asked. "I was hoping to talk you into Sam's. My parents wanted to spend time with you."

His parents wanted to spend time with me? I had a feeling there was more to it than that.

"C'mon, Katie." Alva gave me an imploring look from the passenger seat. "I don't get to go to Sam's very often and it's my favorite. I sure could use another piece of that coconut cream pie."

She had me at *coconut cream pie.*

Not that I could say no to Casey, who refused to budge from outside my door until I nodded. "Okay, we'll meet you there."

"Awesome. See you in a bit." He sprinted across the parking lot toward his truck. I couldn't stop the little sigh that wriggled its way up.

"Look on the bright side, Katie Sue. We'll have a wonderful lunch and then I can nap all the way back to Dallas." She pulled down the visor to block the sun.

Yeah. Sounded dreamy.

As we pulled out of the church parking lot, a call came through my Bluetooth. The moment I heard Brady's voice, I felt my heart rate level out. He always had that effect on me.

"How was church?" he asked.

"Interesting. How was church on your end?"

"We had a guest speaker—some guy from Missouri. Really good stuff. He talked about the seasons we go through. Timely. You can listen to the sermon online when you get back."

"I'd like that." I put on my turn signal to pull out onto the main street. "I miss you, Brady."

"I miss you too, Katie. A lot. Have a piece of coconut cream pie for me when you go to Sam's."

"Wait . . . what? How did you know we were going to Sam's?"

Brady laughed. "That's funny. Anyway, have a slice for me. Talk to you later."

We ended the call just as I pulled my car into the parking lot of Sam's. As I turned the key in the ignition, Alva stirred in her seat. "I just think it's remarkable," she said.

"What?"

"First that gal from San Antonio was on the radio, and now Brady. Seems like those talk show hosts wouldn't be as interested in him now that he's not playing ball, but there he was, on the radio for all to hear."

I didn't even bother to explain. One of these days I'd clue her in about how Bluetooth worked, but not now. No, on this day I wanted to fill up on yummy food at Sam's, then head back to Dallas. Where I belonged.

11

A Guy Is a Guy

I'm tired of being thought of as Miss Goody Two-Shoes . . .
the girl next door, Miss Happy-Go-Lucky.

Doris Day

Spending time with Casey's family at Sam's turned out to be a blast. Funny how I could slip back into the "nothing's changed" gear with such ease. For that hour, I was Katie Fisher from Fairfield—Peach Queen and all-around happy-go-lucky small-town girl.

Mrs. Lawson had apparently forgotten Casey and I weren't dating, because most of her stories revolved around the two of us. Even the waitresses seemed to have forgotten. A couple of different times I had to whisper, "We're not a couple" to the folks who engaged us in conversation as if we were a duo.

Casey was his usual jovial self, acting as if he'd never moved away to Oklahoma in the first place. At one point he slipped his arm over my shoulder. I used that opportunity to get up and walk to the dessert table. I didn't care much for the feelings that swept over me at his nearness and did my best to push them aside.

Alva seemed a little bugged by Casey's attempts to flirt with me, but the coconut cream pie distracted her. By the time we settled into the car for the drive back to Dallas, she seemed to have left her angst behind. She settled in for an afternoon nap.

I spent my time behind the wheel thinking through all that had happened. I felt so conflicted. Half of me really loved being back in Fairfield. The other half could hardly wait to see Brady again.

Brady. The sound of his voice had worked magic on my heart. Now, to get back to where I belonged— the bridal shop.

Unfortunately, the next few days we were so crammed full of work-related things that my sweetie and I hardly had a chance to be alone. We tried, but chaos reigned. I made up my mind to focus on my job. God would take care of my love life.

On Thursday morning at 10:00 a.m., I met bride-to-be Carrie Sanders. As anticipated, she arrived with quite the entourage: her parents, the groom's parents, even the handsome groom-to-be. Very odd. We'd had a few of these gatherings before, but having the groom in attendance never settled well with Nadia or Madge. They were of the opinion that the groom shouldn't see the bride's gown until the moment those back doors of the chapel were opened. I agreed.

Hmm. Brady had seen my gown before. He'd even been

photographed standing next to me when I wore it on the cover of *Texas Bride* magazine.

Not that Brady had proposed.

Carrie was a gorgeous young woman, probably twenty-six or so, with perfectly styled blonde hair and picture-perfect makeup. She looked very stylish in her Dolce & Gabbana jeans and trendy blouse, but what really got me were the cowgirl boots. I wanted to kneel down to take a closer look but didn't dare. I knew Lanciottis when I saw them. Wow.

When the Sanders family entered, I couldn't help but notice the Spurs shirt Mr. Sanders wore. The minute he saw Brady hobbling our way, his eyes widened. "Brady James?" Instead of the usual boisterous welcome we'd come to appreciate from fans, this fellow crossed his arms and remained silent.

"Yes sir." Brady gave him a polite nod and extended his hand. The fellow took it hesitantly. "Welcome to Cosmopolitan Bridal. I'm the acting manager while my mom's in Paris."

"You're Brady James." The groom-to-be extended his hand. "Jimmy Dennison. Great to meet you."

"Nice to meet you too." A smile turned up the edges of Brady's lips.

Mr. Sanders turned and glared at his future son-in-law. "What is this? Some sort of setup?"

Jimmy shook his head. "Hey, I'm completely innocent. I had no idea Brady James would be here."

"I'm thrilled!" The other older man in the group stepped toward Brady and extended his hand. "Marcus Dennison. Father of the groom. I'm a huge Mavericks fan. We all are." He gestured to the group.

"Not *all*." Mr. Sanders turned his glare on Mr. Dennison. "I believe I've made it clear where my loyalties lie."

Oh boy.

Not that Mr. Dennison seemed to notice. He kept his focus on Brady. "So sorry to hear about the knee. We really miss seeing you out there." The fellow placed his hand on Brady's shoulder. "Things just aren't the same without you."

Brady flinched but managed a quiet "Thanks."

"Oh yes, it's such a shame." A lovely woman stepped into place alongside Mr. Dennison. "I'm Julia, by the way. Marcus's wife. We just adore the Mavericks. Always have. We lived in Dallas years ago and fell head over heels for the team. Even had season tickets for a time." She put her hand on Brady's arm. "I do hope your knee will be okay. I tried to get the ladies in my prayer group to add you to our list, but we live in San Antonio. I'm sure you understand."

"They won't pray for a Mavericks player in San Antonio?" Madge asked.

Mr. Sanders gave her a hard glare. "I thought we drove all the way to Dallas to pick out a wedding dress, not talk basketball." He muttered something under his breath about how talking about the Mavericks didn't mean we were truly talking basketball anyway. I prayed Brady didn't hear it.

Unfortunately, someone else did.

"What's that you say?" Stan's voice rang out from behind us. "We have a duel going on here?" He slapped Brady on the back. "Don't worry, folks. One more little surgery to get out of the way and we'll have this boy back on the court."

"You're still under contract?" Mrs. Dennison looked hopeful.

"He will be." Stan plastered on a fake smile. "Next season. Now, if you don't mind, folks, I need to talk to my boy here about an article for the paper. Got to keep his name in front of the fans, you know."

Brady excused himself to his office, but I could read the concern in his eyes. We didn't often get basketball quarrels at the dress shop. Bridal gown quarrels, sure. Money quarrels, always. But, basketball disputes? Never. Here in the Dallas area, it was the Mavericks all the way.

After Brady left, I did my best to reel everyone back in and focus on the bride.

"Let's start by looking at available dresses." I gestured to the rows and rows of gowns. "If you don't find anything you like, we'll involve Dahlia and her team. What's the wedding date again?"

"January 8th." The bride put her hand up. "I know, I know, we don't have long. But we don't want to wait until after the playoffs to get married."

"You're setting the date based on a basketball schedule?" Madge looked mystified by this. "Gracious."

"Now, what about that dress designer?" Mrs. Sanders asked. "Nadia something or other? She's the one who's so famous, right? Everyone raves over her, so we want her to design our Carrie's gown." She giggled. "Can you imagine the look on Janine Parker's face when she finds out that my daughter's dress came from Cosmopolitan? She'll be green with envy."

Alrighty then. That was how this game was played.

"Nadia James is Brady's mother," I explained. "She's the designer you mean. But she's in Paris right now. So Dahlia would be the one to—"

"No mother of a Mavericks player is going to be designing my daughter's dress." Mr. Sanders crossed his arms. "Gotta draw the line somewhere."

"But Mr. Sanders . . ." Wrinkles formed between Jimmy's brows. "It's Carrie's big day and this is what she wants."

The puffed-up father of the bride softened a little at that comment.

"To be honest, Nadia has designed many of the gowns you

see here in the shop," I explained. "So even if Carrie picks out something off the rack, it will likely be Nadia's design."

"Then we might need to rethink this plan. I want the best for my girl, but I'm sure there are plenty of other dress shops between here and San Antonio," Mr. Sanders said.

"Now, Frankie, you're just being silly." Mrs. Sanders patted her husband on the arm. She turned to me and sighed. "He lives, eats, sleeps, and breathes basketball. You should see our house. Everything has the word *Spurs* on it. And we've got season tickets, of course, so dragging him up here to Dallas this late in the season was the equivalent of taking the man for a root canal. Maybe worse."

"That's why we've come on a Thursday morning," Mr. Sanders said. "No game today."

"Ah." So we had to work everything around the bride's father's obsession with the Spurs? And doing so meant that Nadia was out? "Maybe we need to think about choosing something from one of the other designer lines." I pointed to a row of expensive gowns. "These are just in from New York. And we have several from Paris as well. Would you like to start there?"

"I think that's my cue to exit." Jimmy gave his bride-to-be a kiss on the forehead. "My parents and I are headed to the party supply store to pick up some things. We'll be back in a couple of hours. Sound good?"

"Sounds great." Carrie gave him a tender kiss on the lips and waved as they headed out the door. Then she followed on my heels as I pulled several gowns for her to try. In spite of her beautiful figure, none of the dresses seemed just right. She was short-waisted with long legs. Carrie tried on nine gowns in all but couldn't seem to find the perfect one.

After an hour of fretting, her mother came to the only

obvious conclusion. "Honey, I really think we have no choice. We'll have to have something designed just for you." She turned to face her husband. "Don't you agree, Frankie?"

"Not by a woman who produced a Mavericks player." Mr. Sanders shook his head. "Not going to happen."

"Now you see my problem, Katie?" Carrie's eyes flooded with tears. "Welcome to my life."

And what a life it was.

"Just ignore him, Katie," Mrs. Sanders said. "We'll have something special designed for our girl by Nadia James. Carrie will look lovely."

"Like I said, Nadia is in Paris right now," I pointed out. "She's not even here to design the dress. And our other designers are working against the clock for other customers."

"See?" Mr. Sanders said as he approached. "I knew this was a bad idea."

"Oh, but we must have a dress from Cosmopolitan." Mrs. Sanders looked as if she might panic. "We've told *everyone* and they'll be expecting it."

I did my best to keep Carrie's parents calm, finally suggesting they visit the Mexican restaurant next door for an early lunch while I took Carrie to discuss the problem with Dahlia.

Once I was alone with the bride-to-be, she was free to let the tears flow. "See. What. I. Mean?"

"Mm-hmm. How do you do it?"

"Oh, trust me, I don't. I try not to get involved. I'm not even a basketball fan, but please don't tell my parents that. To be honest, Jimmy isn't either. He's an engineer."

What that had to do with anything, I couldn't be sure.

As I led her back to meet with Dahlia, we passed Brady in the hallway. He gave her a warm smile and extended his hand.

"Sorry about all of that," she said. "It's nothing personal

with my dad." She paused. "Actually, I guess it kind of is. If it's not the Spurs, he's not interested. And now that he's retired from the oil and gas business, he has way too much time on his hands."

"We'll work around your dad, and no hard feelings. I'm not playing right now anyway." Brady seemed to flinch as he said those words. "And the Spurs are a great team. I'm good friends with a couple of the players."

"That's good to know. I'll tell him." Her eyes brimmed with tears. "But honestly? This whole wedding experience was supposed to be about me, not about a stupid ball team." She put her hand over her mouth. "Oops. Sorry."

"Again, no offense. Trust me when I say I'm at the point where I'm ready to admit there's a lot more to life than basketball." He shrugged. "I can't believe I can actually say that and mean it, but I can."

I couldn't believe it either, but I was happy to hear it with my own ears.

"Let's see what the design team has to say about coming up with a new dress, okay?" I pushed open the door to the studio.

Had I known what I'd be walking into, I never would have taken Carrie back there. I found Dahlia in a puddle of tears. I rushed her way, alarm bells ringing in my ears. "What happened? Dahlia?"

"Oh, Katie." She threw her arms around my neck and sobbed. And sobbed some more. I tried to calm her down, but she would not be soothed. Carrie came to stand next to me, handing Dahlia tissues. The noise must've alarmed the folks up front because Madge showed up at the door, followed by Twiggy. They all rushed our way.

"Who died?" Madge grabbed a box of tissues and pressed it into Dahlia's hands.

"I—I don't know." Perhaps Dahlia had received bad news from back home in Europe. One thing was for sure—with her carrying on at this rate, we'd never know.

Remarkably, Carrie got her to calm down at last. "Now, tell us what's wrong so we can help."

Dahlia released a slow breath and took a seat in front of her favorite sewing machine. "It's Dewey."

"Dewey?" My heart sailed straight to my throat as she spoke my brother's name. "What's happened to Dewey?"

"He ... he ..." She reverted to sobbing again. Off in the distance Eduardo looked on, his eyes wide. Hibiscus continued to work, but Jane seemed to be in a puddle too.

"Is he okay?" I knelt down next to her chair. "Tell me. Please."

"Physically, yes, he's fine." With a wave of her hand she dismissed any concerns in that area. "But he won't be ... after I kill him!"

12

Here We Go Again

I have found that when you are deeply troubled, there are things you get from the silent devoted companionship of a dog that you can get from no other source.

Doris Day

Okay then. Dahlia planned to kill my brother.

I stood up and tried to gather my thoughts while I willed my hands to stop trembling.

Dahlia threw her tissues on the table in a wad as her words tumbled out. "He. Just. Broke. My. Heart!"

Hmm, maybe someone *needed* to kill my brother.

It took a few minutes to get the rest of the story, but apparently my brother had indeed broken her heart. Not in the "I'm seeing another woman" sort of way, but rather the "Maybe we should take some time to think this through" way. Just like Casey had done to me.

Jerk.

"He said we needed to step back." Dahlia sniffled. "He wasn't sure he could handle the long-distance relationship. Can you believe that? It's only, what—an hour and a half to Fairfield? Two at most?"

"Long distance, my eye," Madge sputtered. "That boy's in Dallas more than he's home in Fairfield. He just needs to get a job here and settle down."

"That's what I told him, but he doesn't want to leave Fairfield and I can't leave the shop. I just can't. He thinks that we should get married and have fourteen kids and live in the country." Dahlia gestured to her trim physique. "Do I *look* like I could carry fourteen kids? And live in the country? I don't think so!" She dissolved into a haze of tears again.

"My goodness, I don't know this man you're referring to, but I do believe he's in need of some wise counsel." Carrie took a seat. "I daresay he needs a swift kick in the backside as well. Not that I know you either, so you can take or leave my advice." She stuck out her hand. "I'm Carrie Sanders, by the way. Just came back to see about having a dress designed."

"Oh no!" Dahlia looked dismayed by this news. "Not another new dress! When do you need it?"

"January 8th." Carrie spoke so softly I had to strain to hear her.

"January 8th?" Dahlia swiped her eyes with the back of her hand. "Are. You. Serious?"

I had to get this train back on track. "Let's go back to what we were talking about. I want to understand, Dahlia. Are you saying that my brother loves you enough to want to marry you, but the two of you can't settle on how you could make it work? Or are you saying that he broke up with you? Because I'm confused."

"Oh, wow." Carrie gazed at me. "The guy who broke her heart is your brother? Awkward."

"I—I guess I broke up with him." Her lashes brimmed with moisture. "Because I can't have fourteen kids. Don't you see that? I just can't."

"I'm sure he doesn't really want you to have fourteen kids," Carrie said. "Likely it's a misunderstanding."

"He wants me to become a . . ." Dahlia cried in earnest now. "A . . ."

"A . . . what?" Carrie sat on the edge of her seat.

"A Baptist!" She seemed to choke on the word. "I can't become a Baptist! All of my people are Lutheran! If I have to leave the Lutheran church, my mother will never forgive me. And my Aunt Regene, God rest her soul . . . she will spit on me from the grave. Don't you see? I can't do it!"

Eduardo, who had kept silent all of this time, rushed Dahlia's way with another box of tissues in hand. Hibiscus and Jane came behind him carrying an open box of imported chocolates.

"This'll make everything better, honey." Jane thrust the box of chocolates in Dahlia's direction.

"Eat two. They're small," Hibiscus added as she grabbed one and popped it into her mouth.

Carrie's eyes widened as Dahlia carried on. I started to apologize but she put her hand up. "Are you kidding me? This makes my situation look like small potatoes. If this poor girl can live through fourteen babies, becoming a Baptist, and having her dead relatives spit on her, then surely I can handle two families that quarrel over basketball."

I wasn't so sure about that last part but didn't say so. Then again, I was a little distracted by Dahlia, who now had chocolate all around the edges of her mouth.

"You are a saint, Dahlia," Carrie said. "Truly."

Dahlia gazed at her with newfound respect. "Here. Come and have a chocolate."

Carrie rose and walked over to grab a couple of chocolates. "Thank you. Don't mind if I do. I tend to agree that chocolate is a cure-all. It makes everything better."

Well, if I couldn't beat 'em . . .

I reached for a chocolate and popped it into my mouth.

Before long calmer heads prevailed. "Dahlia, is there anything I can do?" I asked.

She shook her head.

"I may not be able to solve the problem with my brother," I said, "but maybe it would be a nice distraction to Skype with Nadia after you get Carrie's measurements so that they can talk about design ideas. If you don't have time to make the dress, perhaps one of the others will." I gave Eduardo a hopeful look and he nodded.

Dahlia sniffled and reached for her measuring tape. Less than thirty minutes later, a bright-eyed Dahlia conversed with Nadia over Skype as if nothing had ever happened. Introductions were made and Nadia chatted—like the pro she was—with our young bride-to-be. It didn't take long to settle on a plan. All Nadia had to do was ask the question, "Who's your favorite actress or singer?" to set things in motion.

"Oh, I know you'll think this is crazy, but I'm nuts about Doris Day." Carrie chuckled. "I've seen *Pillow Talk* over a dozen times. Was there ever a sexier man than Rock Hudson?"

We all sighed in unison.

Well, those old enough to know who Rock Hudson was

sighed. This led to a conversation about his life offscreen, which somehow led us back around to Doris Day once again. By the time we ended the call with Nadia, everyone was in good spirits, including Eduardo, who had actually met Doris in person when he lived in Los Angeles in the fifties. Go figure.

Once we finished up with Nadia, Carrie turned my way, eyes lit with joy. "Oh, Katie, I'm so excited! Mama's always been such a huge Doris Day fan and so is Mrs. Dennison. This might be just the ticket. Basketball has separated us but Doris will bring us all together!"

They needed something to bring them all together, no doubt about that. And I was glad Nadia had the insight to ask for the bride's input. Still, I doubted that Doris Day had the power to pull these two families into one cohesive unit.

Minutes later Dahlia—now all smiles—pulled up pictures of Doris Day on the internet. We all pointed out the various dresses that we loved, then gave a common gasp when we saw Doris in a remarkable fitted white gown sparkling with rhinestones on the left shoulder.

"Oh, that's it!" Carrie let out a squeal.

"I know this dress well," Eduardo said from behind me. "Silk sheath, as was her custom. Off-white, though it looks more white in this picture. Ankle-length gown. Notice how the gown is drawn to gather on the left shoulder and how the back plunges downward."

"Yes, it's beautiful." Carrie leaned in to have a closer look.

"Very popular style back in the day," Eduardo said. "And the accessories are perfect. But what really makes the dress come alive is that fitted bodice panel. One rarely sees that anymore, but what a lovely way to accentuate a small waistline." He smiled at Carrie. "Like yours."

"Why, thank you. You think this gown would work for me?"

"Do I? But of course. I would add more sparkle to the top, but the rest would stay the same. Just promise me that you will wear elbow-length gloves in white."

"Ooh, I promise."

"It will be the loveliest gown ever produced at Cosmopolitan Bridal!" Eduardo threw his arms up in the air. "Or my name isn't Eduardo Villa de la Consuela."

Okay then. Looked like everyone was on board.

"It'll be perfect. Just the ticket." As I spoke the word "ticket," I thought about Carrie's father. Hopefully he wouldn't really mind the idea of Nadia designing the gown. Worse things had happened, after all. Who cared if they had opposing views when it came to ball teams?

This made me think about Dewey and Dahlia. Had my brother really given her an ultimatum—move to the country and have fourteen children? If so, I needed to have a "Come to Jesus" talk with him. A real couple worked things out. Even the hard things.

For whatever reason, thinking about them reminded me of Casey—how he'd left me high and dry to move away to Oklahoma. We hadn't worked things out, had we? Then again, we weren't meant to be. I was meant to come to Dallas, to meet Brady James. And Dallas was where I planned to stay.

Unfortunately, the squabbles continued when the families entered the shop once again, though the womenfolk seemed pleased with the whole Doris Day angle. Things didn't get much better when Stan got involved minutes later, insisting Brady sign autographs for the groom's family.

I could read the pain in Brady's eyes as he signed the photos that Stan magically produced from his car. Really? Did the guy carry around photos of the players he represented? Soon after, my youngest brother, Beau, showed up. I hadn't seen him in action as an upcoming agent, but the guy really knew his stuff. At least, he knew enough to get Mr. Sanders more perturbed than ever.

Just when I thought things couldn't possibly get worse, Eduardo made his way out to the front of the store. He'd overheard enough of the conversation to wave his hands in disgust. "I care nothing about basketball. It is a ridiculous sport."

I put my finger to my lips. "Please don't say that so loud, okay?"

"Why should I hide my feelings?" he asked. "I don't need to scream at a television screen to prove my manhood. I prove it just fine by fitting lovely ladies in beautiful dresses. I know a lot of men, young and old, who would kill for such a living. But to create a beautiful gown like the one that Doris wore in *Pillow Talk*? These are the things I live for!"

"To each his own." Stan rolled his eyes. "You can keep your ball gowns. I'll take a basketball any day."

This led to an argument. Great. Just what our customers needed to hear—employees who didn't get along. Not that Stan really worked in the shop, but we couldn't seem to shake him. He wasn't giving up, no matter how problematic Brady's knee situation got. Apparently Eduardo wasn't giving up either. He just kept sharing comment after comment about how much he despised basketball and how Doris would be proud to hear that her gown was making an appearance at a bride's wedding in San Antonio, Texas.

Well, terrific. What a lovely day we were all having.

When everyone finally left, I settled into a chair in Brady's office, relieved to have the whole experience behind me.

"That went well." He laughed.

"The bride got her way in the end. I suppose that's all that matters." I leaned back in the chair and rubbed my neck.

"Yeah. We don't always get our way, do we?" Brady said, a thoughtful look on his face.

"Nope. But I'm completely floored at how brilliant Eduardo is when it comes to designs. Your mom certainly knew what she was doing by hiring him."

"If only we could get him interested in basketball. He'd be the perfect employee." Brady grinned, but just as quickly his smile faded. He busied himself with papers on his desk, but I felt compelled to get to the heart of things once and for all.

I sat up straight in the chair and put one hand on his desk. "Brady, do you mind if we have a little talk?"

"Don't mind a bit." He rose and walked over to the door to close it. "We'll give 'em something to talk about." Before taking his seat, he planted a little kiss on the top of my head. "Now, what's on your mind?"

"I'm worried about you."

"Worried?" He took a seat behind his desk, confusion registering in those gorgeous eyes of his. "Why?"

"You're not yourself lately. You seem kind of . . . down."

"Down? Really?" He looked perplexed. "Not trying to be."

"Oh, I know that. Maybe it's more of a perception. When I first came to Cosmopolitan, you were okay with the idea of *not* playing basketball, at least until your knee healed. But now . . ."

"Now it's more of a struggle." He shrugged. "Part of it is knowing I have to have another surgery. That's like the nail in my coffin. If the first surgery had worked, I would've held on to the hope that I'd be back out on the court in a few months. But the idea of a second surgery . . ." He shook his head. "It changes everything. Mostly my perspective. You heard what I said out there earlier, right? I'm not in love with the sport like I used to be. It's time I start looking at myself as something other than a basketball player."

116

"Not forever, Brady. It's just a season. I've heard you say it yourself. God moves in seasons."

"Yes. It's a season." He rose and winced as he put weight on his left leg. "A long season. And I know what I've said. I still believe all of that. It's just . . . I don't know . . ."

"A little harder than you thought it'd be?"

"A lot harder. And even more on days like today when everyone around me is talking basketball. They all want me back in the game."

Hmm. Not everyone wanted him back in the game. Mr. Sanders, for instance. But I understood his meaning.

"You know how it is." Brady locked eyes with me. "When you're young you have all these dreams about what you want to be when you grow up. Who you want to be. So you set goals. And then you achieve them."

Actually, I'd been raised in Fairfield. My big dream was to make the cheerleading squad in high school and possibly earn the title of Peach Queen before I graduated. I'd achieved both of those goals, thank you very much. Other than that, I hadn't spent a lot of time pondering the whole goals thing.

Oh, wait. I did once have that goal to get a proposal from Casey before I won the wedding dress contest. I hadn't exactly met that goal, but I thanked my lucky stars for that.

Brady was still talking as he moved toward me. Something about basketball. I did my best to focus. He pulled me into his arms and sighed. "I can tell I've lost you, Katie."

"You'll never lose me."

He gave me a little kiss on the cheek. "Promise? 'Cause I'd hate to lose my career and you too."

I admit, it stung a little that he said "you too" instead of "the girl I love" or something to that effect. But I let it roll off me. Mostly. "You haven't lost your career. That's what I was

117

saying before about seasons. This is a long one, yes, but it will pass. Springtime is coming."

"Last time I checked it was November. But I can tell you listened to that sermon online."

"Yeah, it was great. And I got the message loud and clear. It was very fitting. You're facing the death of a dream, but I promise God has new things. Don't give up on your dreams, Brady James. I've never known you to do that and you're not going to start now."

"Listen to the girl." Stan's voice sounded from outside the door.

I laughed. Oh, great. Now Stan was agreeing with me? He'd always considered me a distraction in Brady's life.

The door inched open and Stan stuck his head inside. "Just wanted you to know I've got a meeting with the Mavericks owner in an hour, Brady. No need for you to come. We're just going to talk about . . ." His words drifted off.

"I know. My contract release." Brady shrugged. "Whatever happens, Stan, just remember it's not your fault."

"It's not yours either," I said, giving him a little kiss on the cheek. "You're a team player, Brady. Right now you're just on our team, at Cosmopolitan Bridal."

"Right." His response didn't have much enthusiasm behind it. But I didn't have time to think about that for long because Madge pushed her way into the room and started scolding Stan for bringing food into the shop.

"It's not food," he argued. "It's pizza."

"That's food. And you know better." On and on she went, talking to him like a youngster. Instead of his usual bantering, Stan gave me a little wink and said, "I love it when she talks to me like this."

Okay then. Maybe we weren't all on opposing teams.

Of course, the Sanders and Dennison families kind of were.

And Stan and Eduardo kind of were.

And Dahlia and Dewey kind of were.

Hmm. Maybe this whole teams thing was more than it was cracked up to be.

13

I Said My Pajamas
(and Put On My Prayers)

What she [Doris Day] possessed, beyond her beauty, physical grace, and natural acting ability, was a resplendent voice that conveyed enormous warmth and feeling.

Nellie McKay

On Friday night, the 13th, I drove Alva back to Fairfield for Queenie's lingerie shower, which took place at Bessie May's house. When I picked her up later that night, she was all giggles and smiles and couldn't stop talking about all the nighties Queenie had received.

"I'm just not sure you would believe me if I told you what a couple of them looked like, Katie." My aunt shook her head. "Shocking, really. I don't think Ophelia's eyesight is what it used to be. Surely she wouldn't buy that shade of pink on purpose."

On and on she went, talking about negligees and such, but I didn't want to think about it. I needed to focus on tomorrow's shower, which would take place in the fellowship hall at the Baptist church.

We spent the night at my parents' place again. They were due to return from their latest cruise tomorrow morning, just in time for the shower. I hoped.

I awoke early on Saturday morning, my mind in a whirl. A couple of phone calls came through from Joni and Lori-Lou, who were both on their way to the church. I hurried Alva up and we hit the road, the back of my SUV loaded with supplies.

I happened to pass by the hardware store on my way and smiled when I saw the window display that Crystal and Jasper had come up with. The boxes stacked to look like a tree had been a marvelous idea. I spent so much time looking at it that I must not have noticed the light turning green. The car behind me honked and I moved on my way, anxious to get to the church to help Lori-Lou. We arrived in record time and had the room looking festive and bright in less than an hour. Thanks to Joni, the tables were filled with all sorts of yummy-looking finger foods, not a chicken strip in the mix. By the time the ladies started arriving a few minutes before ten, we were more than ready for them.

Now, I'd been to a lot of bridal showers over the years, but never one that boasted so many elderly women. From what I could gather from the hushed conversations and red faces, last night's lingerie shower was still front and center in everyone's mind. Thank goodness I'd been left off the invitation list.

Right now I didn't have time to think about nighties. I was far too busy playing hostess alongside Lori-Lou, greeting our guests and pointing them toward the food table. The finger foods were being snagged up in record time. No problem, though. Joni refilled the trays, humming a merry tune while she worked.

I couldn't get over the little cake Ophelia had baked. Darling! It boasted four tiny tiers—a wedding cake in miniature. With Prissy Moyer's help, she'd even made some adorable little cookies that looked like wedding dresses. Perfect!

Not everyone was in the best of spirits, though. Mama arrived late with a nasty-looking sunburn. Everything was beet-red except for big round circles around her eyes, where she'd apparently worn sunglasses while on her cruise.

"Don't say it, Katie Sue. I know, I know." She dropped her purse on a chair and turned around. "Could you scratch the middle of my back? I'm peeling."

I couldn't recall ever hearing my mom use those words before, but how could I not scratch her back? The woman had given birth to me, after all.

"I hope I can sit down." She eased her way onto a chair. "The backs of my thighs are crisp. You just haven't known pain until you've had a sunburn in November. All that cold air blowing on your hot skin. So painful."

Hopefully I'd never know.

"Well, you made it back from the cruise just fine."

"Haven't even been home yet. Your father dropped me off. He's headed to the house to unload our bags. The man must've been nuts to think we could handle a cruise to Mexico on the heels of our trip to the Galápagos."

"At least you're seeing the world." I smiled. "That's a good thing."

"I suppose. But I'm missing out here." She gestured to the other ladies, who were all eating little sandwiches. "Anything exciting happen without me?"

"Oh, we just got the ball rolling with the food. In a few minutes we'll cut the cake and then play a couple of games. Then Queenie will open her presents."

"I'd better go say hello to everyone." Mama tried to stand, but apparently her thighs wouldn't cooperate. "Or not." She waved at Queenie, who rose and walked toward us.

"Glad to have you back, Marie." Queenie opened her arms as if ready to give Mama a big hug, but my mother flinched.

"I wish I could hug you, Queenie, but I just can't." My mother squirmed in her seat. "I do wonder if I'll ever be able to hug anyone again."

"How was your trip?" Queenie asked. "Did that son of mine behave himself?"

"If you call eating ten meals a day behaving himself, then yes," Mama said.

Bessie May joined us. She gave a little whistle when she saw Mama's sunburn. "My goodness, Marie. You're crispier than the chicken up at Sam's. Where does one have to go to get a burn like that?"

"Cozumel."

"I thought you were in the Galápagos."

"That was the week before," Mama said, then whispered to me, "Katie Sue, please scratch my back."

"So you decided to do the Cozumel private beach excursion like I suggested?" Bessie May nodded. "Good choice."

"That whole Cozumel experience is a story for another day," Mama said. "But let's just leave it at this: if you ever meet a fellow named Juan Carlos who tries to tell you that he's selling you a Rolex watch, don't fall for it."

"Other than that?" I asked as I gently scratched her back.

"It was nice. But as you can see, I got a bad burn. Did you know that Cozumel is actually closer to the equator than Fairfield?" She wriggled in her seat again. "Apparently it has to do with the effect of the gamma rays . . . or something like that."

Lori-Lou joined us, her eyes growing wide when she saw Mama's burn. "Oh, Aunt Marie. That looks so painful. Can I bring you anything?"

"I bought stock in aloe vera," Mama responded. "So I'm good."

"Would you like some food?" Ophelia appeared from behind Lori-Lou.

"Food. Ugh." Mama groaned, putting her hand on her stomach. "If I never eat again, it'll be fine with me." She looked at me and rolled her eyes. "Your father said he wanted to get his money's worth, so he pretty much ate all day every day."

"Oh my."

"Tell me about it. We started in the Windjammer Café in the mornings, gravitated to the grill on the top deck for lunch, and then had a glorious dinner each night in the main dining room. You've never seen so much food—appetizers, main courses, desserts—anything you like, and as much of it as you'd like."

At this point, every woman in the room was clustered around us, all listening to Mama's story. So much for thinking this would be a shower for Queenie.

"The whole thing sounds wonderful," Lori-Lou said. "Except for the sunburn part. Still, I can't imagine going on a cruise without any of the kids along." She sighed. "For that matter, I can't imagine going anywhere without the kids along."

"Oh?" Mama looked around. "Are they with you today?"

Lori-Lou nodded. "Sort of. Josh is watching them at Dairy

Queen. After that they're going to the park. If it's not too cold, I mean. It's getting chilly out there."

"Well, when you get the chance, take a cruise. But don't eat all day like Herb did. It was terrifying to watch." She faced me again. "I'm pretty sure your father put on ten pounds. I put on five myself. But we had a wonderful time. Mostly. One of these days I'll tell you about the family we met in the dining hall. We had to share a table with them." She shivered, but I couldn't tell if it was from the sunburn or the conversation.

"Back to the party, folks." Ophelia clapped her hands. "We've got a cake to cut."

"And cookies to eat," Prissy said.

"And presents to open!" Lori-Lou added.

"Oh, but first tell me how the lingerie shower went last night, Queenie," Mama said.

At this, my grandmother had to sit down. Several of the other ladies started giggling. In fact, Prissy nearly lost it. Her face turned as red as the buttons on her blouse.

Terrific. And here I'd thought we might get away with not mentioning it.

"We'll tell you everything," Bessie May said. "What do you want to hear first?"

"For pity's sake." Queenie shook her head. "You missed a fiasco. These crazy old women just wanted to shame me."

"Or raise your blood pressure," Ophelia said.

"Trust me, Paul Bradford's blood pressure is surely going to be elevated when he sees her in a couple of those getups we gave her." Prissy slapped her knee. "It's gonna be a humdinger of a honeymoon, we'll just leave it at that!"

If one could judge from the expression on my grandmother's face, she was clearly disgusted with this conversation. "What a ridiculous waste of money," she muttered. "Seriously."

"Now, I thought that white lace nightie was lovely, Queenie," Bessie May said. "Nothing wrong with that one."

"The fabric is thin. I can't abide thin fabric. Give me a good flannel nightgown any day."

"Flannel?" Lori-Lou groaned. "Tell me you're not wearing flannel on your honeymoon, Queenie."

"What I'm wearing—or not wearing—on my honeymoon is nobody's business." My grandmother's face flushed. "Now, let's change the subject, please and thank you. I think we have more important things to discuss than my nightgowns. Didn't someone say there was a cake to be cut? I'd love a slice."

"A small slice, Queenie," Ophelia said. "You don't want to pack on the pounds before you have to wear that hot pink nightie I bought you."

This garnered a groan from Queenie. Or maybe the groan had more to do with the fact that she was attempting to stand. Her knee appeared to give out on her, but Lori-Lou and I caught her before she went down.

"There you go." Queenie released a sigh. "If the nightie doesn't win him over, my slick moves will."

Everyone laughed.

Minutes later Ophelia cut the cake. She and Lori-Lou served up slices while I organized the women into two groups to play our first game.

"Choose one woman from each group to be the bride," I instructed.

The first group chose Prissy Moyer. The second group chose, of all people, Joni. She argued that she wasn't technically a guest at this party, but that argument did her no good.

"Okay, now take the rolls of toilet paper, and when I say go, begin to wrap your bride, making the toilet paper into her wedding gown."

"Toilet paper brides?" Queenie shook her head. "What will they think of next?"

"Ready, set . . . go!" I stood back and watched as the groups dressed their respective brides. I couldn't fathom how they did it, but Joni's group had her looking very bride-like at the end of the challenge. Prissy, on the other hand, looked like a mummy.

Mama pulled out her phone and snapped pictures. "Oh, this'll be perfect to post on Facebook. I can't wait."

"If you dare post a picture of me dressed in toilet paper, I'll sue you, Marie Fisher!" Prissy hollered.

That didn't stop Mama. She continued to take pictures. My favorite was the one with Joni covered in white and holding a toilet paper bouquet. Maybe Levi would take the hint.

Afterward we played another, calmer game. This one was a fill-in-the-blank story that turned out to be a lot of fun. Lori Lou won the game—hardly fair, since she was a hostess, not a guest. But she gave her prize to the bride-to-be, which balanced things out.

Finally the moment arrived.

"Presents!" Ophelia squealed.

"Sure hope they're not as embarrassing as the ones last night," Queenie said.

"You'll never believe what I went through to get that black negligee." Bessie May shook her head. "I bought it online from some site I'd never been to before. And ever since, I've been plagued with spam. Horrible stuff."

"Oh, Spam *is* horrible stuff," Ophelia agreed. "I've never liked it, though my husband—God rest his soul—ate it once a week."

"Not *that* kind of spam, Ophelia." Bessie May rolled her eyes. "Anyway, ever since I ordered the negligee from that site, I get the weirdest pop-ups."

"I had a pop-up for breakfast," Prissy said. "One of those Toaster Strudel things. Still not sure why they call 'em pop-ups. They don't pop up when you bake them."

"My experience on the internet has changed since I placed the order," Bessie May said. "And not in a good way. You would be stunned at the pictures I've seen. I truly didn't know the human body could get into some of those positions."

"Oh my." Mama fanned herself. "Is it getting hot in here?"

"You're sunburned, Marie," Queenie said. "But it is getting warm."

"I wish I could get those pictures to go away." Bessie May shrugged. "I might have to throw my computer out the window and buy a new one. I can't imagine looking at such things every time I want to check my email. Such terrible photos."

The women continued to gab as I passed gifts to Queenie, expressions of glee sounding as she opened one gift after another, and none of them risqué at all. When she got to mine, Queenie gasped and turned my way. "Oh, Katie, it's beautiful." She held up a glittering tiara.

"I know you didn't want a veil, but you're the matriarch of the family. You're our Queenie. So you need a crown."

"Do you think?" A lovely smile lit her face as she examined it.

"It's perfect!" I clasped my hands together, thrilled with her reaction.

"Great. Give her a crown and she'll want a scepter too." Bessie May groaned and then laughed.

"Everyone deserves to be a princess—er, a queen—for a day," I argued. "Especially on her wedding day. Wear it, Queenie. You'll look fabulous." I stood beside her as she fingered the jewels in the crown. I took it from her and eased it into her silver hair. The mesh of silver and crystals against that radiant hair was exquisite.

"I must admit, she does look like royalty," Prissy said.

"I do?" Queenie pulled out her compact and looked at her reflection.

"A royal pain is more like it," Bessie May said. "She's been so stubborn throughout this whole process. Doesn't want anyone to do anything for her. She's so used to calling the shots that she won't take any help from us."

"It's just pride, plain and simple," Ophelia said. "But you know what the Bible says: 'Pride goeth before a fall.'"

"Oh, I won't fall, Ophelia," Queenie said. "I'll be walking down the aisle on my Herb's arm. He's been given strict instructions to hold on tight so I don't fall."

"With all the weight he's put on, I hope he makes it." Mama sighed and took another bite of her cake. And then another.

"And there you go." Ophelia rolled her eyes. "I can see it all now."

I could too, and what I saw brought a smile to my face. Queenie would have her big day, surrounded by people who adored her. Pop would make sure she made it down the aisle without tumbling. And I'd be there to witness the whole thing.

Queenie gave a little wave of thanks. "Ladies, I'm grateful. And thanks for not showering me with embarrassing gifts . . . like last night."

"This is a church shower, after all," Lori-Lou said.

"Humph." My grandmother rolled her eyes. "All of the ladies in attendance last night were church friends and that didn't stop any of them from their shenanigans. Just grateful things played out differently today."

"No shenanigans here, Queenie," I promised.

At least, I hoped not. One never knew what the rest of the day might hold.

Turned out the gifts were pretty tame. A new toaster—

four-slice. A Crock-Pot, because no one can have too many of those. And an iron. Really? Who bought a bride an iron as a gift?

There were some lovely gifts too. A beautiful crystal picture frame for the wedding photo. A scrapbook to memorialize the big day. A pretty serving tray, and even some beautiful toasting glasses from Mama.

"I found 'em in Cozumel," she said. "Got 'em for a song."

"From a guy named Juan Carlos?" I asked.

"Um, no. From a shop that sells high-end glassware. Had a doozy of a time getting them back without breaking."

Queenie proclaimed them to be perfect and said she couldn't wait to use them at the reception. This led to a dissertation from Prissy about the punch recipe she planned to use, which somehow transitioned to a story about how old man Peterson had been picked up on a DWI. I couldn't quite figure out how we'd gotten from one topic to the others, but I was stunned to hear about the arrest.

After Queenie opened her gifts, she thanked her guests and gave a little speech about how much they meant to her. "From the bottom of my heart, I thank you all. This room is filled with the dearest people in the world to me, and I'm honored you've lavished me with your love."

Bessie May wiped away a few tears and said, "Now look what you've done. You've stirred up my allergies." This got a laugh from the others.

I headed to the kitchen to help Lori-Lou with the dishes. I found her in a reflective frame of mind. "I think it's so sweet the way they all support her." Her words were followed by a little sigh. "I hope when we're really old we're still as close as they are."

"Yes, me too. But promise you won't buy me a negligee from a naughty website when I'm old. Pinky swear?"

130

"Pinky swear." She stuck out her pinky and we laughed as we made the promise. Then we tackled the mounds of dirty dishes, tossing the paper ones and putting the rest into the soapy water in the sink.

"You won't be getting married when you're Queenie's age," Lori-Lou said after a few moments. "I have a feeling it won't be long before we're doing all of this for you." She handed me a clean ladle, which I dried with a dish towel.

"Maybe. Not sure." I thought about Brady, about his kisses, his sweet words. Just as quickly, I remembered his upcoming surgery. And the chaos at the bridal shop. And his mother's yearlong stint in Paris. Maybe I wouldn't be getting engaged anytime soon.

We continued to work together, our conversation sweet. Well, until Ophelia interrupted us.

"I'm going to serve up another round of cake," she said. "Sure don't want Queenie to take it home. She'll pack on the pounds between now and the big day, and that will never do."

Before I could say, "No thank you," Mama stuck her head in the door and gestured for me to join her in the reception hall. I tossed the dish towel and followed her.

She engaged me in a conversation on the far side of the room, away from the others. "I've been thinking about what Bessie May said about her computer. All of that stuff about spam and such. We don't often talk about those things in the Baptist church, but perhaps we should."

"O-oh?" Where was she going with this?

"Yes. I believe I'll ask Levi to teach a class on internet safety to the seniors."

"Oh, good idea. But Mama, I sincerely hope you don't tell him Bessie May's lingerie story. It would wreck him."

"It won't wreck him. He won't be shocked at all, I daresay.

He's such a great guy." She gazed across the room, transfixed by something in the distance. "Sometimes a person doesn't have to look far to find the perfect match."

"What do you mean?" I followed her gaze to Joni, who walked from person to person, picking up empty plates and tossing them in the trash can.

"I assume someone's filled you in on the scoop?" Mama whispered.

"Unless you're talking about ice cream, the answer would be a big fat no. What scoop?"

"About Joni."

"Joni? You mean that she's working as a wedding coordinator now? Yes, I know all about that."

"No." Mama shook her head. "Joni. Levi. Dating."

"Oh, right. I know there was some rumor about it, but it's been confirmed?" I asked. "Last I heard, it was just speculation."

"I'd like to believe it's more. He worked as the youth pastor over the summer," Mama explained. "But then, you knew that."

"Um, yes. You tried to hook me up with him after Casey broke my heart."

"True, true. I thought he might be a good option for you, Katie Sue. You can't blame a mama for trying."

Actually, I could, but I didn't choose to do so at the moment. "So what happened?" I asked in an attempt to get Mama back on track.

"Well, Levi was working with the youth, as I said, and Joni was hired by the church to coordinate weddings." Mama paused. "I don't mind admitting we were all a bit . . . surprised. She just didn't seem the wedding-ish type, if you know what I mean. But there they were, Levi and Joni, working at the church together day after day. Before long she was volunteering to help with the youth alongside him, and the rest, as they say, is history."

"Just seems strange. She was so tough in high school. And Levi was a mess back then."

"I suppose that's what they have in common," my mother said. "They've both been through significant changes in their lives. You just never know how things are going to turn out, do you?"

"No, I guess not."

Mama grew silent for a moment. When she did speak, the emotion in her voice took me by surprise. "Katie Sue, you know I love you."

"Well, yes, Mama. I know that." But I also knew that when her conversations started with "You know I love you," she was about to do something to make me question it.

"Jasper and Crystal are doing a fine job at the hardware store. She's settled right in and the people just adore her."

"That's good news, but what does it have to do with me?"

"Well now . . ." She turned to face me, eyes brimming with tears. "I know that your father and I have been away a lot. He's got me gallivanting from one beach to another, and I don't mind admitting the nomad life has been fascinating. Not quite what you read about in books—especially if you're traveling with someone like your father, who tends to throw his dirty clothes everywhere in those tiny cruise ship cabins—but fascinating."

"That's great, Mama."

"But it would make me feel better if I knew you were in Fairfield where you belong."

"I'm sorry—what?"

She reached to grip my hand. "Fairfield is your home. Surely you're not thinking of staying in Dallas forever. Right?"

"I hadn't really thought about forever."

"Of *course* you're thinking about forever. After you and Brady get married, you'll settle down somewhere."

Ah. So that was where this was headed. She thought Brady would marry me and sweep me away to Dallas-land forever. "We're not exactly marching toward the altar just yet. We're not even engaged."

"You will be. It's as plain as the nose on my face. And I don't want my grandchildren raised in the city."

"You don't have any grandchildren."

"Yet. But when I do, I'd like to see them raised here, surrounded by people who love them."

"Mama, you're never home anymore. So when you say 'surrounded' . . ."

"I will be, once the grandchildren start coming. Surely by then your father will be past this phase he's going through. He'll want to be here, building swing sets and taking kids on picnics. That sort of thing."

"It's just a lot to think about. If I do marry Brady—someday— he'll want to be in Dallas because that's where the Mavericks are." Not that he was playing for the Mavericks at the moment, but whatever.

"Just pray, honey."

"I—I do."

"And once those grandbabies start coming, you come home to Mama so I can show you how to raise 'em right, okay?"

I sighed.

She had a point. If and when I had children, I would want them to know their grandparents. If their grandparents ever stayed put. But to bring this up right now, when I wasn't even engaged? My mother might be jumping the gun a little.

I thought about her words for the rest of the day. I'd made

a huge mistake with my first boyfriend, nudging him toward the altar. I wouldn't make the same mistake with Brady. He needed time. And right now, he just needed my support and comfort as he faced one of the biggest challenges of his life. I would walk him through it, no questions about weddings whatsoever. This time it was all about him, not me.

As I thought about all he was facing, my heart filled with such passion, such emotion, that I couldn't hold back the tears. I rushed to the ladies' room to have a good, long cry.

Lori-Lou found me in there soon after. She knocked on the door of my stall and said, "Everything okay in there? Folks are wondering."

"I—I'm just worried about Brady. His surgery is in a few days."

"I know, Katie. And I'm praying. The WOP-pers will pray too."

"The problem is," I said through the closed door, "those WOP-pers don't know how to pray without insisting that God do things their way. They'll probably turn my prayer request into a plea for a proposal from Brady."

"And that would be such a terrible thing?" Lori-Lou asked.

"No. It would be a great thing. But right now I just want to focus on Brady's knee. My prayer—100 percent—is for God to heal his knee and his heart." I opened the door and stepped outside to discover several of the WOP-pers were in the bathroom with Lori-Lou. Oops.

"We'll pray for his healing, Katie," Bessie May said. "I promise. Nothing more and nothing less."

"Not sure I can make that promise," Ophelia interjected, "because I know this football fella with the broken arm is the guy for you. But I'll do my best to pray that God heals up that arm right quick."

"I for one would like to see you happily matched," Prissy said. "So I can't agree to pray only for his arm."

Good grief. "Ladies, I think you're the best. I really do. I just want to do it God's way this time. I tried to push the door open in my previous relationship and failed miserably. I'm tired of trying to make things happen. If God doesn't solidify this relationship with Brady, it's not worth having."

"Oh, he'll solidify it," Lori-Lou said. "I have no doubt about that. But it'll come in his time. His season."

There was that word again—season. Hadn't I just told Brady that he was walking through a season?

"I don't know about the rest of you, but I find it mighty hard to focus in the ladies' room," Ophelia said. "That big mirror is a terrible distraction. All I see is how bad my hair looks, and I can't possibly think of prayer when I'm focused on the terrible job the hairdresser did. Can we shake this joint and have another piece of cake?"

"You and that cake." Bessie May laughed and opened the door. Ophelia walked into the hallway, mumbling all the way about how the hairdresser had botched her 'do. The rest of us followed behind her, all tension relieved.

As we made our way toward the fellowship hall, I looked over at Lori-Lou and laughed. "Oh well. At least they're not mad at me for what I said."

"How could anyone be mad at you, Katie?" Lori-Lou stopped and gave me a warm hug. "Now, if you don't mind, we've got a lot of cleaning to do out there. Josh is on his way back with the kids, and I've got to get off my feet." She rubbed her belly. "This baby girl is giving me fits. Kicking up a storm. And my ankles are swollen." She pointed down at her ankles, and I gasped when I saw just how swollen they were.

"Oh my. Well, you sit down and I'll work with Joni and Josh to get everything done."

"Me? Sit down?" She gave a belly laugh. "That'll be the day. No, Katie, I'll be right beside you every step of the way. That's what friends are for—even friends with really fat ankles."

From up ahead I heard Ophelia say something about how rude it was for us to call her ankles fat, and I couldn't help but laugh. One day that would be Lori-Lou and me, hobbling down the hallway, misunderstanding every other word. Until then . . . well, it looked like we had a big mess to clean up before I headed home to Dallas to see the man I loved.

14

Our Day Will Come

She has style that's her own and when you hear it, you say,
"That's Doris Day!"

Kaye Ballard

The days leading up to Brady's surgery were among the hardest ever, especially with so much going on at the shop. Why oh why had I suggested putting on a bridal extravaganza on Black Friday, with Brady's surgery taking place the week before? I must've been crazy. I needed to focus on my guy, especially with his emotions weaving this way and that. I'd seen glimpses of depression in him before whenever the topic of basketball came up, but not like this.

In the days before the surgery a dark cloud hovered over him, one that was nearly visible to the human eye.

I could only encourage him and pray that the busyness of the shop would serve as a distraction. And talk about busy! Brides came and went in a flurry, but none more than Carrie and her family members. In some ways the Sanders family reminded me of my own: dedicated to one another, all on the same team. But when it came to how they treated the groom's family, civility was thrown to the wind. Clearly these in-laws were going to be facing some tough times once the bride and groom got married. If they got married. I wondered if they would make it all the way to the altar, if warring family members had anything to do with it.

Still, the love between Carrie and Jimmy was obvious. So why would their crazy families get in the way? I pondered that question as I awaited their arrival on the Tuesday morning following Queenie's bridal shower. I walked to the front of the store to have a chat with Madge and Twiggy, needing to get my concerns out in the open before Carrie and her family arrived.

"The Sanders family is coming to meet with Dahlia," I said. "They think she's been working on the sample dress, but she's been too busy."

"Oh dear." Twiggy's nose wrinkled. "Are you saying the sample dress isn't complete?"

"Oh, it's complete, and it turned out great. Eduardo did it. But they don't know that. My big concern is this—Dahlia's up to her eyeballs with another bride and I know she doesn't have time to see Carrie today. What should we do?"

Madge knelt down to pick up a receipt she'd dropped behind the register. "Send her to Eduardo." She rose. Slowly, with her hand on her back. "Man, I'm getting old."

"Puh-leeze. But did you really mean I should send Carrie

and her family to Eduardo? Sounds like a volatile mix of tempers, if you ask me."

"Exactly." Madge stuck the receipt in the drawer. "Send them to Eduardo and let them get a taste of their own medicine. They'll see their own reflection every time they meet with him."

"I think we'll *all* see a reflection," Twiggy said. "Of a building going up in flames. If you get that many combustible people in one room, there's liable to be an explosion."

I had no doubt she was right about that. I did my best not to fret as I awaited the visit from Mr. Sanders. He arrived with his wife and daughter promptly at ten. The arrogant fellow strutted in like a peacock, showing off his Spurs shirt.

"What did you think of that win last night, folks?" he crowed. "Ayres really took it all the way in the last thirty seconds. Have you ever seen anyone shoot a basket from the opposite side of the court? Miraculous, I tell you. The good Lord was aiming that ball straight for the basket." This led to a lengthy conversation about how God favored the Spurs. Lovely.

His wife nudged him with her elbow and shook her head. "Please ignore him, folks. He gets like this."

To my great surprise, Madge kept her mouth shut. Not a word about basketball emerged. She simply greeted them and led the way back to Eduardo's station in the back of the studio. I followed on her heels, anxious to see how she would handle this.

"I think you'll be happy with Eduardo's work," Madge said. "He's got quite the résumé."

"Eduardo?" Mr. Sanders narrowed his gaze, as if sizing up the man who'd been assigned to sew his daughter's wedding gown.

"Eduardo Villa de la Consuela at your service." Ever the suave one, he rose from his sewing machine, took Carrie's hand, and kissed it. His lustrous hair shimmered, every perfect strand sprayed in place. "Happy to attend to your needs. Do you need a bottled water? Perrier? Soda? Have you had lunch?"

"No, I'm fine." Carrie looked around. "I'm sorry, but where's Dahlia? She was supposed to be done with my sample dress."

"Dahlia is with another customer," I said. "But Eduardo will be helping you today. I hope that isn't a problem."

"Oh my." Mrs. Sanders looked a bit alarmed at this news. She couldn't stop staring at Eduardo's hair.

I could read the concern in Carrie's eyes as well. "Well, no, but how do I . . . I mean, how do I handle my fitting with a man?"

"Ah, not to worry." Eduardo put his hand up. "I have pieced together a sample of the gown made out of less expensive material. This we do to ensure the proper fit and design. Once we have established perfection, I will use the pattern pieces to create the real dress. You see? Hibiscus will be helping you into the sample gown today." He flashed a white-toothed smile. "I will be here to make the adjustments. That is all."

"Wait . . . Hibiscus?" Mrs. Sanders looked perplexed. "There's a person named Hibiscus?"

"I'm Hibiscus." The sweet young seamstress waved her hand and giggled. "I'm so excited about this dress. It's going to be gorgeous. You can always tell that when the sample dress is pretty, the real one will be out of this world. And Eduardo's amazing at what he does."

"Great. Mavericks sympathizers and men who sew. We've landed in just the right spot." Mr. Sanders groaned and moved toward the door. "If anyone wants me, I'll be having lunch at the restaurant next door."

"Oh, don't do it, my friend!" Eduardo sprinted across the room. "I've brought tamales. Homemade. Mama's recipe from when I was a boy in Mexico."

"Homemade tamales?" This stopped Mr. Sanders in his tracks. "Really? I love a good tamale."

"Me too," Mrs. Sanders echoed. "But it's too early for lunch."

"Then we'll call it brunch. Please. My treat. You will love my mama's tamales, God rest her soul." Eduardo put his hand on his heart. "I prepared a feast and brought plenty for my friends. Go over to that refrigerator and pull out as many as you like. Warm them in that microwave you see right there." He pointed at the run-down appliance. "And enjoy yourself while I work my magic on your daughter's dress."

"If you say so." Mrs. Sanders walked over to the refrigerator and started fixing plates.

Minutes later Mr. Sanders was caught up in the heavenly bliss of Eduardo's tamales. He ate two and asked his wife for a third. "The man can cook and sew. Eduardo's going to make someone a wonderful wife." He rolled his eyes.

"Frankie Sanders, don't be so rude." His wife reached for the pan of tamales. "If you don't take that back, I will refuse to warm up another one of these wonderful tamales for you."

"I take it back." He pursed his lips.

Hibiscus slipped into the spot next to Mr. Sanders. "If you don't mind, I'd like to share a story with you." She lowered her voice. "You see, Eduardo was married to his wife Natalia for forty years. She passed away a few years back. Being a widower has caused him to rediscover his passion for sewing. When he was a child he worked in a sweatshop in Tijuana. From there he ended up working in Hollywood during the golden age of movies. He's got an amazing story. I wish you had time to hear it all."

The microwave went off, and Hibiscus pulled out the plate holding the steaming tamale and passed it to Mr. Sanders. That seemed to shut him up.

"See, honey?" Mrs. Sanders said. "You can't judge a book by its cover."

"Or a designer by his hairdo," Mr. Sanders responded with a shrug as he took the plate. He dove into the food once again, all smiles.

I could hardly believe my good fortune as the Sanders family settled in with Eduardo, who held them all spellbound with his stories about how he met Doris Day back in the late fifties. I finally felt confident enough to head back to my office to work on the bridal extravaganza.

At lunchtime my phone rang and Mama's voice sounded from the other end of the line. "Katie Sue! When are you coming home?"

"Um, Mama, I was just home for Queenie's shower, remember?"

"Yes, but I meant for good. Remember that long talk we had about you coming back to Fairfield?"

"Yeah, I remember it, but I told you, Mama, this is my home for now. We're right in the middle of planning a bridal extravaganza, and I'm up to my eyeballs in—"

"I just don't understand it, Katie Sue. You've never even been a bride, but you spend all day with wedding dresses? Makes no sense at all."

Gee, thanks a lot, Mama.

She went off on a tangent about something related to Queenie's wedding, but I didn't hear half of it because I found myself distracted by laughter out in the hallway. I peeked outside my door and saw Eduardo with the Sanders family, all of them laughing together about something. *Go, Eduardo!*

"I know you're playing at this whole dress shop thing." Mama's voice brought me back to reality. "But surely you won't stay in Dallas forever."

Right now this conversation felt like it was going on forever. Mama dove into a long dissertation about the goings-on back in Fairfield, claiming I was missing out. "Ophelia has colored her hair the strangest shade of red-orange. Truly. Oh, and Florence Wilson broke her hip getting out of the tub. She's at the hospital having it pinned and plated. And I know I shouldn't gossip, but I don't think Bessie May's doing the best job with the choir. That special they did Sunday was deplorable. Completely flat."

"Mama, you're not heading up the choir anymore, so I suppose it doesn't reflect on you in any way."

"I suppose not, but I can't help but think I might've been able to fix the problem. See, they were flat as a pancake because Bessie May let Mr. Henderson sing in the bass section. The man can't carry a tune in a bucket."

"The Bible just says to make a joyful noise, right, Mama? There's nothing in there about singing on key."

"I feel sure the good King David would have preferred his worship in the appropriate key with the harmonies intact. He was a trained musician, after all."

"And Bessie May is not. But she's taking your place so that you and Pop can travel, so she's really doing this as a favor to you. And it's only in the first service, not the second."

"I suppose." Mama released a little sigh. "And I guess beggars can't be choosers. Oh, and speaking of the contemporary service, Levi and Joni are coleading worship. They've got drums in there. Drums. Can you believe it? I mean, if the Lord wanted drums in a church, he would've put them there, right?"

"Mama, I hardly think you need to fret over—"

"And guitars. Not one but two. Though that second one is really called something else. Maybe a bass? I can't remember. All I know is, I could only handle a couple of minutes listening to them practice. I went straight over to the drugstore and bought myself a pair of earplugs to keep in my purse, just in case I was ever held at gunpoint and forced to attend the second service."

"Well, you and Pop are traveling so much, maybe you won't have to worry about it."

"True." Mama groaned. "Maybe one of these days your father will settle down. I hope. Lose the wanderlust." She started talking about how her sunburn was peeling, and then I heard my father's voice in the background.

"Sorry, honey, but I have to let you go. He's got some wild idea that we're supposed to take off and drive to Galveston for the night."

"In the middle of November?" I asked.

"Exactly. Just my point. Anyway, I don't dare say no to the man. If I do, he'll turn it into a three-day trip, complete with deep-sea fishing. So I'm out of here. Just think about when you can come home to see me."

Before I could say, "You're never home anymore," she ended the call. Oh well. If I had to endure these conversations on a weekly basis, at least they didn't damage my psyche. Much.

I didn't realize anyone else was in the room with me until I glanced up and saw Brady standing in the doorway. "Your mother?" he asked.

"Yeah. I think she's confused."

"About?" Tiny creases formed between his brows.

"She seems to think that having me back home will calm things down. I really think she's hoping that I'll come home and things will go back to normal."

"She's not enjoying their travels?" Brady stepped into the room and sat down in the chair opposite my desk.

"That's just it. I see pictures of Mama and Pop on all of their adventures and she looks happy as a lark. But whenever she's back home in Fairfield, even for a week or two, she's miserable unless I'm there. If I moved back, she'd be gone half the time, so it would be pointless."

"Are you saying you want to move back?" He looked alarmed by this possibility.

"No. I love it here."

His concerns seemed to vanish in an instant. "Good. I'm so glad you want to stay. I don't know what I'd do if you ever decided to go back to Fairfield."

"I certainly wouldn't leave now, anyway. Not with your surgery coming up."

"Day after tomorrow." He leaned back in the chair and stretched out his legs.

"Are you getting anxious?"

He shook his head. "I just want to get it over with and get on with my life. I feel like everything's on hold until then."

"It's not on hold. Not at all. I'm right here, and I'll be with you every step of the way."

"Did you have to say 'every step of the way'?" He groaned. "Anyway, I came in to see if you wanted to go to lunch. Might be our last chance to have some alone time before my surgery day."

"Eduardo might be offended if we take off and leave his tamales uneaten."

"Uneaten?" Brady laughed. "That's a good one. I just stopped back there to snag one and they're all gone."

"You've got to be kidding me."

"Nope. Mr. Sanders. And Mrs. Sanders. And even the bride-to-be. Guess they like Eduardo's tamales."

Better than that, I felt sure they liked Eduardo. Perhaps if he worked his magic on the dress, all of the squabbling would be behind us.

One could hope, anyway.

15

The Last Time I Saw You

I think grief is a very private matter.

Doris Day

Nadia arrived back in town the night before Brady's surgery. From behind the closed door of my office, I shared my concerns with her and Madge seated across the desk from me. I knew Nadia would understand, even sympathize. And I needed someone else to know my thoughts and add their prayers to mine.

"I just can't figure him out," I said. "Half the time he acts perfectly normal. The other half he's quiet and withdrawn and I can't get him to say what he's thinking. Was he like this last time? With the first surgery, I mean?"

Nadia shook her head and appeared to be thinking. "No, last time it all happened so quickly. He was injured and had the surgery shortly thereafter. He didn't have much time to process things. I think that's the problem here—he's had too much time to think." She rose and paced the little office, her heels making a clicking noise as she moved back and forth. "Maybe I made a mistake asking him to take on the shop in my absence. Maybe it's not enough to keep his mind occupied."

"If anyone wants my opinion, I think it's good for him." Madge fiddled with a loose thread on her oversized sweater. "If he wasn't here, what would he be doing? Sitting on the sidelines at the games? Hanging out with his teammates, wishing he could play?" She shook her head and released the thread. "No, I think this is for the best. He's in a completely different world, playing a different game, and staying busy. Busy is good, and trust me when I say the shop has been plenty busy—thanks to Katie."

"It's good up to a point." Nadia's eyes flooded and she stopped pacing. "I just want what's best for him. He's been through so much already."

Seeing her get emotional suddenly got me misty-eyed too. I pondered her words as I tossed and turned later that night, and they stayed with me as I drove to the hospital the following morning with Alva seated next to me, chattering all the way about the weather.

I'd never seen so many people crammed into a waiting room. Me. Nadia. Madge. Stan. Beau. Alva. Who was running the store? Ah yes, Twiggy. And Dahlia. Poor Dahlia. Drowning in alterations and forced to work the front of the shop too. But what else could we do? We had to show Brady our support, didn't we?

Strangely, the person who looked the most nervous was Aunt

Alva. She wore her Mavericks T-shirt, probably not one of her wiser moves. I knew she meant to lend support, but Brady flinched when he saw it. Not that he had time to think about it for long. The pre-op process flew by, and before we knew it, he was whisked away to the operating room and the rest of us were left to our own devices in the surgical waiting area.

"Will they keep him overnight this time?" Stan asked. "Last time he got to go home the same day."

"Depends on the extent of the tear," I said. "The surgeon is being a little more cautious now because the second go-round is trickier than the first. He told us all about it at the last office visit. I think he's really concerned, if you want my take on it."

"Ah." Stan didn't look pleased with my answer, but what could I do?

We all spent the first few minutes quietly talking, but after a while we ran out of words. I picked up an outdated magazine and tried to read it, but stopped cold when I saw an ad for season tickets to the Mavericks. To my right, Alva and Nadia talked about Paris. Nadia made it sound so glamorous, espe-cially the clothing. To my left, Madge and Stan carried on some sort of conversation about a movie they'd both seen. That left one logical candidate to converse with—my brother Beau.

"You doing okay?" He gave me a concerned look.

"Yeah. Just a little worried."

"Don't worry, Katie. You know what the Bible says. Today has enough trouble of its own."

"It's today I'm worried about," I said, then added, "and tomorrow. And the next day."

"Worry doesn't empty tomorrow of its sorrow, it empties today of its strength. Grandpa Fisher used to say that." Beau gave me a sympathetic look. "I guess it's easier to say than to do."

I paused as memories overtook me. "I can't believe you remembered it word for word. He used to say that all the time."

"Yeah. It's also embroidered on a sampler in Queenie's kitchen. I see it every time I'm getting food."

"Oh, *that* explains it." I grinned.

"Grandpa Fisher was great with inspirational sayings." Beau's eyes clouded. "But Grandpa Fisher isn't with us anymore. And Queenie's marrying Reverend Bradford. And becoming a Presbyterian. And Mom and Pop are off on cruises. And you and I live in Dallas."

"Speaking of which, would you believe Mama actually called me and tried to talk me into moving back to Fairfield?"

"Welcome to my world." Beau rolled his eyes. "She used to call me every day. Then it was every other. Then, once she and Pop started traveling, it dropped to once a week. I'm happy to see she's shifted gears to you."

"Do you ever think about going back?" I asked.

"All the time. Fairfield's my home. But my heart is here." A boyish smile lit his face. "Twiggy's here. And my new job is here." He gestured to Stan and Madge, then leaned in close to whisper, "Notice anything stirring over there?"

I had noticed, actually. Madge and Stan, once mortal enemies, were together more than they were apart these days, and the usual quarreling was dissipating. Seemed so strange to see them on the same team. And stranger still that they were talking about a movie they'd both seen. Together, perhaps? Kind of sounded like it. Not that I was listening in. Much.

"I asked him about it a couple of weeks ago and he blew me off." Beau chuckled and reached for a magazine. "But I'm not blind. I can see when someone's twitterpated."

"Twitterpated?" Stan looked up from his conversation with

Madge to give my brother a curious look. "What the heck is twitterpated? Some sort of disease?"

"Yeah, it's a disease, all right." Madge winked at me, and for the first time I realized the truth—she had a crush on Stan. The very man she'd always claimed to hate was in fact the man she adored.

Okay, maybe not adored. Maybe *tolerated* was a better word. But her toleration seemed genuine enough, especially once they started talking about the movie again.

Beau smiled and read his magazine. I tried to do the same, but my thoughts were in a whirl. Before I had time to grab hold of them, the surgeon emerged. He took a seat and talked us through the surgery.

"It went as well as could be expected. The tear has been fixed, but it'll never be perfect. He knows that. He'll compensate for it, so after a while I don't even think people will notice."

"Thank God." Stan swiped his brow with the back of his hand. "You saying he'll play again?"

"That's not what I'm saying at all." The surgeon shook his head. "And because I don't see that as a likelihood—at least in the near future—I'm more worried about Brady's mental state than his physical recovery. I've known Brady awhile and I haven't seen him in this state of mind before. He's going to need a lot of support from all of you while he recovers."

My heart truly felt as if it might break as I listened to the doctor's words. Was Brady really facing the end of his career? If so, how would he handle it?

"What he doesn't need is people trying to make him feel bad because he can't get back in the game." The surgeon gave Stan a pointed look.

"So, are you saying he won't be able to play again?" Stan asked. "As in . . . ever?"

"I don't have any way of knowing that. I'm just saying that jumping back in will cause further damage to the knee. The tear in the meniscus was severe. We had to graft muscle from his hip to piece things together. So only time will tell. But I can guarantee you it won't be soon. I only mention this because people who lose sight of their dream sometimes go into a depression. I'm counting on all of you to keep his spirits up, no matter what he's facing."

These words hit me so hard that I had to excuse myself to go to the ladies' room for a good cry. Nadia and Madge joined me minutes later and we pretty much had a meltdown in triplicate.

After a while Madge blew her nose and then looked at the two of us. "I say we wipe these frowns off our faces and go into that recovery room with all the hope and enthusiasm we can muster."

"He'll see right through us if we're too over-the-top," Nadia said.

"So, hopeful but not hyped up?" I asked. "I think I can do that."

Moments later we were all seated in the waiting room, listening to Aunt Alva snore. Loudly. The recovery room nurse came to fetch us just a few minutes later. I tried to wake Alva, but she wouldn't budge.

Nadia and I followed on the nurse's heels until we reached Brady's little cubicle. I peeked around the curtain just to make sure he was company-ready. The sight of the man I loved lying on a bed with a pained expression on his face left me heartbroken.

Nadia took a seat in the chair next to him. I noticed a lone tear running down her cheek—her right cheek, the one farthest from him. How she managed to control that was a mystery. I walked over to the bed and Brady gazed up at me.

"Hey." I managed a weak smile and felt my hands trembling as I reached out and touched the end of the bed. "How are you doing?"

"Ugh." He shook his head.

The nurse gestured to the plastic bowl at his side. "He's been a little queasy from the anesthesia."

"Understandable."

Brady shifted his position in the bed and grimaced. "Doc says it might take a little longer to get up and running this time. Did he tell you?"

I gave a hesitant nod. "Yeah. But it'll do you some good to rest that knee, Brady. There's no rush to get better."

For whatever reason, he turned his face away. In that moment I wished I could take back what I'd said. Perhaps internally he felt a rush to get better so that he could get back to the business of basketball. Why had I been so inconsiderate?

I didn't have time to drum up an apology because a wave of nausea must have hit him and he got sick—not once but twice. He looked my way and groaned. "Sorry, Katie."

"Don't be. A woman should be able to walk the man she loves through thick and thin."

And there you have it. I'd just told Brady that I loved him. No sooner were the words spoken than he gazed at me with such tenderness that I thought my heart would burst. Just then the nurse appeared with nausea meds in hand, which she injected into his IV. Seconds later his eyes fluttered closed. When he awoke an hour or so later, he was transported to a room. A private room. Likely a move on Stan's part to keep newsmongers away.

"Last time he was in the hospital, he roomed with a fellow who was recovering from shoulder surgery," Nadia said. "Torn rotator cuff. A reporter made his way into the room, claiming to be a relative of the roommate. Poor fellow was so drugged up, I think he really believed that stupid reporter was his cousin Joe. But Brady knew better."

No doubt Brady could spot a fake. And no doubt he could spot sincerity too. I'd meant every word when I'd said I loved him. Surely he realized that. And I wouldn't take it back, even if he didn't reciprocate. Not that the boy could string two words together at the moment. Between the pain meds and the nausea meds, he didn't seem to know his own name. Or why they were wheeling him through the hallways of the hospital. Or why there were butterflies hovering over the stretcher, singing the national anthem.

Yep. Medication was definitely doing its work.

Once they got him settled in his room, he dozed off. Even in his sleep he cried out as he tried to move his leg. My heart twisted into a thousand knots and I felt the sting of tears in my eyes.

"It's going to be okay, Katie," Nadia whispered as she patted my arm. "I promise you. We've been through this before. It'll be over before you know it."

I nodded and tried to get control of my emotions. "I—I know. I just hate to see him in pain."

"Trust me, no man likes to see himself in pain either," Madge countered, her voice a hoarse whisper. "It's humbling to admit that you can't do things without help, no matter who you are. But when you're a pro ball player, it's humiliating."

"I'm sure." I sighed.

"Which is why we need to have a strategy for these next couple of weeks," Madge said. "We have to be prepared to do for him without him realizing he's being done for." She scratched her head. "Does that make sense?"

"Actually, it makes perfect sense." I brightened a bit. "I think

I'll feel better if we have a plan anyway. It'll do me good if I'm focused on how I can make him better. I want him to know that I care about what he's going through."

"He already knows that, sweet girl," Nadia said. "Trust me."

"For one thing, we can't let him know that Sanders fellow is causing problems." Madge's nose wrinkled.

"Again?" Nadia and I spoke in unison.

"Yeah. I had a text message from Dahlia. Sanders called to cancel the dress order."

"What?" I gasped. "But it's too late. He's already paid the down payment, hasn't he?"

"And it's the bride's big day," Nadia said. "She signed off on the agreement."

Madge sighed. "Yeah, but he's paying and he says he didn't sign anything, so it's not going to happen."

"What is the man's problem?" I leaned against the wall, nearly setting off a fire alarm just behind me. I jolted to attention and stood upright.

"It's so stupid." Madge lowered her voice. "From what I understand, the Spurs lost their game against the Mavericks yesterday, so he's in a snit."

Nadia's carefully plucked eyebrows elevated. "Are you saying we're going to have to pray the Spurs into the playoffs so the father of the bride will come to his senses?"

"Won't take much," Madge said. "I mean, the Spurs are a great team. They're probably going to be in the playoffs anyway. But you didn't hear that from me, okay? I mean, around here it's the Mavericks all the way."

"Madge, are you telling me you're a closet Spurs fan?" I couldn't help the words—they slipped right out.

Brady stirred and Madge put her finger over her lips to keep me from saying more. I leaned down to give him a kiss on the forehead. He let out a little whimpering sound and I wondered if he was in pain.

"We're here, honey." Nadia swept in on my left. She brushed the back of her hand along his cheek.

He put his hand on his stomach and groaned.

"Are you sick?" I asked.

He nodded and I passed the little plastic container his way as Nadia pressed the button for a nurse. Seconds later he emptied his stomach once again, right as the nurse entered the room.

"It's just the medicine making you feel sick," she said. "Nothing to be worried about, I promise."

I turned the other way as she tended to him, unable to watch him in pain.

I'd seen Brady James in action on the basketball court.

I'd seen him take charge of the bridal shop.

I'd even seen him impress his fans with kind words and actions.

But I'd never seen him in such a vulnerable position as this. And I hoped—no, I prayed—I never would again.

16

I'll See You in My Dreams

When I was a teeny little girl, I was in dancing school, and I sang. We had to put a dance to a song, so I went to the 10-cent store one day and looked at all the sheet music. It was all laid out, and I picked "Life Is Just a Bowl of Cherries."

Doris Day

The days following Brady's surgery turned out to be a little more complicated than anyone had predicted. An unexpected infection in the surgical site required antibiotics and special care. On the third day he was released from the hospital and would've headed back to his condo, but the second-floor bedroom made that out of the question. The bedrooms at his mother's place were all upstairs too. Nadia

157

couldn't seem to stop fretting over it. She wanted desperately to play a role in his recovery, but with this complication, how could she?

There was only one logical place for the guy to heal: at the home I shared with Aunt Alva. Her place was one story with several available bedrooms. And she couldn't wait to assume the role of hostess and nurse. I secretly wondered how I could balance caring for him with my workload at the shop. With the bridal extravaganza coming up in less than a week, I had my hands full. Nadia agreed to spend every available daytime minute at Alva's place so that my aunt wouldn't be alone when I did have to go to the shop. Perhaps that would solve the problem all the way around.

The nurse wheeled Brady to the hospital lobby, and we all waited while Stan went after the car. My aunt paced the room from end to end, clearly excited about her new guest. "Brady, it's going to be great. You'll take the guest room next to the bathroom. It will be so handy for you. Not that you have to get up and down a hundred times a night like I do, but you know what I mean."

He propped himself up in the wheelchair and smiled. "Oh, I'm sure it'll be great, and thanks for—"

"I do hope you like the color lavender. I painted the room the prettiest shade of lavender in the early nineties. Well, I say *I* painted it, but I really hired someone else to do it—you understand. I never really felt the fellow deserved full payment, though. He only did one coat. If you look closely, you can almost see the design of the wallpaper underneath it, and the seams too. So promise you won't look too closely, okay? I never cared much for that old wallpaper."

"I'm on medication, Alva," he said. "I'll be seeing all sorts of things, but wallpaper won't be one of them."

"If you must look at something when you're in there, look at the drapes. They're lovely, covered in the prettiest purple orchids. Do you like orchids? If not, I have some other drapes that I could hang. They're harvest gold and the sweetest shade of green. Some say those colors went out in the seventies, but I think they're back in style."

"I don't think he's really going to care about the décor, Aunt Alva." I shifted my purse from one shoulder to the other.

"Sure he is. We all respond to our surroundings." She gave him a wink. "I should give you my quilting room. The bed's not as nice but the walls are covered in Mavericks banners and such." She clamped a hand over her mouth. "On the other hand, I don't know if that might depress you. Would it depress you, Brady?"

He shrugged. "Maybe."

At that particular moment a Mavericks fan recognized Brady and stopped to shake his hand. "Wish we had you back in the game, man," the guy said. "Get well soon."

"I'll give it my best shot." Brady offered a weak smile.

"I saw what you did there." The guy laughed. "Best shot. Ha-ha-ha." Off he went across the lobby, laughing so hard that he garnered the attention of others passing by.

Alva didn't seem to pick up on any of this. Her thoughts were still firmly fixed on the drapes. "Never mind. The lavender room it is. And Katie will be right around the corner in her room, should you need anything. She can play nursemaid."

Brady flinched. Ack. Maybe this wasn't such a good idea after all.

"He doesn't need a nursemaid, Alva," I said. "Just knowing people are nearby should be good." I scooted out of the way as a nurse passed by, wheeling a patient out to her car.

"I'll be fine," he said. "And it won't be long before I'm out of your hair, I promise."

"But we don't want you out of our hair, Brady." My aunt leaned over and gave him a peck on the cheek. "We want to spend time with you. In fact, I'm thrilled to have you. It's not often that an old lady like me gets to have a pro basketball player around."

"You see him almost every day, Alva," I reminded her.

"Well, sure, but it's going to be fun to plan his meals." She snapped her fingers. "Oh, I know! I saw the cutest little basketball cookies at the store. I'll pick up some of those. We can eat them when we watch the game tomorrow night."

"Alva, enough with the basketball stuff, okay?" I gave her a warning look, which she obviously ignored.

"And I saw the cutest picture on Facebook the other day—something a friend of mine posted. Little sandwiches cut to look like basketballs. Couldn't figure out what they used to make the stitches, though. Capers, maybe? I've never been a fan of capers, but I might put up with them on this one occasion, just to honor the sport. Do you like capers, Brady?" She clasped her hands together. "Oh, this is going to be so much fun!"

Brady gave her a faint smile, but I could tell he didn't think it sounded like much fun.

After she disappeared into the ladies' room, I sighed. "I'm so sorry, Brady. She means well."

"Trust me . . ." He yawned. "I'm so medicated that I won't remember anything she says. Or does. And I certainly don't think I'll be focused on the color of the walls or the drapes."

"That's good, because the room isn't lavender at all. It's an icky shade of grape popsicle."

"Well, *that* oughta make me feel better." He shifted his position in the chair and grimaced.

Stan arrived with the car a short time later, but Alva was

nowhere to be seen. I went into the ladies' room to fetch her and found her rummaging through her purse for her house keys, which she was sure she'd lost.

"It's okay, Alva. I've got my set. We really need to go. They're waiting on us."

"For pity's sake, we don't want to keep our favorite player waiting." She slung her purse over her left shoulder and her keys slipped out of the side pocket and landed on the floor, along with a tube of lipstick and a package of tissues.

I reached down to pick them up and then touched her arm. "Alva, I really don't think we need to be talking much about basketball in front of Brady. I think it will just depress him." I passed the items back to her and she shoved them into her purse, her lips curling downward in a pout.

"So, does that mean we can't watch the game tomorrow night? I never miss a game."

"Let's let him decide, okay? You can always record it and watch it later."

My aunt looked flabbergasted by this idea.

"Or watch it in your room if he's not keen on it," I suggested.

I tried to change the topic of conversation as we headed through the lobby and out to the car. We got there just in time to see the nurse push the now-empty wheelchair back through the front door of the hospital. She gave us a little wave and said, "Take care of our patient!"

"Oh, I will." Alva waved back. "Can't wait!"

It took a lot longer to get to Alva's house than expected, due to construction on the highway. I could tell by his body position that Brady was uncomfortable in the front seat, but he never complained. Still, he went straight to bed when we reached the house. I don't think the boy even gave the drapes or the walls a second glance. He just climbed into the bed, clothes and all, and passed out cold.

I helped Nadia pull his shoes off and then my phone rang. Glancing down, I saw a familiar name on the screen. I mouthed "Dahlia" to Nadia, who looked concerned.

"I hope everything's all right at the shop," she whispered. "Let me know."

"I'm sure it is." I rushed into the hallway so as not to wake Brady. I took the call and listened as Dahlia carried on about her latest saga with Dewey.

After a moment she gasped. "I'm so sorry. I didn't mean to tell you all of that. I was just calling to check on Brady and to see how Nadia's holding up."

"She's exhausted, and I caught her crying a little earlier."

"Brady's her only child. Not that he's a child, but you know what I mean."

"Yeah, I know." But right now he did seem as vulnerable as a child, at the mercy of the medication.

"I just needed to vent, sorry." Dahlia sighed. "I'm so sorry to interrupt you. I know that Brady's having a hard day. Stan called Madge and she told us that Brady's in a depression."

"I'm not sure I'd call it that. But part of it is the meds. They've got him zonked out most of the time. And when he's not medicated he's in so much pain. It breaks my heart to see him like this. I feel awful."

"Don't blame you, but what can you do other than pray? I'm just hoping he gets through this. Psychologically, I mean." She paused. "I'm so glad he has you, Katie."

"Me too. And I'm glad I've got him."

We said our goodbyes and I stuck my head back in the room. Nadia had almost finished unpacking Brady's suitcase.

I mouthed "Coffee?" and she smiled. Less than a minute later we were seated at the Formica table in the kitchen while my aunt fussed with the coffeepot. I must've been a little too quiet, because Nadia seemed to pick up on my concerns.

"You okay, Katie?" she asked.

"Hmm?" I took my gaze off the coffeepot long enough to glance her way. "Yeah. I will be."

"Worried about the bridal extravaganza?"

Actually, it was the last thing on my mind. "Not really. I still have a few vendors who've left me hanging, but we'll have enough to piece together a real event. And Madge has helped me choose several gowns for the contestants to look through. I think it'll all come together."

"Are you regretting the idea?" she asked.

"No. I only question the timing. I want to be there for Brady, and yet I want to do a good job with this too. If it works out, we might be able to do it every Black Friday. It might be a way to stir up interest in some of our older inventory."

"Good point. And it's a great way to bring in customers who want to buy off the rack, which is where we need to be focused. Dahlia and her team are too busy to take on more designs right now."

"Tell me about it. Hey, speaking of which, the family of that San Antonio bride has really made things interesting."

"The Doris Day bride?" Nadia nodded. "Oh, trust me, I've heard all about her crazy family from Twiggy. They're something else, from what she said."

"Something else is right."

"Would it ease your mind if I passed them off to Madge?" Nadia asked. "Then you could focus on the extravaganza and on Brady. That would be one less thing to worry about."

"Aw, thanks for offering, but I'm actually fine with Carrie. She's really nice. And we'll get through this season. I know we will. I think I'm just . . . confused right now."

"About Brady?" she asked.

"About everything. I care so much about him . . ." The lump in my throat made it nearly impossible to continue. "I hate to see him like this. Like I said, I know it's a season and it will pass, but right now I just can't imagine how he's going to get to the other side of this mountain without giving up."

"He's so blessed to have you in his life." Nadia rose and moved toward me. She leaned down to give me a motherly hug. "I've never been more grateful to have someone love Brady as much as I love him."

"Is it that obvious?"

"Is it *that* obvious?" Alva and Nadia echoed in unison.

Nadia took her seat again, a broad smile on her face. "You couldn't hide it if you tried, Katie. And I love you for loving him."

"Yes, but does he?" I asked. "Love me back, I mean."

"Of course he does." Nadia looked stunned at my question. "What makes you think otherwise?"

I gave my words consideration before speaking them. "He just doesn't voice things the way I do. Maybe I'm expecting too much too soon. His actions are convincing, but the words just haven't come."

"Yet." Nadia reached over and rested her hand on mine. "They haven't come yet. But they have come in a thousand other ways—in expressions and tone of voice."

"Oh, sure, but a girl needs to hear the words. You know?"

"I do."

"Ooh, the two loveliest words spoken between a man and woman!" Alva giggled as she filled our coffee cups. "I do, I do!" She brought Nadia's to the table on a pretty little saucer and set it in front of her. "Sugar? Cream?"

"I'll take a little of both," Nadia said. "And thank you, Alva. The coffee smells wonderful."

I rose and got my cup to save Alva the trip. Before long we were all seated at the table, a holy hush settling over us.

Nadia broke it a couple of minutes later. She held her coffee cup and stared at me. "I need to tell you something, Katie. I don't feel like I'm breaking a confidence or anything."

"What is it?"

She took a sip of her coffee and then released a slow breath as she set the cup back down. "Brady's father was great. He showed his love in a number of ways."

"Yes, I've heard great things about him."

"Such a positive influence on Brady. On everyone he came in contact with. But he did have this one very obvious flaw . . ." She pursed her lips and appeared to be thinking.

"What do you mean?"

"He showed his love, but he wasn't the sort to throw his arms around you and just speak it plain. The words 'I love you' were harder to come by."

"Ah."

"I sense it's a family trait. If you catch my drift." She gave me a knowing look. "But don't let the lack of words get in the way. Promise? Actions speak louder, or so I've always been told. And I know my son really well. He's feeling those words in his heart. Promise you won't give up on him?"

"Give up on him?" I shook my head. "Of course not, Nadia. I could never do that. He's stuck with me. I'm not going anywhere."

"That's good to hear."

From inside my purse, my phone buzzed. I reached inside

and pulled it out, stunned when I saw Casey's name on the screen. Great. Just what I needed. I answered the phone and headed to the hallway for some privacy.

"Hey, sorry to bother you, Katie," he said. "I know you're with Brady right now."

"How did you know that?"

"Oh, Alva called Queenie and she told Bessie May, who saw Prissy when the WOP-pers met for prayer this morning. Prissy ran into Mama at the gas station—did you know you get special points for shopping at Brookshire Brothers?—and Mama called me because she knows I'm a fan of Brady's."

"I see. And the party line lives on."

"Yeah." He released a strained laugh.

"So, what's up, Casey?"

"Well, I'm back in town for the holidays." His words felt rushed, as if he'd rehearsed them or something. "We've shut down the plant in Tulsa until mid-January, so I'll be around for several weeks. Mama wanted me to call and see if you guys wanted to do our usual Thanksgiving game day thing. I know things are a little different this year, but . . ."

A *little* different?

"Our usual thing?" I managed.

"Yeah. Are you going to be home for Thanksgiving?" he asked. "It's just four days from now."

"If everything goes as planned, I'll be home." I'd planned to bring Brady with me, but that couldn't happen now. The idea of leaving him here was upsetting, but missing Thanksgiving? Mama and Pop would kill me.

"So, what do you say? My mother's pumpkin pie? Queenie and your father arguing over football? Yahtzee and Scrabble at the kitchen table?" Casey's voice pulled me back into the conversation.

I had to admit, it all sounded nice. Very nice. Comfortable, even. And right about now I needed something to feel comfortable.

"I'll ask Mama what she's got planned, Casey. I don't really know. But I promise to ask, okay?"

"That's good enough for me," he said. "Oh, and Katie . . . I really am concerned about Brady, and not just because I'm a fan. How is he doing?"

"He's . . ." I probably let the silence go on a bit too long, but I needed to find exactly the right words. "He has the best orthopedist in town, and the surgery went as well as could be expected."

"Great. He'll get back in the game, then?"

I didn't mean to sigh, but I must've.

"More complicated than that?" Casey asked.

"Yeah. A little more complicated than that. Just pray for him, Casey. He needs it."

"O-okay."

We ended the call, and I thought about how strange it was to ask my ex-boyfriend to pray for the man I loved.

The man I loved.

Yes, this journey had solidified that fact, hadn't it? I loved Brady James, and I would stick with him through thick and thin, just as I'd told Nadia. Nothing could tear us apart, not even an ex-boyfriend with a little too much interest in spending time with me.

17

That Old Feeling

The really frightening thing about middle age is the knowledge that you'll grow out of it.

Doris Day

The days leading up to Thanksgiving were a whirlwind. Somehow Eduardo talked Mr. Sanders into reconsidering the dress order by persuading him that Carrie would be the envy of all the other brides in San Antonio. Turned out Mr. Sanders's pride outweighed his basketball leanings. All was saved, thank goodness.

My days were spent driving back and forth from the shop to Alva's place. Half the time I worked on bridal extravaganza details, the other half I spent caring for Brady's needs and helping Nadia shuttle him back and forth to post-op visits.

By the time Wednesday arrived I was a wreck. I worked late into the night with Madge and Twiggy to make sure we had the front of the store set up properly. Dahlia and her team took a break from their design work to help us move several racks of our more expensive gowns to the back, leaving only the giveaways and sale gowns up front. By the time we were finished it was nearly midnight. Did I really have to drive to Fairfield in eight hours, then return less than twenty-four hours later? I must've been crazy to think I could handle all of that.

I awoke early Thursday morning to the smell of coffee and the sound of familiar voices in the kitchen. I'd always loved Thanksgiving morning, but today something seemed amiss.

Ah yes. I couldn't move. I tried to get my legs to cooperate but they refused. After so much work yesterday—moving things around in the shop and hauling boxes to and fro—my muscles had apparently declared a mutiny. Who could blame them?

"Ow, ow, ow!" I did my best to stand and stretch, but the pain was unbearable. And my back wouldn't straighten up.

A rap on my door sounded and Alva popped her head inside. "You okay in here, Katie? I thought I heard a noise."

"Probably the sound of my joints crying out."

She stared at me as I tried again to stand upright. "Oh my. You overdid it this week?"

"To say the least. We spent hours moving things around at the shop in preparation for the Black Friday event tomorrow morning."

She leaned against the open door and shook her head. "I never understood why they called it Black Friday. It's just a shopping day, for pity's sake. And what's with all of that competitive shopping? What sort of people get out at six in the morning to shop? Anyway, I hope you haven't overextended yourself. We have a long day ahead of us, driving to Fairfield."

"And back. I hope you don't mind that I have to come back in the wee hours of the night. I've got vendors arriving at the shop at five in the morning. It won't affect you, I promise. One of the boys will drive you back tomorrow sometime. Probably Dewey."

"You poor girl." She clucked her tongue in motherly fashion. "When this is over you're going to have to sleep for a week."

That sounded mighty good. I stretched my legs and groaned. "I'll be there in a minute. Or two."

Or ten. It certainly took longer than anticipated to slip on my clothes, brush my teeth, and hobble out to the kitchen, where I found Alva and Brady engrossed in an animated conversation about toast.

Toast? Really?

Brady liked his with margarine. Alva couldn't abide anything but butter on hers. I interrupted their conversation with a cheerful, "Happy Thanksgiving!" but couldn't get my hand up to give them a wave. The pain in my shoulders was unbearable.

Brady smiled at me. "Happy Thanksgiving to you too. I hope you won't take this the wrong way, but you look . . ."

"Terrible?" I tried.

"I was going to say sleepy."

"No, I look terrible, but I think I feel even worse." I hobbled over to him and gave him a kiss. "Are you sure you don't feel up to coming with us to Fairfield? I don't want to leave you here alone on Thanksgiving."

"I won't be alone. Madge and Stan are coming by around one to bring turkey and dressing. We'll make a feast of it."

"If you're sure." I gave a little pout. "But I'll miss you."

"I'll miss you too. But I don't want to mess up your plans.

Go home and spend time with your family. Try to make it a normal day, okay?"

"Normal?" I yawned. "When I have a huge event in the morning and I'm fretting over you being here without me?"

"Don't fret over me. Go. Have fun."

And so we did. Alva and I hit the road at eight fifteen, heading toward Fairfield.

Going home for Thanksgiving made me feel like a kid again. In spite of my disappointment about leaving Brady back in Dallas with his mother and Madge, I slipped back into "Katie Fisher, Fairfield resident," with ease. Alva and I arrived at my parents' place just before ten. I carried in the bowl of cranberry salad Alva had made, though my aching joints made the trip up the front walk a difficult one and I nearly lost the bowl more than once. Alva finally took it from me with another cluck of the tongue.

Mama greeted us at the door but was up to her eyeballs with the side dishes, so we offered to help. Not that I was much help in my current condition, but I tried to make myself useful. Mostly I stayed out of the way while Mama and Alva bickered over the ingredients.

Soon after, Queenie and Reverend Bradford arrived carrying in three pies: chocolate, pumpkin, and pecan. Yum. Just one more reason to celebrate coming home for the holidays.

Just a few minutes later Jasper and Crystal arrived. Ever the happy couple, they entered the room hand in hand. I had to give it to those two—they were the stuff love stories were made of. Seeing them together made me think of Brady and miss him all the more.

"Jasper, would you mind going out to the freezer in the garage and checking our ice supply?" Mama asked. "I don't want to run low."

"Sure, Mama." He let go of Crystal's hand, gave her a wistful look, and said, "I'll be right back."

"I'll miss you," she said.

Good gravy.

Mama and Aunt Alva went to work chopping up the celery for the stuffing but ended up in a heated debate. Crystal and I looked at each other, neither of us brave enough to intervene. Finally I could take it no longer. I had to know what all the fuss was about. "Mama? Aunt Alva? What in the world?"

"I *always* put chestnuts in my stuffing." Mama put her hands on her hips. "But she won't let me."

"Can't abide chestnuts." Alva wrinkled her nose. "Can we leave 'em out? I get hives."

"Chestnuts give you hives? Are you allergic?" I asked.

"In theory." She winked. "Just can't stand 'em. I'm allergic to them in my mind."

Mama sighed and tossed the bag of chestnuts aside. "Well, Herb will pitch a fit, but I guess he'll have to deal with it."

"Deal with what?" Pop sauntered into the kitchen, dressed in his undershirt and boxers. "What am I going to have to deal with, Marie?"

"Herbert Fisher, go put on some clothes." Mama pinched her eyes shut and shook her head. "We have guests."

"Just family." My father shrugged. "They don't mind seeing me in my natural habitat."

Actually, I did mind, but it was his house, so who was I to argue?

"That's an *unnatural* habitat if I ever saw one." Queenie slapped him on the arm. "Now, mind your mama and go change into some decent clothes. I raised you better than that."

Alrighty then. My father grunted and headed down the hallway toward his bedroom.

Jasper came back into the kitchen to update us on the ice situation. Then he and Mama began to argue about whether or not we'd be watching the big game later this afternoon. Jasper was all for it, naturally. Mama said that it was sacrilege to watch television on Thanksgiving Day. This led to a debate between Reverend Bradford and Mama about the value—or lack thereof—of football on family holidays.

A short time later the turkey was ready to be carved. Pop, now appropriately dressed, did the honors, as he did every year. He commanded hushed reverence as he sliced, sliced, sliced the bird into manageable pieces. "It's an art form," he explained to all who were listening. "Not just anyone can cut a turkey."

"But anyone can eat it," Jasper said.

"Not if he keeps carving it so slowly." Alva groaned. "At this rate we're not going to have our Thanksgiving dinner until Christmas day."

That got a laugh out of everyone.

Well, almost everyone. Dewey had arrived in a sour mood. I'd have to talk to him later to see why he and Dahlia hadn't worked things out. Not that it was any of my business. Then again, maybe it irked him to see Jasper and Crystal so happy. And Beau and Twiggy looked pretty blissful these days too.

Beau and Twiggy. For the first time all day it occurred to me that they hadn't arrived yet. Mama would throw a fit if Beau didn't show up for Thanksgiving dinner. That had never happened.

Thank goodness they arrived a few minutes later, arms filled with packaged rolls. "I stopped at Brookshire Brothers, just like you said, Mama." Beau put the bags on the counter. "I still can't get over the fact that they're open on Thanksgiving Day."

173

"There was a time when that would've been a criminal offense." Queenie shook her head. "What is this world coming to?"

"I guess it's a good thing they were open or we wouldn't have had any bread to eat."

Queenie carried on a passionate dissertation. Her emotions only intensified when she realized that Alva planned to leave the skin on the potatoes when she mashed them.

"But I don't like to keep the skin on the potatoes when I mash them," Queenie said. "It's hard on my false teeth."

"But the nutrients are in the skin," Alva argued. "And why did you pay good money for teeth that don't chew? I say go back and get yourself some more teeth and then eat potatoes with the skin on."

Mama quietly peeled the potatoes in the background while the two sisters carried on. Alva would just have to live with it.

In the end, we were all willing to live with it. The potatoes, like everything else, turned out great. By the time the table was loaded with food, I could hardly wait any longer. Pop said the blessing and we dove right in, the conversation so erratic and fun that I almost forgot about the bridal extravaganza. Almost.

We ate until our bellies were full. Just about the time we settled down in front of the TV to watch the big game, slices of pumpkin pie in hand, the doorbell rang. I knew who it would be. For as long as I could remember, the Lawsons had joined us for dessert and football on Thanksgiving Day. Yet the idea of spending the afternoon with Casey left me feeling a little conflicted. Okay, not conflicted, really, just . . . odd. And it made me miss Brady more than ever. I would have to remember to call him when things slowed down. *If* things slowed down.

Mrs. Lawson entered with the most gorgeous lemon pie I'd ever laid eyes on.

"My goodness, Charlotte, it's beautiful." Queenie clasped her hands together. "And I'm so glad you brought lemon. I brought several others, but not that. And I don't believe I've ever seen such a pretty meringue."

"She's been watching the Food Network," Mr. Lawson said. "That *Italian Kitchen* show has her hooked."

"Oh my, yes. I just love *The Italian Kitchen*." Mrs. Lawson stepped into the kitchen. "Rosa and Laz are so down-to-earth. Natural. Rustic."

"They sound like my kind of cooks," Alva said. "Bet they leave the skin on *their* potatoes."

"I followed Rosa's recipe to a tee." Mrs. Lawson set the lemon pie on the counter. "And I have a coconut pie in the car. I'll go fetch it now."

Turned out she didn't have to. Casey went for her. I had to give it to him—he'd always been a good son. Actually, he'd been a great boyfriend too. Except that part where he'd broken my heart.

A short time later Joni arrived. Her appearance surprised me a bit. I could tell Mama was caught off guard too, though she greeted our guest with a broad smile.

"There's my favorite wedding planner!" Queenie threw her arms around Joni's neck. "I'm so glad you made it." She looked around. "Levi's not with you?"

"Oh, no ma'am. He's back in Dallas sharing Thanksgiving with a couple of the kids at the college who weren't able to go home to be with their families. You know how dedicated he is to those kids."

I knew, all right. Good old Levi, making all the rest of us look like spiritual slouches.

In spite of the heavy meal we'd eaten, we dove right into those pies. Before long we were all moaning and groaning from the rapid influx of food. Mama and Mrs. Lawson sat on the bar stools talking. Most of the others were in the living room watching the game. I took a seat at the kitchen table next to Casey and Joni, who were already prepping the Yahtzee game.

"I love that feeling you have after eating Thanksgiving dinner," Casey said.

"Miserable?" Joni asked.

"No. Contented."

"And miserable." I rubbed my stomach. "I always feel like I'm in a catatonic state."

"That's what you're supposed to feel like on Thanksgiving," Casey said. "That's half the fun."

"Ugh." Didn't feel like much fun right now. Felt more like I needed to find an antacid.

Aunt Alva took a seat next to me. "It's that spice your mama puts in the dressing, Katie."

"I heard that, Alva." Mama looked over from her conversation with Mrs. Lawson.

"It's true, Marie. I've never used that particular spice before."

"I think it's the lack of chestnuts that made it taste a bit odd," Mama said. "But that's just my opinion." She leaned back in her chair. "I hope no one minds, but I'm just going to sit here for a bit while the rest of you play games and such."

No one seemed to mind. Mrs. Lawson and Queenie struck up a conversation with Joni about the upcoming wedding, and soon we were knee-deep in chatter about the big day. As the volume of the football game intensified, so did the voices of the ladies, who talked over the game. Joni must've forgotten she was playing, but Casey and I continued on, hollering "Yahtzee!" at the appropriate times.

"Sorry it's so noisy in here, Reverend Bradford," Mama called out above the din. "I do hope you'll adjust to our large family."

"I've missed this. When my daughter and son-in-law come to town we have a wonderful time, but it's not like this."

"We're blessed," Queenie said. "Truly. Noise and all. I wouldn't trade it for a thing."

When our game ended, Joni finished her conversation with the older ladies and turned my way. "Did I miss the game?" she asked.

"Yeah." I tried to stifle a yawn.

Casey excused himself to the living room, which left me alone with Joni. Not that I minded. I'd been dying to ask her a question for days now. When I was sure no one else was close enough to hear, I turned our conversation into a private girl-talk session.

"Okay, inquiring minds want to know . . ."

"If I'm dating Levi?" She smiled. "Pretty sure that's what you were going to ask, right?"

"Right."

She shrugged. "He's a great guy and I would be honored to have someone like him in my life, but . . ."

"But?"

"I'm not sure that's where my heart is taking me, and I want to be careful. I don't want to jump headfirst into something just because the WOP-pers think I should. At some point I have to pray and get God's perspective on my own. That's what spiritual maturity is all about."

"Right." She seemed pretty spiritually mature for bringing that up.

"I'll be forever grateful to Levi," Joni said. "He's been such a godsend in my life."

"How so?"

"You know what my life was like. My parents were always so busy with their jobs and then with ministry stuff. I never really had great social skills, so I stuck with sports to find my value. But Levi helped me see past all of that. I broke my arm during that first college game, and it pretty much destroyed my psyche. Levi helped me realize that I'd put too much stock in my performance and not in just being a daughter of the King. I was trying to get my validation in the wrong place."

"Oh, Joni . . . I'm sorry. I didn't even realize you'd broken your arm."

"Yeah." She shrugged. "It was a bad break. Really bad. I was sliding into first and landed wrong. The bones had to be pinned. It destroyed my chances of playing pro."

"I didn't realize you were hoping to go that far with ball. Wow." In that moment, I realized how little I really knew about Joni.

"Anyway, my point is, I had to stop trying to find validation in what I did and start realizing that I was valued simply because of God's love. Does that make sense?"

"Perfect sense." As Casey passed by, I leaned in to whisper, "Would you mind sharing all of that with Brady someday? When he's ready to hear it, I mean?"

"Of course. And in the meantime, I'll be praying for him. God's placed a real burden on my heart to pray for people who feel a little . . . lost." She rested her elbows on the table, a thoughtful expression on her face. "Everyone needs someone like Levi to talk them down from the ledge. I know you're that person for Brady."

"I'm trying. He's just not responding quite the way I'd hoped."

"Don't give up. Promise?"

"Yes, I promise."

"Okay, now tell me how things are going at the shop. I'll bet the wedding biz is a blast."

Strange how quickly panic could hit a person. The minute I thought about the shop, I was reminded of the bridal extravaganza. Oy. I'd have to leave here in the wee hours of the morning and drive all the way back, then work, work, work.

"It's busy," I said after a moment. "Ever since that issue of *Texas Bride* released, the store has been hard-hit with customers."

"Oh yes," Twiggy said as she joined us. "You wouldn't believe how crazy things are. If it wasn't for Eduardo, I don't think Dahlia would've made it."

"Eduardo? Don't think I know that name." Pop walked into the kitchen to get another piece of pie.

"Ask Alva about him." Twiggy winked at my aunt. "I think she could fill you in."

"Hmm? Who? Me?" Alva looked up from her cup of coffee. "What are we talking about?"

"Someone named Eduardo," Pop said. "You know him?"

"Oh. I . . . well . . ." Her cheeks flushed and I had to wonder what was going on in that mind of hers. "I think maybe I'll have another piece of pie."

Interesting.

I didn't really have much time to think about it, though. Mama pulled out some old videos, and before long we were all seated in the living room, watching our memories roll by on the television set. Videos of Casey and me as kids—him on the football field and me in my cheerleading outfit. My three brothers in their teens, playing baseball. Queenie and Grandpa Fisher, the year before he passed away. Mama and Pop at their twenty-fifth wedding anniversary party. Last Thanksgiving with the Lawsons. We watched it all.

The laughter and joy that rang out across the room was blissful. Truly. How long had it been since I'd had a day like this—carefree and fun? Just to celebrate, I had another piece of Mrs. Lawson's coconut pie.

Oh. Yum.

I'd missed her pie. For that matter, I'd missed her. And even though I hated to admit it, I'd also missed her son. Oh, not in a "wow, I'd like to see if we could be an item again" sort of way, but more in a wistful "life was sweet and simple when we were growing up" sort of way.

It was sweet and simple. But a girl had to grow up sometime, right?

I'd think about that tomorrow morning at five o'clock when I arrived at Cosmopolitan Bridal. But right now I had games to play and pie to eat.

18

A Bushel and a Peck

Well, I've been through everything. I always said I was like those round-bottomed circus dolls—you know, those dolls you could push down and they'd come back up? I've always been like that. I've always said, "No matter what happens, if I get pushed down, I'm going to come right back up."

Doris Day

What was I thinking? Those same four words replayed in my mind as I made the drive back to Dallas in the dead of night. With only four hours of sleep to propel me, I did my best to focus on the road.

"You can do this, Katie. You can do this."

I'd better do this! I'd promised Brady, after all.

"Brady." My heart twisted as I whispered his name. How I'd missed him over the past several hours. I should've picked up the phone before the sun went down to wish him a happy Thanksgiving, but caught up in the games and videos, I'd forgotten. Then again, he hadn't called me either, had he?

I tried not to make too much of that as I drove. Surely he'd spent the day with his mom, Madge, and Stan, as they'd planned. No doubt they'd filled up on turkey, watched the game, and then napped the rest of the day away.

Hopefully.

Right now I had to carry on with the show and put on the best bridal extravaganza the city of Dallas had ever seen. Brady was counting on me. Nadia was counting on me.

Everyone was counting on me.

Ack.

The ringer went off over my Bluetooth speaker and I pushed the button on my steering wheel. "Hello?"

"It's Aunt Alva, honey. You left me behind. I'm still in Fairfield."

I bit back a laugh. "Alva, we already discussed this, remember? You're coming back with Dewey later in the day. He agreed to come and help us get the shop put back together after the event."

"For pity's sake. I've been sitting here at Queenie's for an hour, dressed and ready, wondering why you didn't come and fetch me. I could've slept in."

"I'm sorry."

"I wanted to help you at your big shindig."

"Not a good idea, Aunt Alva, though I appreciate your willingness. For one thing, it's freezing outside. And for another, it's mostly physical labor—setting up tables, hauling things around, that sort of thing. Just rest and then come with Dewey later in the morning. He'll fetch you around nine, so be ready."

182

"Well, I'm ready now. Not sure what I'll do with myself between now and then." Off in the distance I heard Queenie's voice ring out. "Oh, never mind, honey," Alva said. "Queenie wants to visit with me about wedding plans. I'm going to be the maid of honor, you know." At that, she clicked off.

Goodbye, Alva.

I arrived at Cosmopolitan at exactly 5:00 a.m., just in time to see the tent go up. I had a quick conversation with the man in charge of that process to make sure he'd brought enough tables for all of the vendors. After I quickly breezed through the tent, I was able to set up a plan for where those tables should be placed. The first vendor arrived minutes later, wedding cake in hand. I panicked as she almost dropped the magnificent four-tiered number with its gorgeous rosettes.

"Don't worry," she hollered out. "It's not a real cake. They're all dummies."

I felt like a dummy myself right about now. Why hadn't I remembered to bring my camera to photograph all of this?

Her table was put into place and she went to work, covering it with a cloth and placing some of the most beautiful faux cakes I'd ever seen on it.

The photographer arrived next with all sorts of framed photos and slide shows to display. He agreed to capture some shots of the day and send them to me in exchange for a plug in our next catalog.

Next came the hair designer. Then the guy with the chocolate fountain. Then the makeup gal. Then a fellow who provided specialty balloons and other fun novelty items for weddings. Then the dance instructor. One by one their tables were set up and decorated. I watched over everything, calling out orders as needed.

Shivering all the while.

At 5:25 Madge arrived with Stan, who offered to help finish setting up tables. Interesting that they'd come together. She headed inside the store to help Twiggy and Beau, who had breezed by me while I helped set up the chocolate fountain. Finally convinced the vendors were okay to wrap up without me, I headed inside.

The next hour was spent finalizing the layout of the store inside while the tables were being set up outside. At 6:00 Nadia and Brady arrived. He hobbled into the store on crutches, carrying on about how great the tent looked.

I rushed his way, greeting him with a kiss. "What are you doing here, Brady?" I waggled my finger at him. "You're supposed to be resting."

"You didn't really think he would miss this, did you?" Nadia shrugged off her designer coat and slung it over her arm. "Surely you know him better than that."

"No way would I miss it." Still, my sweet guy looked bleary-eyed. He yawned. "Too much turkey. Not a good idea to eat turkey when you're already on pain medication. The combination is deadly."

"I'm sure. Why don't you pull up a chair and supervise?"

"Gladly." He yawned again.

Stan arrived with a chair from the studio, which he placed off to the side of the room. "Perfect spot to referee the game."

Brady grimaced as he took a seat.

"It's going to be a great day." I offered a bright smile.

"Yep. Hopefully it'll turn things around in the media." Madge continued working, never missing a beat.

"This whole media thing is just a season anyway, Madge," I said. "They love a sensational story and that bride gave them one. We're going to undo it in just a few short hours. Watch and see."

"Short hours?" Dahlia barreled our way. "What's this about short hours? I know nothing of these words."

"True, true," I said. "Just for the record, Dahlia, you and your team can do your usual thing in the studio while we take care of the extravaganza."

"And miss all the fun?" Her eyes widened in mock horror. "Never! I'll go back and forth, if you don't mind. I don't want to miss out. Besides, Eduardo is going to supervise in the studio. The others know what to do. I want to help out front—it will make me feel normal again." She rubbed her stomach. "If anyone could possibly feel normal after eating so much turkey."

I wanted to ask how her Thanksgiving had gone but didn't have time. She'd been noticeably absent from our get-together yesterday, after all. No doubt Madge had talked her into spending the day with them at Aunt Alva's. I wondered how she would feel about seeing Dewey when he came in a few hours. Maybe it would be better not to tell her just yet.

Hibiscus and Jane arrived moments later, ready to roll.

"Katie, that vendors' area is amazing." Hibiscus clutched her hands to her chest. "I felt like I was at a real wedding! Everyone was there."

Jane cocked her head. "Yeah, and the guests will soon be barreling through the door. What time do we kick this thing off?"

"Eight."

"Tell that to the brides who are already lined up outside," Jane said. "We need someone to keep them out of the tent."

"Ack." Why hadn't I hired security?

Turned out Nadia had. The security guard rolled up at 6:30 to hold back the flow of anxious brides. I gave Nadia a huge hug and thanked her from the bottom of my heart.

"Happy to be of service." She gave me a little wink. "Now, go do what you do."

The next half hour was spent putting the finishing details on things and visiting with the brides, who were about to take the security guard down for not letting them through. By 7:00, I knew we were going to have a glorious day. Every sign pointed to it. And Brady and Nadia seemed to think so too, based on their upbeat chatter.

"This is going to be the best thing that ever happened to the wedding community in Dallas," Brady said.

"And we have Katie to thank." Nadia gave me an encouraging smile, which served to invigorate me.

"You're welcome. But let's don't celebrate just yet. What if the media doesn't show up? The reporter from the *Tribune* was supposed to be here at seven, but there's no sign of him. Or her."

I stopped sweating five minutes later when he finally arrived. "Sorry," he said. "I think I ate too much turkey yesterday. It messed up my brain."

"Tryptophan," Madge said. "Gets you every time."

"I have no idea what that means," the reporter said, "but I'll take your word for it."

By 7:30 the coffee was hot, the one real wedding cake was ready to be sliced, a large bowl of punch was filled to the brim, Nadia was greeting her guests right and left, and the vendors were finalizing their stations.

"We have our own bridal extravaganza." I grinned. "Maybe we'll make this a yearly Black Friday event. What do you think, Brady?"

"I think you've saved the day once again, Katie. And did you see that WFAA sent a camera crew? Now we just have to pray that brides will keep coming."

"Keep coming? To an event that offers free and deeply discounted wedding goods? Trust me, Brady, they'll show up."

And show up they did. We hadn't counted on the massive parking dilemma this event would cause. With the tent taking up so much space, there was no room for the customers to put their vehicles. I made a quick dash to El Burrito, the Mexican restaurant next door, and asked permission to use their space. They agreed, as long as we allowed them to set up a breakfast taco table in the tent. The customers loved it and swarmed them.

Inside we had the time of our lives. I'd never had so much fun. Every fifteen minutes we pulled another number from the hat to announce a winner. By the time eleven o'clock rolled around we'd given away ten gowns, ten pairs of shoes, ten veils, ten free alterations—Dahlia would kill me for that one—and ten tuxedo rentals. We'd also sold thirty-seven off-the-rack wedding gowns, eight veils, two dozen pairs of shoes, and approximately twenty bridesmaid dresses, all marked down for Black Friday. Nadia was beside herself.

Just as we were wrapping up the giveaways, Alva and Dewey showed up. Dahlia, who'd been present in the shop for most of the morning, disappeared into her studio the minute she saw my brother. I could tell it affected his emotional state, but he buried his troubles in hard work, helping us clean up the mess after the extravaganza ended.

I headed outside to the tent to thank the vendors for their participation, offering each of them a gift card for a free lunch at El Burrito. We also gave them our assurance that they would be our go-to vendors when brides asked for a list. All in all, everyone left content and happy.

"All's well that ends well," Twiggy said when I arrived back inside. "I'm exhausted, but that was a blast."

"No kidding. Best day ever." Madge took a look at the store and sighed. "So glad we shut it down at eleven, though."

"We'll keep the sale going through Monday," Nadia said.

"And I'm sure we'll still have customers coming through today looking for sale items," I added, "so let's make sure those are near the front of the store, the first thing they see when they come in."

Madge nodded, then called everyone to attention. "People, we've got a lot of work to do. Remember all of those dresses we pulled into the back room? We've got to get them back out here. And I'll need a couple of you to police the parking lot while that tent is coming down to make sure our customers make it inside without getting knocked upside the head by a tent post."

"I'm here to help," Dewey said.

"Me too," Beau added.

The next three hours were spent whipping Cosmopolitan Bridal back into shape. Brady supervised from a chair off to the side of the room. Several times I caught him trying to lift or lug something and I chastened him and made him sit back down. Nadia scolded him a couple of times too, but he didn't seem to be taking the hint from either of us.

Finally I came to stand next to him, so tired I could barely think straight. That was when I noticed something peculiar going on at the register.

"Well, look at that, why don't you."

"What?" Brady asked.

I pointed to the register where Madge was helping a customer. Standing at her side, his smile as wide as the Rio Grande, Stan rang up the customer.

"Very suspicious." I narrowed my gaze and tried to make sense of what I saw. Why would Stan be helping Madge, and who had taught him to use the cash register?

"What's suspicious?" Brady gazed at the two behind the counter, who seemed to be in deep conversation after the customer left.

"Are you thinking what I'm thinking?" I asked. "I mean, it seems impossible, but then again, God delights in doing the impossible."

"Please." Brady laughed. "Are you really telling me that you haven't known about this? Whatever happened to a woman's intuition?"

"What are you saying, Brady?"

He shook his head. "I'm saying that Stan and Madge have been crazy about each other for more than two years. They've fought it every step of the way, but they're nuts about each other. And I'm completely gobsmacked that you didn't pick up on it. Seriously?"

"Wow." I couldn't believe it. "Wow, wow, wow."

Wow was right. But the proof was in the pudding, as Queenie always said.

I watched as Madge looked around the room and, finding it empty of customers, slipped into Stan's open arms. Seconds later they were kissing. So much for no PDA in the store. The bell above the door rang out, alerting them to the fact that a customer had entered. They backed up and busied themselves once more as if nothing had happened.

"I'm . . . I'm . . ." The words refused to come. I thought I might just be seeing things. I finally managed to eke out, "I'm shocked."

"I'm not," Brady said. "They might not talk about it, but those two are meant to be together."

"But they're as different as night and day," I argued. "They disagree on . . . everything."

"Not everything." Brady grinned and gestured with his head.

I glanced at Madge and Stan, who stole another kiss while the customer wasn't looking.

"Well, there you go." I turned back, shaking my head. "I can truly say I've seen everything now."

"Not quite everything." Alva's voice sounded behind me.

I turned to face her and realized she wasn't alone. Twiggy stood next to her. "What do you mean, Auntie?" I asked.

She shrugged. "If you ever see a fella hanging off my arm, then you can say you've seen everything. But I wouldn't go looking for that just yet. I gave up on the idea of romance a long time ago."

"I think a lot of us did," Twiggy said. "I was starting to wonder if I'd ever find Prince Charming. Then Beau showed up."

"Yes, but you're, what—twelve? I'm in my eighties."

"I'm twenty-seven, thank you very much." Twiggy's lips curled up in a smile. "But it felt like years and years before I found someone."

"Time is relative," Brady said.

"Unless you're old." Alva shook her head. "When you're old, time is not relative. It's anything but." Her nose wrinkled. More than usual. "Anyway, forget I said anything. It's all right. I'm set in my ways. No room in my house for a man."

"If he does show up, you might want to change the drapes in the lavender room." Brady flashed her a playful smile. "Just saying."

"What's wrong with my grape drapes? They're lovely."

"Right, right." Brady wrapped his arms around her. "If you're seriously looking for a man, we'll keep our eyes open. You'd be surprised how many brides come in with fathers in their golden years."

"Golden years, my eye. I need someone in his platinum years. And such a fella doesn't exist."

"You never know, Aunt Alva. Look at Reverend Bradford. Er, Pap-Paul Bradford."

"He's the exception, not the rule." She turned on her heels and headed to the ladies' room, hollering, "This old bladder waits for no one!"

"One day some lucky guy is gonna get a real prize in her." Brady's words seemed teasing, but I could read the seriousness in his eyes. "She's one of the greatest women I've ever known."

"Do you think she really *wants* a husband, though?" I asked.

Brady shrugged. "I would imagine she gets a little lonely sometimes. Her faith is strong and she doesn't seem like the needy sort, so it's probably more of an occasional thought than a deep longing."

I thought about that before responding. "But wouldn't it be fun if God surprised her?"

"He can do it." Twiggy let out a little squeal. "We should all pray."

We turned to look at her.

"No, really. There's power in prayer, right? We should all pray that if God has someone for Alva, he will appear right out of the blue. It could happen."

"Well, yes, but . . ."

"I for one believe in miracles," Twiggy said. "I think we watched one happen today, in fact. So if God cares enough about our bridal shop to make sure we have a terrific day, surely he cares enough about Alva to bring her the perfect man."

Okay then.

About three minutes later, Madge approached. "Hey, Katie, can you come up front for a few minutes? You know that Sanders girl, the one from San Antonio? They've sent her grandfather to pick up her veil. Poor old guy seems clueless. Want to come help him?"

"How old?" Twiggy asked.

"What does he look like?" Dahlia added.

Madge looked back and forth between them. "Too old for the likes of you. And besides, I thought you already had fellas."

"No, not for us." Twiggy laughed. "But I've got to see this for myself. My goodness, the Lord surely moves fast when we pray!"

I didn't think this would be an appropriate time to remind her that we hadn't even prayed yet. If she thought the elderly man at the front of the store was Alva's Prince Charming, so be it.

Before I could head up to the register, some commotion in the hallway caught my attention. Alva had come out of the restroom, wrestling with her girdle. When she turned around I noticed some of the fabric from her dress was hung up in her undergarments in the back. I gestured for her to fix it and she backed her way to the restroom once more.

"If Prince Charming is in the store, we need to get Cinderella ready for the ball," Twiggy whispered. "Maybe I could convince her to put on a little lipstick?"

"Nah." I shrugged. "If it's meant to be, he'll see beyond all of that."

"Seriously?" Dahlia paled. "Well, I suppose that's one school of thought."

I walked to the front of the store with my aunt in tow to visit with Mr. Everett Sanders of the San Antonio Sanderses. Before long we were engaged in conversation, not about wedding tiaras but about basketball. He was a huge basketball fan just like the others in his family. This, of course, bonded him to Alva at once, who had apparently forgotten the family's leanings. On and on they went, talking about basketball.

I heard a noise behind me and turned to see Eduardo approaching, gown in hand. His gaze narrowed when he saw Alva talking to the elderly Mr. Sanders.

"What is she looking at?" Eduardo's eyes narrowed to slits and I could read the disdain in his expression.

"Who?"

He gestured to Alva. "She seems captivated by something."

"Oh, not something . . . someone." I grinned. "I think she's got her eye on that fella over there. He's the grandfather of one of our customers."

Eduardo grunted and swung the gown over his shoulder as he moved toward the register. He mumbled something in Spanish that I couldn't make out. Not that I really had time to focus on Eduardo right now. I had a lot more on my mind where Alva was concerned.

Perhaps we really were witnessing a miracle. Twiggy's faith had brought Mr. Right to Alva's door, just like a fairy tale.

Then again, not all fairy tales had happy endings, did they? Turned out Mr. Sanders was, like his son, not a Mavericks fan. This put Alva in a snit right away. She could hardly look at the man without grimacing. But I had to get the veil so that he could deliver it to his granddaughter.

"Alva, please keep him preoccupied until I get back," I whispered.

She grunted.

When I returned with the veil, the two were embroiled in a dispute. It took Brady showing up to calm things down. When Mr. Sanders looked up, up, up at Brady James, he apparently decided to reconsider his earlier comments about the Mavericks, especially when he saw that Brady was hobbling.

The direction of the conversation shifted a bit, and finally I could tell that things were calming. Thank goodness. I'd hate to see this Spurs/Mavericks thing get out of hand.

"So much for our plans to find a happily ever after for Alva."
Twiggy shrugged. "I suppose it's safe to say those two are *not*
a match made in heaven."

"Oh, I don't know. What about that old saying that tries to
convince us that opposites attract? There's some truth to that,
right? I mean, I'm a small-town girl with no particular sports
leanings who fell in love with a big-city basketball player. It
happens."

Had I really just said the words "fell in love" out loud?
There I went exposing my feelings for all the world to see.
Er, all my co-workers to see. But no one seemed to notice I'd
said anything at all. They were all too busy arguing the finer
points of Alva's love life, or lack thereof.

Minutes later Brady asked if he could talk with me in his
office. I followed behind him as he hobbled on his crutches
into the room, closed the door, and sat behind his desk.

"Have a seat, Katie."

"Am I in trouble?" I eased down into a chair, every muscle
aching.

"No." He laughed. "I just thought you might like to take a
load off. You've worked so hard today and I'm grateful. More
grateful than you know. I feel like a real heel that I couldn't
help more, but I'm so blessed that your brothers showed up
and took care of the physical labor."

"It went great."

"I had a chance to talk to the reporter before he left. He
took great notes. You were right all along, Katie. We didn't
need to dispute the bride who tried to take us down. We just
had to prove to the community that we're here for them. And
today did that."

"I'm so glad it all worked out."

"Just so you know, there's going to be a story on channel

8 tonight. I think they even got a clip of you raffling off that one dress—you know, the one with the pink sash?"

"Ugh, no way! I'm going to be on the news?"

"Yeah." He chuckled. "You were so busy having such a great time that you probably didn't notice the guy with the camera filming you."

"I guess not. But it's fine. It's all for a good cause. Anything I can do to help."

"Speaking of that, I want to talk to you about one more thing." Brady leaned against the desk. "You and Alva have been great to pamper me and treat me like a guest, but I've overstayed my welcome."

"W-what?"

"It's true. I'm getting around pretty good on the crutches now, and I think I'm ready to try this knee out at my own place."

"The drapes getting to you?" I teased.

"No. I just think I need time to . . ." He paused and those beautiful eyes seemed to cloud over. "I don't want you to take this the wrong way, but I kind of need some time to myself."

"Ah." I couldn't really think of anything else to say in response, so I left it at that.

"I have a lot going on in my head right now." Brady rose and took a couple of steps away from me on his crutches.

I stood and walked toward him. "I'm sure you do, but do you really think it's wise to be by yourself right now? Being around other people is probably good for you."

"Only to a certain extent, Katie. I have a lot to think about. And pray about. That's easier to do when I have time to myself."

"I'm just worried about you, Brady. I want you to be okay."

"I want me to be okay too. But I really think it's better if I go back to my place. I think I can manage the stairs with the crutches now. And Stan said he'll come by Alva's tonight and help me get my stuff."

"So you're going tonight?"

"Yeah. I want to sleep in my own bed."

I couldn't fault him for that, but I had a sneaking suspicion there was more going on in that head of his. In spite of his attempts to act upbeat today, I'd noticed glimpses of pain in his eyes. Even during his stay with us, the good and bad moments had been all mixed up together. Some of that could be blamed on the meds. The rest I wasn't so sure of.

Hopefully, time alone would help and not hurt.

19

If I Give My Heart to You

I want to tell the truth, and maybe that's why they trust me.
When I was acting, I believed what I said . . . every line.

Doris Day

I slept until after noon on Saturday. When I awoke, Alva fed
me yummy chicken and dumplings she had prepared from
scratch. Afterward a funny smile lit her face and I could
read the mischief in her eyes.

"I know what you need, sweet girl. You need to go to the
movies."

"The movies?"

"Sure. It's Saturday. As a kid I often went to the show on
Saturday evening. I still love a good movie. And I've heard

you can even get your tickets on the computer now. How do you like them apples? Can we go? Pretty please? You can ask Brady to come with."

"To see a chick flick?" I laughed. "He's a guy, Aunt Alva. Trust me when I say he'd rather not." That, and he'd just told me he wanted to be alone, hadn't he?

Alva cleaned the plates and put them in the dishwasher. "Well now, I don't know . . . Several of the fellas I know love a good romance. I had a long conversation with Eduardo earlier and he told me that he's a fan of Doris Day. He even met her in person."

"Yes, I heard that."

"Do you suppose any Doris Day movies are showing?"

I shook my head. "Um, probably not. We'll have to choose something else."

"I suppose it doesn't matter, as long as there's no cussin' or killin'. I can't abide cussin' and killin'. If I wanted to see that, I'd turn on the evening news."

And that was how we ended up seeing a ridiculously unbelievable romantic comedy starring a couple of Hollywood's most popular twenty-first-century superstars. Alva came out of the theater wide-eyed and a little shell-shocked. "That wasn't what I expected. Whatever happened to good, wholesome family stories? Cary Grant and Rock Hudson? I wasn't quite prepared to see that one scene . . . well, you know the one. For pity's sake, I thought I was going to have to sneak out for a potty break just to avoid the humiliation."

"Yeah, I'm sorry about that, Alva. Unfortunately, there's a lot of that in movies these days."

"Well then, next time we'll just rent the oldies but goodies. *An Affair to Remember. Gone with the Wind.* You know, the good, clean ones."

As we crossed the parking lot toward the car I noticed someone familiar.

"Eduardo!" I raised my hand and waved at him. He took several quick steps in our direction. "Were you just in the theater?"

"Yes." He groaned. "I can't believe I paid almost ten dollars to watch that . . . that . . ."

"Exactly my sentiments." Alva's nose wrinkled. "A waste of good money."

"And time. I could've been working on that Doris Day gown instead of wasting my time on that ridiculous picture." He shrugged. "Anyway, things aren't what they used to be."

"That's for sure," Alva said. "Nothing a double scoop of ice cream won't cure, though. Let's go drown our sorrows."

"But it's freezing outside, Alva."

"I know! That's the perfect time for ice cream."

"What a lovely idea." Eduardo extended his arm to help Alva across the parking lot. "I'll drive my car, if you like. There's an ice cream place not far from here. I know it well. Do you like rocky road, Alva?"

"It's fine, but I prefer mint chocolate chip. Just the right mix of minty and sweet. And it makes my breath kissably fresh."

Kissably fresh? Was my aunt actually flirting with Eduardo?

I didn't have long to think about it because I felt my phone buzzing inside my purse. I saw Brady's number and smiled, then answered with a quick hello.

"Hey, Katie. Just wanted to make sure you got my earlier message about the ad in the *Tribune*. There was a typo in it."

"Ah." Okay, work-related stuff. "I'm sorry."

"I corrected it. And by the way, I don't know if you heard, but that local ad sheet we've been running in the community paper has doubled in price. That's not good news."

"I hadn't heard. Thanks for filling me in. How are you feeling, Brady?"

"Tired. And a little hung over from the medication."

"Well, get as much rest as you can. And don't worry about the *Tribune* or the community paper. I've got them both covered."

The rest of the evening seemed to go downhill after that. I tried to enjoy my ice cream but suddenly felt weary. I just wanted to get back home and sleep once more.

I did manage to crawl out of bed in time to attend church on Sunday. Strangely, Brady turned down my offer to pick him up and drive him there, so I sat alone during the service.

Lori-Lou called later that afternoon to explain that she'd skipped out on church because she wasn't feeling well. Pregnancy-related headaches had her in a quandary. I could hear the stress in her voice as we talked and wished I had time to help her with the kids, but with my workload so high, all I could do was offer to pray for her.

On Monday morning I checked in on Brady as the workday began. I couldn't help but wonder why he hadn't called me on Sunday, but I didn't mention it. Instead, I popped my head in his office door and clucked my tongue at him when I saw him slaving away at his computer. "I can't believe you're here. You should be home resting."

He glanced up, but his fingers never stopped moving on the keys. "I'm going stir-crazy. I need to get my mind back on work. It's a saving grace right now, trust me."

"I understand. And I'm here if you need me."

He gave me a slight nod and went back to work. Maybe I'd better do the same. If I drowned my loneliness in work, all would be well. And boy, did I have a lot to do. The first thing on my agenda today? The Christmas window display—a lovely diversion. I should've done it weeks ago, but the bridal extravaganza had taken precedence. I'd loaded up the window with sale items. Now I had to remove all of those and make a festive wintery display.

I'd planned the whole thing in my head already. I loved working on window displays, after all. A quick trip to the craft store after church yesterday had given me the perfect opportunity to purchase all of the items I needed to transform the window into a thing of beauty. And there was something about the creative process that calmed my heart and stilled my troubled thoughts.

I'd prepped for this all weekend—mentally, anyway—and I couldn't wait to get started. It would be gorgeous. I started by placing mounds of snow-like fluff at the base of the window, then added the adorable snowman I'd purchased. After that I put up twinkling lights—all white, of course. Then I hung the snowflakes. Beautiful, white, shimmering snowflakes.

As I worked I thought about Brady. He definitely wasn't himself lately. Not even close. I'd never seen him so quiet, or so down. His knee seemed to be recovering nicely, but his heart and mind were not. Was he avoiding me? Rethinking our relationship? Or was his withdrawn behavior related to the loss of his career? Were both of those things wrapped up together in his heart? I prayed not.

I buzzed around the shop, preoccupied with my task. I felt my senses come alive as I worked. In fact, the whole thing reminded me of being at home in Fairfield, working on the window display at the hardware store.

Home.

Fairfield.

A wistful feeling came over me, and for the first time in ages I actually felt homesick. I missed the simpler life—leisurely hours after work, hanging out with friends at football games and Dairy Queen. Friday night dinners at Sam's restaurant with the family. These days, my whole world was filled with work, work, work.

Not that I'd ever been averse to working hard, but it seemed like I had no real life outside of my job anymore.

I shook off my concerns and focused on the window. It was coming together nicely, if I did say so myself. As I continued on, my spirits lifted. Suddenly my work didn't feel like work at all. The creative process made it pure joy.

Finally, the pièce de résistance—the lifelike mannequin with the perfect wintery bridal gown. I'd chosen the gown with Dahlia's help—a lovely lace dress sparkling with snow-like crystals from top to bottom. I loved the sheer sleeves and the crystal-embellished sash. The whole thing just cried "winter." And if anyone missed that point, the white faux fur draped across the mannequin's shoulders should seal the deal.

Now, to finish off the whole thing by adding a backdrop. I'd purchased the perfect lace drapes to swag behind the display. They would be open enough to see through into the store, but draped on the sides to frame the display. Perfect.

Twiggy approached just as I turned on the lights. The whole thing sprang to life and we both gasped in unison. "It's gorgeous!" she said.

"You think?" I noticed a couple of things that needing adjusting, so I went back to work, pulling the mannequin slightly to the left and moving the lace curtains so they allowed more of the window display to be seen from the inside of the store.

"Ooh, I knew I forgot something!" I raced to the back of the store and returned with a long veil, which I pinned to the bride's hair. Then I stepped back to give the whole thing one last scrutinizing look.

"What's that song you're singing, Katie?" Twiggy asked.

"Song?" Oops. I didn't even realize I'd been singing out loud.

"Yes. Something about being in your own little corner?"

"Oh, it's from *Cinderella*. Maybe I just need some mice to help me finish this display."

"Mice?" Twiggy paled. "Are you saying we have mice? Here? At the shop?"

"No." I laughed and waved my hand, nearly knocking the mannequin over. "No mice. That I know of. I just like that song."

"Probably because you've got your own prince now." Madge drew close to the window display, giving it an admiring look.

"Hmm." I didn't mean to hesitate, but it couldn't be helped. Madge's words had stopped me in my tracks. With Brady pulling away from me, I had to wonder about the prince comment. Maybe my prince was on sabbatical. Taking a rest from the kingdom for a while.

Madge must've been reading my thoughts. "He'll get through this, Katie." She patted my arm. "Just be patient."

"What else can I be?" I gave a little shrug. "It won't help his situation to fret."

"True. And by the way, the window looks great."

"Thanks. I love doing holiday windows. I got the idea for this one from a fun conversation I had with my brother and Crystal."

"How is Crystal, anyway?"

"Engaged and excited. I think she's settling into the routine at the hardware store fine. She's in her element in a small town."

"I imagine you're right. I always thought she was a bit of a fish out of water here, but we were happy to be her family while she was at the bridal shop."

I pondered the whole "happy to be her family" line. The

folks at Cosmopolitan Bridal had become my family too. And I loved them for adopting me.

Still, it was another family that tugged at my heart as I continued to work. My thoughts kept shifting back to my lunch at Sam's with Casey and his parents. I'd seen the hopefulness in his mother's eyes as she'd talked about the two of us as if we were still a couple. And I couldn't seem to shake the notion that Casey wanted to rekindle things.

Take this morning's text message, for instance. What kind of an ex sent a random "Praying for you" message?

I chided myself for making too much of it. Casey had always been kindhearted, a real sweetie—so good with expressing himself.

Good with expressing himself. Hmm . . . Just the opposite of Brady.

I pushed those thoughts aside to the best of my ability and tried not to let homesickness overwhelm me again.

Before breaking for lunch, I gave the display one last glance, then went outside and took a close look at it through the window. I still needed to move the mannequin slightly to the left, but other than that the whole thing was picture-perfect. I could hardly wait for the customers to take notice.

Speaking of which, I'd better snap a few photos and submit them as part of our weekly ad for the local mailer. I went inside, grabbed my camera, and took as many pictures as I could. Unfortunately, most of them caught my reflection in the glass, so I had to go inside and take several more photos from the back side of the window.

Finally it was time for lunch. Creative work always made me hungry. I passed by Brady's office and noticed the door was closed. Strange. He rarely closed it unless he was on an important call or something. Maybe he just wanted to be alone. Or maybe he was in the studio having lunch with the others.

I walked down the hall and opened the door to the studio. For the first time in ages I didn't find Dahlia in a frenzy. Instead, everyone seemed to be in a relatively pleasant frame of mind. Off in the distance Eduardo worked on Carrie Sanders's gown. I gasped as I saw it on the dress form.

"Oh, Eduardo, it's amazing. Doris would be so proud."

"I will send her a photo when I'm done."

"You'll . . . what?" Was he kidding? He would send Doris a photo?

"We are friends, you know." This led to an animated conversation about the old days in Hollywood.

"I still can't believe you actually know her." Hibiscus gave him a curious look. "I wonder if you're pulling my leg."

"It's the truth." He put his right hand up. "Every word of it."

I warmed my lunch in the microwave and Hibiscus and Jane joined me. I had to laugh when I saw that Jane had changed her hair color again. This week she was sporting a short bob, deep red. And the hippie-style clothing threw me a little. Hadn't bell-bottoms gone out in the seventies?

We took our seats at the little table just as Madge entered the room. She grabbed her lunch from the fridge and warmed it in the microwave, chatting all the while about the customer load out front.

"I'm shocked at how many people we've had come through today, Katie. Spillover from the Black Friday sale. I think we'll get rid of that excess inventory in no time, thanks to your forward thinking."

"I'm glad."

She joined us at the table and we ate our respective lunches while Eduardo continued to work on Carrie's gown. I could barely believe my eyes as I gazed at it. Truly, it looked as beautiful as something Doris would have worn in person. Maybe more so.

I realized I had to say something to the other ladies. I put down my fork and turned to Hibiscus. "I think Eduardo's remarkable. So gifted."

"Yes, more than most of the rest of us put together," Hibiscus said. "And I don't mean that in a putting-us-down sort of way. He's just in a league of his own."

"Yeah." Jane sighed. "It's true. And I just love his televangelist hair. If only my hair looked half that nice." She fussed with her bob.

"I think your hair was fine the old way, Jane," Madge said. "I don't know why women feel like they always have to change. I've had the same hairstyle since the eighties and no one cares." She took a bite of her food and leaned back in her chair.

Jane quirked a brow, then went back to eating her peanut butter sandwich.

"Anyway, who are we trying to impress?" Hibiscus said. "It's not like Mr. Right is going to walk through the door of the sewing room."

"Hi, I'm surprised to hear you talking like this," Jane said. "You're such a free spirit. I thought you were one of those forever-blissfully-single gals."

"Oh, I'm happy. Really. I love my work. It keeps me going." Her smile faded a bit and I read the discontentment in her eyes as she glanced my way. "I guess we're all a little jealous of you, Katie."

"M-me?" I nearly choked on my soda. "Why?"

"Because you're living the fairy tale. Small-town girl comes to the big city and finds the perfect guy. Tall, dark, and handsome, no less. You've got your happily ever after."

I didn't respond at first. I wanted to tell her that fairy-tale romances didn't exist, that even the best relationships went through trials. After considering that I finally shared a few thoughts. "I didn't even know what I was looking for in a guy. I think I just loved the idea of being in love. When I stopped looking, that's when God dropped Brady right in front of me. But honestly, even though it seems like we're living our happily ever after, it's laced with hard realities. Brady's got his share of trials, and I don't always know how to be what he needs me to be."

"Maybe he doesn't need you to be anything," Madge said. "Maybe he just needs you to stick with him and be consistent when nothing else around him is."

Be consistent.

Interesting choice of words.

"His whole world is shifting right now," Madge said. "And he's looking for something to hang on to that isn't moving."

"I'm so glad he's a Christian." As I spoke those words, I felt them deeply. "How do people get through hard situations when they don't know the Lord?"

"I have no idea." Madge took a sip of her drink. "They struggle. There's no rock to hang on to when the seasons are shifting."

Seasons. There was that word again. I thought about the sermon I'd listened to online. It made more sense now than ever.

Hibiscus appeared to be listening closely but didn't comment. Later, after Madge had left, she approached me. "I hear you guys talking about all this Christian stuff a lot. It used to weird me out, but I'm over it now."

"Oh?"

"Yeah. Some of this God-talk stuff is new to me. But something Madge said to you piqued my interest. What was that line about the seasons?"

"Oh, just that we can trust God no matter what season we're in. Is that what you mean?"

"I always considered the changes of life to be the natural ebb and flow of things. Didn't really factor God into them at all. It's just interesting to hear people talk about God like he's right here in the middle of it all."

"Well, he is." I chuckled. "In the very center."

She shook her head. "You people. You've got me looking out of the corner of my eye just in case God pops out."

"Oh, he's popping out, all right," I said. "You just never know when he's going to show up . . . or how."

Hibiscus slinked across the room like a spy on the lookout. "I'll keep my eyes open. I hope he doesn't mind if I'm up to my eyeballs in tulle and lace when he gets here."

I had a feeling he wouldn't mind one little bit.

20

Oh Me! Oh My! Oh You!

I like joy; I want to be joyous; I want to have fun on the set; I want to wear beautiful clothes and look pretty. I want to smile, and I want to make people laugh. And that's all I want. I like it. I like being happy. I want to make others happy.

Doris Day

I'd seen Queenie in just about every situation life could offer: in her grandmotherly role with a stern expression as the children messed up her house with their toys and antics. In an authoritative role as matriarch of the town. In her spiritual role as Bible study teacher and lead WOP-per. I'd seen her pre-surgery and post-surgery and even watched as she transitioned from widow to bride-to-be. But I'd never seen her as happy as the day she walked down the aisle toward Reverend Bradford.

Mama and I sat together in the front row of the Baptist church. In spite of the church being filled with friends and family, I felt lonely without Brady at my side. He'd insisted on coming, but the surgeon gave him a firm no. From what we'd been told, the long drive was too risky. Something about the danger of blood clots. The very idea terrified all of us, so in the end, Brady had acquiesced. Still, he insisted I text him pictures every step of the way. I'd agreed, but it still felt like a part of me was missing.

The music kicked off—Really? Brother Krank was playing the organ?—and the groom entered at the front with all of his groomsmen. I watched as his gaze traveled to the back of the sanctuary.

The back doors of the sanctuary opened. Bessie May sashayed in, wearing a dark blue bridesmaid gown. I had to give it to the old girl—she made that color look good. Or maybe it made her look good. Of course, the loopy makeup job left something to be desired, but who was I to judge an elderly woman's creativity with the eye shadow?

Behind her came Ophelia. Then Prissy. Finally, the moment that made my heart sing—Alva. Queenie's maid of honor. No one could understand the significance of this unless they knew the history. The two sisters hadn't spoken in years until this past summer. To see my aunt assume the role of maid of honor was truly the icing on the cake.

Mmm. Cake. Wouldn't be long now before I could have a yummy slice.

"Ooh, here she comes," Lori-Lou whispered from behind me. "You can do it, girl! Eye on the prize!"

I looked toward the back of the auditorium expecting to see

Queenie but saw Mariela instead. Ah yes. The all-important flower girl. She looked glorious in her white dress with soft blue flowers around the waistline. Perfection.

Well, almost perfection. Mariela got distracted by a kid in the back pew who offered her a stick of gum. Her eyes widened.

"C'mon, Mariela. Stay focused," Lori-Lou whispered. "Just like we practiced."

Mariela shook her head at the kid and kept walking. She dropped one lone petal at a time from her basket, finally passing by our pew and taking her place in line behind the bridesmaids. At this point she began to squirm. I gave her a "be still" look and she sighed.

As the music shifted from "Pachelbel's Canon" to the "Wedding March," the moment we'd all been waiting for arrived at last. I could hardly believe my eyes as the back door of the church opened and Queenie walked through. I'd seen her in the bridal room, but now, in an ocean of powder-puff blue, she looked every bit the radiant queen.

"The dress is perfect, Twiggy." I leaned over to give my friend a smile as I whispered the words. "You were right all along."

She winked.

Mama and I rose and the other guests followed suit as Queenie entered on my father's arm. I'd been to a lot of weddings over the years, but I'd never seen an eighty-two-year-old bride on the arm of her fifty-something son. They both beamed.

I watched as she clung to him and realized she was making this walk without her cane. Good for her. Well, good until they got to the middle of the aisle and her knee appeared to lock up. She stopped and slapped it, then laughed and kept going.

This seemed to generate quite a reaction from folks in the

room, especially Reverend Bradford, who got a kick out of it. Pop deposited Queenie at the front, did the official giving-away thing, and took a seat next to my mother, who already had a box of tissues in hand for the ceremony.

Behind me, Josh and Lori-Lou fussed over their younger children. Little Joshie whimpered and Gilly complained that she was bored. I turned back to see Lori-Lou pop a bottle into Joshie's mouth and place a box of crayons in Gilly's hand, then adjust her pregnant self in the hard pew. Wow. She had this mothering thing down to a science.

We all sat, and the pastor prayed and then went straight for the "I dos."

"I guess when you're in your eighties there's no point in procrastinating," Pop whispered. "Just get right to it."

Maybe. Or maybe the pastor realized that the ladies-in-waiting were having a hard time standing for long. In fact, Bessie May shifted her position so many times I thought she might fall over. No doubt her hip joints were giving her fits again. But they all held the course until the rings were exchanged. Then, at just the right moment, the happy couple was instructed to seal the deal with a kiss.

As they did, the congregation roared with applause. Queenie waved them off and gave her husband another kiss. And then another. Only when the pastor cleared his throat did the new Mr. and Mrs. come up for air.

"And *that's* how they do it in the Presbyterian church," Queenie hollered.

Alrighty then.

Another round of laughs followed, and Queenie appeared to eat it up. She took her bouquet from Alva and waved it in the air, triumphant, then linked her arm through her husband's and they trekked back down the aisle.

Then again, *trekked* was hardly the right word. She gripped his arm and paused twice to shake out her knee. But they made it to the back of the room. By the time the rest of us joined them in the lobby, they were kissing again. And again.

A few photos were taken after that, but most of the wedding party was ready to sit for a while, so off to the fellowship hall we went. The place was crowded with guests, and they cheered as Brother Krank, now playing the role of deejay, announced the entrance of Mr. and Mrs. Paul Bradford. My sweet grandmother and her husband made the rounds greeting the guests, but I was too floored by the room to pay much attention. Joni and Crystal had worked overtime to turn it into a place of beauty. Wow.

"And *that's* how we do it in the Baptist church," my mother said as she gestured to the satin tablecloths and gorgeous serving tables.

I couldn't get over how pretty it all looked. But one thing was noticeably absent—the wedding cake. Weird.

I was just about to ask Mama about that when Crystal approached. "Isn't it bee-*you*-te-ful?" she crooned.

"Definitely."

"Where I come from, back in Georgia, we have a *teen*-sy-tiny little fellowship hall." She raised her voice to be heard about the crowd. "Nothin' this spec-*tac*-u-luh. I had *so* much fun helpin' your mama decorate. It's my passion."

"You're very good at it," I said.

"Let me just tell you, Joni is amazin'. We've become *such* good *free*-unds. She and Levi have dinner with us nearly every Friday evenin'."

"You're still staying at Queenie's place?" I asked.

"Yes." Her nose wrinkled. "But the sweetest thing has happened! Joni has asked me to be her roomie. Isn't that amazin'

213

news? She's livin' in that big ol' house all alone now that her parents are serving full-time as missionaries. You did know about that, didn't you?"

I shook my head. "No. I hadn't heard."

"Zim-*bab*-way. In the deepest, darkest jungles of Africa." Crystal shivered. "Anyway, I'll be movin' my stuff over this week, but it won't be for long." She winked. "You might as well know that I have a little secret of my own."

"One you can share?"

"Yes." Her face lit in a smile just as Bessie May happened by with a plateful of appetizers.

"Let the old people through, if you please!" She pressed her way between Crystal and me and we both laughed.

"Don't eat all of the chicken strips, Bessie May!" Ophelia's voice sounded from across the room. "Save some for the rest of us."

Crystal gestured for me to lean in close. "Jasper and I have set a date! The second Saturday in May." She put her finger over her lips. "We decided we don't want to wait long. I mean, when you find the person you're supposed to be with forever, you want forever to begin right away. Isn't that how the old sayin' goes?"

Yes, that was exactly how the old saying went. Only, now I couldn't stop thinking about Brady. I somehow gathered my wits about me and congratulated Crystal with a warm hug.

"I know where to get my weddin' gown," she said. "And I know just the design. I'm crazy about Scarlett O'Hara. It's going to be a full-out Southern ball, Katie. You'll have to help me with the details."

"Of course. I want to be there for you."

She put her finger to her lips again, then smiled. "Remember, it's top secret."

"I won't breathe a word."

Crystal slipped off through the crowd and I thought through everything she'd told me. Wedding. May. Southern. My heart swelled with joy for my brother and his fiancée, but at the same time I felt a little niggle of defeat when I thought about the fact that he would beat me to the altar. Not that this was a race.

"Penny for your thoughts." Casey's voice sounded from behind me. I turned, nearly breathless as I saw him standing there dressed in a suit and tie.

"Well now, don't you clean up nice." I instinctively reached out to straighten his tie, then quickly pulled my hand back. Oops.

"Very funny." He tugged at his tie. "Not my favorite way to dress, but anything for Queenie. When you care about someone, you'd do just about anything for them." He gazed at me with such intensity that I felt my face grow hot. I pulled the wedding program out of my purse and started fanning myself.

"What did you think of the ceremony?" I asked.

"I thought Bessie May was going to faint, and I was pretty sure Queenie was going to lose it coming up the aisle. But all's well that ends well."

"I thought it was great." I gave a contented sigh. "The perfect wedding."

"Almost as much fun as the Franklins' wedding. Remember that one? I think we were twelve at the time."

"Thirteen," I said.

"Yes. Thirteen. And the flower girl stepped on the bride's train and ripped it off? Left her backside exposed?"

I cringed remembering, then laughed. "Yes, well, thank goodness for Queenie. She saved the day, remember?"

"Like I could forget! She wrapped her lace shawl around the bride's waist and told her to keep going and ignore the laughter."

"So many great memories."

"And most of them involve food. Are you hungry?"

"Starved." I rubbed my stomach as it rumbled.

"We'd better get in line if we stand a chance of getting any food. You know how it is at the Baptist church."

I knew, all right. Wedding or not, folks attacked the tables just like they did the monthly potluck. I trailed behind Casey until we found ourselves at the end of a long line. I watched as Queenie and Reverend Bradford laughed and smiled with the pastor and his wife. What fun to see the two reverends getting along so well. It did my heart good.

Casey said something about the weather, but I didn't hear it. I was way too distracted by Joni, who approached wearing the most gorgeous blue dress I'd ever seen. I let out a whistle. "Girl! Wow."

"You like it?" She did a little twirl and her skirt swished.

"It's amazing."

Clearly Casey thought it was amazing too. I caught him glancing at her more than once. I had to admit, she was a woman transformed. Our little softball-playing caterpillar had morphed into a butterfly.

The line inched forward a bit, giving us hope that we would soon reach the table. "Hope there's still food left by the time you get there." Joni gave us a little wave and headed across the room to talk to Levi.

"Wow." I shook my head, unable to put into words how I felt. "She's a beauty."

"She is." Casey didn't appear to be looking at Joni anymore, though. Ack.

I turned my attention to the food table as we finally reached the front of the buffet line. "Looks like we'll get to eat after all."

"Interesting assortment of foods." Casey reached for a

couple of empty plates and passed one to me. "Chicken strips from Dairy Queen? Peach preserves from Cooper Farms? Barbecue from Sam's?"

"Yeah, I know. Everyone and their brother contributed something, from what I've been told."

We filled our plates and reached the dessert table, where we found slices of peach pie but nothing else. So strange.

"No wedding cake?" Casey looked perplexed.

"I was sure Ophelia was making one. Maybe she . . ." Oh no. Maybe she'd dropped it. I'd have to ask Mama about it—quickly.

I gestured to a nearby table. Casey followed on my heels and we both sat down and dove right in. I saw Mama and Pop talking with Mr. and Mrs. Lawson off in the distance. It felt good to have everyone together again. Really good.

"Hey, remember that one potluck dinner where Mrs. Franklin brought a pot roast that tasted suspiciously like motor oil?" Casey set his fork down and laughed.

"Um, yeah." I used my paper napkin to wipe gravy from my lips. "Hadn't her husband just stolen the pan to drain the oil from his old Chevy truck or something?"

"Yeah. She was clueless. But I distinctly remember someone saying we all got an oil and lube job that day."

I started laughing and couldn't stop. When I finally got myself under control, I managed to say, "I remember it well."

Casey gazed into my eyes and took my hand, giving it a squeeze. "I remember a lot of things well, Katie. All good memories."

A lump rose in my throat and I couldn't seem to speak around it.

"What's so funny over here?"

I looked up to see that Mama was standing next to my

chair. I pulled my hand out of Casey's, my face heating up as if I'd done something wrong. Which I hadn't of course. Still, judging from the expression on my mother's face, I might as well have.

"We're just talking about old times, Mrs. Fisher. Good times." Casey took another bite of his chicken strip.

"Hmm." Her gaze traveled back and forth between the two of us.

Time to change the subject. "Mama, I'm almost scared to ask, but where's the cake?"

"At the Methodist church, naturally." She plopped down into a chair to my right and fanned herself. "Is it getting hot in here or am I just having my own personal summer?"

"W-what? Did Ophelia accidentally take the cake to the wrong place?" I knew the poor old soul was getting a little forgetful, but taking the cake to the wrong church? That was really something.

"Of course not." Mama looked at me like she thought I'd lost it. "We're all headed to the Methodist church after we eat."

"We—we are?"

"Well, sure. I thought you knew that."

"No. I'm pretty sure I would've remembered that little detail." I looked at Casey. "Did you know?"

"Nope. I guess the gossip train hadn't reached Mama yet on this one."

"Gossip, my eye. It's common knowledge." Mama pursed her lips.

"Like everything else in this town," Casey whispered in my ear, chuckling.

"Mama, do you mind if I ask *why* we're going to the Methodist church? This is a perfectly wonderful place for the reception. It makes no sense to move down the street."

"There's a perfectly good explanation, Katie. The Methodist church allows dancing, and Queenie and Reverend Bradford—er, Dad Bradford—wanted to offer their guests the opportunity to celebrate on the dance floor."

Casey looked perplexed by this notion. "Um, I hate to ask the obvious, but why not go to the Presbyterian church for that?"

"They don't allow dancing there either." Mama leaned in close to whisper the next part. "Big brouhaha at the Presbyterian church when Reverend Bradford brought it up in a board meeting. Trust me, you don't want to get into all of that. Anyway, that leaves us with the Methodists. And maybe the charismatics, but I'm pretty sure that dancing in the Holy Ghost isn't the same thing as the Texas two-step."

I shook my head as I tried to make sense of this. "So, let me get this straight. We're having food at the Baptist church and then cake and dancing at the Methodist church."

"And punch." Mama stood and smoothed out her skirt. "But whatever you do, don't drink much. I heard a rumor that Prissy Moyer is planning to spike it. I guess they allow that at the Methodist church too." My mother sighed. "That last part is only hearsay, of course."

"Of course." Casey grinned.

"This whole thing just seems so strange," I said. "No one in our family is Methodist."

"Strange or not, it's where we're headed next, and I need to grab a ride from you in that fancy new car of yours because the heater's gone out in my car."

"O-okay."

After eating our fill, we all packed up and headed over to First United Methodist Church, where Prissy greeted us in a fellowship hall equally as decked out with lovely tables and beautiful blue floral centerpieces. She gestured to an exquisite table in the center of the room. There, in the very middle of the table, stood the most gorgeous wedding cake I'd ever seen, five tiers tall, trimmed out in soft blue roses that matched the color of Queenie's wedding gown perfectly.

To the right of the cake stood an elaborate punch fountain. The lights in the center column and base showed off the gorgeous red punch as it flowed, flowed, flowed, the trickling sound reminiscent of a mountain stream. Off in the distance a love song played, and Brother Krank, still in deejay mode, called out a welcome from the stage in the corner.

Mama looked a little floored by the sheer beauty of the room. Not Prissy, though. As she passed by, I'm pretty sure I heard her say, "And *that's* how we do it at the Methodist church!"

21

I'm Beginning to See the Light

Ronnie [Ronald Reagan] is really the only man I've ever known who loved dancing.

Doris Day

Brother Krank cranked up one of Queenie's favorite songs—"When I Fall in Love"—and the bride and groom headed out on the dance floor arm in arm. I'd seen my fair share of dances over the years, both high school proms and square dances at the civic center, but I'd never seen anything like the sight before me now. My grandmother looked positively radiant. And in that moment, when her husband swept her into his arms for their first spin around the dance floor as a newly married couple, I barely noticed the knee issue. All I saw was the smile on her face and the look of pure bliss in her husband's eyes.

After their dance, she shared a special dance with my dad. Then Reverend Bradford danced with his daughter, who had arrived in town just in time for the ceremony. I watched all of this in awe, my heart moved by the emotion of the day. Finally Brother Krank opened up the dance floor to everyone. Most of the couples were in their sixties and older. Even Mama and Pop joined in, though they were among the younger set. I smiled as they danced to "Dream a Little Dream of Me."

All morning long I'd observed Dewey and Dahlia hanging on the fringes, watching each other without saying much. I sensed the awkwardness between them but also picked up on the affection in my brother's eyes every time he glanced her way. It didn't take much courage for me to approach Dahlia to nudge her into his arms.

"Dahlia?"

She looked up from her glass of punch, which had almost touched her lips, but not quite. "Hmm?"

"You love my brother."

Her eyes filled with tears and she stared down at the floor.

"And my brother loves you." I spoke the words with conviction. "This separation thing is just plain silly. Get yourself over there and ask him to dance." I took the cup away from her and set it down on a table.

She glanced up and I could see her trying to find Dewey through the crowd.

"He's right there." I pointed over to the punch table. "And he's by himself. You're going to be miserable until you get this over with."

"I don't know, Katie."

I extended my hand and she stared at me, clearly confused. "What?"

"Come with me." I looped my arm through hers, marched across the room, and moved her directly in front of Dewey. I could read the surprise in his eyes, but it was coupled with delight.

"Dahlia?"

"Yeah." She looked down at the floor. Finally she looked up, grabbed Dewey by the hand, and said, "You're going to dance with me."

He stared at her for a moment. Then he led her to the dance floor. Less than a minute later, they were kissing. And kissing. And kissing some more.

I really should take up matchmaking.

I didn't mean to say the words aloud, but I obviously had.

"You'd make a great matchmaker, Katie." Casey must've been listening in. He pointed at Dewey and Dahlia, who were now cheek to cheek on the dance floor. "What's going on with those two?"

"He wants to marry her."

Casey tipped his head a bit to the right and watched them. "That's a good thing, right?"

"Yeah, but he wants her to move to Fairfield. She's opposed to that idea."

"I see. The distance thing is a dilemma."

"And he wants her to have fourteen kids."

"Fourteen?" Casey's eyes grew wide.

"Approximately. But I think, based on how comfortable they look together, they'll come to some sort of compromise."

"Seven kids?" Casey tried. "And maybe they could live halfway between Fairfield and Dallas? I hear Waxahachie is nice. That's about halfway."

"Yeah. Maybe."

We watched, mesmerized, as my brother and Dahlia continued smooching as they danced. When the song ended, she kissed him soundly, and as soon as she realized the entire roomful of people was watching, she gave a cheeky smile and hollered, "And *that's* how we do it at the Lutheran church."

"Okay then." Alva stepped beside me and fanned herself. "I might have to convert."

"There's a mighty lot of converting going on around here already." Bessie May walked over with a glass of punch. "Queenie's becoming a Presbyterian, Dewey's going to end up a Lutheran, and Lori-Lou and her husband have gone off and joined one of those rock-and-roll churches in Dallas. What about you, Katie? You converting too?"

I put my hands up. "Don't ask, Bessie May. You'll just be disappointed to hear I've been trying out a community church."

"Don't tell me you're a rock and roller too, Katie." She slapped herself on the forehead. "We raised you on the hymns."

"And I still love hymns. But I love contemporary worship songs too."

"For pity's sake."

"I love the church I go to in Dallas. It's different than the one I grew up in, but not in the ways that really matter. People still love on each other. The gospel is still preached. Sure, the music's a little different . . . okay, a lot different. And we meet in a building that's about five times the size of the Baptist church. And we don't have pews—we sit on chairs. But if you don't count all of that, it's just the same. Except for the lights. They put on a crazy-cool light show during some of the worship songs. Very ambient."

"Ambient, my eye." Bessie May grunted. "I'd have to close my eyes to keep from getting seasick."

"But it's the kind of church where I feel comfortable, where I can grow. And isn't that the point? Shouldn't we all find the place where we feel like we're part of something bigger than ourselves, where we've got people to lift our arms?"

In that moment, as I spoke those words, it hit me—it really, really hit me—why Brady was so devastated about not playing pro basketball anymore. He'd always been a team player. Now he had no team. For a guy accustomed to being surrounded by teammates, he must feel completely lost without them.

Bessie May fanned herself and walked away, mumbling something about how the whole world was going to pot now that the Baptists were dancing in the Methodist fellowship hall, the Lutherans were kissing the Baptists, and the community church folks were lifting their arms.

Casey couldn't seem to stop laughing. Before long I'd joined in. It felt so good to laugh. Great tension reliever, and the past few weeks had been filled with their share of tension.

"Want to take a spin around the dance floor, Katie?" Casey took hold of my hand. "For old times' sake?"

I hesitated, but then Casey tugged me to the center of the dance floor as "Unforgettable" played overhead. "It's our song," Casey whispered in my ear as he pulled me into his arms.

Correction. It used to be our song.

Still, as the lyrics rooted themselves in my heart, I found myself caught up in the moment. I settled into Casey's familiar, comfortable embrace and was whisked back in time to the days when we were young and in love.

Out of the corner of my eye I caught a glimpse of Mama staring at me. She turned and whispered something to Pop. No doubt I'd hear about this later. But there was nothing wrong with a girl dancing with an old friend, right?

When the dance ended I shook off my ponderings and headed over to the punch bowl to cool down. Casey's mother lifted an empty glass and filled it for me. "So, you and Casey . . . I'm happy to see the two of you together again."

"Oh, we're not together, Mrs. Lawson. We're just friends."

Her eyebrows elevated as she passed the glass my way. "I see." She lifted another glass for the next guest and I moved out of the way, intrigued by the punch. It appeared to be some sort of reddish-purple fruit drink mixed with sherbet, just like the punch we always had at our church events. So why did Prissy say she was using a family recipe if it was the same old same old?

I'd just started to take a sip when Bessie May rushed my way. "Don't drink the punch!" She snatched the cup out of my hand and set it on a table.

"But I'm thirsty," I said.

She waggled her finger at me. "It's not Baptist-approved."

"Huh?"

"There's a water fountain in the hall. Don't drink the punch."

Okay then. I trotted off to the hallway to the water fountain, where there was quite a line. Weird.

Minutes later I watched as Lori-Lou—visibly pregnant—and Josh danced. Mariela tugged at her skirt as she reached down to pick up Gilly. Off in the distance Alva held little Joshie, who took bites of a cookie. Looking at that cookie made me wonder when—or if—we'd ever get a slice of that yummy-looking cake. Thank goodness Brother Krank's voice came over the sound system, announcing the time had come to cut it.

Queenie looked pretty winded by now. For that matter, Reverend Bradford—er, Pap-Paul—did too. But they made quite a show out of cutting the cake, bragging about the amazing job Ophelia had done.

"I helped her put it together." Prissy planted her hands on her hips. "And I set out the plates."

"Thank you, Prissy." My grandmother held her little plate of cake with a shaky hand. She lifted a piece with her fingers and aimed it at her husband's mouth. Would she do it?

"Oh my." Lori-Lou busted out laughing. "Well, look at that, why don't you."

I couldn't stop looking, actually. Queenie had smeared cake all over the good reverend's face, but he responded by kissing her. When he came up for air, they were both a sticky mess.

Mrs. Lawson handed them cups of punch. I wanted to say, "Don't drink it!" but Queenie took a big sip and then licked her lips.

"Yum. Tastes different this time. Just what the doctor ordered, though."

She got distracted talking to a guest, and Prissy started slicing the cake.

"I know what you're thinking," Casey whispered in my ear.

"You do?" I was thinking I needed a trip to the ladies' room after all the water I drank, but I couldn't remember where it was.

"Yes. You're thinking you want a piece of cake with one of those blue buttercream roses on it."

I faced him. "You remembered. I love extra frosting."

"Of course I remembered. I remember everything about you, Katie. About us."

"Chocolate or white cake, Katie?" Prissy's voice interrupted my thoughts.

"Hmm?"

"There are only two tiers left, girl, so speak now or forever hold your peace. One tier is white, the other is chocolate. What's your poison?"

"Actually, I think the poison's in the punch bowl," I whispered to Casey. "I'll take the white cake," I said to Prissy.

She cut a tiny sliver—*Really? That's all I get?*—and I carried it to the table to devour it.

Casey settled into the chair next to mine. Hanging out with him was getting to be a habit, one that suddenly felt a little strange. I swallowed down the cake and then headed off to find the ladies' room. It was just past the water fountain, which still boasted an exceptionally long line.

When I got inside the bathroom, I heard a familiar voice coming from inside one of the stalls.

"Alva?"

"Yes, honey?"

"Are you singing in there?"

"I just can't help it." She giggled. "They keep playing some of my favorite old songs from days gone by. Just sets my toes to tapping and my heart to singing."

"So you're enjoying the day?"

"Very much." She came out of the stall and washed her hands at the sink. I glanced at our two reflections in the large mirror.

"I saw you dancing with Casey out there," she said.

"Yeah. Don't read too much into it, though, okay?"

She dried her hands and then spoke to my reflection in the mirror. "Listen to me, girl, and listen good." Her voice took on a tone I rarely heard, sort of a chastening sound. "You can't let the little foxes spoil the vine."

"I'm sorry—what?" I turned to face her.

"The little foxes." This time she talked to me rather than my reflection. "It's a verse in the Bible. Look it up. I can't remember the reference or I'd tell you straight up. But it's there. Little foxes get in and spoil the vine."

"What does this have to do with me, Alva?"

"The little foxes are trying to worm their way into your relationship with Brady. To bring confusion. But don't be confused, honey. The Bible says you don't have to be confused."

"It does?"

"Well, something like that. It doesn't specifically say, 'Katie Sue Fisher, you don't have to be confused.' But the point is, you've got to shoo away those little foxes before they ruin everything. They'll eat up all the good grapes, and before long there won't be any left to make a fine wine."

"We don't drink wine in the Baptist church, Alva."

"I'm just trying to say that you need to be on the lookout. The enemy prowls around like a roaring lion, seeking whom he may devour."

"I thought we were talking about foxes."

"Foxes. Lions. It's all the same. Point is, if you want something badly enough, you have to fight for it. You can't let anything—or anyone—steal it away. Even if he's young and handsome and someone you grew up with." She put her hands on her hips. "Got my drift, or do I need to just come out and say it?"

"Alva, is that what you're thinking? You're worried that Casey and I are . . ." I shook my head. "I knew I shouldn't have danced with him."

"I'm just saying that the little foxes try to confuse us. I know, because I've walked a mile in your shoes." She adjusted her girdle. "Well, not in your shoes exactly. I could never wear heels like that, not with my bunions. But I've been in a place where I lost a relationship with the most important person in the world to me, my sister."

"That was completely different, Alva. And I'm not breaking up with Brady. I'm just . . ."

"Confused. Like I said. A common feeling, I know. And Brady's not making it any easier with his pity partying. I'd like to throw that boy a bottle of hope and pray he catches it. But only God can do that. Your mission, should you choose to accept it, is to pray. And to pull out your BB gun."

"My BB gun?"

"It's on the top shelf of your bedroom closet. Shoot those foxes in the backside. Send 'em running." She looked over as Mama entered the ladies' room. "Then I promise you, you'll have fine wine to drink and no confusion at all."

"What's all this talk about wine?" My mother walked over to us. "Is that punch spiked or isn't it? The rumors are rampant."

Alva slapped herself on the forehead. "If it is, don't blame it on me. I'm just a visitor here."

"You're never a visitor in Fairfield, Alva." Mama looped her arm through my aunt's. "You're family."

"Yes, I know. But that wasn't the point. Honestly, some people just aren't as quick on the draw. I suppose I should be blunt, but I've never been one to use a blunt approach." Alva walked out of the ladies' room, muttering under her breath.

"She hasn't?" Mama moved toward a stall. "Sometimes I get so confused."

She wasn't the only one. I found myself a little discombobulated at the moment, but it had nothing to do with the punch.

From inside the stall Mama talked about how beautiful the service had been, but I couldn't stop thinking about Alva's speech. What in the world did all of that chatter have to do with anything?

Okay, so maybe she had a point. Brady's strange back-and-forth behavior over the past few days had left me reeling.

I headed back to the reception hall. Casey took several steps in my direction, his eyes wide. "There's a rumor going around that the punch is spiked." He held up his cup. "Should I go for it?"

"It's your call. You're a Presbyterian. I only know the Baptist protocol."

He took a little sip, his eyes narrowing. He licked his lips. "It's definitely not the same old punch we always had as kids. But I don't think it's spiked. It's something unusual. Kind of . . . gross."

"Tequila? Prissy just got back from a trip to Juarez last month, you know."

He shook his head and chuckled. "No, not tequila. Something else. Something . . . weird. But I think you're safe to try it. Who knows? You might think it's great."

"Not likely, but I'll give it a shot. I'm thirsty."

He filled glasses for both of us and we headed to the far side of the room to sit for a while. I nudged my purse aside, then heard ringing coming from it. Had I really forgotten to turn off the ringer during the ceremony? Ack! Thank goodness it hadn't gone off then. I reached to grab the phone, and my heart leaped when I saw Brady's number. Just as I took the call, Casey settled into the chair next to mine.

"Hey." I did my best to steady my voice. "How are you, Brady?"

As soon as I said Brady's name, Casey's smile faded.

"Feeling better today." In fact, Brady sounded pretty much like his old self. "How's the wedding?"

"It was great. You should've seen her, Brady. She looked like a princess."

"Send me some pictures. Then I can feel like I was there," he said. "I was there in spirit. And I prayed for both of them at exactly ten o'clock."

"That's sweet. Those prayers worked."

"Yeah. That's really why I called. I wanted to tell you that I've had a lot of time to think and to pray since I've been back home."

"O-oh?"

"I want to apologize for pulling away from you, Katie. Please forgive me. But I think God has made good use of the time to really do some serious work in my heart."

My own heart softened immediately. "There's nothing to forgive, Brady." I softened my voice and turned away from Casey. "You've been in pain."

"I have. But that's no excuse to push people away. If I ever needed the people I love, it's right now."

The people I love? Had he really just said that?

"When you get back in town, I'm going to show you the old Brady, I promise. God and I had a long talk, and I need to shake off this depression and have a different perspective."

"He can give you that, Brady. I know he can."

"He's already doing it. But I wanted you to know that I'm sorry I've been such a downer. It's not like me. Ask anyone."

"I don't have to. I know it from personal experience. And you have nothing to apologize for. I'd probably be a mess if I were in your shoes."

"My shoes are a size 13. If you were in them you'd trip over yourself." He laughed long and loud.

Out of the corner of my eye I watched as Casey walked across the room toward Joni. He extended his hand and she took it, then followed him to the dance floor. Interesting.

Not that I really had time to watch them. No, I was far too busy talking to Brady to notice much else.

When our conversation ended, I finally decided to take a swig of the punch. Yuck! Something thick and pulpy greeted

232

me. Very strange. One sip was more than enough to convince me to stick to water.

Mama showed up at just that moment. She took one look at the glass in my hand and pinched her eyes shut. "You drank some?"

"Unfortunately."

Her eyes popped open. "I guess you didn't get the memo?"

"About the punch?"

"About the secret ingredient."

"We've been trying to figure it out all afternoon. What's going on, Mama? What is it?"

"You sure you want to know, Katie?"

"Well, of course."

"You might want to put that down first." She took my glass and tossed it into a nearby trash container. "Because what you're drinking there, sweet girl, is guaranteed to set your stomach on fire."

"Mama, are you saying it's really . . ."

"Yep. You've got it." Mama paled as she whispered, "That punch is 100 proof prune juice."

22

A Very Precious Love

She [Doris Day] was always gracious no matter what the situation. There are such people whose very presence seems to make life a little brighter.

Leo Fuchs

Somehow I survived the prune juice saga, though I heard that several others, including Queenie herself, had a rough twenty-four hours after the fact. By the time I headed back to Dallas on Sunday afternoon, the whole town was recovering. Many were also on the prowl looking for Prissy, who—it was rumored—had decided to take a last-minute trip to the Panhandle. Coward.

I gathered my things, along with Aunt Alva, and loaded up

my car. We hit the road around three o'clock, though it felt more like evening to me due to my exhaustion. Our peaceful trip was interrupted by a call from Carrie, who always managed to get me when I was on the road. Thank goodness for Bluetooth. I answered with a cheerful "Hello?" and her voice rang out over the car's speaker. Alva perked right up when she heard the familiar voice.

"I'm so excited about seeing the dress." Carrie giggled. "Tomorrow, three o'clock? Do you think Eduardo has made enough progress for me to try it on?" Before I could respond, she rattled off a thousand reasons why it just had to work out for her to try that dress on tomorrow.

"I really like this program, Katie." Alva sat on the edge of her seat, hands on her knees. "It reminds me a lot of those old radio dramas we used to listen to when I was a kid, and it always leaves you hanging at the end. Until the next episode, I mean. I've always loved a good cliff-hanger."

"Excuse me?" Carrie said. "Did someone say something about hangers? For the dress?"

"Sorry, Carrie." How could I fix this? "Aunt Alva and I are driving back to Dallas today. My grandmother got married yesterday."

"Oh, that's right." Carrie's voice grew more animated. "You told me! And she got her dress from Cosmopolitan too, right?"

"Yes."

"Anyone who's *anyone* gets their wedding dress from Cosmopolitan. Mama's friends are going to be green with envy."

Alva looked at me, eyes narrowed. "Is this a commercial break from the regularly scheduled program?"

"What?"

She pointed at the radio. "Sounds like that woman's doing a commercial for the bridal shop."

"Oh, I could. I so could." Carrie giggled. "But we'll save that for a later date. Right now all I can think about is my dress. Can't wait to see it."

Time to give this girl a reality check. "I think Eduardo's made great strides with the gown, Carrie, but don't be too disappointed if you see bits and pieces of it missing still." I put on my turn signal to exit onto 287. "These things take time, you know."

"Oh, I won't be disappointed. Much." She giggled. "And speaking of Eduardo, that man is so awesome. And talented. And gracious. And sweet on the ladies. Anyway, I'm looking forward to seeing you again, Katie." Her voice raised as she said, "And you too, Alva." At that, the call ended.

Alva gasped. "Merciful heavens, how did that radio show know *I* was in the car?" Her tone grew more intense. "The government has spies watching us from all over. I read all about it in an article on that book face site."

"Facebook?" I tried.

"No, I don't want to put my face into a book. But I guess that's part of their evil plan. They are probably photographing us now."

"What?"

"I'm telling you, that radio show—that drama about the wedding dress—is really an inside job from the government. They're watching us." She pointed at the screen in the middle of my console. "I wouldn't be a bit surprised if they knew where we were at all times."

I pointed at the GPS. "They kind of do. And they make it easy for us to know too."

"Ack." She scooted down in her seat. "If they want any more information about me, they're going to have to come and beat it out of me." Alva leaned her head back on the seat and closed her eyes. "And how dare that woman add Eduardo as a character to her radio show. Did you hear all of those things she said about him? I do agree that he's suave. A woman would have to be blind not to notice that. But all of those other things? You would think she was trying to steal him away, and isn't she already engaged to someone else?"

"Well, yes, but—"

"That's the problem with these soap operas." Alva yawned. "Nobody cares if they're engaged or married to one person. They're off having affairs with another. I refuse to saturate my mind with that garbage. Turn it off, Katie, if you please."

"But it's not a . . . oh, never mind." I turned the radio to a station that played worship music and listened to it all the way back to Dallas. When we arrived at Alva's house, I woke her up and she yawned and stretched.

"That was a short little catnap." She sat up and then let out a gasp. "Ooh, my bladder's about to burst. Better get inside. Pray I make it."

She made it. I did too. And though I didn't feel like cleaning out my car, I decided I'd better. Tomorrow would be crazy, especially if Carrie and her crew came to the shop.

I slept like a log in my own bed that night. Well, the bed that I'd adopted after moving in with Alva. I had the strangest dreams, though. Brides. Grooms. Bridesmaids. Prune juice. Ick.

The next morning I awoke refreshed and ready to face a new week. Hopefully Brady would be in good spirits. I could hardly wait to see him. I showered and dressed, then headed to the kitchen, where I found Alva fumbling with an old radio she'd placed on the kitchen counter. "What station is that program on, Katie?"

"Program?"

"The one we always listen to in the car. They've hooked me with that Eduardo character. I want to listen to it again."

Good grief. "I have a better idea, Alva. Why don't you come to work with me today?"

She looked flabbergasted by this idea. "Why?"

"Because Carrie Sanders, the star of that program, is coming in person to the shop."

"No!" Alva clasped her hand over her mouth. "Seriously?"

"Seriously. And you can meet her firsthand, and her crazy family."

"I'll be ready in two shakes of a lamb's tail." Alva practically sprinted out of the room. She came back a few minutes later, fully dressed with a bit of makeup on. I let out a whistle.

"My, don't you clean up nice."

"I want to look my best. It's not every day one meets a movie star."

"She's hardly a movie star, Alva."

"Still . . ."

We made the drive to Cosmopolitan with my aunt talking a mile a minute. I'd planned to fill her in, to explain how the Bluetooth worked and share the truth—that Carrie was just a gal from San Antonio who happened to be purchasing her gown from us. But I never got the chance, thanks to chatterbox Alva. Hopefully I could get it all straightened out before day's end. No point in stringing her along much longer.

We arrived at the store at eight forty-five, just behind Madge, who was unlocking the front door.

"The most wonderful news, Madge!" Alva hurried through the door of the shop. "We're meeting superstars today."

"Superstars?" Madge tossed the keys on the front counter. "And who would that be?"

"Have you invited Doris Day to join us?" Eduardo asked as he entered the store. "Is that what this is about?"

"No, not Doris. It's some actress named Carrie. She does a radio show." Alva grabbed Eduardo's hand. "She's turned you into a character, but I'm not sure I like where the plot is heading." She gripped his hand and he gazed into her eyes.

"Really?" Eduardo gave her hand a squeeze. "I daresay I do like where the plot is heading. Now, why don't you come into the studio and tell me all about it."

She followed on his heels, chattering all the way.

By now Twiggy, Dahlia, Hibiscus, and Jane had joined us. They stood wide-eyed as my aunt sauntered back into the studio with Eduardo.

"Well, if that doesn't beat all." Madge tossed her purse on the counter.

"Am I the only one who's noticed that Alva's wearing makeup?" Hibiscus asked.

"No, I noticed too." Twiggy opened the cash register and a little ding sounded. She slammed it shut. "Weird."

"What's up with that, Katie?" Hibiscus asked.

"Oh, she heard that someone famous was coming today, so she got gussied up for the occasion."

"Someone famous? Who?" Madge asked. "I don't remember hearing anything about that."

"No one, actually. It was a big misunderstanding. But she just got prettied up to see someone special."

"So strange." Madge shrugged and got busy arranging veils on a nearby rack.

I was just about to say more when Eduardo entered the shop from the back hallway, gown in hand. He sang "Feliz Navidad" at the top of his lungs as he hung the dress on a rack between several others. Alva's voice rang out in perfect harmony from the far end of the hall. Eduardo smiled, then the two headed back to the studio, singing all the way, their voices perfectly blended.

We all froze. Dahlia broke the silence first with an "Oh my goodness."

"Are you thinking what I'm thinking?" Twiggy asked.

Everyone nodded. I'd never given the notion a second's thought, but there it was, staring all of us in the face: Eduardo and Alva. Two peas in a pod. Him with his televangelist hair and her with her frizzy 'do and Mavericks T-shirts.

"That's it!" Hibiscus giggled. "Eduardo is the 'someone special' she got gussied up for. Surely you've seen signs, Katie. These things don't just happen overnight."

"She has been talking a lot about Prince Charming, but mostly about how he doesn't exist. But you're right about the makeup. She got all dolled up for the wedding. Lori-Lou talked her into putting her hair up and wearing a little lipstick and blush. And eyeliner. That was really some feat."

"Oh my." Jane shook her head. "Even I still struggle with that."

"Yes, that didn't end well, but the point is, she wanted to give it a shot, and she had a lot of compliments on her looks at the reception, which she seemed to like."

"Why does a woman who's never worn makeup suddenly want to look nice?" Twiggy put her hands on her hips. "Only one reason, and we just saw it with our own eyes. She wants to impress Eduardo."

"Maybe," I said. "Or maybe wearing makeup makes her feel better about herself. I'm not disputing the notion that she has a crush on Eduardo, but maybe there's more to it than that. We all know that doing the best we can with what's on the outside makes us feel better on the inside."

At this, Jane grew quiet. She swung her purse over her shoulder and headed toward the studio. "I guess I'd better get back to work." She hurried down the hallway, never looking back.

I glanced at Dahlia, who seemed a bit puzzled by this behavior. "What was that about?" I asked.

"Not sure. I think you struck a nerve."

We had to end the conversation because a customer entered. I headed back to my office, deep in thought about the conversation with the ladies. Surely they were imagining the situation with Alva and Eduardo, right? Then again, she had perked up at his appearance on the "radio show."

Brady arrived around eleven and greeted me in my office with a kiss and a bundle of red roses.

"What are these for?" I asked.

"Because, Katie Sue Fisher, I'm layin' claim to you, remember?"

"Oh, that's right. Well, these ought to seal the deal."

"Hope so. Hey, do you have a few minutes to talk?" He leaned his crutches against the wall and hopped over to a chair to sit down.

"Sure."

"First, I really meant what I said on the phone the other day. You've been the most patient person on the planet where I'm concerned. I've been so worried about my stupid career and my bum knee that I didn't think you would want to commit to a long-term relationship with me."

"Surely you didn't really think that?" I took a seat in the chair across from him.

He leaned forward and put his elbows on the desk. "I didn't know if I could offer you the kind of life you deserve. When I'm out on the court, I'm in my element. I'm in the zone. Doing what comes naturally to me. And I'm earning a great income.

I don't want to make too much of that, but it's a blow to the pocketbook to have my career come to an end, you know?"

"But you do well at the shop, right?"

"Yeah. But I'm kind of a fish out of water here. I think I just wanted you to be proud of me."

"I *am* proud of you, Brady. You've done exactly what a good son would do—swept in and made things right for your mom while she's off in Paris fulfilling her dream."

"And all the while, I've felt like my own dream is dying."

"Oh, Brady . . ."

His eyes glistened. "There's nothing worse than the death of a dream. I spent most of this past season acting like it didn't affect me. But trust me when I say that it has. It's not just the pain. I can live with that. It's the not knowing if I'll have a shot again, and I don't mean that as a pun."

"I—I know."

"If they don't renew my contract, then a piece of my identity will be forever missing."

"But Brady, your identity isn't in basketball. It's in Christ."

"I know that." He reached across the desk for my hands and I placed them in his. "I do. And I've memorized those lines, trust me. I want to be confident in that. And if working in a bridal shop is what he has for me, then I need to be okay with it. But I don't know if I can honestly say that I'm giving the woman I love the best possible life if I'm not content with it. You know?"

Wait. Did he just say "the woman I love"?

I rose from my chair and walked around to his side of the desk, then knelt beside him, unable to control my tears. "Brady James, listen to me. You're the best man I've ever known. You've shown me how to be strong when I felt weak. You've shown me what it means to stick with your family, even when it's hard. And you're even teaching me how to transition from one stage of life to another. We don't know for sure that you won't play again. Maybe this is just a season. But the truth is, we have to trust God with the seasons."

"There's that sermon again." He smiled and kissed me. And kissed me again. In fact, he kept kissing me until every doubt I'd ever had about our relationship was completely washed away.

When we finally came up for air, I let out a whistle. "Wowza."

"Yeah. Sorry, got carried away. But it's hard to hide my feelings when you're around, Katie."

"Because . . ."

Crinkles formed around his eyes as he smiled. "Because I love you. I've loved you ever since that first day we went to the stockyard together to scope out a location for the cover shoot. And I love you even more now than I did then. Any more questions?"

"Only one." I reached over and picked up the roses. "Do we have a vase somewhere? I want to show off these flowers."

He laughed. "Try the studio. They keep all sorts of things in the kitchen back there."

"I will. Oh, one more thing before I go."

"Yes?"

I snaked my arms around his neck and planted a kiss on him that he wouldn't soon forget. "Just that," I said when I released my hold on him. "Just that."

23

Cuddle Up a Little Closer

There were times when I wasn't always up. Everything could be calm and peaceful, then the next day the bottom dropped out. What can you do? Moan and groan and feel sorry for yourself? No, you pull yourself up by your bootstraps and you get on with life.

Doris Day

I headed back to the studio to find something that might work as a vase. I found Aunt Alva and Eduardo side by side, working on Carrie's gown.

"Ooh, you got red roses, honey." Alva moved toward me and sniffed them. "Luscious. Would you believe no one has ever given me flowers? Oh, but these are perfect. Let me help you find a glass to put them in."

A couple of minutes later she located a tall glass just sturdy enough to hold them. I filled it with a few inches of water and settled the stems inside, then stood back to have a look.

"Exquisite." Alva clasped her hands to her chest. "Just the sweetest thing ever."

I had to agree. My gaze shifted to Eduardo. "How's it going, Eduardo? Are you going to be ready for Carrie by three?"

"Should be. Not finished, obviously, but we're making progress."

"We?"

Alva squared her shoulders. "He put me to work gluing on sequins."

"Austrian crystals," he said.

"Right. Crystals. Whatever." Alva shrugged. "Point is, I'm exhausted and starving. We skipped breakfast this morning, remember? When you're my age you can't afford to skip a meal."

"I'm hungry too."

"Good." She clapped her hands and spoke to everyone in the room. "Who wants to go out for Mexican food? I love the tamales at El Burrito."

"Sounds yummy," Hibiscus said.

Jane shook her head. "No thanks. I brought a peanut butter sandwich."

"Oh, but one day away from your sandwich won't hurt you. I just love the food at El Burrito." Alva carried on about her now-favorite restaurant.

"El Burrito." Eduardo went off in Spanish about how much he hated the Mexican restaurant next door. Not that I spoke Spanish, but the look on his face made it pretty clear how he felt about Tex-Mex fast food. He turned to face Alva. "If you want real Mexican food, come to my place. Saturday. Seven o'clock."

My aunt's face turned as red as the bridesmaid dress Hibiscus was altering. "C-come to y-your place?"

"I'll show you Mexican food. Real Mexican food." He looked my way. "You too, Katie. Come. Bring Brady. I'll cook my mama's tamales and taco soup."

"I don't know if I'm free Saturday night." My aunt fanned herself. "There's a game on."

"A game?" He rolled his eyes. "You're going to let a ball game stand between you and the best Mexican food this side of the Rio Grande? What's wrong with you, woman?"

At this point Eduardo and Alva got into a bit of an argument about whether or not she could watch the game at his place. They lost me about halfway into it. I was far too distracted watching Jane, who had paused from her work to walk to the refrigerator. Something was up with that girl. I just knew it.

I moved toward her, hoping to catch a few words with her before we left for lunch.

"Jane?"

She turned around and I saw a mist in her eyes. "Hmm?"

"Jane." I lowered my voice. "What's going on? Are you okay? Was it something I said earlier?"

She glanced over at Alva and Eduardo, who were still going at it, and sighed. "I think maybe I just need some time to think."

"About what?"

She gestured to her dark red hair and exaggerated lip- and eyeliner. "I think I've been trying to change my outward appearance so that I'll feel better about myself. What you said about the outside matching the inside hit me the wrong way. Or the right way. I'm not sure which."

"You're a beautiful girl, Jane." I rested my hand on her arm.

"I'm a caricature."

"What?"

"I heard Eduardo say it. He didn't know I heard but I did. The day we had the extravaganza. He told Hi that I keep changing costumes and hairdos because I'm not happy with the real me."

"It's none of his business," I said.

"Right. It's not." She chewed on her lower lip. "But I think it's true. Maybe a little bit." She slapped herself on the forehead and mumbled, "Okay, it's a lot true."

"But why?" I asked. "You're one of the most wonderful people I've ever known. Everyone thinks so."

She took a seat and rested her elbows on the table. "I think I just want to be memorable. So I'm always changing things up because maybe then people will say, 'Oh yeah, she's that girl who has a different color hair every time I see her.'" She gave me a pensive look. "Does that make sense? They'll remember me if I stand out. Only, now I'm not sure that's really the kind of memory I want people to have." She released a slow breath and looked at me so intently I almost felt uncomfortable. "I think I'm a little jealous of you, Katie."

"What? You're jealous of . . . me?"

"Yeah."

"Ordinary Katie from Fairfield? Didn't-even-go-to-college Katie? Katie-who-wasn't-sure-she'd-ever-leave-her-small-town Katie? Why in the world would you be jealous of *me*?"

"Because you are like a rock. You hold steady, no matter what changes are going on around you."

"I do?" It took me by complete surprise that she saw me this way. "I kind of thought I freaked out at every little thing. Rocks don't panic."

"But look at you," she said. "All this stuff with Brady, and you're right there, holding firm. And the stuff going on back in Fairfield—you're right there, helping your grandmother with everything she needs. And here at the shop? When things are in trouble, who comes to the rescue? Katie. You're constant. You never feel like you have to change anything."

"Are we talking hair and makeup here or something else?"

"Something else. Remember that conversation with Madge? The one where you said that life moves in seasons?"

"Yeah. Had a similar conversation with Brady about that very thing just now. Everything is seasonal."

"Well, that's my point. I guess I'm a little jealous that you seem to survive the seasons better than I do. They change but you don't. Me? I change even when the seasons don't." She gave a strained laugh. "Change, change, change."

"Wow. I don't even know what to say." As I thought about the chaos of the past few weeks, tears sprang to my eyes. "I'm not constant, Jane. I'm not. But God is. And if I've learned anything, it's that I can trust him in the seasons. When things are hard, I always tell myself, 'It's winter, but springtime is coming.' Because if you think about it, spring always comes. Even when dreams are dying or relationships are ending, springtime is coming. So we can't give up."

I caught a glimpse of Dahlia as she took a few steps in our direction. "Okay, sorry. I didn't mean to listen in." Her cheeks flushed. "Or maybe I did. But I have to say something here." She looked at Jane. "First of all, I liked your hair when you were a brunette, but I guess that's off the point."

"Really?" A smile turned up the edges of Jane's lips. "'Cause that's my favorite too. Actually, that's my natural color."

"I know." Dahlia stuck a pin in the pincushion on her wrist. "But what I wanted to say was this: I've spent this whole crazy season in a panic. I thought I wasn't going to make it through all of those Loretta Lynn gowns. And I let that panic affect other areas of my life, like my relationship with Dewey." Her eyes took on a faraway look. "That precious guy wouldn't give up on me."

"Are you saying you've decided to marry him and have fourteen children and live in the country?" Jane looked stunned by this possibility.

"No. I'm saying that I let a few things he told me get blown out of proportion, and in my mind that's what I thought he wanted. Turns out he just wanted to talk about options. He's okay with whatever happens, as long as it happens to us together."

"What are you saying, Dahlia?" Jane asked.

The most beautiful smile brightened Dahlia's countenance. "I'm saying we're a couple again, and it's because of the very thing you said, Katie. I realized the season I was walking through—with all the craziness at the shop—would eventually come to an end. All seasons do. They morph into a different season. So springtime is coming for me and Dewey."

"What about the whole Baptist-Lutheran thing?" Jane asked. "Did you get that settled?"

"Yes. This week we're going to start looking for a church here in the Dallas area that we both love. We'll keep searching until we hit the one that makes sense. We're both Christians. We'll find the right home." A contented look came over her.

"Wow." Jane sighed. "Now I'm a little envious of both of you."

"You don't have to be," I said. "The kind of peace that she's talking about is just God's grace. It's there for anyone who wants it."

"It's a lot to take in. But right now I just have to figure out when I should take my hair back to its natural color."

"Don't be in a rush to change it on our account," I said.

"But do go back to brunette." Dahlia gave her a knowing look.

Across the room Alva and Eduardo had gone back to work on the dress. They were all laughter and smiles.

"So, did you hear him invite her over for dinner?" Dahlia whispered. "I think maybe we're onto something."

"No, I think maybe *they're* onto something." Jane gestured with her head to Eduardo, who held the wedding gown up in front of Alva as if trying to envision it on her.

Alrighty then. Enough with all of that.

"I'm ready for lunch, Auntie!" I called out. "Who's up for some Mexican food?"

That seemed to work. She pried herself away from the workstation and we headed next door—Alva, Dahlia, Hibiscus, Twiggy, and me—for some girl time. I made a point not to mention Eduardo, but Twiggy took advantage of every opportunity to bring up his name. Auntie played dumb, but I could read through her act. She liked him. She really, really liked him.

When lunch ended we got back to work. By the time Carrie arrived at three, I was almost caught up with my paperwork and this week's flyer. She breezed into the store completely alone, and I led her back to the studio.

"Can you believe I'm here by myself?" Carrie asked. "It took a miracle, but I managed it. My parents are celebrating their anniversary tonight and Jimmy is out of town on a business trip. So I decided this would be the perfect day to—" She stopped cold when she saw her wedding gown on the dress form. "Oh!" Her hand flew to her mouth and tears sprang to her eyes. "Th-that's mine?"

Eduardo walked our way and held out his hand. She took

it and he kissed the back of her hand. "Miss Carrie, your wedding gown awaits." He led her to the dress, gushing over how beautiful it would look on her.

"I . . . I just can't believe it." She reached out to touch the crystals on the bodice. "It's the most beautiful thing I've ever seen." She continued to gush, finally reaching over to give Eduardo a hug. "Oh, I knew we did the right thing by coming here. Yes, this was Nadia's idea—having a Doris Day dress—but you're the one, Eduardo, who made it happen for me. I've never been this happy . . . In. My. Life!"

"Glad to be of service, my dear." He gave a little bow.

"Eduardo is quite the artiste, is he not?" Dahlia walked over to join us. "He's probably the most brilliant designer I've ever known, next to Nadia, of course."

"She should make you a partner." Carrie fingered the brooch on the left shoulder of the gown. "She really, really should. You're worth far more than whatever she's paying you."

"Yes." Eduardo's gaze narrowed. "So I have told her." A glorious laugh followed his words. "I am joking, friends! To work for Nadia is a privilege. I am blessed to be in this wonderful place with these amazing people." For whatever reason, his gaze landed squarely on Alva, not the seamstresses.

Dahlia reached for the gown, unfastening the buttons that ran down the side. "Now, as Eduardo said, it's not done yet. We'll be pinning up the hem today, so I hope you're wearing heels."

"Oh, I am." Carrie showed us her beautiful gold pumps and Eduardo gasped.

"Exquisite."

"We'll also be looking at several alterations on the waistline, I think," Dahlia said. "So don't be disappointed if the fit isn't perfect just yet. It will be, I promise. And the draping will need some adjustment. We'll also need to check the back to make sure the fabric plunges to just the right spot."

Turned out the fit was nearly perfect already. Inside the small dressing room Dahlia and I helped Carrie into the gown and fastened the buttons, then we examined the glorious dress from every angle.

"This is about as close as we've ever come to perfection," Dahlia said. "Just a couple of nips and tucks . . ." She pulled three straight pins out of the pincushion on her wrist and stuck one in the right shoulder and one on either side of the waistline. "Have you lost a little weight since your first fitting?"

"Nerves." Carrie turned to look at the dress's train. "Oh, but I had nothing to worry about. This dress solves everything. My father will finally have to admit that we made the right decision, and Mama will be happy because she'll get to brag to her friends that she bought my dress from Cosmopolitan. It's a win-win situation."

"But how do you feel about it, Carrie?" I asked. "I mean, factoring your parents out, how does the dress make *you* feel?"

Another glance in the mirror and her eyes flooded with tears. "It makes me feel like bursting into a Doris Day song. Something joyous. Something positive."

"'Que Sera, Sera'!" Alva's voice rang out from the other side of the dressing room. Seconds later she and Eduardo were both singing at the top of their lungs in perfect harmony.

"Well, there you go." I laughed. "Your dress has musical powers."

Dahlia opened the door and led us back to the studio. Eduardo took one look at Carrie and burst into tears. "It's not manly to cry, I know." He sniffled. "But I cannot help myself. This is one of the finest moments of my life, and you, my dear, are the picture of perfection, the ideal bride-to-be in the dress of any man's dreams."

"When you put it like that . . ." Tears brimmed over Carrie's lashes.

Alva went to find some tissues and returned to press them into Eduardo's hands. Minutes later he'd gotten things under control and was busy pinning the hem of the dress.

"When should I return to pick up the dress?" Carrie asked.

"The week after Christmas," Eduardo said. "If that works for you."

"It does. Oh, I can't wait until Jimmy sees me coming down the aisle in this gown. You've saved the day, Eduardo. Everyone will be so happy."

They continued to chat as he tucked the right shoulder seam. After she changed back into her regular clothes, she lingered in the studio to fill us in on the details of her big day, describing in detail the venue, the flowers, even the music.

"January 8th. It's going to be the best day of my life." She sighed. "And nothing and no one can stop it."

"Who would want to, beautiful girl?" Alva wrapped her in a warm hug. "You deserve the very best."

"And I've got it." Her eyes flooded again. "The best groom, the best dress . . ." She looked at all of us. "And the best design team on the planet. You've truly become friends to me, and I'm so happy to have all of you in my life."

She left a few minutes later, but her joy had lifted us all to a new level. I could feel the energy in the room.

"And *that's* how we do it in the Cosmopolitan studio," Dahlia said and then laughed.

Everyone went back to work, and Eduardo put Carrie's gown back on the dress form. He seemed a bit distracted, though.

"Are you all right, Eduardo?" Alva asked.

He turned to face her. "Yes. But when will you stop being so stubborn, old woman?"

"W-what?" Alva stopped in her tracks. "What did you call me?"

"Stubborn." He fussed with the buttons on the dress.

"No, the other part."

He turned to face her and reached for her hand. "When will you come to my house for tamales? I invited you, but you didn't give me a proper answer. You argued with me about basketball, but you never agreed to spend the evening with me. What do I have to do to make that happen?"

That stopped her in her tracks. I'd never seen Aunt Alva speechless before, but that pretty much did it.

"The invitation stands. You are all invited to Eduardo's place on Saturday night for dinner. Seven o'clock. There will be no basketball. None. We will watch Doris at her finest, wearing the gown that I re-created for our beautiful bride. And you . . ." He gave Alva's hand a squeeze. "You will be my guest of honor."

"Well then." Alva giggled. "How could a girl say no to an invitation like that?"

How indeed?

24

Teacher's Pet

I grieve for Doris Day and the ignorance that regards her as old-fashioned.

David Thomson

I'd seen my aunt in an agitated state before, but nothing compared to the days leading up to her date with Eduardo. She must've gone through every item in her wardrobe a dozen times, looking for just the right ensemble. In the end I took her shopping for a new blouse and slacks. Then I took her to the salon to have her hair styled. When the stylist finished, I gasped. "Alva! You look like Queenie."

"I do, don't I?" She fussed with her hair as she gazed at her reflection in the mirror. "We are sisters, after all."

"This style is so becoming on you. It's perfect." I nudged her with my elbow. "You're going to knock Eduardo off his feet."

"Oh, I hope not. I'd like to keep him upright. At our age, a fall like that could break a hip."

On Saturday afternoon I thought she was going to back out. She made herself sick with nerves. But when it came time to leave to pick up Brady, she hopped into my car, ready to roll. Well, hopped might not be the most accurate word to describe it, but at least she landed in the passenger seat.

"Now, I don't want to hurt your feelings, Katie Sue, but please don't turn on the radio today, all right? I don't think I have the energy to get caught up in that program. I'll spend the whole evening wondering what's going to happen next instead of focusing on our host."

As if anything could keep her mind off Eduardo.

We stopped at Brady's condo to pick him up, and I had to laugh when he came out dressed in a rather dapper outfit from the fifties.

"Don't ask." He groaned as he got into the backseat. "I'm under strict orders from Eduardo to wear this . . . or else."

"Or else what?" I asked.

"Who knows." Brady tugged at the scarf around his neck and closed the door. "But I wouldn't go against it. I'm surprised he didn't give you some sort of dress code."

"If he did, we missed it."

My GPS led me straight to Eduardo's house. I'd never given one second's thought to the kind of home he might have, so I was stymied when we pulled into the most magnificent neighborhood I'd ever seen.

"Wow." Alva sat up straighter in her seat. "Do you think we're in the right place?"

"Yeah, it's right," Brady said. "Eduardo had quite the life in Los Angeles. Worked in movies for years. So he accumulated quite a bit of wealth."

"That would be an understatement," I said.

"Oh dear." Alva looked as if she might be sick. "I hadn't counted on that."

"What should it matter, Alva?" Brady asked.

"Why would a wealthy bachelor with all of the beautiful starlets from LA to choose from be interested in a middle-class gal like me, one who can't even pick out her own outfit?"

"You're a prize catch," Brady said. "He's lucky to have you."

She giggled. "He doesn't exactly have me just yet. This is just our first date, after all. And I'm so thrilled you two were willing to double with us."

Brady nodded. "Happy to be of service."

To enter the gated community I had to show my ID to a guard. He nodded and let us through. Moments later we pulled up in front of a glorious Spanish-style home with wrought-iron embellishments and grandiose windows.

"Wowza." I let out a whistle.

"Here goes nothin'." Alva opened her door before I even had a chance to put the car into park.

"Hold your horses there, Alva," Brady said. "Let me be a gentleman and get your door."

"Hurry it up, then." She sat in place until Brady hobbled to her door in his walking boot.

We hadn't even made it to the front door when Eduardo met us on the front patio dressed in the most interesting getup, a pink cardigan and wool flannel pants in a dark gray. Even the loafer-style shoes were costume-like. But nothing came close to the hair. I'd seen it televangelist style, smoothed over to the side, but never slicked back in James Dean fashion.

"Ooh, you look just like Rock Hudson!" Alva said as she headed his way.

"That's the idea, my dear." He extended his arm and she looped hers through it. "Now, let me show you inside."

I'd come across some eccentric houses in my day, but nothing like Eduardo's world. On nearly every wall hung photos of women in beautiful dresses from the 1930s to present day. He had it all.

Brady let out a whistle. "Man. No wonder Mom wanted Eduardo to come to Texas so badly. This is all right up her alley."

"Yes, up her alley, all right." Eduardo reached to take Alva's coat. "She knows that I specialize in dresses from the old days. My life was—and is—the movies. I just adore the women of old."

"Then you're in luck tonight," Alva said.

That got a laugh out of everyone.

He showed us around the fabulous home and then led us to the dining room where a waiter—Really? A waiter?—tended to our every need while we ate homemade tamales. They were, as he'd said, the yummiest I'd ever eaten. And the taco soup was divine.

Alva didn't manage to eat much. I had a feeling this whole thing was a bit much for her. The poor old girl was a nervous wreck, though Eduardo did everything possible to put her at ease. After we ate our dinner, we topped it off with homemade sopapillas.

Then Eduardo rose and gestured for us to join him. "Now, my friends, let's go to the theater."

"Oh, I've been asking Katie for weeks to take me back to a picture show," Alva said. "A good clean one this time, of course. None of that hanky-panky. So where are we headed? One of those newfangled places with the seats that recline?"

"The seats recline, yes," Eduardo said. "But we won't have to go far, I assure you."

He led the way down the hall and up the massive rounded stairway to a hallway upstairs. There, to our right, was a flashing marquee. "Welcome to the Theater de la Consuela," Eduardo said.

"For pity's sake." Alva leaned against the wall. "You have a theater in your home?"

"Certainly. I couldn't live without it. I spend a lot of hours in here, dreaming up dress designs and reliving the old days. Like the day I met Doris for the first time, for instance. We were on the set of *Pillow Talk* together, you know."

"I think I might have to sit down." Alva fanned herself with her hand. "You actually worked on that movie? I had no idea."

"I worked in the costume department. Then again, I was a peon at the time. A nobody. But I met them all. Do you need to sit, Alva?"

"Eventually. Give me a minute to let this sink in."

"You met Rock Hudson?" Now Brady seemed genuinely interested.

"I did. But I worked on the costumes for Doris alongside Jean Louis, one of the greatest designers ever to grace the movie world."

"He's making all of this up." Alva looked my way. "C'mon, Eduardo. Seriously?"

"I assure you, I am not. And I have the proof." Eduardo pointed to a photo just outside of the theater. Doris Day. A signed copy. Next to her stood a startlingly handsome young man who looked just like a younger version of . . .

"Eduardo?" I pointed to the photograph. "That's you?"

"Well, twenty pounds and fifty-six years ago, yes. I was

young. Invincible. Nothing could stop me." He appeared to drift off into his thoughts. Until he happened to gaze at my aunt.

"I don't know what to say." Alva stared at him as if seeing him for the first time. "Who else did you meet?"

"It might be easier to tell you who I didn't meet." He paused. "Back then, everyone knew everyone. We were all one big happy family on the movie sets. So before we watch the show, please allow me to show you my photos from the old days." He led the way into the theater and I gasped as I saw three rows of upscale theater seats. And the walls! They were decked out with signed photographs. Nearly every famous star from the fifties, sixties, and seventies made an appearance.

"Eduardo, you knew all of these people?" I stood in front of an exquisite photo of Audrey Hepburn surrounded by a gilded frame.

"But of course."

"John Wayne?" Brady pointed to an elaborately framed picture of the great actor.

"Quite a challenge to fit into costumes, but yes. Wonderful man. Very talented."

"And of course . . ." Alva squinted as she took in a photo of Doris Day. "Just as you said. You really knew Doris Day."

"We were closer than most," he said. "I haven't spoken to her for some time, but she was once a true friend, which is why I was so pleased to work on the bridal gown for Miss Sanders." He paused next to Alva. "You see what she's wearing? Doris was such a role model for young women of her day."

"Women of this day too," Alva said.

Eduardo pointed at the photo. "She became known for the sheath dress—or the wiggle dress, as many called it."

"Wiggle dress?" Brady looked perplexed.

"Yes." Eduardo chuckled. "It fit to the woman's figure in such a way that every wiggle showed. Thanks to Doris, this style really took off. Before we knew what hit us, women all over the country wanted the wiggle dress. Quite popular in its day, I daresay."

"I owned quite a few myself." Alva laughed. "Back when my wiggle was a bit . . . well . . . less wiggly."

"I would love to create a gown for you, Alva." Eduardo gazed into her eyes. "It would be my great honor." He took hold of her hands and held them tight.

"Is it warm in here?" Alva looked as if she might faint.

"I will adjust the thermostat." He did so and then showed off several more photos of Doris, each in a different dress or coat. "She was the original urban sophisticate," he said. "And the queen of turtlenecks. Did you ever notice how many turtlenecks she wore?"

"Never paid much attention, I guess." Alva gave the photos a closer look.

Eduardo's right eyebrow elevated. "What do you suppose she was trying to say with those turtlenecks?"

"She was cold?" I tried.

"Hardly. It was a symbol of her purity. Covered up from the chin down. See what I mean? An article of clothing can speak volumes." Eduardo went on to talk about her penchant for little bobbed hats, beautiful coats, and glorious collars. I'd never given a moment's thought to any of this, but I made up my mind to pay attention as we watched the show.

"Before we begin, I want to fill you in on Doris. Her last name wasn't Day originally. She was born Doris Mary Ann von Kappelhoff."

"That's quite a mouthful," Alva said. "No wonder she went with Day."

"She was born in Ohio and started as a singer with Les Brown in the forties. Anything else you want to know?"

"You've sure memorized a lot of facts about her," Brady said.

"I study a film's actors before I ever watch it and try to commit to memory their real-life stories, which, to my way of thinking, are even more fascinating than the characters they play."

"My goodness." Alva shook her head. "I just go to the movies, eat my popcorn, and watch the show. Never thought about all of that."

"Just my habit," Eduardo said. "Now, are we ready for the movie? I'll pop some popcorn, if so."

"You have a popcorn machine?" Alva asked. She mouthed, "Wow."

"I'm a sucker for movie popcorn," he said. "It's my weakness."

"Mine too." They gazed at each other in complete silence as if frozen in time. Well, until Brady snorted. I didn't blame him. The whole thing was pure cheese, but what fun!

Eduardo told us to choose our seats. Alva settled on one in the second row and Brady and I took a couple of seats in the third. Eduardo got the popcorn going and soon the luscious scent filled the room. Not that I had room in my stomach for one more bite of food, but I never turned down popcorn.

Minutes later he settled into the recliner next to Alva. I peeked over the edge of the seat and caught a glimpse of him taking her hand. The lights in the room went dim as the movie started. Before long we were all laughing . . . and sighing . . . and laughing. I found myself caught up in the moment, and all the more when Doris appeared in that glorious white dress.

"Ooh, she looks just like our young bride," Alva said. "Only the dress you made is even prettier, Eduardo."

"Bless you, lovely lady." He lifted her hand and kissed it.

A few minutes later Alva began to squirm in her seat. "Would you mind pausing the movie for a minute or two so this old lady can take a little break?" She tried to stand but couldn't get the recliner into the correct position. Eduardo rose, adjusted her seat, and extended his hand.

"My lady. But of course." He gave her a little wink and her cheeks flushed as she tottered off down the hallway in search of the restroom.

Eduardo paused the movie and looked our way. "So, what do you think of it? The movie, I mean?"

"Doris is fabulous in this one," I said, "Then again, she was great in every movie."

"Yes, but that poor girl was pigeonholed," he said. "She knew it, and the rest of us did too."

"What do you mean?" I asked.

"She played the same character in nearly every movie. And I'm not sure she liked it either. I have a feeling she wanted something different from her life."

"Doesn't everyone?" Brady asked.

"Oh, but that's why we love her movies so much," I said. "We know just what we're gonna get. She's always paired up with the wrong fella. And she always has to somehow convince herself that the wrong fella is the right fella."

"Yes." Eduardo nodded. "They are perfect for each other, but they are polar opposites. Funny how God works, isn't it?"

As if to punctuate his words, Alva chose that very moment to reenter the room. She stopped and stared at all of us when we looked her way.

"What did I miss?"

"Just saying that opposites attract, sweet lady." Eduardo extended his hand and she took it.

They settled back into their recliners—hands tightly clutched—and the movie started again. I reached for Brady's hand, my thoughts fixed on what Eduardo had said. Yes indeed, opposites did attract. And the fella seated directly to my left? Well, he and I were living proof of that.

25

$\mathcal{R}$eady, Willing and Able

She [Doris Day] was always smiling and had the rare quality
of making people feel good just by being near her.

Martha Hyer

On the afternoon of December 24th, with Nadia on
a plane back to Paris, Brady and Alva and I made
the drive to Fairfield to spend the holiday with my
family. Technically, I drove while Brady listened to a game on
the radio and Alva snored in the backseat. We arrived at my
parents' house around three and I lugged my gifts into the
house with Brady's help. Now that his knee was healing up, I
could ask for his assistance without feeling guilty.

That evening we ate at Sam's—our usual place to dine on

Christmas Eve—then went to the service at the Methodist church. Might've seemed a bit weird, a bunch of Baptists and Presbyterians going to church with the Methodists, but they were the only ones who had a Christmas Eve service and we loved attending. As long as no one served us that infamous prune juice punch. I still couldn't get that taste out of my mouth. Or my mind.

On Christmas Eve night Brady slept on the sleeper sofa in my dad's office and I shared my childhood bedroom with Aunt Alva, who kept me up most of the night tossing and turning and talking in her sleep. When she started talking out loud to Eduardo, who was spending the night at the Super 8 and would be joining us for the Christmas festivities, I couldn't help but giggle. I had to put the pillow over my head to keep from waking her.

The following morning I awoke early, as I'd done so many other Christmases in the past. I slipped on my robe and headed to the kitchen to help Mama with breakfast—our usual Christmas morning fare, crepes with strawberries and whipped cream. I loved this tradition.

"I'm so glad you and Pop are home for Christmas." I prepped the skillet and poured some crepe batter inside.

"I wouldn't miss it. It's fun to travel—and we have a lot of adventures ahead, trust me—but there's no place like home for the holidays."

Aunt Alva's warbling voice rang out behind us, sounding a bit off-key. I didn't mind a bit. A cheery "Good morning" kicked off my conversation with her.

"Good morning to you too, Katie Sue." A smile turned up the edges of her lips. "Merry Christmas. I sure hope everyone slept as well as I did. I had the loveliest dreams."

Um, yeah. Should I tell her she'd called me Eduardo? Nah, better not.

Speaking of Eduardo, the doorbell rang seconds later and I opened the door to find him on the other side, arms loaded with gifts. "Merry Christmas, Katie! Would you help me with these?"

"Oh, you shouldn't have, Eduardo," I scolded as I took several of the presents from the top of the stack.

"I have ulterior motives, trust me." He grinned. "A few of those are for someone special. And I have something else for her in the car. I must go get it."

"Just let yourself back in. We'll be in the kitchen. She's helping Mama with the crepes."

"Such a kind woman, that Alva." He headed back to his car, and I went into the kitchen.

"So, what's the plan around here?" Alva asked. "This is my first Christmas with the family."

"I guess it is, isn't it?" Mama stopped her work to give Alva a pensive look. She slipped her arm around Auntie's shoulders. "You're such a natural part of the family that it feels like you've been with us for ages. I can't believe this is your first Christmas with us."

"Glad to be here. You have no idea. My Christmas mornings were usually pretty quiet. Lonely. The first few years, anyway. After a while I started working at a homeless shelter, handing out gifts and feeding folks. I really learned to appreciate the spirit of giving. But being with family would always be my first choice. Just don't let me get in the way."

"Never."

"What can I do to help?" she asked.

"We're pretty laid-back in the morning, if you want the truth of it. We don't open presents until after lunch. You okay with that?"

"Yep. That reminds me—I left all of my presents in the trunk of Katie's new car."

"Nope, Brady brought them in last night, Aunt Alva," I said. "He put them all under the tree."

"Oh dear. I forgot to put name tags on a few of them. Hope we get it all sorted out. Might be a big fiasco if we don't."

"I'm sure it'll be fine." Mama started more batter for the crepes. "I'm surprised Queenie and Reverend Bradford aren't here yet. I could've sworn I heard someone at the door a few minutes ago. They're supposed to bring the strawberries. I can't abide crepes without fresh fruit on top."

"They are newlyweds, you know." Alva winked. "Perhaps they're preoccupied."

That stopped Mama in her tracks. "Well, if they don't come soon we'll have to thaw some blueberries from the freezer. Just remember, Crystal is bringing scones. She should be here soon."

Just about the time we'd given up on Queenie and Reverend Bradford, they arrived. I couldn't help but notice that my grandmother didn't appear to be limping as much as before. Her knee was healing, thank goodness. I knew that Alva and Mama would probably pressure them for details about their honeymoon in Galveston, but I stayed out of it. Well, as much as possible.

"Merry Christmas, Fisher family!" Queenie set the berries down on the kitchen counter and waited for her new husband to take her coat. He helped her off with it and then carried it to the coat closet in the front hall.

"You've certainly got him trained." Alva gave an admiring nod. "Nice work, if I do say so myself. Does he happen to have an available brother, perhaps? A cousin?"

We all laughed.

Okay, not everyone laughed.

"There will be no need for a brother or a cousin." Eduardo's voice rang out from behind the throng of people.

"W-what?" Alva looked perplexed. "Who said that?"

The waters parted, and he walked straight up to Alva and handed her an exquisite bouquet of red roses. "Merry Christmas, Alva. I thought these would brighten the room."

"I . . . I . . ." She stared at the roses, unable to speak. Her eyes flooded with tears. "I'm a million years old and I've never received flowers from a man before."

"I recall hearing that once before." Eduardo gave her a wistful look. "And I'm glad to be the one to break that cycle."

"For pity's sake." She stood there holding the flowers as if frozen in place.

Brady broke the silence when he entered the room, still looking a little groggy. "What did I miss?" His gaze shifted to the flowers in Alva's hands. "Aw, you shouldn't have, Alva."

"I—I didn't." Her eyes flooded with tears.

"Let's put those in some water." Mama eased them out of Alva's hands and reached into one of the upper cabinets for a vase. "This'll do just fine. We'll use these as a centerpiece." She fussed over the flowers, finally marching them to the dining room and putting them squarely in the middle of the table, alongside the plastic nativity set. "That's just fine."

"It's more than fine." Alva still stood rooted, eyes brimming. "It's . . . it's downright lovely."

"Why, thank you. I'll take that as a compliment." Eduardo slipped his arm around her shoulder. "I'm glad you like them, Alva."

"What's not to like? They're perfect."

"Just like their recipient."

"Looks like Eduardo's a gentleman, like my Paul," Queenie

said. "I never have to ask him to do things like that. He opens doors for me, gets my coat, even takes out the trash."

I heard the sound of male voices and turned to discover my brothers had arrived with their respective ladies. Jasper didn't have far to travel, his bedroom being on the second floor and all. Same with Dewey, but he hadn't shown up last night, so I had a sneaking suspicion he'd spent the night in Dallas at Beau's place. Nevertheless, they were all here now, the boys and their girls.

"I hope you're paying attention, boys," Queenie said. "A woman wants a man who'll take out the trash."

"Take out the trash." Jasper yawned and rubbed his eyes. "Got it."

"And opening doors for a lady might not be fashionable, but it's still a grand idea, to my way of thinking," Queenie said. "Capiche?"

"Capiche." Jasper nodded. "Trust me, Crystal's got me trained. She's from the South, so she's used to manners."

"You might have to work on that Dahlia girl a bit, Dewey," Queenie said. "She's not from around these parts, so she might not cotton to a fella who treats her like a princess. But she'll come around in time."

"Yep. Got it. Treat her like a princess. I think she'll be okay with that." Dewey gave us a thumbs-up.

"We don't have to tell you a thing, do we, baby boy?" She pinched Beau on the cheeks. "Such a sweet one you are. I know you're treating Twiggy like a lady."

The other boys rolled their eyes.

Everyone looked at Brady as if expecting him to chime in. He put his hands up in the air. "Hey, all I can say is I try to remember to be a gentleman. I don't always get it right, but I try. My mama raised me right."

"Is it getting weird in here?" Pop entered the kitchen still dressed in his pajamas with his hair sticking up on top of his head. "People are being too nice. Mostly the guys."

"They are just being gentlemen, Herb." My mother rolled her eyes. "Is it so hard to believe some men treat their ladies in gentlemanly fashion?"

"Hey now . . ." He scratched his backside and yawned. "Who else took his woman on a cruise to see the turtles in the Galápagos Islands?" His gaze traveled from Reverend Bradford to Eduardo and then back again. "I see there's silence in the court. Yours truly did that, thank you very much." He gave Mama a passionate kiss, then slapped her on the rear end. "You're welcome."

"Well, I never!" Mama's face turned pink.

"Nope. I guess you never got kissed like that in front of the family, but it's high time they see that the old people still have their spark."

"Speak for yourself," Mama said.

"I am." Pop gave her a wink and left the room.

Eduardo turned to look at me, his eyes widening. "And that, I assume, is your father?"

"Um, yeah. He should've come with a warning label."

"What he lacks in gentlemanly skills, he certainly makes up for in passion." Mama adjusted the collar of her blouse. "My goodness, it's hot in here."

Brady started laughing and couldn't seem to get control of himself. He finally had to leave the room. In fact, all of the guys took that as their cue to head to the living room for some guy time. That left us ladies alone in the kitchen.

"So, married life is agreeing with you, Queenie?" Twiggy asked. "You sure look radiant." She giggled.

My grandmother's response surprised me. Her eyes welled with tears. "Indeed. I feel like a young bride. It's all been so wonderful."

"*All* of it?" Alva asked, her thinly plucked brows elevating with mischief.

"There's not time to tell the whole tale right now," Queenie said. "But I will give you one word of advice: if you ever visit the Tremont Hotel in Galveston, do not ask for the honeymoon suite."

"Why not?" Mama asked.

"Let's just leave it at this: the bed was high off the ground. Now, I'm a tall woman, but having to climb steps to get into bed, when your knee is as locked up as mine? Quite the conundrum. And don't even get me started on the marble floor in the bathroom. We got out of the—I mean, I got out of the shower and slid all the way across the bathroom floor."

We stared in silence at her, eyes wide.

"C-crepes, anyone?" Mama's voice cracked as she held up the platter.

Several minutes later we gathered around the table. Pop said the blessing and Jasper attempted to steal the first scone while no one was looking. But I was looking—just a little peek. I stuck out my tongue at him and he chuckled, which caused Queenie to clear her throat. All of this mid-prayer.

To my left, Brady sat quietly. Well, until Pop said, "Amen." Then he reached for my hand and gave it a squeeze. I thought about how different today was from Thanksgiving four short weeks ago. Having Brady here made everything better. He was the strawberry topping on my crepe, the whipped cream on my scone, the butter on my . . .

Anyway, he made everything better.

The conversation around the breakfast table centered on two things: the gifts we would be opening and lunch, which would be served at one o'clock. Ham, au gratin potatoes, green bean casserole, and a variety of other dishes. I kept an eye on Brady, who really seemed to be enjoying himself. Every few minutes he would look my way and give me a reassuring smile. How far he'd come in the past few weeks. He'd made tremendous strides. I could feel it.

When breakfast ended, the guys disappeared into the yard to look at Pop's old boat. That left us ladies alone in the kitchen to clean up. I didn't really mind. Apparently Mama and Alva still had quite a few questions for Queenie, who seemed oblivious.

"So?" Alva tossed her a dish towel. "Spill it."

"Spill what?" Queenie grabbed a clean plate and dried it with the towel.

Alva put her hands on her hips and stared her sister down. "Are you serious?"

"About what?" Queenie kept drying the plate, not even looking our way.

"Do I have to spell it out for you?" Alva asked. "You tell us that you and Paul slide out of the shower and nearly kill yourselves on the marble floor, but you stop the story right there? Well, what was it like?"

"What was *what* like?" Queenie's brows wrinkled more than usual. Just as quickly a flash of recognition lit her face. "Oh, you want to know about the wedding night?"

"Duh!" Mama, Alva, Twiggy, Crystal, and Dahlia spoke in unison. I did my best to keep putting dishes away to avoid the embarrassment that was yet to come. Were we really about to go there?

"I'll start by sharing one huge relief." Queenie put the plate down and gestured with her index finger for us to listen close. "I didn't have to worry about my mushy old body. Not one little bit."

"You mean he didn't care about the saggy boobs and such?" Alva's eyes widened. "That gives me great hope."

"Nope." Queenie slapped her thigh and laughed. "I didn't mean it like that exactly. I'm just saying that once the man took his glasses off, he couldn't see a thing. For all he knew, I was Angelina Jolie."

We all busted out laughing. All but Queenie, who shook her head. "Then again, the man has hands, and I'm pretty sure this old skin doesn't feel anything like Angelina Jolie's." She grabbed hold of her hips and jiggled them. "See there? See what I mean? There's a lot of elastic in this old skin. Angelina doesn't have to deal with that."

"Yet." Mama quirked a brow.

Queenie shrugged and gestured to her hips. "Well, there's more of me than there used to be, we'll just leave it at that."

"The better to cuddle with you, my dear." Reverend Bradford's voice sounded from behind us and we all let out a gasp.

Queenie turned, her face redder than the painted rooster on the cookie jar. "Paul Bradford, were you eavesdropping?"

"Not on purpose. I just had to come in to see what all the laughing was about." He gently kissed her on the cheek. "But just so you know, I love a woman who's soft—inside and out."

"Well, you get half of that with Queenie, at the very least." Alva laughed.

My grandmother glared at her. "Now there's a fine response."

"No, she's a softie, all the way to the core." Reverend Bradford's eyes misted over. "I think it just took a little bit of love to bring it out."

"You're so sweet, Rev—" I sighed, unsure of how to finish.

Reverend Bradford put his hand on mine. "Katie, I've been meaning to talk to you and your brothers about that. I know you're struggling with what to call me."

"Yeah."

"I'm Reverend Bradford to the community, but I'm more

than that to you. We're family now. I'd love it if you would call me by a meaningful name, something of your choosing."

"Like Pap-Paul," Queenie said. "That's my suggestion."

"Just sounds more like something a child would call a grandfather," I countered. "You know?"

"We'll have children one day." Brady's voice sounded from the other side of the room. His words caught me totally off guard. I turned to face him, my heart pounding wildly in my chest. "I think they would love to call him Pap-Paul. So let's stick with that."

Wow. You could've heard a pin drop in that room for the next ten seconds. Everyone looked back and forth from Brady to me.

"I think that'll do fine," Pap-Paul said with a smile. "I like it. And it'll be fun to have children calling me that. Someday."

This whole conversation put me in such a jolly frame of mind that I threw my arms around his neck. "Welcome to the family, Pap-Paul!"

"Thank you. You've all made the transition so easy. I feel like I've been a part of things for years."

In a way he had. We'd known him for years, anyway.

"You seem to fit right in too, Brady," Pap-Paul said. "It's nice to be part of a big family, isn't it?"

Brady's response to this was so tender that it took me by surprise. "Definitely. I'm an only child with a mother who always worked around the clock, so my Christmas mornings weren't like this." He gestured to the overcrowded living room. "They weren't like this at all."

"Aw, I'm sorry, Brady." I walked over and slipped into his arms. He pulled me into a warm embrace.

"Just saying a guy could get used to this."

"Well, I certainly have," Pop interrupted us. "Anyone see that tray of scones? Don't tell me Jasper ate the last one."

"Hey, don't blame it on me, Pop. It was Crystal." Jasper pointed at her and she feigned innocence.

"You ate enough on our cruise to last a month, Herb." Mama waved a spoon in his face. "Enough with the carbs already."

"But it's Christmas!" He took the spoon and swatted her on the rear end. This resulted in a chase around the kitchen. Oh boy. Brady looked on, doubled over in laughter.

Before long everyone was arguing.

All but Queenie and Pap-Paul, who were smooching in the breakfast room.

And Alva and Eduardo, who were holding hands as they walked toward the living room.

And Dewey and Dahlia, who were snuggled on the love seat.

Oh, and Brady James and yours truly. With our lips locked, I found nothing whatsoever to argue about.

26

The More I See You

I don't even like parties.

Doris Day

We put together the yummiest lunch ever, then gathered around the table to eat. Afterward we opened presents. By the time all was said and done, the living room was covered in wrapping paper. Mama fussed and fussed as she picked it up and scooped it into trash bags. Then she plopped down onto the sofa, clearly exhausted.

Judging from the look on Pop's face, he had something to say to the group. He rose and paced the room, then stopped to face us all. "We have some news."

"You're having another baby?" Jasper tried.

"Bite your tongue!" My mother looked horrified at the very idea. "No, this is another one of your father's harebrained ideas."

"Harebrained, my eye. It's a stroke of brilliance." Pop crossed his arms as if satisfied with himself. "Your mother and I have purchased an RV."

A collective gasp went up from all in attendance.

"Technically, it's a fifth wheel," Mama said. "Which can be attached to your father's truck and hauled from state to state."

"State to state?" Beau looked perplexed. "Is that the plan?"

"Yes, but there's more to the story than that," my father said. "See, I would like to say I've been to all fifty states before I die."

"You're driving to Hawaii in a fifth wheel?" Dewey asked.

"No. We're driving to all of the states in the continental United States. Then someday we'll go on cruises to Alaska and Hawaii."

"Don't forget about Puerto Rico," Eduardo said. "It's not technically a state, but it's worth the visit."

Pop rolled his eyes. "Anyway, the point is, we won't be home much."

"You're already gone from home a lot," Jasper said. "I guess we'll need to finalize the paperwork related to the hardware store."

"Yes, and that leads me to my next point." My father turned to Jasper and Crystal. "I know you two are saving up for your wedding and you've been wondering about where to live. What if we sold the house to you?"

"W-what?" Crystal's hand flew to her mouth and her eyes filled with tears. "Oh, that's a *luv*-lee i-*de*-a, Papa Fisher!" She sprang to her feet and threw her arms around his neck.

Jasper looked a bit more reserved. "How much you asking for the place, Pop? I'm not sure about getting a loan for a house just yet."

"We're asking a dollar." Pop put his hands on his hips. "Do you think you can swing that, son? I know you have a wedding to pay for and all, so we didn't want to strap you."

"A—a dollar?" Jasper gasped. He looked at Pop and then back at Crystal. "Seriously?"

Pop was never one to get terribly emotional. Not many guys in the hardware business were. But his eyes filled with tears as he spoke. "You've done such a great job taking over the hardware store, son. I'm very proud of you. And you've stayed put in Fairfield, something you never thought you'd be interested in."

"So you're rewarding me for staying put while you run away?" Jasper grinned. "Cool. I can live with that."

"Not sure I can," Dewey grumbled. "Doesn't seem fair."

"Oh, don't worry, Dewey," Mama said. "You'll get your fair share of the inheritance someday too. If we don't spend it all gallivanting around the country." She turned to us ladies. "Do you think I'll need a new wardrobe? I don't know what Herb is thinking, taking me on a road trip across all fifty states in the middle of winter. I think he's lost his mind. If you find my body frozen solid to a porta-potty at some RV camp, please bury me in the blue dress that I wore to Queenie's wedding. It's my new favorite."

This led to a discussion about her dress. Naturally.

"Mama, I'm surprised you're going along with this," I said. "I thought you were getting tired of traveling."

"I want your father to be happy. And I had no idea the man had so many secret desires." She fanned herself. "I found out about his passion for RVing the hard way, in front of fifteen hundred people."

"Excuse me? You found out that Pop wanted an RV in front of fifteen hundred people?"

"Yes. On the cruise ship. See, there I was, looking like a lobster because of too much fun in the sun, and your father decided we needed to volunteer to be on the Newlywed Game."

"The Newlywed Game? That makes no sense at all. You're not newlyweds."

"I know, right? Anyway, it's a game—really, more of a contest—where they choose couples to come on the stage and answer questions about each other." Her gaze shifted downward. "I don't mind telling you it was terribly embarrassing. I won't even tell you the kinds of questions they asked, but needless to say, everyone on board the ship got to know us because we won the whole thing."

"You won the Newlywed Game?" I said. "Very cool."

"Not really, because it pushed us into the spotlight, and everywhere we went people were talking to us . . . and *about* us. I can fill you in on all that later. But my point is, one of the game questions I couldn't answer. They asked your father, 'What is one secret desire you have that your wife knows nothing about?' Now, I felt sure he would say, 'Go to Paris and see the Eiffel Tower,' but he didn't. He told that man—in front of fifteen hundred folks in the audience—that he wanted to buy an RV and travel the country."

"Wow."

"Yep. So I answered it wrong and they corrected me, and I felt so foolish, but mostly because I didn't know my own husband well enough to *know* that he wanted to buy an RV. Isn't that sad?"

"Well, you have to admit that Pop has been springing a lot of new things on you lately, Mama, so I wouldn't feel too bad."

"I didn't, until after that stupid Newlywed Game was over. From that point on, every place we went on that ship, people came up to me and said, 'Buy that man an RV.'" She sighed.

"Peer pressure. It happens at every age, no matter where you are. Even at sea."

"So you came home and bought him an RV?" I asked.

"Yep. I mentioned it to Dad Bradford, and it turned out he and his first wife had one, a 2007 model, still in perfectly good shape because they'd hardly used it. So he sold it to us."

"How sweet is that! Queenie didn't mind?"

"Mind? Can you picture your grandmother on a road trip?" Mama laughed. "Then again, I couldn't picture myself on one just a few short weeks ago, but I suppose that's beside the point."

"I wish I had time to travel." Eduardo's words took me by surprise. "But my workload is so high it seems impossible at the moment."

I thought about his beautiful home. Surely the man didn't need to work. And he was certainly well above retirement age. Maybe he could work something out with Nadia—a part-time position with Cosmopolitan that gave him time to travel. Or maybe, if she made him a partner, he could come and go like she did. Yes, the two of them sharing the responsibilities of ownership might be just the thing. I'd have to suggest it to Brady.

My thoughts were so wound around this idea that I barely heard my phone ringing in my purse. Only when Brady alerted me to the fact did I jump up and run for it. I caught it on the last ring but didn't recognize the number.

"Katie?" A man's voice greeted me. A shaky voice.

"Yes?"

"This is Frankie Sanders, Carrie's dad."

Seriously? On Christmas? What are you mad about now?

He definitely sounded upset, but not in the usual way. He spoke a few more words, but I could barely understand him.

About thirty seconds into the conversation, however, I'd heard enough to stop me in my tracks.

"Mr. Sanders, did you say that Carrie and Jimmy were in an accident?"

At this point, everyone in the room stopped talking. Jasper muted the sound on the TV.

"Yes." His voice was still shaking. "They were driving to our house for Christmas Eve and had just exited the interstate. A large truck was going too fast . . ." His words faded.

I wanted to ask the obvious, "Are they all right?" but couldn't seem to summon the words.

"It's Jimmy. He's in bad shape."

My heart felt as heavy as lead. "I'm so sorry, Mr. Sanders. I really am. We'll be praying for both of them. Is Carrie . . . I mean, is she . . . all right?"

"She has a broken hand from where she hit the dashboard and some cuts on her face from the windshield, but she's very lucky."

"Thank God."

"Yes, we're all doing that down here. And we'll be doing a lot more of it when Jimmy pulls through." A long pause followed. I looked across the room at my family and friends, who all waited for me to fill them in. They would have to keep waiting until this call ended.

"I know that Eduardo is expecting Carrie to pick up her dress next week, but that's just not possible. In fact . . ." He stopped again and I thought I'd lost him. "I don't know how they can possibly go through with the wedding in two weeks. The doctor said it might take two or three months for Jimmy to walk again."

"Oh, Mr. Sanders, I'm so sorry."

"No, Katie, I'm the one who's sorry. I made such a big deal

out of the rivalry between our families, and now . . ." His voice cracked as he added, "We have to work together to get the kids through this. We have to."

"And you will." I did my best to sound encouraging. "Please don't worry about the dress. If it would make Carrie feel better to have it—if seeing it would give her hope—then I'll have it shipped. Or I'll drive it to San Antonio myself."

"I don't know. The dress might be a painful reminder of what hasn't happened, what isn't going to happen for a long time."

"She might not wear that dress in two weeks," I said. "But she *will* wear it. And in the meantime, I'm going to pray that God heals Jimmy completely and quickly. I won't stop praying either."

"Thank you, Katie, for everything."

As we ended the call I turned to face my family and friends. They'd picked up on most of the conversation through my end of it, but I could tell Eduardo was particularly shaken.

"Is she going to be okay?" he asked.

"She is. But they're really concerned about Jimmy. I didn't get a lot of details, but I think the doctors are worried he might not walk for quite some time."

"Then we're going to pray." Brady rose and reached for my hand. He gestured for the others to join us. "The Bible says there's power in corporate prayer."

"Where two or three are gathered . . ." Pap-Paul said as he stood alongside Brady and took his hand.

"There's power in numbers," Queenie added.

We gathered in a circle and held hands—the Baptists, the Presbyterians, the Lutherans, and even those of us from the community church. In that moment, as we lifted Jimmy's name before the throne of God, the things that separated us didn't matter. The things that united us did.

27

$\mathcal{P}$erhaps, Perhaps, Perhaps

I've never met an animal I didn't like, and I can't say the same
thing about people.

Doris Day

The weeks after Christmas were strangely calm. I kept
my regular hours at the shop, but we had few customers. Several times I thought about what Madge had said
a while back, about seasons of plenty and seasons of want.
We'd just come through a crazy-busy season. Now things were
slowing down, as they were prone to do. That was okay with
me. The busyness had left most of us exhausted, and if we ever
needed a chance to catch our breath, it was after Christmas.

I needed the chance to do something else too. Pray. With

so much stirring in my heart, I had to keep God in his right-ful place—at the very center. It was hard to stay focused at times. I kept thinking about Carrie and Jimmy, wondering what I could do to help. We'd sent flowers and we'd all signed a card, which had been mailed the day after Christmas. But I wanted to do more. This feeling hit me especially hard on Friday, January 8th, when Brady and I met in his office to talk.

"This was supposed to be their wedding day."

"Yeah." He sat on the edge of his desk. "I remember."

"I talked to Mrs. Sanders a couple of days ago. She said that Jimmy's been moved to a rehab hospital. Did you know they had him in a medically induced coma for a few days after the accident?"

"Yeah. I actually called Mr. Dennison to talk to him a while back. They're a great family."

"I just wish there was something we could do. Every time I see that dress in the studio I want to send it to her, but I've won-dered if it would be the right thing to do. And I hate to bring this up, but there's still a balance due on the dress—$3,500."

"Since you did bring it up, I've come up with a great idea." Brady rose and took a few steps across the room, his knee in fine working order now. "I think my mom will go along with it."

"What's that?"

"After talking to Mr. Dennison the other day, it occurred to me that what they're going through won't last forever. Jimmy will recover and they will get married, and they'll probably go on to have 2.5 children and live in a house with a white picket fence."

"Debatable, but what's your idea?"

"I want to give her the wedding dress." He folded his hands together, clearly pleased with himself for coming up with this idea.

"Wait—give it to her? That's a five-thousand-dollar dress."

"Yep. I know. And I want to give it to her. I even want to refund the deposit. The dress will be our gift to the two of them, and I truly believe it will give them hope that things are going to get better. Sometimes that's all people need— something to hang their hope on."

"Do you really think your mom will give away a five-thousand-dollar dress? I mean, we just gave away ten five-hundred-dollar dresses on Black Friday. You know? Can the shop afford to do this?"

"We can't afford not to. Oh, and I have some news. Related to the shop, I mean."

"Please don't tell me we have a hundred orders for the Doris Day gown. I don't think my heart can take it."

"No." He chuckled and eased himself down into the chair behind his desk. "I know you're not going to believe this, but remember that angry bride, the one who went to the newspaper with her story?"

"How could I forget her?"

"She called this morning to let me know that she's broken up with her fiancé. Kaput. Finished."

"No way."

"Yes. Just a week before the ceremony she decided she couldn't go through with it. So now she wants to return her dress for a full refund."

"Oh, Brady. What did you do?"

"I told her we'd be glad to take the dress back and would give her a full refund. And she's as happy as a lark. She even said she's going to go back to the paper to recant her story."

"That's going to cost the shop even more money," I said.

"But we'll make money in the end because happy customers bring in more happy customers. See?"

"Yeah, but giving away a five-thousand-dollar dress on the same day you offer to refund a bride for another gown? Your mom's gonna flip."

"Nah. I learned from the master. She'll be thrilled that I'm being so generous. Generosity has its rewards."

"So, all's well that ends well?" I asked.

"Yeah, except now we have this random dress coming back to the shop and no one to wear it."

I could certainly relate to that statement. I had a random dress hanging in Queenie's cedar closet and no reason to wear it.

"Don't worry, Brady. It'll sell. The dress is gorgeous, and it's in an easy-to-sell size—a ten."

"Yeah, I'm sure it will sell. Just thought the whole thing was so strange. It's weird how women—er, people—can change moods so quickly."

"Um, women?" He was a fine one to talk. These past few weeks he'd been up and down like a yo-yo.

"Okay, okay, I get your point." He put his hands up in the air as if caught. "We all go through highs and lows."

"Thankfully, more highs than lows."

"Yes. And we all move on."

His words made me think of Casey. I'd definitely moved on from him, hadn't I? "Yes, we do."

As he leaned back in his chair, it squeaked. Other than that little noise the room went quiet for a moment. Brady finally broke the silence. "Speaking of moving on, I, um . . . I wanted you to be the first to know that I'm about to sign my official release papers from the Mavericks. I mean, we knew it was coming, but I got the forms this morning. Stan faxed them over."

"Oh, Brady." A rush of air left my lungs. "Are you . . . I mean, are you okay?"

"Yeah, actually, I am. I mean, it took a while for the idea to sink in, but I think I'm okay with it. God might open a door for me to play pro ball in the future, or he might not, but the Bible says I'm supposed to be content in whatever state I'm in."

"You're in Texas, boy. Everyone's content in Texas!" Madge's voice sounded from the open doorway.

I laughed out loud. "Well, she has a point."

"Everything's better in Texas!" Alva appeared next to Madge.

"Which is precisely why I moved here," Eduardo chimed in beside Alva.

"Looks like the gang's all here," Brady said. "Did someone call a meeting?"

Madge shook her head. "No, but I was about to. We just had a call from Carrie Sanders. She wanted to thank us for the fruit basket that arrived this morning." Madge's eyes narrowed as she looked back and forth between Brady and me. "I don't recall sending a fruit basket. Does that ring a bell with either of you?"

"Ooh, I love fruit," Alva said. "I'm especially fond of nectarines."

"Me too." Eduardo clasped his hands together. "I should take you to California some day, Alva, to taste the sweet nectarines from Orange County."

"I would love that," she said. "But wouldn't people talk if the two of us headed off on a vacation together?"

"Let them talk." He lifted his chin.

"Well, I don't know." She looked concerned. "A single man? A single woman? Heading off on an adventure together without a chaperone?" She glanced my way. "Ooh, that's the answer. We'll take Katie with us. How would you like to go to California, Katie?"

"That's random," I said. "I'd have to think about it."

"I do see another solution." Eduardo slipped his arm over Alva's shoulders. "One that would keep people from talking."

"Oh?" She looked at him.

"Yes, but we can talk about that privately." He gave her a kiss on the cheek.

Okay then.

"So, back to that fruit basket . . ." Madge wrinkled her nose. "You set that up, boss? Then I'm assuming you're also the one who scheduled more flowers to be delivered tomorrow to the Dennison home? I saw the receipt come through on the company email account."

"Yep." Brady nodded. "I want them to know we're thinking of them."

Madge waggled her finger in the air. "Brady James, you are a good, good boy. Your mama raised you right. Of course, I had a little something to do with your raising too. I think I did a fine job, if I do say so myself. I hate to brag. That would just be wrong. But you did turn out to be quite the gentleman." She crossed her arms. "Even if you are a little over-the-top generous."

"I think this situation with Jimmy really struck a nerve. I feel bad for him. He's lying in a hospital in far worse shape than I've ever been." Brady rose and paced the room, pausing to rub his knee for a moment. "What if we gathered the troops and made a trip to San Antonio to deliver the dress in person?"

"Right now?" Madge looked stunned by this idea.

"Yes." Brady stopped in place. "Right now. It's Friday. The shop is closing in a couple of hours."

"Are you sure?" I asked.

"Ooh, I want to go." Alva raised her hand. "You're talking about the girl from that radio program, right?"

"He's talking about Carrie Sanders," Eduardo said. "And if you don't mind, I'd like to go too. I would love to deliver that dress in person."

"Yes, I think it would be nice if we all showed up together," Madge said. "I do hope it's not too much for Carrie to have the dress, considering . . ."

"This visit isn't about a dress," Brady said. "It's about giving them hope. And extending a hand of friendship."

"Even if they don't like the Mavericks?" Alva asked.

"That doesn't even factor in," Brady said. "Never did."

Less than an hour later we were all pressed into my SUV, Brady in the front seat with me and Alva, Eduardo, and Madge in the backseat. The gorgeous Doris Day gown had been carefully bagged and laid out in the very back of the vehicle. I couldn't believe we were leaving this late in the afternoon to drive all the way to San Antonio, but I was open to an adventure. Out of the corner of my eye I peeked at Brady, who seemed to come alive as he talked about how we would go about giving them the news. I hadn't seen him this excited in a while.

"It feels good to shift the attention off myself," he said. "And if anyone needs our attention right now, it's this couple. They've really been through it."

Yes, they had. And how good of him to care this much.

Brady made a call to Mr. Dennison, who gave him the address of the rehab hospital. When the call ended, Brady gave us our marching orders. "Okay, he's in room 104 and Carrie is there with him. He should be wrapping up therapy on his legs when we arrive, so the timing would be perfect."

We arrived at the rehab hospital at six o'clock, just as the sun was starting to set. I was happy to stretch my legs. Alva was happy to look for a bathroom. When we walked inside the lobby, the guy behind the front desk looked up, his eyes widening when he saw Brady.

"Dude, you're Brady James." The fellow stared up at Brady in awe, then extended his hand across the desk.

"I am." Brady shook his hand. "And you are?"

"Oh, sorry. Jeff Blaine. I play for the Wildcats. Northwest Vista College."

"I've heard a lot of great things about the Wildcats."

"Really?" Jeff looked at our little group, clearly confused. The sight of Alva searching for a bathroom probably didn't help. "What are you doing here in San Antonio?"

"Came to see a friend who's rehabbing after an accident."

"Ah. You're brave, man."

"Brave?"

"Yeah. Big game tonight. Spurs. Mavericks. You know."

Brady's eyes widened. "Would you believe I forgot about that? I really did."

"Wow." Jeff laughed and pointed Alva in the direction of the ladies' room. "Well, no one around here has forgotten about it, trust me, so you might want to get out of town while the gettin's good."

"I think we'll see our friend first. Could you tell us how to get to room 104?"

"Better yet, I'll show you. Just let me get someone to cover the front desk, okay?"

A couple of minutes later an older man took Jeff's place—after scowling at Brady. We waited for Alva, the tension a little thick as the man muttered something under his breath about the Mavericks, and then headed to Jimmy's room. Eduardo carried the bag with the gown inside.

When we arrived, Jeff knocked on the door and I heard Carrie call out, "Come in."

We eased open the door and her eyes widened when she saw us standing there.

"Oh!" Tears sprang to her eyes. She jumped up and rushed toward us. "I can't believe you came all this way."

"We have a special gift to deliver." Eduardo lifted the bag that held the gown. "For a very special lady."

"My—my dress." Her expression shifted from surprise to concern. "I . . . I don't know what to say."

"No need to say anything." Eduardo hung the dress on the empty IV pole next to the bed. "We wanted you to have it."

"This was supposed to be our wedding day." She stared at the bag, a somber expression on her face.

"I know." I put my arms around her and held her in a warm hug. "That's why we came today. Brady decided we should bring the dress. And we've been wanting to see Jimmy."

She pointed to the empty bed. "He should be coming back from therapy any minute now. They wanted to try it without me in the room today. He seems to work harder when I'm not there." She shrugged.

"How is he doing, Carrie?" I took the seat next to her as she sat down. "And how are you?"

"It's going to be a long journey," she said. "Maybe another month or two before he's able to put any weight on those legs. I'm all healed up . . . on the outside. My hand will recover. But my heart . . ." She looked up at the dress bag once more. "I'm not so sure."

"Maybe this news will make things a little easier." Brady walked over to join us. "We want to give you the dress. No balance due."

"W-what? Are you sure?" She put her hand over her mouth.

"Very sure. And not only that . . ." Brady turned to Madge,

who handed him an envelope. "We want to return your deposit. The dress is our gift to you. You will wear it at just the right time."

"And it will be perfect." Eduardo knelt down in front of her. "Because the perfect bride will be wearing it. The one I designed the gown for. The one who was destined to wear it all along. She will have her day and she will be beautiful. And we will all celebrate alongside her, not just for the vows she's taking but for the road she's walked that's led her to that moment."

Carrie began to weep. Madge passed her a box of tissues. Eduardo tried to stand but couldn't get up until Brady and I helped him.

Just then the door opened and a nurse nudged Jimmy's wheelchair into the crowded room. "What's going on in here?" she asked.

Carrie's tears raised immediate concerns with Jimmy. "Carrie? What's happened?"

"My dress!" She pointed to the gown.

"Ah." He gazed at the bag and then looked back at her. "I see."

"They gave it to me, Jimmy. Gave it to me. No cost."

"Wow." He gave Brady an admiring look. "I knew I was rooting for the right team."

This seemed to awaken something in the nurse, who pointed at Brady. "That's it! You're Brady James. You play for the Mavericks."

"*Played* for the Mavericks. I don't play anymore." He pointed down. "Bad knee."

"Bummer." She helped Jimmy out of his wheelchair and into the hospital bed. "Sounds like we've all had our share of hard knocks."

"Yeah." A reflective look came over Brady's face. "I don't

know if I'll ever play basketball again. But I've been thinking about that a lot. The Bible says I'm supposed to be content in whatever state I'm in." He gestured to his knee. "I haven't been. I've been angry. Sad. Depressed. But definitely not content."

Jimmy struggled to get comfortable in the bed. He let out a little grunt, then said, "Tell me about it."

Brady walked to the side of the bed and spoke to him friend to friend. "This morning I got to thinking about all of the people who've faced the loss of a dream but kept going. People who thought life was going to take them in one direction but ended up taking them in another. God redirected them. We have a choice to get bitter or get better. I know you, Jimmy. At least, I think I know you, based on the few times we've met. You're going to get better. And this season will be behind you sooner than you think."

"Not sure I would accept that speech from just anyone." Jimmy adjusted his pillows and tried to get comfortable. "But knowing what you've been through, Brady, I think I can handle it from you. You're one of the few people who really under-stands what I'm going through, I guess."

"I don't suppose it matters in the long term if I shoot the winning basket or not," Brady said. "I guess it doesn't even matter if I ever get back out on that court. What does matter is how I choose to live my life, how I face adversity. I want to be an overcomer, not someone who gives in to defeat. And I know you want that too, Jimmy. That's why I came, to remind you that you're going to get through this."

You could've heard a pin drop as he wrapped up his speech.

"Wow." The nurse fussed with the covers around Jimmy's legs. "Maybe you should take up preaching."

"Maybe I should." Brady chuckled.

The nurse put her hands on her hips. "In spite of that lovely speech, I say you're brave to come to San Antonio tonight. That shirt will *never* fly here." She pointed to his Mavericks T-shirt and grimaced.

"Yeah." Brady shrugged. "That's me. Brave."

He was brave. Truly one of the bravest men I'd ever known. I had witnessed it the day of his surgery and saw even more evidence of it right now, as he talked about the end of his career without any evidence of pain in his eyes. I loved this brave guy. And I would go on loving him no matter how many dreams were gained and lost along the way.

28

By the Light of the Silvery Moon

I'm always looking for insights into the real Doris Day because
I'm stuck with this infatuation and need to explain it to myself.

John Updike

We made the drive back to Dallas that same night.
Brady and I talked quietly while worship music
played on the radio.

"You want me to drive for a while?" he asked.

"Nah. I'm doing okay. Enjoying it, really." I was enjoying
more than just the drive. Our sweet conversation was just

what we needed. I kept a watchful eye on the road, but the late hour provided us with smooth sailing.

A call came through from Lori-Lou on the Bluetooth. Alva had been sleeping soundly in the backseat but awoke the minute she heard her great-niece's voice coming through the car's speaker.

"Oh my goodness!" Alva let out a squeal, which woke Eduardo. "They've hired Lori-Lou to be on our program!"

"What program?" Eduardo yawned. "What did I miss?"

"Our *program*," Alva repeated. "But I can't believe she would take on a job right now, what with the new baby coming and all."

"New job?" Lori-Lou said. "I don't have a job, Aunt Alva. In fact, that's why I'm calling."

"Calling?" Alva echoed.

"Yes." I could hear the anxiety in her voice. "Katie, I'm calling because I need your help."

"Help? With what?" *Please don't say the kids. Please don't say the kids.*

"The kids. I can't believe I'm saying this, but the doctor has put me on bed rest."

"Why?" Madge, Alva, and I spoke in unison.

"Because I'm having Braxton Hicks contractions. They're not productive or anything."

"I have no idea what that means, Lori-Lou." I eased the car into the next lane and slowed my speed.

"It means my body is wanting to go into labor, even though Iris isn't due for two months."

"This show just gets more and more exciting!" Alva squealed. "So glad I woke up in time to tune in."

"Are you serious?" I asked.

"Yes." Lori-Lou's voice trembled. "You know me, Katie. I

don't get shaken up about a lot of things. But I'm really scared. The doctor says I have to take it easy. Look at me. Look at my life. You know that's impossible. How can I lounge around in bed all day with three kids to take care of? The girls fight all day and Joshie is into everything. It's just a stage, I know, and all stages pass. But man, this is a tough one. And I'm all by myself over here. Well, I'm never all by myself, but I feel like it, if that makes any sense."

"I just don't know how much I can—"

"I'm not trying to make you feel bad," Lori-Lou said. "I'm really not." She began to sniffle. "I think it's the h-h-hormones. Pregnancy makes me a little c-c-crazy."

In the backseat Madge cleared her throat. Brady shifted his gaze out the window, probably to keep from laughing.

I kept a close eye on the road, my thoughts now tumbling. "I'll come and help you tomorrow after work. We'll figure out a plan."

"Lori-Lou, if you stop working for the radio station, you can spend more time resting," Alva shouted from the backseat.

That got Brady tickled. He couldn't seem to stop laughing.

"I'm telling you, Aunt Alva, this isn't a radio program. It's a phone call. I think Katie has me on speakerphone."

"Speakerphone?" Alva said. "Are you telling me there's some sort of contraption that makes the phone come to life so everyone can hear?"

"Yes, Alva," we all said in unison.

"For pity's sake. So this is really you, Lori-Lou? And you're really on bed rest? It's not some sort of act?"

"I wish it was an act, but it's really me and I really need help."

"Well then, I have the perfect solution," Alva said. "I'll come and help with the kids."

"But you don't drive, Alva."

"Eduardo will take me. I know he will." She leaned over to ask him, "You will, won't you?"

"Anything for you, my dear," he responded.

"He's a fine man and he will be happy to drive me over to your place. I know Katie Sue's busy with the shop."

"Well, technically Eduardo's busy too," I added, "but I'm sure Dahlia wouldn't mind if he takes some time off."

"He doesn't work around the clock, Katie Sue." Alva's voice sounded like she was scolding. "He's well past his retirement years and needs to take it easy."

"Eduardo loves his job," I argued.

Alva cleared her throat. "One can speculate that people work to stay busy. But when one isn't lonely anymore, one doesn't have to fill that void. Is this as clear as mud?"

It was clear, all right, though she'd lost me at the mud part.

"Hello, people. I am still in the car." Eduardo's voice had a hint of laughter in it.

"Does anyone remember that I'm still on the phone?" Lori-Lou's voice rang out through the speaker.

"Of course I remember," Alva said. "And I'm your solution. I'm the perfect candidate to come and play with the children. In fact, I might just stay there with you instead of coming and going. If you don't mind my gentleman friend coming for a visit every now and again. During daytime hours, I mean."

"That would be lovely," Eduardo said. "I would like that very much."

"Do I have your permission to allow a male visitor in your home while I'm there, Lori-Lou?" Alva continued to raise her voice. "If not, then all bets are off."

My cousin sounded like she was choking on the other end

of the line. Finally she said, "Certainly you're welcome to have a visitor, Aunt Alva. No problem at all."

"I promise to behave myself," Alva said. "In front of the children, anyway." This led to a hearty laugh from my aunt, who slapped her knee and then groaned in pain. "I always forget about this stupid knee. Must be a storm coming. It's aching something fierce."

There was a storm coming, all right, but not the kind she referred to. I couldn't picture Aunt Alva putting up with Lori-Lou's three kids for more than a few hours before throwing in the towel, and I certainly couldn't picture Eduardo handling them.

On the other hand, she might have them walking the straight and narrow in no time. And who knew? Maybe Eduardo secretly longed for grandchildren to spoil.

"You've got room in that new house of yours, don't you? I can stay in Joshie's room on that air mattress you're always talking about."

"You're planning to sleep on an air mattress, Alva?" I shook my head. "It's not easy to get up and down from that thing. Trust me. I slept on it for weeks when I first moved to Dallas."

"Then we'll put in a proper bed. I'll stay at your place as long as you need, Lori-Lou. That's what family is for, right?"

So I'd be at Alva's house by myself. That might be a little weird.

"Oh, one more thing before I go," Lori-Lou said. "The game just finished. The Mavericks pulled it out in the end. I hear Spurs fans are beside themselves."

"Wow." Brady chuckled. "Guess we got out of San Antonio just in time then."

Lori-Lou ended the call and I turned the radio back up. A familiar worship song was playing.

"I'm so relieved to hear that Lori-Lou has quit that radio program." Alva yawned. "I would hate to see her overtaxed."

"But Alva, surely you heard her say that—"

"Yes, I heard her say that she's on bed rest, and that's a good thing. When I'm at her place I'll make sure she gets the TLC she needs. But promise me one thing, Katie."

"Anything."

"Promise me you won't listen to our radio program without me. It's getting *so* good!"

Good gravy. After all of that, she still didn't get it? My poor auntie. Clearly her mind was starting to slip.

"I don't mind admitting I am a wee bit confused," Eduardo said.

Join the club.

"Oh, it's the most intriguing program. You would love it, Eduardo. I know you would. It's kind of like a soap opera. There's a girl who's ordering a wedding gown and her family doesn't get along. It was just getting to the good part when we had to turn it off, so I'm feeling a little conflicted about how the story is going to end."

"I can assure you, it will end with a happily ever after." Eduardo's words had a loving tone. "They always do."

"Yes, they do, don't they?"

Soon gentle snores followed from both of them.

I kept my gaze on the road in front of me, but the guy in the seat next to me—the one who couldn't stop laughing—proved to be quite the distraction. One of these days I'd explain it all to Alva. Or maybe I wouldn't. Maybe I'd let her go on thinking that life was a radio program, filled with highs and lows, cliff-hangers and breathtaking moments. Because, after all . . . it really was all of those things and more.

29

Sentimental Journey

There was something very special about walking onto the set and seeing Doris Day. It was just electrifying. Just looking at her.

Philip Brown

By the time we reached mid-January the shop was filled with customers again. On a particularly busy day I received a call from Carrie Sanders. In spite of my crazy schedule I was happy to hear from her. I closed the door to my office so I could hear above the din coming from the shop.

"Carrie!" I did my best to focus on her. "How are you?"

"Good. Making progress."

"And Jimmy?"

"He's out of the rehab hospital. He won't be doing any marathons, but that's okay, since he's not a runner." She laughed.

"I'm glad he's better. So glad. We've been praying."

"Thank you so much, Katie. He's graduated to home care, so it's time for us to think about the wedding. I thought you'd want to know we've set a new date."

"You have?"

"Yes. Palm Sunday weekend. But I have the best surprise ever. I guess some guy at *Texas Bride* magazine somehow found out about our story."

"Is his name Jordan Singer, by any chance?"

"Yes, how did you know?"

"I have a sneaking suspicion I might know how he got your name, but keep going."

"Well, he called me and wanted to know if they could bring a camera crew to photograph us. Jimmy and I are going to be on the cover of *Texas Bride*! In March, I think. Or maybe April? I wasn't clear on that part, but they want a shot of me in that amazing Doris Day dress. Can you believe it?"

"I can. And Eduardo will be tickled pink."

"We all are. But the best news? My dad has been the one helping take care of Jimmy. He goes to his house every day and spends time with him, runs errands for him, that sort of thing. It's really gone a long way in mending fences between our families. This accident could have taken us down, but it's only made us stronger."

"You've survived the season."

"I guess you could put it that way."

Yep. I could put it that way, because that was the way it was.

I had to end the call with Carrie quickly because another call came through—this one from Mama. I knew that she and

Pop would be leaving tomorrow for their big RV road trip, so I wanted to hear what she had to say.

"Mama, are you packed and ready?"

"As ready as I'll ever be. I still can't believe we're going to do this. Your father has some crazy idea that we might buy an RV park. Can you picture that?"

"You haven't even been to an RV park yet. How does he know if he'll like it?"

"Exactly what I said. But you know the man—crazy as a loon. He's been working up a sweat loading the RV—er, fifth wheel—and I'm trying to stock the kitchen. Can't imagine making all of our meals in that teensy-tiny cracker box of a kitchen, but I guess I'll try."

"And you can eat out while you're on the road."

"Humph. Your father and food. Between the cruises and eating out at so many restaurants, he's going to be as big as a house. We'll have to squeeze him through the door of the fifth wheel. But anyway, I just wanted to call to say goodbye. Next time you hear from me we'll be in New Mexico. I think. And then Arizona. After that I'm not really sure. California, likely."

"Ooh, Alva might be going to California with Eduardo. She wants me to go with. Maybe we could all meet up."

"W-what? Alva's traveling with that sewing fella now? I thought she was staying with Lori-Lou until the baby comes."

"Oh, she is. The California trip would be later . . . if at all."

"I guess Alva and Eduardo are a couple, then?"

"He's fallen head over heels for her, and vice versa."

"As I live and breathe. I guess it's true what they say—love knows no age." Mama paused and then her tone changed. "And apparently it knows no boundaries either."

"Boundaries? You think Alva and Eduardo need boundaries? That's why they've invited me to go along on their trip, to serve as chaperone."

"Oh, sorry." My mother sighed. "I wasn't thinking about Alva and Eduardo at all when I said that. My thoughts were on someone else entirely. Well, a couple of someones."

"Mama, shoot straight with me. Who are you talking about? I'm so confused."

"Poor Levi," she said. "Poor, poor Levi."

"Poor Levi? What do you mean?"

"That poor boy just doesn't seem to have any luck with women."

"Joni told me a while back that she wasn't really dating him. Are the WOP-pers disappointed by that news?"

"Maybe a little. The WOP-pers believe they have an inside track to the Almighty, and they were pretty sure about that one. But they were wrong. Wrong, wrong, wrong."

"Joni and Levi are still good friends," I said.

"Yes, God bless Levi. You know how he is. He's always been the forgiving sort. And he seems to bounce back no matter what life throws his way. Must be all that ministry training."

"I'm so confused, Mama. What does he have to forgive?"

"Joni's gone off the deep end. She's dating someone else entirely."

"Who?"

"Well, I really hate to say."

"Mama."

"Okay. Casey. Casey Lawson."

For a moment there I thought I'd heard wrong. Surely I'd heard wrong. "Mama, did you say Casey Lawson?"

"Yep. I don't know how he did it, but that wolf in sheep's

clothing came in through the back gate and stole Levi's girl. Right there in front of God and everybody."

"Well, she must've wanted to be stolen."

"The way I hear it—and I'm not one to gossip, so forgive me if I get this wrong—he stayed after at Queenie's wedding to help clean up. Joni was there working at the Methodist church and Levi had gone back to the Baptist church."

"You're saying they hooked up because of the two different churches?"

"I'm not blaming it on the churches. Just saying that Levi went back to the Baptist church and Joni and Casey were there at the Methodist church. They struck up a conversation."

"But Casey and Joni? They're as opposite as two people can be. Casey always thought Joni was, well . . ."

"I know, I know. But clearly she's woman enough for him now. And they've been spotted all over town, even taking a drive down to the lake. Folks are saying it won't be long before she has a ring on her finger. The WOP-pers are saying it, so I'm guessing they'll be hitched soon."

Wait—ring on her finger? Casey's ring? How many times over the years had I envisioned him putting a ring on *my* finger? And now, could it really be true?

As soon as those thoughts emerged, I pushed them down. I had nothing to be jealous of. Nothing whatsoever. My feelings for Casey had faded ages ago, never to return.

"I think the WOP-pers need to pray for Joni," Mama said. "Can you imagine her being stuck with that heartbreaker Casey Lawson for the rest of her life?"

"Actually, there was a time when I could've imagined it for myself. But you know what, Mama? Maybe God really brought Joni and Casey together. Just like he brought together Queenie and Pap-Paul. Jasper and Crystal. Dewey and Dahlia.

Beau and Twiggy. Alva and Eduardo. Me and Brady. Maybe this was all meant to be. Not everything in life turns out the way we think it will."

"Sometimes . . ." I heard Brady's voice behind me. "Sometimes it turns out better." He slipped his arms around my waist and pulled me close, planting kisses in my hair.

"What's going on over there, Katie Sue?" Mama asked. "I'm hearing static on the line."

She was hearing static, all right. Brady kissed the top of my ear and I giggled. "Mama, I have to go. I'm . . . working."

"Doesn't sound like you're working." She sighed. "Just pray for Joni. I guess you know this is more than just a marriage. We're losing her to the Presbyterians."

"Oh, that's right. Casey's a Presbyterian."

"And she was such a great wedding planner at the Baptist church. What a loss."

"Look on the bright side, Mama. Maybe Casey will convert and become a Baptist."

"Not sure we want him. Wolf in sheep's clothing. We have enough of those already," she said. "Anyway, I have to go now. Your father wants to show me some great deal he found online on an RV park in Ruidoso, New Mexico. Can you picture me living in New Mexico? Because I surely can't. I hope they have Wi-Fi at this place so I can stay in touch with my children. I'm going to want to help Jasper and Crystal plan their wedding. It's so hard to believe they're getting married soon and I won't be here to help. But you will be, Katie. Promise you'll be there for them. I'll feel so much better knowing you're helping."

"Well, actually, I—"

"Ugh. Your father wants me to hang up. He's got this RV park idea on his mind and you know how he is. I swear, I don't know what's wrong with that man. He's gone nutso. Someone needs to reel him in."

Someone was reeling me in right now . . . with his eyes. I ended the call and threw my arms around Brady's neck, all giggles and smiles.

"I'd love to know what that was all about." He gestured to the phone I had just shoved into my purse.

"Um, kind of a long story. It involves a Baptist, a Presbyterian, and a God-ordained moment at the Methodist church."

"I see. I think."

He didn't, but it didn't really matter. All that mattered right now was melting into the sweet kisses of the man I loved.

30

I'll Never Stop Loving You

I liked being married instead of the girl who's looking for a guy.

Doris Day

On the morning of Valentine's Day, just before leaving for church, I got a call from Jordan Singer, reporter at *Texas Bride*.

"I just wanted you to know that I decided to go ahead with the photo shoot with Carrie Sanders, even though her fiancé couldn't join us. It went great. I think I snagged the perfect picture for the magazine cover, really captured the gown and her personality. I know Carrie and Jimmy had to reschedule their ceremony, which stinks, but I do think our readers will appreciate hearing about everything this couple has been through. So please thank Brady for introducing me to them. It's the perfect story for our publication."

"I'll tell him. Oh, and how's this for coincidence. Guess where Brady and I are headed this afternoon after church? Back to the stockyards where we did our photo shoot last summer."

"I'll never forget that day." Jordan laughed. "Pretty sure it was a game changer for all of us."

"It certainly was for me." I couldn't help but smile as memories flooded over me.

Later that afternoon Brady and I strolled the main street of the historic stockyard area in Fort Worth. As we walked, we reminisced about the day we'd come here for our photo shoot. I'd been a different girl then, a nervous wreck. But I'd discovered my love for Brady on that day.

As we reached the area where the photo shoot had taken place, I gasped. "Brady, look."

The whole area had been set up in exactly the same way it had that day, complete with photographer. "W-what? Jordan?"

He grinned and extended his hand. "Good to see you again, Katie."

"But I thought you were in San Antonio."

"I was. Yesterday. But now I'm here in Fort Worth."

My mind reeled as I tried to take in all of this. "I'm so confused."

"That . . ." Brady kissed my nose. "Was . . ." He kissed my cheek. "The idea." He kissed me on the lips.

"My phone call this morning was meant to throw you off," Jordan said. "Did it work?"

"Um, yeah." I gazed at him and then shifted my attention to Brady. "What is this?"

"Oh, just a little something I planned as a Valentine's gift." He took my hand and led me to the very spot where we'd been photographed months before. "I thought it would be fun to re-create a few photos. Do you mind?"

"In regular clothes?" I pointed to my shirt and jeans.

"Yep. In regular clothes."

"But why?"

"Because, Katie, we need to mark the day."

"Mark the day?" This made no sense at all. Well, no sense until he reached into his pocket and came out with a little box.

"I would love to drop down on one knee, Katie," he said. "But that's a technical impossibility right now. So I'm going to do the next best thing." He gestured to a wooden crate, the same one I'd stood on during our original photo shoot. "Would you mind stepping up, my dear?"

"W-what?"

"Climb up on the crate, Katie," Jordan said. "I want to get a shot."

"O-okay." So I did. It didn't exactly put Brady below me, him being so tall and all. In fact, we were face-to-face, but that was just fine with me. I shivered, half from the cold and half from nervous anticipation.

Brady gazed into my eyes and then back down at the box, which he popped open. Inside, the loveliest diamond ring shimmered in the afternoon sunlight.

"Oh, Brady! How did you know?"

"Alva. She busted into your diary."

"What?"

"Kidding. She told me that you've always talked about having a princess-cut diamond. Oh, and she said you've got photos from *Texas Bride* pinned to your wall."

"Oh, right." I giggled. "Well, I have been planning my wedding since I was, like, twelve."

"Perfect. Now you have something to plan for." He pulled

the ring from the box. "If you feel the way I do, I mean." Off in the distance I heard the click of cameras. I could hardly contain my joy as I gazed into Brady's eyes.

"Oh, I do." I laughed. "I mean, I do feel the same. I *really* do."

"Good. Then I have a question for you, Katie Sue Fisher." He held the ring up and grinned. "Would you do me the honor of becoming Mrs. Brady James?"

"Would I!"

He slid the ring on my finger and I realized a crowd had gathered around us. I looked down at the gorgeous gem and then flung myself into Brady's arms, forgetting about his bad knee. Fortunately, he managed to keep standing. Oh, but what sweet kisses followed. As I lingered in the arms of the man I loved, I thought about my life—my amazing, crazy life—and how far I'd come over the past year. What a blissful ride!

The cameras kept clicking. No doubt we were getting some fun shots. And the crowd seemed to be enjoying it, so we kept giving them more and more fodder.

Finally we came up for air. Through the sea of faces I saw Alva. And Queenie and Pap-Paul. And Mama and Pop. What? Weren't they supposed to be in New Mexico? And Nadia. Whoa! When did she get back from Paris? And my brothers. And their respective leading ladies. I saw Stan pass a handkerchief to Madge, who dabbed her eyes. Then my gaze traveled back to Brady . . . and there it stayed. Well, until he pulled me close and planted a kiss on me that would've made Doris Day swoon. The crowd went a little crazy after that.

A few moments later I was surrounded by loved ones all talking at once.

My grandmother was the first to get my attention. "I guess you know what this means, Katie Sue."

"What, Queenie?"

"You've got to come and get that wedding dress out of my cedar closet."

"Oh, that's right. But we haven't even set a date yet. And I don't know where we'll get married."

"Fort Worth is lovely for weddings," Nadia suggested.

"Over my dead body." Queenie gave me a knowing look. "Katie will get married at the Baptist church in Fairfield, naturally. Where she belongs."

"Oh, but we won't be living in Fairfield, Queenie. Surely you know that."

"I know, I know." She waved her hand. "But please make this old lady happy by sealing the deal in the church you grew up in. Promise?"

"But you're a Presbyterian now. Why would that matter to you?"

"It just matters. Then again, if you want to dance, we'll have to have the reception at the Methodist church. That might be problematic."

"We can talk about all of that later."

Mama got involved at this point. "Ooh, if you had a summer wedding, you could have your reception outdoors at city hall, right across the street from the hardware store. We could set up picnic tables and invite the whole town."

That sounded wonderful to me, but I'd have to run all of it by Brady. He might have different ideas altogether.

"Of course, I'll have to talk your father into staying home long enough to attend your wedding." Mama rolled her eyes. "I do hope he gives up on that RV park idea. You're my only daughter, Katie, and I'm going to be there for you no matter what."

Off she went on a tangent, talking about Pop and his wanderlust. Not that I really heard any of it. Through the crowd

I caught a glimpse of Brady talking to Jordan Singer. He gestured for me to join him and I wove my way through my friends and family members to his side. He took my hand—the one with the ring on it—and gave it a kiss à la Eduardo.

"You sure you can handle being Mrs. Brady James?" he asked. "My life is pretty crazy."

"*Your* life is crazy?" I gestured to the crowd of people behind us. "Most of those people are from my side."

He gazed at me with intensity. "No more sides, Katie. It's not about Fairfield or Dallas. It's not about the Mavericks or Spurs. It's not even about the Baptists or Presbyterians. From now on, we're on the same team."

"Ooh, I like the sound of that."

He pulled me into his arms and kissed me soundly. The crowd gathered around us once again. I could hear Queenie bickering with Alva about where the wedding would be held. Mama and Pop argued about the timing of the wedding and how that would interfere with his latest plan to buy an RV park. Twiggy and Dahlia fretted over who would run the store if Brady and I left to go on a honeymoon. And Eduardo and Nadia called dibs on who would get to make my wedding gown.

Should I remind them that I already *had* a wedding gown hanging in Queenie's cedar closet? It, like the girl who would wear it, had been waiting quite some time.

But as I gazed up, up, up into Brady's gorgeous eyes, I had to admit the truth. Some things were definitely worth the wait.

Acknowledgments

The writing of this story came at a difficult time in our family's journey. Just a few months after celebrating the news that a granddaughter was on the way, we received the devastating news that little Evie Joy didn't make it. We didn't learn until after the fact that she had Turner's syndrome, a chromosomal condition that affects one in every two thousand live births and is responsible for nearly 10 percent of all miscarriages. I was in the middle of writing this happy-go-lucky story at the very time we were mourning her loss. When I contacted my editor, Jennifer Leep, to let her know that I needed extra time to complete the book as a result, she responded with such kindness and grace. This is such an example of the body of Christ at work in the real world. It's one thing for people to say, "I'm a believer." It's another thing to see them prove it with their actions. I'm so grateful for the role Jennifer has played in my writing career, but I'm even more grateful for her kindness. She's walked me through countless trials.

Speaking of editors, I'm so blessed to have my line/copy editor, Jessica English. Jessica, I marvel at your ability to keep up with all of my characters. And the timelines! You're a marvel. Please don't ever leave me!

To my awesome marketing team at Revell: Michele Misiak, Erin Bartels, Lanette Haskins, and many others. Thanks so much for helping me market my books. Those blog tours are amazing! Thanks for rallying around me at book launch time. I love the creative things we come up with.

Speaking of teams, I'm forever grateful to my Dream Team. You put up with my prayer requests, my crazy marketing ideas, and my wacky stories. You are my biggest fans, and vice versa. What a gift you are to me!

I want to offer a kind word for my agent, Chip MacGregor. He came up with the idea for this story and has celebrated its success every step of the way. Chip, I'm so glad to have you in my life. You're a terrific cheerleader.

Finally, to my Lord and Savior, Jesus Christ. You've called me to go outside of the box and write romantic comedy instead of the "serious stuff." Though I don't always understand this amazing call on my life, I'm grateful for it. It's such a relief to be who you've called me to be.

COMING SUMMER 2016

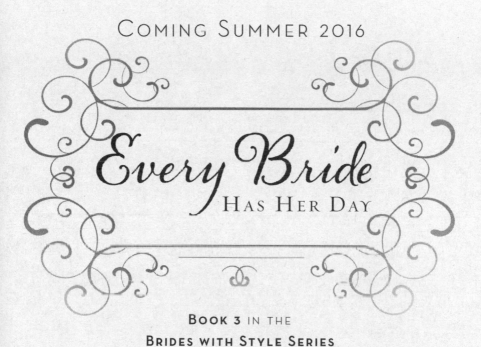

Every Bride
HAS HER DAY

BOOK 3 IN THE
BRIDES WITH STYLE SERIES

1

ℋappy Girl

I believe in pink. I believe that laughing is the best calorie burner. I believe in kissing, kissing a lot. I believe in being strong when everything seems to be going wrong. I believe that happy girls are the prettiest girls. I believe that tomorrow is another day and I believe in miracles.

Audrey Hepburn

Y ou. Are. An. Engaged. Woman." I spoke to my reflection in the mirror on the Monday morning after the love of my life popped the question. "Engaged!" A little giggle followed as I reflected back on the moment when my sweetie had slipped that gorgeous, perfect-for-me ring on my finger. The flawless princess-cut diamond was almost as amazing as the fella who'd given it to me. Almost. Then again, Brady James was in a class of his own. Comparing him to anything—even something as precious as a diamond—just felt wrong. What I'd ever done to deserve such a guy, I could not say, but he was mine all the same.

Mine.

Engaged!

I needed to get busy planning a wedding. Oh, but right now I just wanted to dance down the hallway to the kitchen, eat breakfast with Aunt Alva, then head off to work at Cosmopolitan Bridal, where I would see my fiancé in person. A few sweet kisses would start my workday off right.

I did a happy little Texas two-step all the way from my bedroom to the Formica table in the kitchen, where I greeted my elderly aunt with a kiss on the cheek. "G'morning, Auntie!" I sang, my words coming out like a Disney musical in the making. "How are *you* today?"

"Well, aren't we happy this morning, Katie Sue." Aunt Alva's soft wrinkles seemed even more pronounced as her lips curled up in a smile. "Love is in the air, I see."

"Indeed, it is!" I trilled, my melodic words filling the tiny kitchen. "Birds are singing, flowers are blooming, and all's right with the world!"

"Love does make you feel young, doesn't it?" She attempted to stand, but her arthritis slowed things down a bit. "Well, never mind getting up. I guess you'll just have to fix your own plate. I'm so worn out from taking care of Lori-Lou's kids all week I can hardly move."

"No doubt."

"Feels good to be home, even if it's just for the weekend. And nice to cook in my own kitchen again. I made pancakes, honey. I know how much you love them and figured they'd hit the spot."

"Yum! And don't fret, Auntie. I'll fix my own."

"Before long you'll be fixing breakfast for two." A look of concern shadowed her face. "In your own house. On the other side of town. Far away from me. Not that I'm complaining about you and Brady getting hitched. I'm just worried about living on my own again after having someone as sweet as you share my home."

I slipped my arms around her shoulders and leaned in close. "Think about it, Aunt Alva. I'm not the only one with a beau. I think we both know that Eduardo is planning to pop the question soon, and his house is near Brady's. We'll be neighbors."

Auntie brightened at this notion. "I do hope he'll hurry up. I'm eighty-plus years old. I don't have time to dawdle." She tried again to stand, this time managing the feat. "But if I move into that ridiculously large house of his, you'll probably have to send in a search party to find me. At least here I know the way to the bathroom." She toddled off down the hallway as if to prove her point.

As I filled my plate with food, I thought about all of the changes in our lives of late. Moving from Fairfield to Dallas. Meeting Brady. Landing a dream job at his mother's bridal salon. Moving in with my aunt. Falling head over heels for the greatest guy in the world. Had I really only been away from my hometown of Fairfield less than a year? Seemed like forever. Oh, but what a joy to start my life over again in a place with endless possibilities!

My happily-ever-after attitude continued to propel me as I drove to work later that morning. I entered Cosmopolitan Bridal, my home away from home, and was greeted by my co-worker Twiggy, who let out a deafening squeal the moment she clapped those overly-made-up eyes of hers on me. "Katie! I still can't believe you're engaged! I mean, I know you are. I was there. I saw it firsthand. But it seems like a dream. Ooh, speaking of dreams, let me see your ring again."

I extended my left hand to show off the diamond and she gasped. "Wowza! Is it heavy? Have you set a date? Are you guys getting married at your church here in Dallas or back home in Fairfield? Where are you going on your honeymoon? Don't go on a cruise. I've heard terrible stories about those tiny cabins. Not good for honeymooning. Have you chosen your bridesmaids?" A hopeful look sparked in her eyes at that last question.

Before I could say, "We haven't had time to think about all of that," the store manager approached. "So, Brady finally popped the question." Madge gave me a motherly look as she crossed her arms at her chest. "It's about stinkin' time. I've been laying on some pretty thick hints over the past few weeks, but he didn't seem to be taking them. I was starting to think Brady James planned to stay single the rest of his life, just like that stubborn agent of his." A hint of pain clouded Madge's eyes. "Some fellas are confirmed bachelors, I guess."

"I was just waiting for the perfect moment, Madge." Brady's voice sounded from behind me. I turned, my lips curling up in a smile as I gazed into my handsome fiancé's face. "And I'm pretty sure Stan isn't a confirmed bachelor. Time will prove that."

Madge rolled her eyes. "Whatever. And who was talking about Stan anyway? What does your agent have to do with this conversation?"

"Maybe that's a discussion for another day." Brady gave her a knowing look.

"Enough about confirmed bachelors. We have a wedding

shower to plan!" Twiggy seemed delighted at this possibility. "What themes do you like, Katie?"

"Themes?" I gave a little shrug. "No idea. What do you mean?"

"Oh, bridal showers these days are all themed. Tiffany. Shabby chic. Chevron. Everything's built on the theme. So what's it going to be? Everything has to be planned out."

"Well, in Fairfield all of the bridal showers are just alike. We meet at the Baptist church, drink punch, eat cake, and open presents. There's always a toaster. And a blender. And my grandmother always puts together a basket of cleaning products, though I've never understood why you would give cleaning products as a gift. I guess she's just trying to send some sort of message to the bride to keep a clean house?"

"Humph. Well, maybe that's how they do it in a small town, but it's not going to happen on my watch." Twiggy waggled her finger in the air. "We can do a sure sight better than that."

"We sure can." My boss, Nadia, sashayed into place alongside Brady. "My boy deserves a top-notch wedding. And his fans will expect it to be grand. What about the Gaylord, honey? You've loved that place since you were a kid."

"Well, it's a great hotel, Mom." Brady pursed his lips and I tried to read his thoughts. "But this is really more about making the bride happy. You know?"

"Katie will be happy as long as you're happy." Nadia stared at me so intently that I felt beads of sweat pop out on my neck. "Right, honey?"

Before I could say, "But I've never even been inside the Gaylord," Nadia headed off to her office, muttering something about how she would pull a few strings to get us the grand ballroom for a midsummer wedding. Lovely.

Twiggy clasped her hands together in obvious glee. "Ooh,

the Gaylord! Perfection! I'm going to throw you the bridal shower of the century. I know the other girls will help me. Dahlia loves to design things. Hibiscus too. Crystal's probably a little too busy planning her own wedding right now to get very involved, but I could ask Jane." Her nose wrinkled. "No, on second thought, I doubt Jane would be terribly interested."

"I think it's a little early to be worrying about all of that," I said.

"Oh, it's never too early. Now, the first order of business is to look for ideas. Fresh. New. Hip. Cool. Nothing too overdone." Twiggy swept her hair back with her hand. "We want something fashion-forward, not something from a magazine. By the time that magazine goes to print, the trend is already passing. We want something fresh, something perfect for Katie."

"Well, I'm a small-town girl, so—"

"Everything has to jive with the theme for the wedding. And if you're getting married at the Gaylord—"

"Are you saying my wedding has to be themed too?" I slapped my palm against my forehead. "Really? Can't we just call it 'typical wedding theme' and leave it at that?"

"Typical wedding theme?" Twiggy stared at me as if I'd lost my mind. "I guess some girls still do that. But don't you worry, Katie. I'll start a wedding board for you on Pinterest, and I'll pin all sorts of ideas to share with you."

"Wait." I shook my head. "You're coming up with ideas for the shower or the actual wedding? Because I really want to do that my—"

"Both! It's going to be great." She sauntered down the hallway toward the design studio with Madge on her heels. I could hear them talking about my wedding as they disappeared from view.

Brady slipped his arms around my waist. "You don't have

to listen to a word they say. They're just trying to be helpful, in their own intrusive way."

"It's not that, Brady." I leaned my head against his shoulder and sighed. "I'm just so embarrassingly small-town that I don't know much about how to do things in a big way. And if that's really what you want, what you expect, then . . ."

"All I expect is for you to be there, ready to take my hand in yours. Other than that, I couldn't care less. Just tell the planning committee that you want to go simple."

"Right. Is there such a thing as simple chic? Something that doesn't involve pictures from the internet? Or big hotels?"

"Yep. But you'd better tell them quickly. I have a feeling Mama's already mapping out the reception hall, and I'm guessing Twiggy is back in the studio by now, involving Dahlia and Hibiscus."

I shook my head and pinched my eyes shut. Maybe I should let them enjoy the moment. And perhaps I should look at whatever plans they came up with. They might just surprise me with something that felt right, after all. Just because we always did things the simple way in my small town didn't mean I wasn't open to change.

"I've already got my dress, anyway." I offered Brady a delighted smile. "Thanks to you."

"No, thanks to *you* and that prize-winning essay you wrote."

"Yes, the essay." I pursed my lips as I remembered the emotions I'd felt as I'd penned the winning essay. Felt like a lifetime ago. "But I guess my point is this: the dress is a Loretta Lynn style, which is simple. Country. Sweet."

"I like simple. Country. Sweet."

"Which explains why you fell for me, I suppose." I gave him a little kiss on the cheek. "But I'm trying to say that the theme of our wedding could be just that. Simple. Country. Sweet."

"Yep." His word came out with a slow Texas drawl. Brady then tipped his imaginary hat, gave me a little wink, and headed off to his office. I decided I'd better get to my office as well. In spite of my enthusiasm for the wedding, there was still work to be done. Cosmopolitan Bridal wasn't paying me to plan my wedding, they were paying me to do marketing and PR for the store.

Several minutes later, as I was comfortably seated at my desk, my phone rang. I answered on the second ring. "Cosmopolitan Bridal, home of the Loretta Lynn gown. How can I help you?"

"You can help me by taking a break from your work and talking to me about your wedding." I recognized my mother's voice. "Pop and I are so excited about your big day. I'm sorry we couldn't stick around and help you plan it, but you know how he is. He wanted to get back on the road again, headed west."

"Oh, no problem. I've hardly had time to think about it since Brady popped the question. It's been a whirlwind weekend for sure."

"Well, I hope you don't mind, but I took it upon myself to see when the church is available. I figured you'd want to do a springtime wedding, though that wouldn't give you much time, this being February and all. If spring is too short notice, then summer would be nice too."

"Well, actually, we—"

"I called the church, and they've got VBS taking place the second week of June, so you can't use the fellowship hall that weekend. And, of course, there's the annual Peach Festival. You'll have to work around that. But I understand every weekend in July is open. Of course, it's hot as blue blazes in July and the AC isn't great in the fellowship hall, but maybe we could bring in a couple of window units? Those are loud, though. Might be kind of hard to celebrate with all that racket. What do you think?"

"I think Brady and I haven't even talked about dates yet. Plus we attend a great church here in Dallas, Mom. And just so you know, Brady's mom has her heart set on—"

"Dallas?" She spoke the word as if it brought her great pain. "Please tell me you're not thinking about getting married in Dallas. The people you love live in Fairfield."

"Well, half of them." I sighed. "The other half—the people I see every day at work—live here. And the girls at the bridal shop are already very invested, trust me. They're making plans as we speak."

"You're letting total strangers plan your wedding?" Mama sounded flabbergasted at this idea.

"They're not strangers, they're good friends. And they're not planning the wedding for me. They're just working on ideas. On Pinterest."

"Pinterest?" Mama groaned. "You don't need the internet to plan a lovely home-grown wedding, honey. And you certainly don't need to tie the knot in the big city. Dallas is just so far away from home." Her voice grew tense. "Don't you want the people you grew up with to attend your wedding?"

"Mama, Dallas is an hour away from Fairfield, not halfway across the country. If people really care about me, they would probably travel here. Not that I'm asking them to . . . at least not yet. Please don't fret. I'm sure Brady will agree that getting married in Fairfield is the best plan. And I'm pretty sure Queenie would kill me if I didn't get married at the Baptist church where I grew up."

"Maybe not. Queenie's a Presbyterian now. Did you forget?" Mama's voice held that crisp edge of disapproval she'd become known for.

The phone grew warm against my ear, so I shifted it to the other one. "I know she is, but her heart is still at the Baptist church."

"That's what getting hitched to a man of the cloth will do to you, I guess. You marry him and the next thing you know, everything's changing." Mama sniffled. "Kind of like what's happening to you, now that you're engaged."

"Brady's not a man of the cloth, Mama. He's a basket-ball player." Even as I spoke the words, I wished I could take them back. With his post-surgery knee still bothering him, my sweetie's professional basketball career was taking a backseat to helping out at the bridal shop. "He's not a Presbyterian either," I added. "We both attend a community church now."

Mama released an exaggerated groan. "I guess that proves my point. Everything's changing. The signs are all there. I've been trying to ignore them, but it's getting harder every day. You've left home for good."

"Left home?" I did my best not to laugh out loud. "Where are you calling me from, Mama?"

A short pause followed before she finally replied, "We're headed to the Texas Panhandle, Palo Duro Canyon area. We planning to see that wonderful outdoor musical I've heard so much about."

"Yep. And where will you be next week?"

"Ruidoso, New Mexico."

"After that?"

"I believe we're headed to Colorado. Or maybe Arizona. You know how your father is, Katie. He's got the wanderlust."

"And wherever he wanders, you happily follow."

"He's my husband."

"Exactly." I did my best to punctuate the word.

A lengthy pause followed on my mother's end. "Well, I suppose, when you say it like that . . ." Her voice trailed off.

"I'm just saying that when two people become one, they start carving their own path. Doing their own thing."

"Could you carve your path a little closer to Fairfield? At least for the wedding day?"

"I'm sure we'll get married in Fairfield, Mama, as I said. And I'll be calling the church myself to talk to Joni about setting a date."

"Joni's not at the Baptist church anymore, honey. Remember? Now that she's dating your ex-fiancé, she's changed churches too."

"Casey was never my fiancé, Mama, but thanks for the reminder about Joni switching churches. I guess I'll have to call Bessie May then. She's still Baptist, isn't she?"

"Yes, but stop avoiding the obvious. You and Casey were very nearly engaged once upon a time, before he started dating Joni. And I suppose it could be argued that he's the one responsible for nudging you off to Dallas. I still haven't quite forgiven him for that, you know."

"Well, it's time you did. He and Joni are happily matched, and so are Brady and me. It will all work out in the end, you know. So you and Pop enjoy yourself in New Mex—"

"The Texas Panhandle."

"The Texas Panhandle. And don't take any wooden nickels."

"I've never understood that expression." My mother laughed. "But if I've heard your father use it once, I've heard him use it a thousand times. 'Don't take any wooden nickels, Marie.'" She laughed a little louder. "Every time old man Harrison would come into the hardware store, your father would say it loud enough for everyone in the place to hear."

"I remember."

"I . . ." She seemed to drift away for a moment. "I miss our days at the hardware store. Do you, Katie Sue?"

"Mama, you and Pop just passed off the store to Jasper and Crystal a few months back. And from what Jasper tells me, Pop is still trying to manage things, even from the RV."

"It's not technically an RV, honey. It's a fifth wheel."

"Well, you get my point. You haven't lost ties with the hardware store, and I don't see that happening . . . ever. It'll always be a part of us, as will the wooden nickel phrase."

"Okay, okay." Mama disappeared for a minute, then returned, breathless. "Hate to run, honey, but your father is about to drive us off the road and into a canyon. I have to help him with the GPS."

"Dumb thing gets it wrong every time!" my father hollered.

"Pretty sure he's talking about the GPS, not me," Mama said. "But I can't be sure."

"Be safe and have fun, Mama. And don't worry about a thing. I will get married in Fairfield and you will be in the center of the plans, I promise. I won't leave you out."

"Thank you, honey." Mama ended the call.

I put the phone down and laid my head on my desk, my thoughts in a whirl.

"Things are that bad already?" Brady's voice roused me from my ponderings. I sat up straight and released an exaggerated sigh as I saw him standing in the open doorway.

"Just more people trying to plan our big day. That's all."

"I see." He moved toward my desk, his gorgeous eyes twinkling. "Well then, let's just run off and elope. What do you think of that idea?"

"I think they would all kill us. We'd be murdered in our sleep."

"But at least we'd be in each other's arms."

"True, that." I offered a weak smile. Still, I couldn't help but fret. Wedding planning wasn't supposed to be stressful, was it? I mean, all of the bridal magazines made it look like so much fun. Our engagement was just one day old and we were already talking about running off to elope? What would the next few months hold?

I rose and took a few steps in Brady's direction. He slipped his arms around me and I nestled against him, all of my woes about the wedding slipping away. There, in that safe place, there were no cares, no anxieties.

Well, until Madge popped her head in the door and hollered, "I've got it, you two! Let's do a Hawaiian-themed wedding, luau and all! I'll bring the roasted pig!"

The groan I gave was pretty loud, but it was drowned out by the sound of Brady's laughter. "Now *there's* an idea," he whispered in my ear, his breath sending tingles all the way down my spine. "We'll elope . . . in Hawaii!"

Funny. That idea sounded better to me than all of the others put together.

Award-winning author **Janice Thompson** enjoys tickling the funny bone. She got her start in the industry writing screenplays and musical comedies for the stage, and she has published over ninety books for the Christian market. She has played the role of mother of the bride four times now and particularly enjoys writing lighthearted, comedic, wedding-themed tales. Why? Because making readers laugh gives her great joy!

Janice formerly served as vice president of Christian Authors Network (CAN) and was named the 2008 Mentor of the Year for American Christian Fiction Writers (ACFW). She is active in her local writing group, where she regularly teaches on the craft of writing. In addition, she enjoys public speaking and mentoring young writers. She recently opened an online bakery, Nina's Cakes and Cookies, where she specializes in wedding-themed sweets.

Janice is passionate about her faith and does all she can to share the joy of the Lord with others, which is why she particularly enjoys writing. Her tagline, "Love, Laughter, and Happy Ever Afters!" sums up her take on life.

She lives in Spring, Texas, where she leads a rich life with her family, a host of writing friends, and two mischievous dachshunds. She does her best to keep the Lord at the center of it all. You can find out more about Janice at www.janicea thompson.com or www.freelancewritingcourses.com.

Come Meet

Janice Thompson

at www.JaniceAThompson.com

Read her blog, book information, and fun facts!

Follow Janice on Facebook and Twitter

Somewhere in a sea of tulle and taffeta, satin
and crepe, Katie Fisher needs to find the
key ingredient of the perfect wedding—the groom.

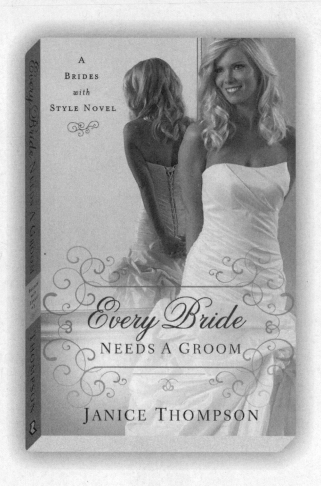

Don't Miss **Book 1** in the **Brides with Style** series!

If you are looking for a romantic comedy that will have you laughing all day, grab the *Weddings* BY *Bella* series!

"I fell in love with the Rossi clan, a delightful collection of quirky characters who feel as passionately about their pizza as Texans do about chili."

—**Virginia Smith**, author, *Third Time's a Charm*

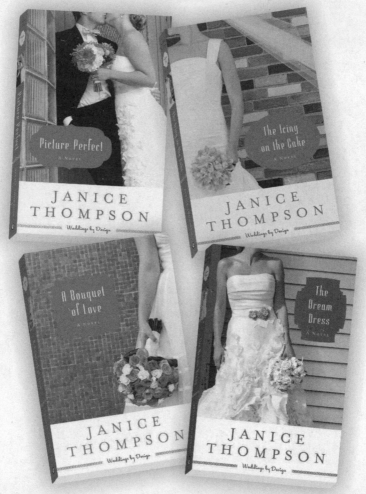